A VERY GOTHIC CHRISTMAS

Two novellas

CHRISTINE FEEHAN

MELANIE GEORGE

POCKET BOOKS
New York London Toronto Sydney Singapore

CRITICS PRAISE CHRISTINE FEEHAN:

THE SCARLETTI CURSE

"The characters and twists in this book held me on the edge of my seat the whole time I read it. If you've enjoyed Ms. Feehan's previous novels, you will surely be captived by this step into the world of Gothic romance. . . . Once again, Ms. Feehan does not disappoint!"

—*Under the Covers Book Reviews*

DARK CHALLENGE

"The exciting and multifaceted world that impressive author Christine Feehan has created continues to improve with age."

—*Romantic Times*

DARK MAGIC

"With each book Ms. Feehan continues to build a complex society that makes for mesmerizing reading."

—*Romantic Times*

DARK GOLD

"The third in Christine Feehan's Carpathian series is her best to date. *Dark Gold* is imbued with passion, danger, and supernatural thrills."

—*Romantic Times*

MORE PRAISE FOR CHRISTINE FEEHAN:

DARK PRINCE

"For lovers of vampire romances, this one is a keeper. . . .
I had a hard time putting this book down. . . . Don't miss
this book!"

—*New-Age Bookshelf*

RAVE REVIEWS FOR MELANIE GEORGE:

DEVIL MAY CARE

"Humor, passion, and rising sexual tension merge beautifully in Melanie George's allegorical tale. . . . Carefully
constructed and well told, this story's readers will adore
the characters. . . . With sensuality akin to Robin Schone,
Devil May Care sparkles and will garner Ms. George
many new fans."

—*Romantic Times*

"Ms. George has given us a rare gift in this delightful
story. Please don't miss getting to know [her unique char-
acters]. Damien has two brothers, Nicholas and Gray, and
I'm looking forward to their stories."

—*Old Book Barn Gazette*

An *Original* Publication of POCKET BOOKS

 POCKET BOOKS, a division of Simon & Schuster, Inc.
1230 Avenue of the Americas, New York, NY 10020

After the Music copyright © 2001 by Christine Feehan
Lady of the Locket copyright © 2001 by Melanie George

ISBN: 0-7434-4271-1

First Pocket Books printing November 2001

10 9 8 7 6 5 4 3 2 1

POCKET BOOKS and colophon are registered trademarks of Simon & Schuster, Inc.

For information regarding special discounts for bulk purchases, please contact Simon & Schuster Special Sales at 1-800-456-6798 or business@simonandschuster.com

Cover art by Lisa Litwack

Printed in the U.S.A.

contents

AFTER THE MUSIC

Christine Feehan

dedication

For Manda and Christina, may you always be survivors.
Much love.

acknowledgments

Special thanks to Dr. Mathew King for all of his help with
the research needed for this book. Also to Burn Survivors
online. Thank you for your courtesy and patience and all
the offers of help. And of course, to Bobbi and Mark
Smith of the Holy Smoke Band, who gave me their time
and help with my persistent questions.

chapter

1

JESSICA FITZPATRICK WOKE UP screaming, her heart pounding out a rhythm of
terror. Fear was a living, breathing entity in
the darkness of her room. The weight of it crushed her,
held her helpless; she was unable to move. She could taste
it in her mouth, and feel it coursing through her bloodstream. Around her, the air seemed so thick that her
lungs burned for oxygen. She knew something mon-
strous was stirring deep in the bowels of the earth. For a
moment she lay frozen, her ears straining to hear the
murmur of voices rising and falling, chanting words in
an ancient tongue that should never be spoken. Red,
glowing eyes searched through the darkness, summoning
her, beckoning her closer. She felt the power of those eyes
as they neared, focused on her, and came ever closer. Her
own eyes flew open, the need to flee was paramount in
her mind.

The entire room lurched, flinging her from the narrow
bunk to the floor. At once the cold air brought her out of
her nightmare and into the realization that they were not

safe in their beds at home, but in the cabin of a wildly pitching boat in the middle of a ferocious storm. The craft, tossed from wave to powerful wave, was taking a pounding.

Jessica scrambled to her feet, gripping the edge of the bunk as she dragged herself toward the two children, Tara and Trevor Wentworth, who clung together, their faces pale and frightened. Tara screamed, her terrified gaze locked on Jessica. Jessica managed to make it halfway to the twins before the next wild bucking sent her to floor again.

"Trevor, get your life jacket back on this minute!" She reached them by crawling on her hands and knees, and then curled a supporting arm around each of them. "Don't be afraid, we'll be fine."

The boat rose on a wave, teetered and slid fast, tossing the three of them in all directions. Salt water poured in a torrent onto the deck and raced down the steps into the cabin, covering the floor with an inch of ice-cold water. Tara screamed, and clutched at her brother's arm, desperately trying to help him buckle his life jacket. "It's him. He's doing this, he's trying to kill us."

Jessica gasped, horrified. "Tara! Nobody controls the weather. It's a storm. Plain and simple, just a storm. Captain Long will get us safely to the island."

"He's hideous. A monster. And I don't want to go." Tara covered her face with her hands and sobbed. "I want to go home. Please take me home, Jessie."

Jessica tested Trevor's life jacket to make certain he was safe. "Don't talk that way, Tara. Trev, stay here with Tara while I go see what I can do to help." She had to shout to make herself heard in the howling wind and booming sea.

Tara flung herself into Jessica's arms. "Don't leave me—we'll die. I just know it—we're all going to die just like Mama Rita did."

Trevor wrapped his arms around his twin sister. "No, we're not, sis, don't cry. Captain Long has been in terrible storms before, lots of them," he assured. He looked up at Jessica with his piercing blue eyes. "Right, Jessie?"

"You're exactly right, Trevor," she agreed. Jessica had a firm hold on the banister and began to make her way up the stairs to the deck.

Rain fell in sheets; black clouds churned and boiled in the sky. The wind rose to an eerie shriek. Jessica held her breath, watched as Long struggled to navigate the boat through the heavier waves, taking them ever closer to the island. It seemed the age-old struggle between man and nature. Slowly, through the sheets of rain, the solid mass of the island began to take shape. Salt water sprayed and foamed off the rocks but the sea was calmer as they approached the shore. She knew it was only the captain's knowledge of the region and his expertise that allowed him to guide the craft to the dock in the terrible storm.

The rain was pouring from the sky. The clouds were so black and heavy overhead that the night seemed unrelentingly dark. Yet Jessica caught glimpses of the moon, an eerie sight with the swirling black of the clouds veiling its light.

"Let's go, Jessie," Captain Long yelled. "Bring up the

kids and your luggage. I want you off this boat now." The words were nearly lost in the ferocity of the storm, but his frantic beckoning was plain.

She hurried, tossing Trevor most of the packs while she helped Tara up the stairs and across the slippery deck. Captain Long lifted Tara to the dock before aiding Trevor to shore. He caught Jessica's arm in a tight grip and pulled her close so he could be heard. "I don't like this—Jess, I hope he's expecting you. Once I leave you, you're stuck. You know he isn't the most pleasant man."

"Don't worry," she patted his arm, her stomach churning. "I'll call if we need you. Are you certain you don't want to stay overnight?"

"I'll feel safer out there," he gestured toward the water.

Jessica waved him off and turned to look up at the island while she waited to get her land legs back. It had been seven years since she'd last been to the island. Her memories of it were the things of nightmares. Looking up toward the ridge, she half expected to see a fiery inferno, with red and orange flames towering to the skies, but there was only the black night and the rain. The house that once had sat at the top of the cliff overlooking the ocean was long gone, reduced to a pile of ashes.

In the dark, the vegetation was daunting, a foreboding sight. The weak rays of light from the cloud-covered moon were mottled as they fell across the ground, creating a strange, unnatural pattern. The island was wild with heavy timber and thick with brush; the wind set the trees and bushes dancing in a macabre fashion. Naked branches bowed and scraped together with a grating sound. Heavy evergreens whirled madly, sending sharp needles flying through the air.

Resolutely, Jessica took a deep breath and picked up her pack, handing Trevor a flashlight to lead the way. "Come on, kids, let's go see your father."

The rain slashed down at them, drenching them, drops piercing like sharp icicles right through their clothes to their skin. Heads down, they began to trudge their way up the steep stone steps leading away from the sea toward the interior of the island where Dillon Wentworth hid from the world.

Returning to the island brought back a flood of memories of the good times—her mother, Rita Fitzpatrick, landing the job as housekeeper and nanny to the famous Dillon Wentworth. Jessica had been so thrilled. She had been nearly thirteen, already old enough to appreciate the rising star, a musician who would take his place among the greatest recording legends. Dillon spent a great deal of his time on the road, touring, or in the studio, recording, but when he was home, he was usually with his children or hanging out in the kitchen with Rita and Jessica. She had known Dillon in the good times, during five years of incredible magic.

"Jessie?" Trevor's young voice interrupted her reflection. "Does he know we're coming?"

Jessica met the boy's steady gaze. At thirteen, Trevor had to be well aware that if they had been expected, they wouldn't be walking by themselves in the dead of night in the middle of a storm. Someone would have met them by car on the road at the boathouse.

"He's your father, Trevor, and it's coming up on Christmas. He spends far too much time alone." Jessica slicked back her rain-wet hair and squared her shoulders. "It isn't good for him." And Dillon Wentworth had a responsibility to his children. He needed to look after them, to protect them.

The twins didn't remember their father the way she did. He had been so alive. So handsome. So everything. His life had been magical. His good looks, his talent, his ready laugh and famous blue eyes. Everyone had wanted him. Dillon had lived his life in the spotlight, a white-hot glare of tabloids and television. Of stadiums and clubs. The energy, the power of Dillon Wentworth were astonishing, indescribable, when he was performing. He burned hot and bright on stage, a man with a poet's heart and a devil's talent when he played his guitar and sang with his edgy, smoky voice.

But at home . . . Jessica also remembered Vivian Wentworth with her brittle laugh and red, talon-tipped fingers. The glaze in her eyes when she was cloudy with drugs, when she was staggering under the effects of alcohol, when she flew into a rage and smashed glass and ripped pictures out of frames. The slow, terrible descent into the madness of drugs and the occult. Jessica would never forget Vivian's friends who visited when Dillon wasn't there. The candles, the orgies, the chanting, always the chanting. And men. Lots of men in the Wentworth bed.

Without warning, Tara screamed, turning to fling herself at Jessica, nearly knocking her off the stairs. Jessica caught her firmly, wrapping her arms around the girl and holding her close. They were both so cold they were shivering uncontrollably. "What is it, honey?" Jessica whispered into the child's ear, soothing her, rocking her, there on the steep stairs with the wind slashing them to ribbons.

"I saw something, eyes glowing, staring at us. They were red eyes, Jess. Red, like a monster . . . or a devil." The girl shuddered and gripped Jessica harder.

"Where, Tara?" Jessica sounded calm even though her stomach was knotted with tension. Red eyes. She had seen those eyes.

"There," Tara pointed without looking, keeping her face hidden against Jessica. "Through the trees, something was staring at us."

"There are animals on the island, honey," Jessica soothed, but she was straining to see into the darkness. Trevor valiantly tried to shine the small circle of light toward the spot his twin had indicated, but the light couldn't penetrate the pouring rain.

"It wasn't a dog, it wasn't, Jessie, it was some kind of demon. Please take me home, I don't want to be here. I'm so afraid of him. He's so hideous."

Jessica took a deep breath and let it out slowly, hoping to stay calm when she suddenly wanted to turn and run herself. There were too many memories here, crowding in, reaching for her with greedy claws. "He was scarred terribly in a fire, Tara, you know that." It took effort to keep her voice steady.

"I know he hates us. He hates us so much he doesn't ever want to see us. And I don't want to see him. He *murdered* people." Tara flung the bitter accusation at

Jessica. The howling wind caught the words and took them out over the island, spreading them like a disease.

Jessica tightened her grip on Tara, gave her a short, impatient shake. "I *never* want to hear you say such a terrible thing again, not *ever*, do you understand me? Do you know why your father went into the house that night? Tara, you're too intelligent to listen to gossip and anonymous phone callers."

"I saw the papers. It was in all the papers!" Tara wailed.

Jessica was furious. *Furious.* Why would someone suddenly, after seven years, send old newspapers and tabloids to the twins? Tara had innocently opened the package wrapped in a plain brown paper. The tabloids had been brutal, filled with accusations of drugs, jealousy, and the occult. The speculation that Dillon had caught his wife in bed with another man, that there had been an orgy of sex, drugs, devil worship, and murder, had been far too titillating for the scandal sheets not to play it up long before the actual facts could come out. Jessica had found Tara sobbing pitifully in her room. Whoever had seen fit to enlighten the twins about their father's past had called the house repeatedly whispering horrible things to Trevor and Tara, insisting their father had murdered several people including their mother.

"Your father went into a burning house to save you kids. He thought you were both inside. Everyone who had gotten out tried to stop him, but he fought them, got away, and went into a burning inferno for you. That isn't hate, Tara. That's love. I remember that day, every detail." She pressed her fingers to her pounding temples. "I can't ever forget it no matter how much I try."

And she had tried. She had tried desperately to drown out the sounds of chanting. The vision of the black lights and candles. The scent of the incense. She remembered the shouting, the raised voices, the sound of the gun. And the flames. The terrible greedy flames. The blanket of smoke, so thick one couldn't see. And the smells never went away. Sometimes she still woke up to the smell of burning flesh.

Trevor put his arm around her. "Don't cry, Jessica. We're already here, we're all freezing, let's just go. Let's have Christmas with Dad, make a new beginning, try to get along with him this time."

Jessica smiled at him through the rain and the tears. Trevor. So much like his father and he didn't even realize it. "We're going to have a wonderful Christmas, Tara, you wait and see."

They continued up the stairs until the ground leveled out and Jessica found the familiar path winding through the thick timber to the estate. As islands went, in the surrounding sea between Washington and Canada, it was small and remote, no ferry even traveled to it. That was the way Dillon had preferred it, wanting privacy for his family on his own personal island. In the old days, there had been guards and dogs. Now there were shadows and haunting memories that tore at her soul.

In the old days the island had been alive with people, bustling with activities; now it was silent, only a caretaker lived somewhere on the island in one of the smaller houses. Jessica's mother had told her that Dillon tolerated only one older man on his island on a regular basis. Even in the wind and rain, Jessica couldn't help noticing the boathouse was ill-kept and the road leading around and up toward the house was overgrown, showing little use. Where there had always been several boats docked at the pier, none were in sight, although Dillon must still have had one in the boathouse.

The path led through the thick trees. The wind was whipping branches so that overhead the canopy of trees swayed precariously. The rain had a much more difficult time penetrating through the treetops to reach them, but drops hitting the pathway plopped loudly. Small animals rustled in the bushes as they passed.

"I don't think we're in Kansas anymore," Trevor quipped, with a shaky smile.

Jessica immediately hugged him to her. "Lions and tigers and bears, oh, my," she quoted just to watch the grin spread across his face.

"I can't believe he lives here." Tara sniffed.

"It's beautiful during the day," Jessica insisted, "give it a chance. It's such a wonderful place. The island's small, but it has everything."

They followed a bend, stumbling a little over the uneven ground. Trevor's flashlight cast a meager circle of light on the ground in front of them, which only served to make the forest darker and more frightening as it surrounded them. "Are you certain you know the way, Jess? You haven't been here in years," he asked.

"I know this path with my eyes closed," Jessica assured

him. Which wasn't exactly the truth. In the old days, the path had been well manicured and had veered off toward the cliff. This one was overgrown and led through the thick part of the forest toward the interior of the island, rising steadily uphill. "If you listen, you can hear the water rushing off to our left. The stream is large right now, but in the summer it isn't so strong or deep. There are ferns all along the bank." She wanted to keep talking, hoping it would keep fear at bay.

All three of them were breathing hard from the climb, and they paused to catch their breath under a particularly large tree that helped to shelter them from the driving rain. Trevor shined the light up the massive tree trunk and into the canopy, making light patterns to amuse Tara. As he whirled the light back down the trunk, the small circle illuminated the ground a few feet beyond where they were standing.

Jessica stiffened, jammed a fist in her mouth to keep from screaming, and yanked the flashlight from Trevor to shine it back to the spot he had accidentally lit up. For one terrible moment she could hardly breathe. She was certain she had seen someone staring at them. Someone in a heavily hooded long black cloak that swirled around the shadowy figure as if he were a vampire from one of the movies the twins were always watching. Whoever it was had been staring malevolently at them. He had been holding something in his hands that glinted in the flash of light.

Her hand was shaking badly but she managed to find the place where he had been with the flashlight's small circle of light. It was empty. There was nothing, no humans, no vampires in hooded cloaks. She continued to search through the trees, but there was nothing.

Trevor reached out and caught her wrist, pulling her hand gently to him, taking the flashlight. "What did you see, Jess?" He sounded very calm.

She looked at them then, ashamed of showing such naked fear, ashamed the island could reduce to her to that terrified teenager she once had been. She had hoped for so much: to bring them all together, to find a way to bring Dillon back to the world. But instead she was hallucinating. That shadowy figure belonged in her nightmares, not in the middle of a terrible rainstorm.

The twins were staring up at her for direction. Jessica shook her head. "I don't know, a shadow maybe. Let's just get to the house." She pushed them ahead of her, trying to guard their backs, trying to see in front of them, on both sides.

With every step she took, she was more convinced she hadn't seen a shadow. She hadn't been hallucinating. She was certain something, *someone* had been watching them. "Hurry, Trevor, I'm cold," she urged.

As they topped the rise, the sight of the house took her breath away. It was huge, rambling, several stories high with round turrets and great chimneys. The original house had been completely destroyed in the fire and here, at the top of the rise, surrounded by timber, Dillon had built the house of his boyhood dreams. He had loved the Gothic architecture, the lines and carvings, the vaulted ceilings, and intricate passageways. She remembered him talking with such enthusiasm, spreading pictures on the counter in the kitchen for her and her mother to admire. Jessica had teased him unmercifully about being a frustrated architect and he had always laughed and replied he belonged in a castle or a palace, or that he was a Renaissance man. He would chase her around with an imaginary sword and talk of terrible traps in secret passageways.

Rita Fitzpatrick had cried over this house, telling Jessica how Dillon had clung to his dreams of music and how he had claimed that having the house built was symbolic of his rise from the ashes. But at some point during Dillon's months at the hospital, after he'd endured the pain and agony of such terrible burns and after he realized that his life would never return to normal, the house had become for him, and all who knew him, a symbol of the darkness that had crept into his soul. Looking at it, Jessica felt fear welling inside her, a foreboding that Dillon was a very changed man.

They stared at the great hulk, half expecting to see a ghost push open one of the shutters and warn them off. The house was dark with the exception of two windows on the third story facing them, giving the effect of two eyes staring back at them. Winged creatures seemed to be swarming up its sides. The mottled light from the moon lent the stone carvings a certain animation.

"I don't want to go in there," Tara said, backing away. "It looks . . ." she trailed off, slipping her hand into her brother's.

"Evil," Trevor supplied. "It does, Jess, like one of those haunted houses in the old movies. It looks like it's staring at us."

Jessica bit at her lower lip, glancing behind them, her

gaze searching, wary. "You two have seen too many scary movies. No more for either of you." The house looked far worse than anything she had ever seen in a movie. It looked like a brooding hulk, waiting silently for unsuspecting prey. Gargoyles crouched in the eaves, staring with blank eyes at them. She shook her head to clear the image. "No more movies, you're making me see it that way." She forced a small, uneasy laugh. "Mass hallucination."

"We're a small mass, but it works for me," there was a trace of humor in Trevor's voice. "I'm freezing; we may as well go inside."

No one moved. They continued to stare up at the house in silence, at the strange animating effect of the wind and the moon on the carvings. Only the sound of the relentless rain filled the night. Jessica could feel her heart slamming hard in her chest. They couldn't go back. There was something in the woods. There was no boat to go back to, only the wind and piercing rain. But the house seemed to stare at them with that same malevolence as the figure in the woods.

Dillon had no inkling they were near. She thought it would be a relief to reach him, that she would feel safe, but instead, she was frightened of his anger. Frightened of what he would say in front of the twins. He wouldn't be pleased that she hadn't warned him of their arrival, but if she had called, he would have told her not to come. He always told her not to come. Although she tried to console herself with the fact that his last few letters had been more cheerful and more interested in the twins, she couldn't deceive herself into believing he would welcome them.

Trevor was the first to move, patting Jessica on the back in reassurance as he took a step around her toward the house. Tara followed him, and Jessica brought up the rear. At some point the area around the house had been landscaped, the bushes shaped, and beds of flowers planted, but it looked as though it hadn't been tended in quite a while. A large sculpture of leaping dolphins rose up out of a pond on the far side of the front yard. There were statues of fierce jungle cats strewn about the wild edges of the yard, peering out of the heavier brush.

Tara moved closer to Jessica, a small sound of alarm escaping her as they gained the slate walkway. All of them were violently shivering, their teeth were chattering, and Jessica told herself it was the rain and cold. They made it to within yards of the wraparound porch with its long thick columns when they heard it. A low, fierce growl welled up. It came out of the wind and rain, impossible to pinpoint but swelling in volume.

Tara's fingers dug into Jessica's arms. "What do we do?" she whimpered. Jessica could feel the child shivering convulsively. "We keep walking. Trevor, have your flashlight handy—you may need it to hit the thing over the head if it attacks us." She continued walking toward the house, taking the twins with her, moving slowly but steadily, not wanting to trigger a guard dog's aggressive behavior by running.

The growl rose to a roar of warning. Lights unexpectedly flooded the lawn and porch, revealing the large German shepherd, head down, teeth bared, snarling at them. He stood in the thick brush just off the porch, his gaze focused on them as they gained the steps. The dog took a step toward them just as the front door was flung open.

Tara burst into tears. Jessica couldn't tell if they were tears of relief or fear. She embraced the girl protectively.

"What the hell?" A slender man with shaggy blond hair greeted them from the doorway. "Shut up, Toby," he commanded the dog.

"Get them the hell off my property," another voice roared from inside the house.

Jessica stared at the man in the doorway. "Paul?" There was utter relief in her voice. Her shoulders sagged and suddenly tears burned in her own eyes. "Thank God you're here! I need to get the kids into a hot shower and warm them up immediately. We're freezing."

Paul Ritter, a former band member and long-time friend of Dillon Wentworth, gaped at her and the twins. "My God, Jess, it's you, all grown up. And these are Dillon's children?" He hastily stepped back to allow them entrance. "Dillon, we have more company. We need heat, hot showers, and hot chocolate!" As wet as she was, Paul gathered Jessica in his arms. "I can't believe you three are here. It's so good to see you. Dillon didn't say a word to me that you were coming. I would have met you at the dock." He shut the door on the wind and rain. The sudden stillness silenced him.

Jessica stared up at the shadowy figure on the staircase. For a moment she stopped breathing. Dillon always had that effect on her. He lounged against the wall, looking elegant and lazy, classic Dillon. The light spilled across his face, his angel's face. Thick blue-black hair fell in waves to his shoulders, as shiny as a raven's wing. His sculptured face, masculine and strong, had that hint of five o'clock shadow along his jaw. His mouth was so sensual, his teeth amazingly white. But it was his eyes, vivid blue, stunningly blue, burning with intensity that always mesmerized everyone, including Jessica.

Jessica felt Tara stir beside her, staring up in awe at her father. Trevor made a soft sound, almost of distress. The blue eyes stared down at the three of them. She saw joy, a welcoming expression of surprise dawning on Dillon's face. He stepped forward and gripped the banister with both hands, a heart-stopping grin on his face. He was wearing a short-sleeved shirt and his bare hands and arms were starkly revealed as if the spotlight had picked up and magnified every detail. Webs of scarred flesh covered his arms, wrists, and hands. His fingers were also scarred and misshapen. The contrast between his face and his body was so great it was shocking. That angel's face and the twisted, ridged arms and hands.

Tara shuddered visibly and flung herself into Jessica's arms. At once Dillon slipped back into the shadows, the welcoming smile fading as if it had never been. The burning blue eyes had gone from joyful to ice-cold instantly. His gaze raked Jessica's upturned face, slid over the twins, and came back to her. His sensual mouth tightened ominously. "They're freezing, Paul; explanations can wait. Please show them to the bathrooms so they can get out of those wet clothes. You'll need to prepare a couple more bedrooms." He started up the darkened stairway, taking care to stay well in the shadows. "And send Jess up to me the minute she's warm enough." His voice was still that perfect blend of smoke and edginess, a lethal combination that could brush over her skin like the touch of fingers.

Her heart beating in her throat, Jessica stared after him. She turned to look at Paul. "Why didn't you tell me? He can't play, can he? My God, he can't play his music." She knew what music meant to Dillon. It was his life. His soul. "I didn't know. My mother never brought me back. She came the one time with the twins, but I was ill. When I tried to see him on my own, he refused."

"I'm sorry." Tara was crying again. "I didn't mean to do that. I couldn't stop looking at his hands. They didn't look human. It was *repulsive*. I didn't mean to do that, I didn't. I'm sorry Jessie."

Jessica knew the child needed comfort badly. Tara felt guilty and was tired, frightened, and very cold. Shaken by what she had discovered, Jessica had to fight back her own tears. "It's all right, honey, we'll find a way to fix this. You need a hot shower and a bed. Everything will be better in the morning." She looked at Trevor. He was staring up the stairway after his father as if mesmerized. "Trev? You okay?"

He nodded, clearing his throat. "I'm fine, but I don't think he is."

"That's why we're here," she pointed out. Jessica looked at Paul over Tara's bent head. She didn't believe for a minute that they'd find a way to fix the damage Tara had done, and looking at Paul's face, she guessed, neither did he. She forced a smile. "Tara, you might not remember him, you were just a little girl, but this is Paul Ritter.

He was one of the original members of the *HereAfter* band, right from the very beginning. He's a very good friend of your family."

Paul grinned at the girl. "The last time I saw you, you were five years old with a mop of curly black hair." He held out his hand to Trevor. "You had the same mop and the same curls."

"Still do," Trevor said, grinning back.

chapter 2

THICK STEAM CURLED through the bathroom, filling every corner like an unnatural fog. The tiled bathroom was large and beautiful with its deep bathtub and hanging plants. After her long, hot shower, Jessica was feeling more human, but it was impossible to see much with the steam so thick. She towel-dried the mirror, staring at the reflection of her pale face. She was exhausted, wanting only to sleep.

The last thing she wanted to do was face Dillon Wentworth looking like a frightened child. Her green eyes were too big for her face, her mouth too generous, her hair too red. She had always wished for the sophisticated, elegant look, but instead, she got the girl-next-door look. She peered closer at her reflection, hoping she seemed more mature. Without make-up she appeared younger than her twenty-five years. Jessica sighed, and shook her head in exasperation. She was no longer a child of eighteen, but a grown woman who had helped to raise Tara and Trevor. She wanted Dillon to take her seriously, to listen to what she had to say and not dismiss her as he might a teenager.

"Don't be dramatic, Jess," she cautioned aloud, "don't use words like 'life and death'. Just be matter-of-fact." She was trembling as she pulled on a dry pair of jeans, her hands shaking in spite of the hot shower. "Don't give him a chance to call you hysterical or imaginative." She hated those words. The police had used them freely when she'd consulted them after the twins had been sent the old tabloids and the phone calls had started. She was certain the police thought her a publicity-seeker.

Before she did anything else, she needed to assure herself the twins were being taken care of. Paul had shown her to a room on the second floor, a large suite with a bathroom and sitting room much like in a hotel. Jessica knew why Dillon had his private home built that way. In the beginning, he would have clung to the idea that he would play again. He would compose and record, and his home would be filled with guests. She ached for him, ached for the talent, the musical genius in him that must tear at his soul night and day. She couldn't imagine Dillon without his music.

She wandered down the wide hallway to the curving staircase. The stairs led up another story or down to the main floor. Jessica was certain she would find the twins in the kitchen and Dillon up on the third floor so she went downstairs, delaying the inevitable. The house was beautiful, all wood and high ceilings and stained glass. It had endless rooms that invited her to explore, but the sound of Tara's laughter caught at her and she hurried into the kitchen.

Paul grinned at her in greeting. "Did you follow the smell of chocolate?" He was still as she remembered him, too thin, too bleached, with a quick, engaging smile that always made her want to smile with him.

"No, the sound of laughter." Jessica kissed Tara and ruffled her hair. "I love to hear you laugh. Are you feeling better, honey?" She looked better, not so pale and cold.

Tara nodded. "Much. Chocolate always helps, doesn't it?"

"They're both chocolate freaks," Trevor informed Paul. "You have no idea how scary it gets if there's no chocolate in the house."

"Don't listen to him, Mr. Ritter," Tara scoffed. "He loves chocolate, too."

Paul burst out laughing. "I haven't had anyone call me Mr. Ritter in years, Tara. Call me Paul." He leaned companionably against the counter next to Jessica. "I had the distinct feeling Dillon had no idea you were coming. What brought you?"

"Christmas, of course," Jessica said brightly. "We wanted a family Christmas."

Paul smiled, but it didn't chase the shadows from his dark eyes. He glanced at the twins and bit off what he might have said. "We have more company now than we've had in years. The house is full, sort of old home week. Everyone must have had the same idea. Christmas, huh?" He rubbed his jaw and winked at Tara. "You want a tree and decorations and the works?"

Tara nodded solemnly. "I want a big tree and all of us decorating it like we did when Mama Rita was alive."

Jessica looked around the large kitchen, closer to tears

than she would have liked. "It looks the same in here, Paul. It's the same kitchen that was in the old house." She smiled at the twins. "Do you remember?" The thought that Dillon had had her mother's domain reproduced exactly warmed her heart. They had spent five happy years in the kitchen. Vivian had never once entered it. They had often joked that she probably didn't even know the way. But Tara, Trevor, and Jessica had spent most of their time in or near that sanctuary. It was a place of safety, of peace. A refuge when Dillon was on the road and the house was no longer a home.

Trevor nodded. "Tara and I were just talking about it with Paul. It feels like home in here. I expected to find the cupboard I scratched my name into."

Paul caught Jessica's elbow, indicating with a jerk of his head to follow him out of the room. "You don't want to keep him waiting too long, Jessie."

With a falsely cheery wave at the twins, she went with him reluctantly, somersaults beginning in the pit of her stomach. Dillon. She was going to face him after all this time. "What did you mean, old home week? Who's here, Paul?"

"The band. Even though Dillon can't play the way he used to, he still composes. You know how he is with his music. Someone got the idea to record a few songs in his studio. He has an awesome studio, of course. The sound is perfect in it, all the latest equipment, and who could resist a Dillon Wentworth song?"

"He's composing again?" Joy surged through her. "That's wonderful, just what he needs. He's been alone far too long."

Paul matched her shorter strides on the stairs. "He's having a difficult time being around anyone. He doesn't like to be seen. And his temper . . . He's used to having his own way, Jessica. He isn't the Dillon you remember."

She heard something in his voice, something that sent alarm bells ringing in her head. She looked sideways at him. "I don't expect him to be. I know you're warning me off, trying to protect him, but Trevor and Tara need a father. He may have gone through a lot, but so did they. They lost their home and parents. Vivian might not have counted, they barely knew her and what they remember isn't pleasant, but he abandoned them. Add it up any way you like, he retreated and left them behind."

Paul stopped on the second floor landing, looking up the staircase. "He went through hell. Over a year in the hospital, so they could do what they could for his burns, all those surgeries, the skin grafts, and through it all, the reporters hounding him. And, of course, the trial. He went to court covered in bandages like a damned mummy. It was a media circus. Television cameras in his face, people staring at him like he was some freak. They wanted to believe he murdered Vivian and her lover. They wanted him to be guilty. Vivian wasn't the only one who died that night. Seven people died in that fire. They made him out to be a monster."

"I was here," Jessica reminded him softly, her stomach revolting at the memories. "I crawled through the house on my hands and knees with two five-year-olds, Paul. I pushed them out a window and followed them. Tara rolled down the side of the cliff and nearly drowned in the ocean. I didn't get her out of the sea and make my way

around to the other side of the house in time to let Dillon
know we were safe." She had been so exhausted after battling to save Tara who could barely stay afloat. She had
wasted precious time lying on the shore with the children, her heart racing and her lungs burning. While she'd
been lying there, Dillon had fought past the others and
run back into the burning house to save the children. She
pressed a hand to her head. "You think I don't think of it
every day of my life? What I should have done? I can't
change it, I can't go back and do it over." Guilt washed
over her, through her, so that she felt sick with it.

"Jessica." Dillon's voice floated down the stairs. No one
had a voice like Dillon Wentworth's. The way he said her
name conjured up night fantasies, vivid impressions of
black velvet brushing over exposed skin. He could weave
spells with that voice, mesmerize, hold thousands of people enthralled. His voice was a potent weapon and she
had always been very susceptible.

Jessica grasped the banister and went up to him. He
waited at the top of the stairs. It saddened her to see that
he had changed and was wearing a long-sleeved white
shirt that concealed his scarred arms. A pair of thin black
leather gloves covered his hands. He was thinner than in
the old days, but still gave the impression of immense
power that she remembered so vividly. He moved with
grace, a sense of rhythm. His body didn't just walk across
a stage, it flowed. He was only nine years older than she,
but lines of suffering were etched into his face, and his
eyes reflected a deep inner pain.

"Dillon." She said his name. There was so much more,
so many words, so many emotions rising up out of the

ashes of their past. She wanted to hold him close, gather him into her arms. She wanted him to reach for her, but she knew he wouldn't touch her. Jessica smiled instead, hoping he would see how she felt. "I'm so glad to see you again."

There was no answering smile on his face. "What in the world are you doing here, Jessica? What were you thinking, bringing the children here?"

His face was a mask she couldn't penetrate. Paul was right. Dillon wasn't the same man any longer. This man was a stranger to her. He looked like Dillon, he even moved like Dillon, but there was a cruel edge to his mouth where before there had been a ready smile and a certain sensuality. His blue eyes had always burned with his intensity, his drive, his wild passions, his joy of life. Now they burned a piercing ice-blue.

"Are you taking a good look?" He had a way of twisting his words right at the end, a different accent that was all his own. His words were bitter but his voice was even, cool. "Look your fill, Jess, get it out of your system."

"I'm looking, Dillon. Why not? I haven't seen you in seven years. Not since the accident." She kept her voice strictly neutral when a part of her wanted to weep for him. Not for the scars on his body, but the ones far worse, the ones on his soul. And he was looking at her, his gaze like a rapier as it moved over her, taking in every detail. Jessica would not allow him to rattle her. This was too important for all of them. Tara and Trevor had no one else to fight for them, for their rights. For their protection. And neither, it seemed, did Dillon.

"Is that what you believe, Jessica? That it was an accident?" A small, humorless smile softened the edge of his mouth but made his eyes glitter like icy crystals. He turned away from her and led the way to his study. Dillon stepped back, gestured for her to precede him. "You're much more naive than I ever gave you credit for being."

Jessica's body brushed up against his as she stepped past him to enter his private domain. At once she became aware of him as a man, her every nerve ending leaping to life. Electricity seemed to arc between them. He drew in his breath sharply and his eyes went smoky before he turned away from her.

She looked around his study, away from him and his virility, and found it to be comforting. It was more like the Dillon she remembered. All warm leather, golds and browns, warm colors. Books were in floor-to-ceiling shelves, glass doors guarding treasures. "The fire was an accident," she ventured, feeling her way carefully with him.

The ground seemed to be shifting out from under her feet. This house was different, and yet the same as the one she remembered. There were places of comfort that could quickly disappear. Dillon was a stranger, and there was something threatening in his glittering gaze. He watched her with the same unblinking menace of a predator. Uneasily, Jessica seated herself across from him with the huge mahogany desk between them, feeling she was facing a foe, not a friend.

"That's the official verdict, isn't it? Funny word, official. You can make almost anything official if you write it up on paper and repeat it often enough."

Jessica was uncertain how to reply. She had no idea

what he was implying. She twisted her fingers together, her green eyes watching him intently. "What are you saying, Dillon? Do you think Vivian started the fire on purpose?"

"Poor neglected Vivian." He sighed. "You bring back too many memories, Jess, ones I can do without."

In her lap, her fingers twisted together tightly. "I'm sorry for that, Dillon. Most of my memories of you are wonderful and I cherish them."

He leaned back in his chair, carefully positioned to keep his body in the deeper shadows. "Tell me about yourself. What have you been doing lately?"

Her green gaze met his blue one squarely. "I have a degree in music and I work at Eternity Studios as a sound engineer. But I think you know that."

He nodded. "They say you're brilliant at it, Jess." He watched her mouth curve and his body tightened in reaction. Actually hardened, in a heavy, throbbing ache. He was fascinated by her mouth and his fascination disgusted him. It brought up too many sins he didn't want to think about. Jessica Fitzpatrick should never have walked back into his life.

"You moved the house away from the cliffs," she said.

"I never liked it there. It wasn't safe." His blue eyes slid over her figure, deliberately appraising. Almost insulting. "Tell me about the men in your life. I presume you have one or two? Did you come here to tell me you've found someone and you're dumping the kids?" The idea of it enraged him. A volcanic heat that erupted into his bloodstream to swirl thick and hot and dangerous.

There was an edge to him, one she couldn't quite nail down. As soon as she focused on something, he shifted

nd moved so that she was thrown off balance. Their
onversation seemed more like one of the chess matches
ney'd often played in her mother's kitchen so many years
arlier. She was no match for him in sparring and she
new it. Dillon could cut the heart out of someone with a
mile on his face. She'd seen him do it, charming, edgy,
aying the one thing that would shatter his opponent like
lass.

"Are we at war, Dillon?" Jessica asked. "Because if we
re, you should lay out the rules for me. We came here to
pend Christmas with you."

"Christmas?" He nearly spat the word. "I don't do
hristmas."

"Well, we do Christmas, your children, your family,
illon. You remember family, don't you? We haven't seen
ou in years; I thought you might be pleased."

His eyebrow shot up. "Pleased, Jess? You thought I'd be
leased? You didn't think that for a minute. Let's have a
ttle honesty between us."

Her temper was beginning a slow smolder. "I doubt if
ou know the meaning of honesty, Dillon. You lie to
ourself so much it's become a habit." She was appalled at
er own lack of control. The accusation slipped out
efore she could censor it.

He leaned back in his leather chair, his body sprawled
ut, lazy and amused, still in the shadows. "I wondered
hen your temper would start to surface. I remember the
ld days when you would go up in flames if someone
ushed you hard enough. It's still there, hidden deep, but
ou burn, don't you, Jess?"

Dillon remembered it all too vividly. He'd been a

grown man, for God's sake, nearly twenty-seven with two children and an insane drug addict for a wife. And he'd been obsessed with an eighteen-year-old girl. It was sick, disgusting. Beyond his every understanding. Jessica had always been so alive, so passionate about life. She was intelligent; she had a mind that was like a hungry sponge. She shared his love of music, old buildings, and nature. She loved his children. He'd never touched her, never allowed himself to think of her sexually, but he had noticed every detail about her and he detested himself for that weakness.

"Are you purposely goading me to see what I'll do?" She tried not to sound hurt, but was afraid it showed on her face. He always noticed the smallest detail about everyone.

"Damn right I am," he suddenly admitted, his blue eyes glittering at her, his lazy, indolent manner gone in a flash. "Why the hell did you bring my children all this way, scaring the hell out of them, risking their lives . . ." He wanted to strangle her. Wrap his hands around her slender neck and strangle her for wreaking havoc with his life again. He couldn't afford to have Jessica around. Not now. Not ever.

"I did not risk their lives." Her green eyes glared at him as she denied the charge.

"You risked them in that kind of weather. You didn't even call me first."

Jessica took a deep breath and let it out slowly. "No, I didn't call. You would have said not to come. They belong here, Dillon."

"Jessica, all grown up. It's hard to stop thinking of you

s a wild teen and accept that you're a grown woman."
His tone was sheer insult.

Her chin lifted. "Really, Dillon, I would have thought
you would have preferred to think of me as a much older
woman. You certainly were willing to leave Trevor and
Tara with me after Mama's death, no matter what my
age."

He rose from his chair, moving quickly across the
room, putting distance between them. "Is that what this
is about? You want more money?"

Jessica remained silent, simply watching him. It took a
great deal of self-control not to get up and walk out. She
allowed the silence to stretch out between them, a taut,
tension-filled moment. Dillon finally turned to look at
her.

"That was beneath even you, Dillon," she said softly.
"Someone should have slapped your face a long time ago.
Are you expecting me to feel sorry for you? Is that what
you're looking for from me? Pity? Sympathy? You're
going to have a long wait."

He leaned against the bookcase, his blue eyes fixed on
her face. "I suppose I deserved that." His gloved fingers
slid along the spine of a book. Back and forth. Whispered
over the leather. "Money has never held much allure for
you or your mother. I was sorry to hear of her death."

"Were you? How kind of you, Dillon, to be sorry to
hear. She was my mother and the mother of your children, whether you want to acknowledge that or not. My
mother took care of Tara and Trevor almost from the day
they were born. They never knew any other mother. They
were devastated at losing her. I was devastated. Your kind

gesture of flowers and seeing to all the arrangements . . . lacked something."

He straightened, pulled himself up to his full height, his blue eyes ice-cold. "My God, you're reprimanding me, questioning my actions."

"What actions, Dillon? You made a few phone calls. I doubt that took more than a few minutes of your precious time. More likely you asked Paul to make the phone calls for you."

His dark brow shot up. "What did you expect me to do, Jessica? Show up at the funeral? Cause another media circus? Do you really think the press would have left it alone? The unsolved *murders* and the fire were a high profile case."

"It wasn't about you, Dillon, was it? Not everything is about you. All that mattered to you was that your life didn't change. It's been eleven months since my mother's death and it didn't change, did it? Not at all. You made certain of that. I just stepped right into my mother's shoes, didn't I? You knew I'd never give them up or let them go into foster care. The minute you suggested hiring a stranger, maybe breaking them up, you knew I'd keep them together."

He shrugged, in no way remorseful. "They belonged with you. They've been with you their entire life. Who better than you, Jessica? I already knew you loved them, that you would risk your life for them. Tell me why I was wrong not to want the best for my children?"

"They belong with you, Dillon. Here, with you. They need a father."

His laughter was bitter, without a trace of humor. "A

father? Is that what I'm supposed to be, Jessica? I seem to recall my earlier parenting skills. I left them with their mother in a house on an island with no fire department. Do you remember that as vividly as I do? Because, believe me, it's etched in my brain. I left them with a mother who I knew was out of her mind. I knew she was flying on drugs, that she was unstable and violent. I knew she brought her friends here. And worse, I knew she was fooling around with people who were occultists. I let them into my home with my children, with you." He raked gloved fingers through his black hair, tousling the unruly curls so that his hair fell in waves around the perfection of his face.

He pushed away from the bookcase, a quicksilver movement of impatience, then stalked across the floor with all the grace of a ballet dancer and all the stealth of a leopard. When had his obsession started? He only remembered longing to get home, to sit in the kitchen and watch the expressions chasing across Jessica's face. He wrote his songs about her. Found peace in her presence. Jessica had a gift for silences, for laughter. He watched her all the time, and yet, in the end, he had failed her, too.

"Dillon, you're being way too hard on yourself," Jessica said softly. "You were so young back then, and everything came at once—the fame and fortune. The world was upside down. You used to say you didn't know reality, what was up or what was down. And you were working, making it all come together for everyone. You had so many others who needed the money you generated. Everyone depended on you. Why should you expect that you would have handled everything so perfectly? You weren't responsible for Vivian's decisions to use drugs nor were you responsible for any of the things she did."

"Really? She was clearly ill, Jess. Whose responsibility was she if not mine?"

"You put her in countless rehabs. We all heard her threaten to commit suicide if you left her. She threatened to take the kids." She threatened a lot more than that. More than once Vivian had rushed to the nursery, shouting she would throw the twins in the foaming sea. Jessica pressed a hand to her mouth as the memory rose up to haunt her. He had tried to get her committed, to put her in a psychiatric hospital, but Vivian was adept at fooling the doctors, and they believed her tales of a philandering husband who wanted her out of the way while he did drugs and slept with groupies. The tabloids certainly supported her accusations.

"I took the easy way out. I left. I went on the road and I left my children, and you, and Rita, to her insanity."

"The tour had been booked for a long time," Jessica pointed out. "Dillon, it's all water under the bridge. We can't change the things that happened, we can only go forward. Tara and Trevor need you now. I'm not saying they should live with you, but they should have a relationship with you. You're missing so much by not knowing them, and they're missing so much by not knowing you."

"You don't even know who I am anymore, Jess," Dillon said quietly.

"Exactly my point. We're staying through Christmas.

That's nearly three weeks and it should give us plenty of time to get to know each other again."

"Tara finds me repulsive to look at. Do you think I would subject a child of mine to my own nightmare?" He paced across the hardwood floor, a quick restless movement, graceful and fluid, so reminiscent of the old Dillon. There was so much passion in him, so much emotion, he could never contain it. It flowed out of him, warmed those around him so that they wanted to bask in his presence.

Jessica was sensitive to his every emotion, she always had been. She could practically see his soul bleeding, cut so deeply the gash was nearly impossible to heal. But agreeing with his twisted logic wouldn't help him. Dillon had given up on life. He had locked his heart from the world and was determined to keep it that way. "Tara is only thirteen years old, Dillon. You're doing her an injustice. It was a shock to her, but it's unfair to keep her out of your life because she had a childish reaction to your scars."

"It will be better for her if you take her away from here."

Jessica shook her head. "It'll be better for you, you mean. You aren't thinking of her at all. You've become selfish, Dillon, living here, feeling sorry for yourself."

He whipped around, taking her breath away with his speed. He was on her before she had a chance to run, catching her arm, his fingers wrapping around it so tightly she could feel the thick ridges of his scars against her skin, despite the leather of his glove. He dragged her close to him, right up against his chest, pulled her tight so that every soft curve of her body was pressed relentlessly against him. "How dare you say that to me." His blue eyes glared at her, icy cold, *burning* with cold.

Jessica refused to flinch. She locked her gaze with his. "Someone should have said it a long time ago, Dillon. I don't know what you're doing here all alone in this big house, on your wild island, but it certainly isn't living. You dropped out and you don't have the right to do that. You *chose* to have children. You brought them into this world and you are responsible for them."

His eyes blazed down into hers, his mouth hardened into a cruel line. She felt the change in him. The male aggression. The savage hostility. His hand tangled in the wealth of hair at the nape of her neck, hauled her head back. He fastened his mouth to hers hungrily. Angrily. Greedily. It was supposed to frighten her, to punish her. To drive her away. He used a bruising force, demanded submission, in a primitive retaliation designed to send her running from him.

Jessica tasted the hot anger, the fierce need to conquer and control, but she also tasted dark passion, as elemental as time. She felt the passion flood his body, harden his every muscle to iron, soften his lips when they would have been brutal. Jessica remained passive beneath the onslaught, her heart racing, her body coming alive. She didn't fight him, she didn't resist, but she didn't participate either.

Dillon lifted his head abruptly, swore foully, dropped his hands as if she had burned him. "Get out of here, Jessica. Get out before I take what I want. I'm damned selfish enough to do it. Get out and take the kids with you, I won't have them here. Sleep here tonight and stay the hell out of my way, then go when the storm passes. I'll have Paul take you home."

She stood there, one hand pressed to her swollen lips, shocked at the way her body throbbed and clenched in reaction to his. "You don't have a choice in the matter, Dillon. You are perfectly within your rights to send me away, but not Tara and Trevor. Someone is trying to kill them."

chapter

3

"WHAT THE HELL are you talking about?"
All at once Dillon looked so menacing, that
Jessica actually stepped back.

She held up her hand, more frightened of him than
she had ever conceived she could be. There was something merciless in his eyes. Something terrifying. And for
the first time, she recognized him as a dangerous man.
That had never been a part of Dillon's makeup, but
events had twisted him, shaped him, just as they had
shaped her. She had to stop persisting in seeing him as
the man she had loved so much. He was different. She
could feel the explosive violence in him swirling close to
the surface.

Had she made a terrible mistake in coming to Dillon?
In bringing the children to him? Her first duty was to
Trevor and Tara. She loved them as a mother would, or, at
the very least, an older sister.

"What the hell are you up to?" he snapped.

"What am I . . ." Her voice broke off in astonishment.
Fear gave way to a sudden wave of fury. She stopped

backing away and even took a step toward him, her fingers curling into fists. "You think I'm making up a story, Dillon? Do you think I dragged the children out of a home they're familiar with, away from their friends, in secret, in the dead of night, to see a man they have no reason to love, who *obviously* doesn't want them here, on a whim? Because I felt like it? For what? Your stupid, pitiful money?" She sneered it at him, throwing his anger right back in his face. "It always comes back to that, doesn't it?"

"If I *obviously* don't want to have them here, why would you bring them?" His blue eyes burned with a matching fury, her words obviously stinging.

"You're right, we shouldn't have come here, it was stupid to think you had enough humanity left in you to care about your own children."

Their gazes were locked, two combatants, two strong, passionate personalities. There was a silence while Jessica's heart hammered out her fury and her eyes blazed at him. Dillon regarded her for a long time. He moved first, sighing audibly, breaking the tension, walking back to his desk with his easy, flowing grace. "I see you have a high opinion of me, Jessica."

"You're the one accusing me of being a greedy, grasping, money-hungry witch," she pointed out. "I'd say you were the one with a pretty poor opinion of me." Her chin jutted at him, her face stiff with pride. "I must say, while you're throwing out accusations, you didn't even have the courtesy to answer my letter suggesting the children come live with you after my mother died."

"There was no letter."

"There was a letter, Dillon. You ignored it like you

ignored us. If I'm so money-hungry, why did you leave your children with me for all these months? Mom was dead, you knew that, yet you made no attempt to bring the children back here with you and you didn't respond to my letter."

"You might remember when you're stating things you know nothing about that you are in my home. I didn't turn you out, despite the fact that you didn't have the courtesy to phone ahead."

Her eyebrow shot up. "Is that a threat? What? You're going to kick me out into the storm or even better, send me to the boathouse or the caretaker's cottage? Give me a break, Dillon. I know you better than that!"

"I'm not that man you once knew, Jess, I never will be again." He fell silent for a moment watching the expressions chase across her face. When she stirred, as if to speak, he held up his hand. "Did you know your mother came to see me just two days before she died?" His voice was very quiet.

A chill went down her spine as she realized what he was saying. Her mother had gone to see Dillon and two days later she was dead in what certainly wasn't an accident. Jessica didn't move. She couldn't move as she assimilated the information. She knew the two incidents had to be connected. She could feel his eyes on her, but there was a strange roaring in her ears. Her legs were all at once rubbery and the room tilted crazily. *She had brought Trevor and Tara to him.*

"Jessica!" He said her name sharply, "Don't faint on me. What's wrong?" He dragged a chair out and forced her into it, pushing her head down, the leather covering his palm feeling strange on the nape of her neck. "Breathe. Just breathe."

She inhaled deeply, taking in great gulps of air, fighting off dizziness. "I'm just tired, Dillon, I'm all right, really I am." She sounded unconvincing even to her own ears.

"Something about your mother's coming here upset you, Jess. Why should that bother you? She often wrote or called to update me on the progress of the kids."

"Why would she come here?" Jessica forced air into her lungs and waited for the dizziness to subside completely. Dillon's hand was strong on her nape; he wasn't going to allow her to sit up unless she was fully recovered. "I'm fine, really." She pushed at his arm, not wanting the contact with him. He was too close. Too charismatic. And he had too many dark secrets.

Dillon abruptly let her go, almost as if he could read her thoughts. He moved away from her, back around the desk, back into the shadows, and hid his gloved hands below the desk, out of her sight. Jessica was certain his hands had been trembling.

"Why should it upset you that your mother came to see me? And why would you think someone might want to harm the twins?" The anger between them had dissipated as if it had never been, leaving his voice soft again, persuasive, so gentle it turned her heart over. "Does it hurt to talk about her? Is it too soon?"

Jessica gritted her teeth against his effect on her. They had been so close at one time. He had filled her life with his presence, his laughter, and warmth. He had made the entire household feel safe when he was home. It was difficult to sit across from him, thrown back to those days of camaraderie by his smoky voice, when she knew he was a different person now.

"My mother's car had been tampered with." Jessica blurted it out in a rush. She held up her hand to stop his inevitable protest. "Just hear me out before you tell me I'm crazy. I know what the police report said. Her brakes failed. She went over a cliff." She was choosing her words carefully. "I accepted that it was an accident but then other accidents started happening. Little disturbing things at first, things like the fan on a motor ripping loose and tearing through the hood and windshield of *my* car."

"What?" He sat up straight. "Was anyone hurt?"

She shook her head. "Tara had just gotten into the backseat. Trevor wasn't in the car. I had a few scratches, nothing serious. A mechanic explained the entire thing away, but it worried me. And then there was the horse. Trevor and Tara ride every Thursday at a local stable. Same time, every week. Trev's horse went crazy, bucking, spinning, squealing, it was awful. The horse nearly fell over backward. They discovered a drug in the horse's system." She looked straight at him. "I also found this in the horse's stall, sticking out of the straw." Watching his face she handed him the guitar pick with the distinctive design made for Dillon Wentworth as a gift so many years ago. "Trevor admitted that it might have been in his pocket and fallen out. That and other things were sent anonymously to the kids."

"I see." He sounded grim.

"The stable owners believe it was a prank on the horse, that it happens sometimes. The police thought Trevor did it, and grilled him until I called an attorney. Trevor would never do such a thing. But it felt wrong to me, two accidents so close together and only a few months after my mother's car went out of control." Jessica tapped her fingernail on the edge of his desk, a nervous habit when she was worried. "I might have accepted the accidents had that been the end of it, but it wasn't." She watched him very, very closely, trying to see past the impassive expression on his face. "Of course, the incidents didn't happen one on top of the other, a couple of weeks elapsed between them." She wanted desperately to read his blue eyes, but she saw only ice.

Jessica shivered again, experiencing a frisson of fear at being alone in the shadowy room with a man who wore a mask and guarded the darkness in his soul as if it were treasure.

"What is it, Jess?" He asked the question quietly.

What could she say? He was a stranger she no longer trusted completely. "Why did my mother come here and when?"

"Two days before her death. I asked her to come."

Her throat tightened. "In seven years you never asked us here. Why would you suddenly ask my mother to travel all the way out here to see you?"

One dark brow shot up. "Obviously because I couldn't go to see her."

The alarm bells were ringing in her mind again. He was sidestepping the question, not wanting to answer her. It was too much of a coincidence, her mother's visiting Dillon at his island home and two days later her brakes mysteriously failing. The two events had to be connected.

She remained silent, suspicion finding its way into her heart.

"What else has happened? There must be more."

"Three days ago the brakes on my car failed, too. It was a miracle we all lived through it. The car was totaled. Someone also has been phoning the house and sent old newspaper accounts of the fire to the children. That's when the guitar pick was sent. The phone calls were frightening. That, along with the other incidents over the last few months, made me decide to bring them here to you. I knew they would be safe here." She injected a note of confidence into her voice which she no longer felt. Her instincts were on alert. "Christmas was a natural, a perfect excuse should anyone question why we decided to visit you." She had been so certain he would be softer at Christmastime, more vulnerable and much more likely to let them into his life again. She had run to him for protection, for healing, and she was very much afraid she had made an enormous mistake.

Dillon leaned toward her, his blue eyes vivid and sharp. "Tell me about these phone calls."

"The voice was recorded like a robot's voice. Whoever was calling must have prerecorded it and then played it when one of the twins answered. They said terrible things about you, accused you of murdering Vivian and her lover. Of locking everyone inside the room and starting the fire. Once he said you might kill them, too." She could hear her own heart beating as she confessed. "I stopped allowing the twins to answer the phone and I made plans to come here."

"Have you told anyone else about this?"

"Only the police," she admitted. She looked away from him, afraid of seeing something she couldn't face. "The minute they realized Trevor and Tara were your children, they seemed to think I was looking to grab headlines. They asked if I was planning to sell my story to the tabloids. The incidents, other than the car, were minor things easily explained away. In the end they said they would look into it, and they took a report, but I think they thought I was either a publicity-seeker or the hysterical type."

"I'm sorry, Jess, that must have been painful for you." There was a quiet sincerity in the pure sensuality of his voice. "I've known you all of your life. You've never been one to panic."

The moment he said the words aloud, her heart slammed hard in her chest. Both of them froze, completely still while the disturbing memories invaded, crowding in, filling the room like insidious demons crawling along the floor and the walls. A sneak attack, uninvited, unexpected, but all-invasive. The air seemed to thicken with the heavy weight of memory. Evil had come with the mere mention of a single word and both of them felt its presence.

Jessica did indeed know panic intimately. She knew complete and utter hysteria. She knew the feeling of being so helpless, so vulnerable, so stripped of power she had wanted to scream until her throat was raw. Humiliation brought color sweeping up her face and her green gaze skittered away from Dillon's. No one else knew. No one. Not even her mother. She had never told her mother the entire truth. The nightmare was too real, too ugly, and she couldn't look at it.

"I'm sorry, Jess, I didn't mean to bring it up." His voice was ultra soft, soothing.

She managed to get her shaky legs under her, managed to keep from trembling visibly, although her insides were jelly as she pushed away from his desk. "I don't think about it." But she dreamt about it. Night after night, she dreamt about it. Her stomach lurched crazily. She needed air, needed to get away from him, away from the intensity of his burning, all-seeing eyes. For a moment she detested him, detested that he saw her so naked and vulnerable.

"Jessica." He said her name. Breathed her name.

She backed away from him, raw and exposed. "I *never* think about it." Jessica took the coward's way out and retreated, whirling around and fleeing the room. Tears welled up, swimming in her eyes, blurring her vision, but somehow, she made her way down the stairs.

She could feel Dillon's eyes on her, knew he followed her descent down the stairs but she didn't turn around, didn't look at him. She kept moving, her head high, counting in her head to keep the echo of the long ago voices, of the ancient, hideous chanting from stealing its way into her mind.

When she reached her room, Jessica shut the door firmly, and threw herself, face down, onto the bed, breathing deeply, fighting for control. She was no child, but a grown woman. She had responsibilities. She had confidence in herself. She would not, *could* not let anything or anyone shake her. She knew she should get up, check on Tara and Trevor, make certain they were comfortable in the rooms Paul had provided for them, on either side of her room, but she was too tired, too drained to move. She lay there, not altogether asleep, not altogether awake, but drifting, somewhere in between.

And the memories came to take her back in time.

There was always the chanting when Vivian and her friends were together. Jessica forced herself to walk down the hallway, hating to go near them, but needing to find Tara's favorite blanket. Tara would never go to sleep otherwise. Her heart was pounding, her mouth dry. Vivian's friends frightened her with their sly, leering smiles, their black candles, and wild orgies. Jessica knew they pretended to worship Satan, they talked continually of pleasures and religious practices, but none of them really knew what they were talking about. They made it up as they went along, doing whatever they pleased, each trying to outdo the other in whatever outrageous perverted sexual ritual they could envision.

As Jessica moved past the living room, she glanced inside. Black heavy drapes darkened the windows, candles were lit in every conceivable space. Vivian looked up from where she sat on the couch, naked from the waist up, sipping her wine while a man lapped greedily at her breasts. Another woman was naked while several men surrounded her, touching and grunting eagerly. The sight sickened and embarrassed Jessica and she looked away quickly.

"Jessica!" Vivian's voice was imperious, that of a queen speaking to a peasant. "Come in here."

Jessica could see the madness on Vivian's flushed face, in her hard, over-bright eyes, and hear it in her loud, brittle laugh. She made herself smile vaguely. "I'm sorry, Mrs.

Wentworth, I have to get back to Tara immediately." She kept moving.

A hard hand fell on her shoulder, another hand clapped over her mouth hard enough to sting. Jessica was dragged into the living room. She couldn't see her captor, but he was big and very strong. She struggled wildly, but he held her, laughing, calling out to Vivian to lock the door.

Hot breath hit her ear. "Are you the sweet little virgin Vivian is always teasing us with? Is this your little prize, Viv?"

Vivian's giggle was high-pitched, insane. "Dillon's little princess." Her words slurred and she circled Jessica and her captor several times. "Do you think he's had her yet?" A long-tipped fingernail traced a path down Jessica's cheek. "You're going to have such fun with us, little Jessica." She made a ceremony of lighting more candles and incense, taking her time, humming softly. "Tape her mouth, she'll scream if you don't." She gave the order and resumed her humming, stopping to kiss one of the men who was staring at Jessica with hot, greedy eyes. Jessica fought, biting at the hand covering her mouth, a terrified cry welling up. She could hear herself, screaming in her head, over and over, but no sound emerged.

She struggled, rolled over, the sound of ugly laughter fading into terrified weeping. She woke completely, sobbing wildly. She pushed the pillow harder against her face, muffling the sound, relieved it was a nightmare, relieved she had managed to wake herself up.

Very slowly she sat up and looked around the large, pleasant room. It was very cold, surprisingly so when Paul had turned on the heater to take the chill off.

Pushing at her long hair, she sat on the edge of the bed with tears running down her face and the taste of terror in her mouth. She hadn't come back to the island with the sole purpose of keeping the children safe. She had come back in the hopes of healing herself, Dillon, and the children, of finding peace for all of them. Jessica rubbed her hand over her face, resolutely wiping the tears away. Instead the nightmares were getting worse. Dillon wasn't the same man she had known seven years ago. She wasn't the same hero-worshipping girl.

She had to think clearly, think everything through. Tara and Trevor were her greatest concern. Jessica flicked on the lamp beside the bed. She couldn't bear to sit in the dark when her memories were so raw. The curtains fluttered, danced gently, gracefully in the breeze. She stared at the window. It was wide open, fog and rain and wind creeping into her room. The window had been closed when she'd left the room. She was absolutely certain of it. A chill crept down her spine, unease prickling her skin.

Jessica looked quickly around the room, her gaze seeking the corners, peeking beneath the bed. She couldn't stop herself from looking in the closet, the bathroom, and the shower. It would be difficult for anyone to enter her room through the open window, especially in a rainstorm, because it was on the second floor. She tried to convince herself one of the twins must have come into her room to say goodnight and opened the window to let in some air. She couldn't imagine why, it didn't make any sense, but she preferred this explanation to the alternative.

She crossed the room to the window, stared out into

the forest, and watched the wind as it played roughly in the trees. There was something elemental, powerful about storms that fascinated her. She watched the rain for a while, allowing a certain peace to settle back over her. Then, abruptly, she closed the window and went to check on Tara.

The bedside lamp was on in Tara's room, spilling a soft circle of light across it. To Jessica's surprise, Trevor lay on the floor wrapped in a heap of blankets, while Tara lay on the bed beneath a thick quilt. They were talking in low tones and neither looked at all astonished to see her.

"We thought you'd never come," Tara greeted, moving over, obviously expecting Jessica to share her bed.

"I thought I was going to have to go rescue you," Trevor added. "We were just discussing how to go about it since we didn't exactly know which room you were in."

Warmth drove out the cold in her soul, pushing away her nameless fears and the disturbing remnants of old horrors. She smiled at them and rushed to the bed, jumping beneath the covers and snuggling into the pillow. "Were you really worried?"

"Of course we were," Tara confirmed. She reached for Jessica's hand. "Did he yell at you?"

Trevor snorted. "We didn't see any fireworks, did we? If he yelled at her we would have seen the Fourth of July."

"Hey, now," Jessica objected. "I'm not that bad."

Trevor made a rude noise. "Flames fly off you, Jess, if someone gets you angry enough. I can't see you being all mealymouthed if our own father didn't want us for Christmas. You'd read him the riot act, probably knock

im on his butt and march us out of his house. You'd
nake us swim back to the nearest city."

Tara giggled, nodding her head. "We call you Mama
Tiger behind your back."

"What?" Jessica found herself laughing. "Total exag-
eration. Total!"

"You're worse. You grow fangs and claws if someone is
mean to us," Trevor pointed out complacently. "Justice
or the children." He grinned at her. "Unless you're the
ne getting after us."

Jessica threw her pillow at him with perfect aim. "You
ttle punk, I never get after you. What are you doing
wake, it's four-thirty in the morning."

The twins erupted into laughter, pointing at her and
mimicking her question. "That's called getting after us,
ss," Tara said. "You're worse than Mama Rita was."

"She spoiled you rotten," Jessica told them haughtily,
aughter brimming over in her green eyes. "All right, fine,
ut nobody in their right mind is up at four-thirty in the
morning. It's silly. *And* it was a perfectly *reasonable* ques-
on."

"Yeah, because we're not in some spooky old house
ith total strangers and a man who might want to throw
s out on our butts or anything like that," Trevor said.

"Taking you off upstairs to do some dastardly deed
e've never heard of," Tara said, adding her two cents.

"When did you two become such smart alecks?"
ssica wanted to know.

"We talked to Paul for a while downstairs," Trevor said
hen the laughter had subsided. "He's really nice. He said
e knew us when we were little."

Jessica was aware of both pairs of eyes on her. She caught the pillow Trevor tossed to her and slipped it behind her back as she sat up, drawing up her knees. "He and your father were best friends long before the band was put together. Paul actually was the original singer for their band. Dillon wrote most of the songs and played lead guitar. He could play almost any instrument. Paul played bass guitar, but he sang the songs when they first started out. Brian Phillips was the drummer and I think it was his idea to form the band. They started out in a garage and played all the clubs and made the rounds. Eventually they became very famous."

"There were a couple of other band members, Robert something," Trevor interrupted. "He was on keyboard and for some reason I thought Don Ford was the bass player. He's on all the CD covers and in the old magazine articles written on *HereAfter*." There was a note of pride when he said the band's name.

Jessica nodded. "Robert Berg. Robert's awesome on the keyboard. And yes, Don was brought in to play bass. Somewhere along the line, Paul picked up a big drug habit."

Tara wrinkled her nose. "He seemed so nice."

Jessica pushed back her hair. "He is nice, Tara. People make mistakes, they get into things without thinking and then it's too late to get out. Paul told me he began using all the time and couldn't remember the lyrics to the songs during their live performances. Your father would step up and sing. Paul said the crowds went wild. Paul was on a downward spiral and eventually the band members wanted him out. He was doing crazy things, tearing places up, not showing up for scheduled events, that sort of thing, and they said enough."

"Just like you read in the tabloids," Trevor pointed out.

There was a small silence while both children looked at her. "Yes, that's true. But it doesn't make the things they wrote about your father true. Remember, this was all a long time ago. Sometimes when people become famous too fast, have too much money, they have a hard time handling it all. I think Paul was one of those people. It overwhelmed him. Girls were throwing themselves at him all the time, there was just too much of everything. Anyway, Dillon wouldn't give up on him. He made him go into rehab and helped him recover."

"Is that when they picked up another bass player?" Trevor guessed.

Jessica nodded. "The band really took off while Paul was cleaning himself up and they had to have another bass player, so Don was brought in. Dillon's voice rocketed them into stardom. But he wouldn't leave Paul behind. Your father gave Paul a job working in the studio and eventually made a place for him in the band. And when Dillon needed him most, Paul came through."

"Did Paul know Vivian?" Tara's question was hesitant.

Jessica realized Vivian still managed to bring tension into a room years after her death. "Yes he did, honey," she confirmed gently. "All of the members of the band knew Vivian. Paul didn't do all the tours with them so he often stayed here, seeing to things at home. He knew her better than most." And despised her. Jessica remembered the terrible arguments and Vivian's endless tirades. Paul had tried to keep her under control, tried to help Rita and Jessica keep the twins safe when she brought her friends in.

"Does he think my father murdered Vivian and that man she was with, like the newspaper said?"

Jessica swung her head around, her temper rising until she saw Tara's bent head. Slowly she let her breath out. How else was Tara going to learn the truth about her father if she couldn't ask questions? "Honey, you know most of those tabloids don't tell the truth, right? They sensationalize things, write misleading headlines and articles to grab people's attention. It wasn't any different when your father was at the height of his career. The tabloids twisted all the facts, made it sound as if Dillon found your mother in bed with another man. They made it sound like he shot them both and then burned down his own house to cover the murders. It didn't happen like that at all." Jessica curved her arm around Tara's shoulders and pulled her close, hugging her. "Your father was acquitted at the trial. He had nothing to do with the shooting or the fire. He wasn't even in the house when it all happened."

"What did happen, Jess?" Trevor asked, his piercing blue gaze meeting hers steadily. "Why wouldn't you ever tell us?"

"We're not babies," Tara pointed out, but she cuddled closer to Jessica's warmth, clearly for comfort.

Jessica shook her head. "I would prefer your father tell you about that night, not me."

"We'll believe you, Jess," Trevor said. "You turn beet red if you try to lie. We don't know our father. We don't know Paul. Mama Rita wouldn't say a word about it. You know it's time you told us the truth if someone is sending us newspapers filled with lies and calling us on the phone telling more lies."

"It's the three of us, Jessie," Tara added. "It's always been the three of us. We're a family. We want you to tell us."

Jessica was proud of them, proud of the way they were attempting to handle a volatile and frightening situation. And she heard the love in their voices, felt the answering emotion welling up in her. They weren't babies anymore, and they were right, they deserved to know the truth. She didn't know if Dillon would ever tell them.

Jessica took a deep breath, then she began. "There was a party at the house that night. Your father had been gone for months on a world tour and Vivian often invited her friends over. I didn't know her very well." The fact was, Jessica had never understood Dillon's relationship with his wife. Vivian had left the twins with Rita from almost the moment they were born so she could tour with the band. She rarely returned home the first three years of their lives. Yet during the last year of her life she had stayed home, the band's manager refusing to allow her to travel with them due to her violent mood swings and psychotic behavior.

"You've gone quiet again, Jessica," Trevor prompted.

"The fact is, Vivian drank too much and partied very heavily. Your father knew about her drinking, but she threatened him with you. She said she'd leave him, take you with her, and get a restraining order so he couldn't see you. She knew people who would take money in return for testimony against Dillon. He was often on the road, and bands, especially successful ones, always have reputations."

"You're saying he was afraid to risk a court fight," Trevor said, summing it up.

Jessica smiled at him. "Exactly. He was afraid the court would say you had to live with Vivian and he wouldn't be able to control what was happening to you if he didn't have custody. By staying with her, he hoped he could keep her contained. It worked for a while." Vivian didn't want to be home, she preferred the nightlife and the clubs of the cities. It was only during the last year, when the twins were five, that Vivian had returned home, unable to keep up appearances.

"That night, Jess," Trevor prompted.

Jessica sighed. There was no getting around telling them what they wanted to know. The twins were very persistent. "There was a party going on," she chose her words very carefully. "Your father came home early. There was a terrible fight between him and your mother, and he left the house to cool off. He made up his mind that he would leave Vivian and she knew it. There were candles everywhere. The fire inspector said the drapes caught fire and it spread fast, because there was alcohol on the furniture and the walls. The party was very wild. No one knows for certain where the gun came from or who shot whom first. But witnesses, including me, testified that Dillon had left the house. He ran back when he saw the flames and he rushed inside because he couldn't find you."

Jessica looked down at her hands. "I had taken you out a window on the cliff side of the house and he didn't know. He thought you were still inside so he went into the burning house."

Tara gasped, one hand covering her mouth to stop any sound but her eyes were glistening with tears.

"How did he get out?" Trevor asked, a lump in his throat. He couldn't get the sight of his father's terrible scars out of his mind. "And how could he make himself go into a burning house?"

Jessica leaned close to them. "Because that's how courageous your father is, how absolutely dependable, and that's how much he loves both of you."

"Did the house fall down on him?" Tara asked.

"They said he came out on fire, that Paul and Brian tackled him and put out the flames with their own hands. There were people on the island then, guards and groundskeepers who had all come to help. The helicopters had arrived I think. I just remember it being so loud, so angry . . ." her voice trailed off.

Trevor reached up and caught her hand. "I hate that sad look you get sometimes, Jess. You're always there for us. You always have been."

Tara kissed her cheek. "Me, too, I feel the same way."

"So no one really knows who shot our mother and her friends," Trevor concluded. "It's still a big mystery. But you saved our lives, Jess. And our father was willing to risk his life to save us. Did you see him after he came out of the house?"

Jessica closed her eyes, turned her head away from them. "Yes, I saw him." Her voice was barely audible.

The twins exchanged a long look. Tara took the initiative, wanting to wipe away the sorrow Jessica was so clearly feeling. "Now, tell us the story of the Christmas miracle. The one Mama Rita always told us. I love that story."

"Me, too. You said we were coming here for our miracle, Jess," Trevor said, "tell us the story so we can believe."

"We're all going to be too tired to get up tomorrow," Jessica pointed out. She slipped beneath the covers and flicked off the light. "You already believe in miracles, I helped raise you right. It's your father who doesn't know what can happen at Christmas, but we're going to teach him a lesson. I'll tell the story another time, when I'm not so darned sleepy. Goodnight you two."

Trevor laughed softly. "Cluck cluck. Jessica hates it when we get sappy."

The pillow found him even in the dark.

chapter

4

BRIAN PHILLIPS WAS FLIPPING pancakes in the kitchen when Jessica entered the room with Tara and Trevor early the next evening. She grinned at him in greeting. "Brian! How wonderful to see you again!"

Brian spun around, and missed a pancake as it came flying down to splat on the counter. "Jessica!" He swooped her up, hugged her hard. He was a big man, the drummer for *HereAfter*. She had forgotten how strong he was until he nearly broke her ribs with his hard, good-natured squeeze. With his reddish hair and stocky body, he always had reminded Jessica of a boxer fresh from Ireland. At times she even heard the lilt in his voice. "My God, girl, you look beautiful. How long has it been?" There was a moment of silence as both of them remembered the last time they had seen one another.

Jessica resolutely forced a smile. "Brian, you must remember Tara and Trevor, Dillon's children. We were so exhausted we slept the day away. I see you're serving breakfast for dinner." She was still in the circle of Brian's arms as she turned to include the twins in the greeting. Her smile faltered as she met a pair of ice-cold eyes over the heads of the children.

Dillon lounged in the doorway, his body posture deceptively lazy and casual. His eyes were intent, watchful, focused on her, and there was a hint of something dangerous to the edge of his mouth. Jessica's green gaze locked with his. Her breathing was instantly impaired, her breath catching in her lungs. He had that effect on her. Dillon was wearing faded blue jeans, a long-sleeved turtleneck shirt and thin leather gloves. He looked unmercifully handsome. His hair was damp from his shower and he was barefoot. She had forgotten that about him, how he liked to be without shoes in the house. Butterfly wings fluttered in the pit of her stomach. "Dillon."

Jessica ripped out his heart, whatever heart he had left, with her mere presence in his home. Dillon could hardly bear to look at her, to see her beauty, to see the woman she had become. Her hair was a blend of red and gold silk, falling around her face. A man could lose himself in her eyes. And her mouth . . . If Brian didn't take his hands off of her very, very soon Dillon feared he might give in to the terrible violence that always seemed to be swirling so close to the surface. Her green eyes met his across the room and she murmured his name again. Softly. Barely audible, yet the way she whispered his name tightened every muscle in his body.

The twins whirled around, Tara reaching out to take Trevor's arm for support as she faced her father.

Dillon's gaze reluctantly left Jessica's face to move

broodingly over the twins. He didn't smile, didn't change expression. "Trevor and Tara, you've certainly grown." A muscle jerked along his jaw but otherwise he gave no indication of the emotions he was feeling. He wasn't certain he could do this, look at them, see the look in their eyes, face up to his past failures, face the utter and total revulsion that he had seen in Tara's eyes the night before.

Trevor's gaze flickered uncertainly toward Jessica before he stepped forward, thrusting out his hand toward his father. "It's good to see you, sir."

Jessica watched Dillon closely, willing him to pull his son into a hug. To at least smile at the boy. Instead, he shook hands briefly. "It's good to see you, too. I understand you're here to celebrate Christmas with me." Dillon glanced at Tara. "I guess that means you'll be wanting a tree."

Tara smiled shyly. "It's sort of an accepted practice."

He nodded. "I can't remember the last time I celebrated Christmas. I'm a little rusty when it comes to holiday festivities." His gaze had strayed back to Jessica and he silently damned himself for his lack of control.

"Tara will make sure you remember every little detail about Christmas," Trevor said with a laugh, nudging his sister, "it's her favorite holiday."

"I'll count on you, then, Tara," Dillon said with his customary charm, still watching Jessica intently. A smile slipped out. Menacing. Threatening. "If you can manage to take your hands off Jess, Brian, maybe we can all share those pancakes." There was a distinct edge to his voice. "We keep strange hours here, especially now that we're recording. I prefer to work at night and sleep during the day."

Tara glanced at her brother and mouthed, "Vampire."

Trevor grinned at her, covering for his twin with a diversion. "I take it we get pancakes for dinner."

"You'll grow to love them," Brian assured. He laughed heartily and squeezed Jessica's shoulders quickly before dropping his arms. "She's turned into a real beauty, Dillon." He leered at Jessica. "I don't know if I mentioned to you or not, that I'm recently divorced."

"Ever the lady's man," Jessica patted his cheek, determined not to let Dillon shake her confidence. "What was that, your third or fourth wife?"

"Oh the pain of the arrows you sling, Jessica girl," Brian clutched his heart and winked at Trevor. "She never lets anything slip by, I'll bet."

Trevor grinned at him, wide and engaging, that famous Wentworth smile that Jessica knew so well. "Not a single thing, so be careful around her," he cautioned. "I'm a fairly good cook. I can help you with the pancakes. Don't let Jessie, even if she offers. The mere thought of her cooking anything is scary." He shuddered dramatically.

Jessica rolled her eyes. "He should be in acting." She was aware of Tara inching closer to her for comfort, aware of the tension in the room despite the banter. Trying to ignore Dillon, she drew the child to her and hugged her encouragingly as her father should have done. "Trevor turns traitor when he's in the company of other men, have you noticed?"

"I'm stating a fact," Trevor denied. "She sets the

popcorn on fire in the microwave whenever we let her pop it."

"It's not my fault the popcorn behaves unpredictably when it's my turn to pop it," Jessica pointed out.

She stole a glance at Dillon. He was watching her intently, just as she suspected he was. When she inhaled, she took his clean, masculine scent into her lungs. He dominated the room simply by standing there, wrapped in his silence. Awareness spread through her body, an unfamiliar heat that thickened her blood and left her strangely restless.

"Can anyone join in the fun?"

The blood drained out of Jessica's face. She felt it, felt herself go pale as she turned slowly to face that strident voice. Vivian's voice. The woman was tall and model thin. Platinum blond hair was swept up onto her head and she wore scarlet lipstick. Jessica noticed her long nails were polished the exact same shade. Jessica swallowed the sudden lump in her throat and looked to Dillon for help.

"Brenda." Dillon said the woman's name deliberately, needing to wipe the fear out of Jessica's eyes. "Jess, I don't believe you ever had the chance to meet Vivian's sister. Brenda, this is Jessica Fitzpatrick and these are my children, Trevor and Tara."

The twins looked at one another and then at Jessica. Trevor put his arm around Tara. "We have an aunt, Jessie?"

"Apparently," Jessica said, her gaze on Dillon. She had never seen Brenda in her life. She had a vague recollection of someone mentioning her, but Brenda certainly had never come to see the children.

"Of course I'm your aunt," Brenda announced, waving her hand airily. "But I travel quite a bit and just haven't gotten around to visiting. No pancakes for me, Brian, just coffee." She walked across the kitchen and threw herself into a chair as if she were exhausted. "I had no idea the little darlings were coming, Dillon." She blew him a kiss. "You should have told me. They certainly take after you, don't they?"

"Must have been a lot of traveling," Trevor muttered, leaning into Jessica. He quirked an eyebrow at her, half amused, half annoyed, in a way that was very reminiscent of his father.

Jessica felt Tara tremble and immediately brushed the top of her head with a kiss. "It isn't quite dark yet, honey, would you like to go for a short walk? The storm's passed over us and it would be fun to show you how beautiful the island is."

"Don't leave on my account," Brenda said, "I don't get along with kiddies. I make no apologies for it. I need coffee, for heaven's sake, can't one of you manage to bring me a cup?" Her voice rose, a familiar pitch that was etched for all time in Jessica's memory. "Robert, the lazy slug, is still in bed." She yawned and leveled her gaze at Dillon. "You've turned us all around so we don't know whether it's morning or night anymore. My poor husband can't get out of bed."

"Are you here for Christmas?" Trevor ventured, uncertain what to say, but instinctively wanting to find a way to smooth out the situation.

"Christmas?" It was Brian who answered derisively. "Brenda doesn't know what Christmas is, besides a day she expects to be showered with gifts. She's here for more money, aren't you, my dear? She's gone through Robert's money and the insurance money, so she dropped by with her hand out."

"So true," Brenda shrugged her shoulders, unconcerned with Brian's harsh assessment of her. "Money is the bane of all existence."

"She has an insurance policy on everyone, don't you, Brenda," Brian accused. "Me, Dillon," he indicated the twins with his jaw, his eyes glittering at her, "the kids. Poor Robert is probably worth far more dead than alive. What do you have on him, a cool million?"

Brenda raised one eyebrow, blew another kiss at him. "Of course, darling, it's just good sense. I figured you'd go first with your horrendous driving abilities, but, alas, no luck so far."

Brian glared at her. "You're a cold woman, Brenda."

"You didn't used to think so, babe."

Jessica stared at her. *Insurance policy on the kids. On Dillon.* She didn't dare look at Dillon, he would know exactly the suspicion going through her mind.

Brenda gave a tinkling laugh. "Don't look so shocked, Jessica, dear. Brian and I are old friends. It ended badly and he can't forgive me." She inspected her long nails. "He actually adores me and still wants me. I adore him, but choosing Robert was a good decision. He balances me." She lifted her head, moaning pathetically, her eyes pleading. "I could *kill* for a cup of coffee."

Jessica turned over the information in her mind. Insurance money. It had never occurred to her that someone other than Dillon or the children might have profited monetarily from Vivian's death. She remembered her mother talking about it with Dillon's lawyer after the fire. The lawyer had said it was good that Dillon didn't have a policy on his wife because an insurance policy was often considered a reason for murder.

Reason for murder. Could an insurance policy on Tara's and Trevor's lives be the motive behind the accidents? Jessica looked at Brenda, trying to see past her perfect makeup to the woman beneath.

"How could you have an insurance policy on Vivian, Brenda?" Jessica asked curiously. "Or on Brian or Dillon or the twins? That's not legal."

"Oh please," Brenda waved her hand, "I'm dying for coffee and you want to talk legalities. Fine, a little lesson, kiddies, in grown-up reality. Viv and I went together to get insurance on each other years ago. With consent it can be done. Dillon gave his consent," she blew him another kiss, "because we're family. Brian gave consent when we were together and Robert's my husband, so *of course* I have insurance on him."

"And you're so good at persuading people to let you have those policies, aren't you, Brenda," Brian snapped.

"Of course I am," Brenda smiled at him, in no way perturbed by his accusations. "You're becoming so tedious with your jealousy. Really, darling, you need help."

"You're going broke paying your insurance premiums," Brian sniped.

Brenda shrugged and waved airily. "I just call Dillon and he pays them for me. Now, stop being so mean, Brian, and bring me coffee; it won't hurt you to be nice for a change," Brenda wheedled, slumping dramatically over the table.

"Yes, it would," he said stubbornly. "Doing anything for you is bad karma."

"But how would you manage to take out a policy on the twins?" The very idea of it repulsed Jessica.

Brenda didn't lift her head from the tabletop. "My sister and Dillon gave me permission of course. I'm not talking anymore, without coffee! I'm fading here, people."

Jessica glared accusingly at Dillon across the room. He flashed a heart-stopping rather sheepish smile and shrugged his broad shoulders. Brenda groaned loudly. Jessica gave in. It was clear that Brian wasn't going to get Vivian a cup of coffee and Dillon looked unconcerned. She found the mugs in a cupboard and did the honors. "Cream or sugar?"

"You don't have to do that, Jess," Dillon snapped suddenly, his mouth tightening ominously. "Brenda, get your own damn coffee."

"It's no big deal." Jessica handed the cup to Brenda.

"Thank you, my dear, you are a true lifesaver." Her eyes wandered over Jessica's figure, an indifferent, blasé appraisal, then she turned her attention to Tara. "You look nothing like your mother, but fortunately you inherited Dillon's good looks. It should take you far in life."

"Tara is at the top of her class," Jessica informed the woman, "her brains are going to take her far in life."

Trevor wolfed down a pancake without syrup. "Watch yourself now, Jessica's got that militant look in her eye."

His voice changed, a perfect mimic of Jessica's. "School is important and if you mess around thinking you can get by on good looks or charm, or think you're going to make it big in the arts, think again buddy, you're going nowhere if you don't have a decent education." He grinned at them. "Word for word, I swear, you opened a can a worms."

"Looks have gotten me what I want in life," Brenda muttered into her coffee cup.

"Maybe you weren't aspiring high enough," Jessica said, looking Brenda in the eye.

Brenda shuddered, surrendering. "I don't have the energy for this conversation. I told you I wasn't good with kiddies or animals."

"Tara," Jessica said, as she handed the girl a plate of pancakes, "you are the kiddie and that brother of yours is the animal."

Trevor grinned at her. "Too true, and all the girls know it."

Dillon watched them bantering back and forth so easily. *His* children. *His* Jessica. They were a family, basking in each other's love. He was the outsider. The circle was tight, the bond strong between the three of them. He watched the expressions chasing across Jessica's face as she snapped a tea towel at Trevor, laughing at him, teasing him. The way it should have been. The way it was supposed to be.

Jessica was aware of Dillon every moment that they stayed in the same room. Her wayward gaze kept straying to him. Her pulse raced and he affected her breathing. It was aggravating and made her feel like a teenager with a crush. "We want to go for that walk before it gets dark, don't we, Tara?" Now *she* wanted to escape. Needed to escape. She couldn't stay in the same room with him much longer.

"The grounds haven't been kept up, Jess," Dillon informed her. "It might be better if you amuse yourselves inside while we work."

Her eyebrow shot up. "Amuse ourselves?" She ignored Trevor's little warning nudge. "What did you have in mind? Playing hopscotch in the hall?"

Dillon looked at his son's face, the quick, appreciative grin the boy couldn't hide fast enough. Something warm stirred in him that he didn't want to think about or examine too closely. "Hopscotch is fine, Jess, as long as you draw the boxes with something we can erase easily." He said it blandly, watching the boy's reaction.

Trevor threw his head back and laughed. Brian joined in. Even Brenda managed a faint smile, more, Jessica suspected, because Trevor's laugh was infectious than because Brenda found anything humorous in Dillon's reply.

Jessica didn't want to look up and see Dillon smiling but she couldn't stop herself. She didn't want to notice the way his face lit up, or that his eyes were so blue. Or that his mouth was perfectly sculpted. Kissable. She nearly groaned, blushing faintly at the wild thought. The memory of his lips, velvet soft, yet firm, pressing against hers was all too vivid in her mind.

She had to say something, the twins would expect her to hold her own in a verbal sparring match, but she couldn't think, not when his blue eyes were laughing at her. Really laughing at her. For one brief moment, he looked happy, the terrible weight off his shoulders. Jessica glanced at the twins. They were observing her hopefully. She took a deep breath and deliberately leaned close to Dillon, close enough that she could feel electricity arcing between them. She put her mouth against Dillon's ear so that he could feel the softness of her lips as she spoke. "You cheat, Dillon." She whispered the three words, allowing her warm breath to play over his neck, heat his skin. To make him as aware of her as she was of him.

It was a silly, dangerous thing to do, and the moment she did it, she knew she'd made a mistake. The air stilled, the world receded until there was only the two of them. Desire flared in the depths of his eyes, burning hot, immediate. He shifted, a subtle movement but it brought his body in contact with hers. Hunger pulsed between them, deep, elemental, so strong it was nearly tangible. He bent his dark head to hers.

No one breathed. No one moved. Jessica stared into the deep blue of his eyes, mesmerized, held captive there, his perfect mouth only a scant inch from hers. "I play to win," he murmured softly, for her ears alone.

The sound of a creaking chair, as someone shifted restlessly, broke the enchantment. Jessica blinked, came out of her trance, and hastily stepped away from the beckoning heat of Dillon's body, from the magnetic pull of his sexual web. She didn't dare look at either of the children. Her heart was doing strange somersaults and the butterflies were having a field day in the pit of her stomach.

Dillon ran his gloved hand down the length of her hair

in a gentle caress. "Were you and the children comfortable last night?"

Tara and Trevor looked at each other, then at Jessica.
"Very comfortable," they said in unison.

Jessica was too wrapped up in the sound of his voice to
answer. There was that smoky quality to it, the black velvet that was so sexy, but it was so much more. Sometimes
the gentleness, the tenderness that came out of nowhere
threw her completely off balance. Dillon was a mixture of
old and new to her, and she was desperately trying to feel
her way with him.

"That's good. If you need anything, don't hesitate to
say so," Dillon poured the rest of his coffee down the
sink and rinsed the cup out. "We're all pitching in with
the chores as the housekeeping staff is gone on vacation
this month. So I'll expect you kids to do the same. Just
clean up after yourselves. You can have the run of the
house with the exception of the rooms where the others
are staying, my private rooms and the studio. That's
invitation only." He leaned his back against the sink and
pinned the twins with his brilliant gaze. "We keep odd
hours and if you get up before late afternoon, please
keep quiet because most of us will be sleeping. The
band is here to try recording some music, just to see
what we can come up with. If it works, we hope to have
a product to pitch again to one of the labels. It requires
a great deal of time and effort on our part. We're *working*, not playing."

Trevor nodded. "We understand, we won't get in the
way."

"If you're interested, you can watch later, after we've

worked out a few kinks. I'm heading to the studio now, so if you need anything, say so now."

"We'll be fine," Trevor said. "Getting up at four or five o'clock in the afternoon and staying up all night is an experience in itself!" His white teeth flashed, an engaging smile, showing all the promise of his father's charisma. "Don't worry about us, Jess will keep us in line."

Dillon's blue gaze flicked to Jessica. Drank her in. She made his kitchen seem a home. He had forgotten that feeling. Forgotten what it was like to wake up and look forward to getting out of bed. He heard the murmur of voices around him, heard Robert Berg and Don Ford laughing in the hall as they made their way together to the kitchen. It was all so familiar yet completely different.

"Well, we have a houseful." Robert Berg, the keyboard player for the band, entered and crossed the kitchen to plant a kiss on the nape of Brenda's neck. Robert was short and compact with dark thinning hair and a small trim goatee gracing his chin. "This can't be the twins, they're all grown up."

Trevor nodded solemnly. "That happens to people. An unusual phenomenon. Time goes by and we just get older. I'm Trevor." He held out his hand.

"With the smart mouth," Jessica supplied, frowning at the boy as he shook hands with Robert. "Good to see you again, it has been a while." She dropped her hands onto Tara's shoulders. "This is Tara."

Robert smiled at the girl, saluted her as he snagged a plate and piled it high with pancakes. "Brian's been doing the cooking, Jessica, but maybe now that you're here we can have something besides pancakes."

Trevor choked, went into a coughing fit and Tara burst out laughing. Dillon's heart turned over as he watched Jessica tug gently on Tara's hair, then mock strangle Trevor. The three of them were so easy with one another, playfully teasing, sharing a close camaraderie he had always wanted, but had never found. He had been so desperate for a home, for a family, and now when it was in front of him, when he knew what was important, what it was all about, it was too late for him.

"*Men* are the supreme chefs of the world," Jessica replied haughtily, "why would I want to infringe on their domain?"

"Here, here," Brenda applauded. "Well said."

"You coming, Brian." Dillon made it a command, not a question. "I'll expect the rest of you in ten minutes and someone get Paul up."

There was a small silence after Dillon left. It had always been that way, he dominated a room with his presence, the passion and energy in it had flowed from him. Now that he was gone there seemed to be a void.

Don Ford hurried in, his short brown hair spiked and tipped with blond and his clothes the latest fashion. "Had to get in my morning smoke. Dillon won't let us smoke in the house. Man, it's cold out there tonight." He shivered, rubbing his hands together for warmth as he looked around and caught sight of the twins and Jessica. He shoved small wire rim glasses on his nose to peer at them. "Whoa! You weren't here when I went to bed or I'm giving up liquor for all time."

"We snuck in when you weren't looking," Jessica

admitted with a smile. She accepted his kiss and made the introductions.

"Am I the last one up?"

"That would be Paul," Robert said, shoving cream and sugar across the counter toward Don.

Paul sauntered in, bent to kiss Jessica's cheek. "You're a sight for sore eyes," he greeted. "I'm here, I'm awake, you can cancel the firing squad." He winked at Tara. "Have you already made plans to go hunting for the perfect Christmas tree? We won't have time to go hunting one on the mainland so we'll have to do it the old-fashioned way and chop one down."

Brenda yawned. "I hate the sound of that. What a mess. There might be bugs, Paul. You aren't really going to get one from the wilds, are you?"

Tara looked alarmed. "We are going to have a Christmas tree, aren't we, Jessica?"

"*Jessica* doesn't have a say in the matter," Robert pointed out, "Dillon does. It's his house and we're here to work, not play. Brenda's right, a tree from out there," he said, gesturing toward the window, "would have bugs and it would be utterly unsanitary. Not to mention a fire hazard."

Tara flinched visibly. Trevor stood up, squared his shoulders and walked straight over to Robert. "I don't think you needed to say that to my sister. And I don't like the way you said Jessica's name."

Jessica gently rested her hand on Trevor's shoulder. "Robert, that was uncalled for. None of us need reminders of the fire, we were all here when it happened." She tugged on Trevor's resistant body urging him away from Robert. "Tara, of course you'll have a tree. Your father has already agreed to one. We can't very well have Christmas without one."

Brenda sighed as she stood up. "As long as I'm not the one dealing with all of those needles that will fall off it. You need such energy to cope with the kiddies. I'm glad it's you and not me, dear. I'm off to the studio. Robert, are you coming?"

Robert obediently followed her out without looking at any of them. Don drained his coffee cup, rinsed it carefully and waved to them. "Duty calls."

"I'm sorry about that, Jessie," Paul said. "Robert lives in his own little world. Brenda goes through money like water. Everything they had is gone. Dillon was the only one of us who was smart. He invested his share and tripled his money. The royalties on his songs keep pouring in. And because he had the kids he carried medical and fire insurance and all those grown-up things the rest of us didn't think about. The worst of it is, he tried to get us to do the same but we wouldn't listen to him. Robert needs this album to come about. If Dillon composes it and sings and produces it, you know it will go straight to the top. Robert is between a rock and hard place. Without money, he can't keep Brenda, and he loves her." Paul shrugged and ruffled Tara's hair. "Don't let them ruin your Christmas, Tara."

"Whose idea was it to put the band back together?" Jessica asked. "I had the impression that Dillon wanted to do this, that it was his idea."

Paul shook his head. "Not a chance. He's always composing, music lives in him, he hears it in his head all the time, but up until last week, he hadn't worked with anyone but me since the fire. He can't play instruments any more. Well, he plays, but not anything like he used to play. He doesn't have the dexterity, although he tries when he's alone. It's too painful for him. I think Robert talked to the others first and then they all came to me to see what I thought. I think they believed I could persuade him." His dark eyes held a hint of worry. "I hope I did the right thing. He's doing it for the others, you know, hoping to make them some money. That was the pitch I used and it worked. He wouldn't have done it for himself, but he's always felt responsible for the others. I thought it might be good for him but now, I don't know. If he fails . . ."

"He won't fail," Jessica said. "We'll clean up in here. You'd better go."

"Thanks, Jess," he bent and dropped a kiss on the top of her head. "I'm glad you're all here."

Trevor grinned at her the moment they were alone. "You're getting kissed a lot, Jess. I was thinking there for a few minutes when you were . . . er . . . *talking* with my dad, I might even get my first lesson in sex education." He took off running as Jessica madly snapped a tea towel at him. His taunting laughter floated back to her from up the stairs.

chapter 5

JESSICA SLOWED MIDWAY up the staircase, the smile fading from her face. It was the smell. She would never forget the smell of that particular incense. Cedarwood and alum. She inhaled and knew there was no mistake. The odor seeped from beneath the door to her room and crept out into the hallway. Jessica paused for just a moment, allowing herself to feel the edginess creep back into her mind. It seemed to be there whenever she was alone, a warning shimmering in her brain, settling in the pit of her stomach.

"Jess?" Trevor stood at the top of the stairs, puzzlement on his face. "What is it?"

She shook her head as she walked past him to stand in front of the door to her room. Very carefully she pushed it open. Ice-cold air rushed out at her, and with it, the overpowering odor of incense. Jessica stood in the doorway of her room, unmoving, her gaze going immediately to the window. The curtains fluttered, floating on the breeze as if they were white, papery thin ghosts. For one moment there was vapor, a thick white fog permeating her room. She blinked and it seemed to dissolve, or merge with the heavy fog outside the house.

"It's freezing in here, why did you open the window?" Trevor hurried across the room to slam it closed. "What is that disgusting smell?"

Jessica had remained motionless in the doorway, but when she saw his shoulders stiffen, it galvanized her into action. She hurried to his side. "Trev?"

"What is that?" Trevor pointed to the symbol ground into the throw rug near the window.

Jessica took a deep breath. "Some people believe that they can invoke the aid of spirits, Trevor, by using certain ceremonies. What you're looking at is a crude magician's ring." She stared, mesmerized, at the two circles, one within the other, made from the ash of several sticks of incense.

"What does it mean?"

"Nothing at this point, there's nothing in it." Jessica's teeth tugged at her bottom lip. Two circles meant nothing. It was simply a starting point. "Some people believe that you can't make contact with spirits without a magic circle drawn and consecrated. The symbols invoking the spirit and also for protection would be inside." She sighed softly. "Let's check Tara's room and then yours, just to be on the safe side."

"You're shaking," Trevor pointed out.

"Am I?" Jessica rubbed her hands up and down her arms, determined not to scream. "It must be the cold." She wanted to run to Dillon, to have him hold her, to comfort her, but she knew the minute he saw that symbol he would throw each and every one of the band members out. And he would never try to make his music again.

"I want to go get Dad," Trevor said, as they entered Tara's room. "I don't like this at all."

Jessica shook her head. "Neither do I, but we can't tell your father just yet. You don't know him the way I do. He has an incredible sense of responsibility." She took his arm as they entered Tara's room. "Don't shake your head—he does. He didn't leave you alone because he didn't love you. He left you alone because he believed it was the right thing to do for you."

"Baloney!" Trevor poked around the room, making certain the window was securely closed and that no one had disturbed his sister's things. "How could he believe that leaving was the right thing to do, Jessie?"

"After the fire he spent a year in the hospital, and then he had over a year of physical therapy. You have no idea how painful it is to recover from the type of burns your father suffered. The kinds of things he had to endure. And then the trial dragged on for nearly two years. Not the actual trial, but the entire legal process. No one actually found the murderer so Dillon wasn't freed from suspicion. You had to know him. He took responsibility for everyone. He took the blame for everything that happened. He's his own worst enemy. In his mind he failed Vivian, the band, you kids, even my mother and me. I don't want to take a chance that he might quit his music. Someone wants us to go away and they know what frightens me. But they directed this prank at me, not at you."

"I knew you thought someone was trying to hurt us." Trevor shook his head as they walked into his room. "You should have told me. That's why you brought us to him."

She nodded. "He would never allow anything to happen to you. Never."

They finished the examination of Trevor's room. It was immaculate; he hadn't even pretended to be using it. "What was all that business about insurance money? Does Brenda really have a policy on us? Can she do that? It freaks me out."

"Unfortunately, it sounds as if she has. I intend to talk to your father about it at the earliest opportunity." Jessica sighed again. "I don't understand any of this. Why would someone want us gone enough to try to scare us with a magic circle? They all know Dillon, they must realize he'd throw off the island whoever is trying to scare me. If the music is so important to them, why risk it?"

"I think it's Brenda," Trevor said. "Robert doesn't have any more money and she's looking at my dad. You come along and Dad's looking at you. Jealousy rears its ugly head. Case solved. It's the cold-hearted woman looking for the cash every time."

"Thank you, Sherlock, blame it on the woman, why don't you. Let's go back downstairs and find Tara. She's probably already cleaned the kitchen."

"Why do you think I'm stalling up here?"

Jessica was glad the tea towel was still in her hand. She snapped it at him as she followed him downstairs.

To Trevor's delight, Tara had tidied the kitchen so the three of them spent the next couple of hours exploring the house. It was fun discovering the various rooms. Dillon had antique and brand-new musical instruments of all kinds. There was a game room consisting of all the

latest video and DVD equipment. Jessica had to drag
Trevor out of a poolroom. The weight room caught her
interest, but the twins dragged her out. Eventually they
settled in the library, curled up together on the deep
couch surrounded by books and antiques. Jessica found
the Dickens Christmas classic and began to read it aloud
to the twins.

"Jess! Damn it, Jess, where are you?" The voice came
roaring out of the basement. Clipped. Angry. Frustrated.

Jessica slowly put the book aside as Dillon called for
her a second time.

Tara looked frightened and reached for Jessica's hand.
Trevor burst out laughing. "You're being yelled at, Jessie.
I've never heard anyone yell at you before."

Jessica rolled her eyes heavenward. "I guess I'd better
go answer the royal command."

"We'll just go along with you," Trevor decided, striving
to sound casual as Dillon roared for her again.

Jessica hid her smile. Trevor was determined to protect
her. She loved him all the more for it. "Let's go then,
before he has a stroke."

"What did you do to make him so angry?" Tara asked.

"I certainly didn't do anything," Jessica replied indignantly. "How could I possibly make him angry?"

Trevor flicked her red-gold hair. "You could make the
Pope angry, Jessie. And you bait him."

"I do not!" Jessica chased him along the hall leading to
the stairs. "Punky boy. An alien took you over in your
sleep one night. You were good and sweet until then."

Trevor was running backward, dancing just out of her
reach, laughing as he neared the top of the stairway. "I'm

still good and sweet, Jessie, you just can't take hearing the truth."

"I'll show you truth," Jessica warned, making a playful grab for him.

Trevor stepped backward onto the first stair and unexpectedly slipped, his foot going out from under him. For a moment he teetered precariously, his hands flailing wildly as he tried to catch the banister. Jessica could see the fear on his young face and lunged forward to grab him, choking on stark, mind-numbing terror. Her fingers skimmed the material of his shirt, but missed. Tara, holding out both hands to her twin, screamed loudly as Trevor fell away from them.

Dillon rushed up the stairs, taking two at a time, furious that Jessica hadn't answered him when he knew *damn* well she'd heard him. Strangling her might not be a bad idea *after* she explained to that idiot Don what he was looking for. What was so difficult about hearing the right beat? The right pause? As Tara's scream registered, he glanced up to see Trevor falling backward. For one moment time stood still, his heart lodged in his throat. The boy hit him hard, squarely in the chest, driving the air out of his lungs in one blast. Protectively he wrapped his arms around his son as they both tumbled down the stairs to land heavily on the basement floor.

Jessica started down the stairs, Tara in her wake. The moment her foot touched the first stair, she felt herself slide. Clutching the banister, she caught Tara. "Careful, baby, there's something slippery on the stair." They both clung to the banister as they rushed down.

"Are they dead?" Tara asked fearfully.

Jessica could hear muffled swearing and Trevor's yelp of pain as Dillon ran his hands none too gently over his son to check for damage. "Doesn't sound like it," she observed. She knelt beside Trevor, her fingers pushing his hair from his forehead tenderly. "Are you all right, honey?"

"I don't know," Trevor managed a wry grin, still lying on top of his father.

Dillon caught Jessica's hand, his thumb sliding over her inner wrist, feeling her frantic heartbeat. "He's fine, he fell on top of me. I'm the one with all the bruises." Fear, mixed with anger, pulsed through his body. He hadn't experienced such panic and dread in years. The sight of Trevor falling from the top of the stairs was utterly terrifying. "I can't breathe, the kid weighs a ton." Dillon didn't know whether to hug Trevor or to shake him until his teeth rattled.

Jessica pushed back the unruly waves of hair falling into the center of Dillon's forehead. "You're breathing. Thanks for catching him."

Her touch shook him. Dillon's blue gaze burned over her face hungrily. It was painful to be jealous of his son, of the tender looks she gave him, the way she loved him. The way she was so at ease with him. Dillon wanted to drag her to him right there in front of everybody and kiss her. Devour her. Consume her. She was wreaking havoc with his body, breaking his heart and reopening every gaping laceration in his soul. She was making him feel things again, forcing him to live when it was so much better to be numb.

"And it was a great catch," Trevor agreed.

Dillon shoved the boy to one side, glaring at him, furious that he had been so terrified, furious that his life was being turned upside down. "Stop fooling around, kid, you could have really been hurt. You're too old to be playing so carelessly on the stairway. Roughhousing belongs outside, that way you don't break things that don't belong to you or injure innocent parties with your stupidity."

The smile faded from Trevor's face and color crept up his neck into his face. Tara gasped, outraged. "Trevor didn't hurt your stupid staircase."

"And you need to learn how to speak to adults, young lady," Dillon concluded, switching his glare to her furious little face.

Jessica stood up, drawing Tara up with her. She reached down to help Trevor to his feet. "Trevor slipped on something on the stairs, just as I did, Dillon," she informed him icily. "Perhaps, instead of jumping to conclusions about Trevor's behavior, you should ask your other guests to be more careful and not spill things on the stairs that will send people flying."

Dillon climbed to his feet slowly, his face an expressionless mask. "What's on the stairs?"

"I didn't stop and check," Jessica answered.

"Well, let's go see." He started up the stairs with Jessica following him closely.

The top stair was shiny, a clear, oily substance covering it. Dillon hunkered down and studied it. "Looks like cooking oil, right out of the kitchen." He glanced down at the twins who were waiting at the bottom of the stairs as if suspecting them.

"They didn't spill oil here. They were with me," Jessica snapped. She reached past him, touched the oil with a fingertip and brought it to her mouth. "Vegetable oil. Someone must have poured this oil onto the stair." Oil was used in magical ceremonies to invoke spirits. She remembered that piece of information all too well.

"Or accidentally spilled some and didn't realize it." Dillon's blue gaze slid over her. "And I wasn't accusing the kids, it didn't occur to me they did this. Don't jump to conclusions, Jess."

"Let's go ask the others," she challenged him.

He sighed. "You're angry with me." He held out his leather-covered hand to her, an instinctive gesture. The moment he realized what he'd done, he dropped his hand to his side.

"Of course I'm angry with you, Dillon, what did you expect?" Jessica tilted her head to look up at him. "Don't treat me like a child, and don't use that infuriating patronizing voice on me either. I told you the accidents that have been happening at home could easily be explained away. I'll guarantee you, no one in this house is going to admit to spilling cooking oil on the stairs."

He shrugged. "So what if they don't? This wasn't directed at Trevor and Tara—how could it be? We're recording down there. Why would anyone think the kids would come down? No one could possibly have predicted that I would be calling for you."

"I disagree. I love music and I'm a sound engineer, and everyone here knows it. And you mentioned earlier in the kitchen that the twins could come down later and watch."

He raised his eyebrow at her. "Everyone, including Brenda, is in the studio. How do you explain that?"

"The twins were with me the entire time, Dillon," Jessica countered, her green eyes beginning to smolder, "how do you explain that? And speaking of Brenda, why in the world would you give your consent to allow that woman to hold an insurance policy on you and your children?" .

"She's family, Jessie, it's harmless enough, although costly," he shrugged carelessly, "and it makes her feel a part of something."

"It makes me feel like a vulture is circling overhead," Jessica muttered. She followed him back down the stairs to where the twins waited expectantly.

"Hey, we're wasting time," Brian called. "Are you two going to come and work or are you going to discuss the positive versus the negative flow of the universe around us? What's going on out there?"

"We fell down the stairs," Dillon said grimly. "We'll be right there." He leaned close to Jessica. "Take a breath, Mama Tiger, don't rip my head off," Dillon teased, searching for a way to ease the tension between them. "Pull in the claws." Her instant, fierce defense of his children amused and pleased him.

Jessica glared at the twins. Both backed away innocently, shaking their heads in unison, awed that their father knew their secret pet name for Jessica. "I didn't tell him. Honest," Trevor added, when she kept glaring. "And he didn't mention fangs."

"Does she have fangs?" Dillon asked his son, his eyebrow shooting up. He was so relieved the boy hadn't hurt himself in the fall.

"Oh, yeah," Trevor answered, "absolutely. In a heart-beat. Fear for your life if you mess with us."

Dillon grinned suddenly, his face lighting up, mischief flickering for a brief moment in the deep blue of his eyes. "Believe me, son, I would."

Trevor stood absolutely still, shaken at the emotion pouring into him at his father's words. Jessica's hand briefly touched his shoulder in silent understanding.

"Come on, Jessica, we could use a little help." Dillon caught her arm and marched her down the hall as if she were his prisoner. He leaned close to her as they walked, his breath warm against her ear. "And I am *not* volatile." He glanced back at the twins, beckoning to them. "If you two can keep quiet, you can come and watch. Brenda! I have a job for you."

Jessica made a face at Trevor behind Dillon's back that set the children laughing as Dillon dragged her into the sound room.

"A job?" Brenda stretched languidly as she stood up. "Surely not, Dillon. I haven't actually worked in years. The idea is a bit on the daunting side."

"I think you'll find it easy enough. There's oil on the stairway, a large amount of it. It makes the stairs danger-ous and it needs to be cleaned up. My household staff is gone, we're all pitching in, so this is your task for the day."

Brenda widened her eyes in shocked dismay. "You can't possibly be serious, Dillon. It was a terrible decision to allow your staff to leave. What were you thinking to do such a crazy thing?"

"That it was Christmastime and they might want to be with their families," Dillon lied. The truth was he hadn't wanted anyone to witness him falling flat on his face while he worked with the band. It was terrifying to think of the enormity of what he was doing. "You knew there was no staff, that we would be working. You agreed to help with the everyday chores if I allowed you to come."

"Well, chores, of course. Fluffing the towels in the bathroom, not cleaning up a mess on the stairs. You," she pointed to Tara, "surely you could do this little job."

Before Tara could reply Dillon shook his head. "You, Brenda, get to it. Tara and Trevor, sit over there. Jessica, take a look at my notations and listen to the tracks and see if it makes any sense to you. I'm ready to pull out my hair here." He pulled Jessica over to a chair, pressing down on her shoulders until she sat. "It's a nightmare."

Jessica waited until he was safely in the studio before muttering her reply. "It is now. Working with Dillon Wentworth is going to be pure hell." She winked at the twins. "Wait until you see him. He's all passion and energy. Quicksilver. And he yells when he doesn't get *exactly* what he wants."

"Big surprise there," Trevor said drolly.

Brenda threw a pencil onto the floor, a small rebellion. "That man is an overbearing, dominating madman when he's working. I don't know where he gets the mistaken idea he can boss me around."

"True, but he's a musical genius and he makes lots and lots of money for everyone," Jessica reminded, frowning down at the sheets of music. It was obvious Dillon's smaller motor skills were lacking, his musical notations were barely legible scratches.

Brenda sighed. "Fine then, it's true, we need our wonderful cash machine, so I'll do my part to make him happy. One of you kiddies should take a picture of me scrubbing the stairs like Cinderella. It might be worth a fortune." She gave her tinkling laugh. "I know Robert would certainly love to see such a thing, but then, it would ruin his image of me and I can't let him think I'm capable of working." She winked at Trevor. "I'm trusting you not to say a word to him. If you both want to come with me, I'll even pass on smoking, which the master has decreed I can't do in his house."

"Well, you shouldn't smoke. It's not good for you." Tara pointed out judiciously.

Brenda made a face at her. "Fine, stay here and listen to your father yell at everyone, but it won't be nearly as entertaining as watching me." Her high heels tapped out her annoyance as she left.

Jessica spent an hour deciphering Dillon's musical notations then listening through the tracks he had already recorded, trying to find the mix Dillon was look-ing for. The problem was, the band members weren't hearing the same thing in their heads that Dillon was hearing. Don was no lead guitarist; his gift lay in his skill with the bass. It was apparent to Jessica that the band needed a lead, but she wasn't altogether certain who could play Dillon's music the way he wanted it to be played. Most musicians had egos. No one was going to allow Dillon to tell him how to play.

She saw that the band had once more ground to a halt. Brian grimaced at her through the glass. Paul shook his head at her, worry plain on his face. She leaned over to flip the switch to flood the room with sound. Dillon paced back and forth, energy pouring out of him, filling the studio, flashes of brilliance, of pure genius mixed with building frustration and impatience.

"Why can't any of you hear it?" Dillon smacked his palm to his head, stormed over to the guitar leaning against the wall. "What's so difficult about anticipating the beat? Slow the melody down, you're rushing the riff. It isn't to show what an awesome player you are alone, it's a harmony, a blending so that it smokes." He cradled the guitar, held it lovingly, almost tenderly. The need to play what he heard in his head was so strong his body trembled.

Watching him through the glass, Jessica felt her heart shatter. She could read him, and his need to bring the music to life, so easily. Dillon had always been exacting, a perfectionist when it came to his music. His passion came through in his composing, in his lyrics, in his playing. It was what had shot the band to the top and all of them knew it. They wanted it again, and they were banking on him to find it for them.

Dillon glared at Don. "Try again and this time get it right."

Visibly sweating, Don glanced uneasily at the others. "I'm not going to play it any differently than I did the last time, Dillon. I'm not you. I'll never be you. I can't hear what you want me to hear just by you telling me about blending and smoke and strings. I'm not you."

Dillon swore, his blue eyes burning with such intensity Don stepped away from him and held up his hand. "I want this, I do. I'm telling you, we need to find someone else to play lead guitar because it's not going to be me.

And no matter who we get, Dillon, it still won't be you. You aren't ever going to be satisfied."

Dillon winced as if Don had struck him. The two men stared at one another for a long moment and then Dillon turned and abruptly stalked out of the room. He stood in the sound room, head down, breathing deeply, trying to push down despair. He never should have tried, never should have thought he could do it. Aloud, he cursed his hands, cursed his scarred, useless body, cursed his passion for music.

Tears swam in Tara's eyes and she buried her face against her brother's shoulder. Trevor put his arm around his sister and looked at Jessica.

The movement snapped Dillon back to reality. Jessica was fiddling with a row of keys, concentrating intently, not looking at him. "Jess!" The sight of her was inspiring, a gift! He stalked across the room like a prowling panther, caught her arm and pulled her to him. "You do it, Jess, I know you hear what I hear. It's there inside of you, it's always been there. We've always shared that connection. Get in there and play that song the way it's meant to be played." He was dragging her toward the door. "You've been playing guitar since you were five."

"What are thinking? I can't play with your band!" Jessica was appalled. "Don will get it right, stop yelling at him and give him time."

"He'll never get it right, he doesn't love the melody. You have to love it, Jessica. Remember all those nights we sat up playing in the kitchen? The music's in you, you live it and breathe it. It's alive to you the same way it is for me."

"But that was different, it was just the two of us."

"I know you play guitar brilliantly, I've heard you. I know you would never give up playing, you hear it the same way I hear it." He was shoving her, actually pushing her as she mulishly tried to dig in her heels.

Jessica looked to the twins for support but they were wearing identical grins. "She plays every day, sometimes for hours," Tara volunteered helpfully.

"Little traitor," Jessica hissed, "you've been hanging around with your brother too long. Both of you have dish duty for the next week."

"*Both* of us?" Trevor squeaked. "I'm innocent in this. Come on, Tara, let's leave them to it. We can explore that game room a little more."

"Deserters," Jessica added. "Rats off the sinking ship. I'll remember this." She was holding the door to the studio closed with her foot.

"Actually, I think it will be fun to catch Aunt Brenda cleaning the goop off the stairs," Tara said mischievously. She flounced out with a little wave and Trevor sauntered after her, grinning from ear to ear.

"It's obvious that you raised them," Dillon said, his lips against her ear, his arm hard around her waist. "They both have smart mouths on them."

"Stop making such a spectacle! You have the entire band grinning at us like apes!" Jessica pushed away from him, made a show of straightening her clothes and smoothing her hair. Her chin went up. "I'll do this, Dillon. I think I have an idea of what you're looking for, but it will take some time to pull it out of my head. Don't yell at me while I'm working. Not once, do you understand? Do not raise your voice to me or I will walk out of that room so fast you won't know what hit you."

"I'd like to get away with saying that," Brian observed.

"You all can take a break. Jessica is going to save the day for us."

"I am *not*." She glared at Dillon. "I'm just going to see if I can figure it out and if I can get it, I'll play it for you. Do you mind, Don?"

"I'm grateful, Jess." Don smiled for the first time since entering the studio. "Yell very loud if you need help and we'll all come running."

"Great, the place is soundproof." Jessica picked up the guitar and idly began to play a blues riff, allowing her fingers to wander over the strings, her ear tuning itself to the tones of the instrument, familiarizing herself with the feel of it. "You're leaving me with Dillon, just remember that."

JESSICA CLOSED HER EYES as she played, allowing the music to move through her body. Her heart and soul. It wasn't right, there was something missing, something she wasn't quite hitting. It was so close, so very close, but she couldn't quite reach it. She shook her head, listening with her heart. "It's not quite what it should be. It's almost there, but it isn't perfect."

There was frustration in her voice, enough that Dillon checked what he would have said and waited a heartbeat so that his own frustration wouldn't betray him. She didn't need him raging at her. What she needed was complete harmony between them. Unlike Don, Jessica was aware of what he wanted, she heard a similar sound in her own head, but it wasn't coming through her fingers. "Let's try something else, Jess. Pull it back a bit. Hold the notes longer, let the music breathe."

She nodded without looking at him, intense concentration on her face as her fingers lovingly moved over the strings. She listened to the flow, the pitch, a moody, introspective score, opening slowly, building, until the pain and heartbreak swelled, spilled over, filling the room until her heart was breaking and there were tears in her eyes. Her fingers stopped moving abruptly. "It's not the guitar, Dillon. The sound is there, haunting and vivid, the emotions pouring out of the music. Listen, right here, it's right here," she played the notes once, twice, her fingers lingering, drawing out the sounds. "This isn't a piece where we can just lay a track and have bass and drums doing their thing. It isn't ever going to be enough."

He snapped his fingers, indicating for her to play again, his head cocked to one side, his eyes closed. "A saxophone? Something soft and melancholy? Right there, cutting into that passage, lonely, something lonely."

Jessica nodded and she smiled, her entire face lighting up. "Exactly, that's it exactly. The sax has to cut in right there and take the spotlight for just a few bars, the guitar fading a bit into the background. This melody is too much for just bass and drums. We just aren't looking at the entire picture. When we mix it, we can try a few things, but I'd like to hear what it would sound like with Robert giving us synthesized orchestra sounds on the keyboard. This song should have more texture to it. The vocal will add the depth we need."

Dillon paced across the room, once, twice, then stopped in front of her. "I can hear the saxophone perfectly. It has to come in right on the beat in the middle of the buildup."

She nodded. "I'm excited—I think it will work. I've got the ideas for mixing. Don can come in and play it . . ."

"No!" He nearly bit her head off, his blue eyes burning at her.

He looked moody, dark. Intriguing. Jessica nearly groaned. She looked away from him, wishing she didn't find him so attractive. Wishing it was only chemistry sizzling between them and not so many other things.

"Don will never have your passion, Jess. He knows that, he as much as said so. He told me to find another lead."

She leaned the guitar very carefully against the wall. "Well, it isn't going to be me. I can't play the way you want—I don't have enough experience. And even if I did, this is a men's club. Very few musicians want to admit that a woman can handle a guitar."

"You'll have the experience when we need it. I'll help you," he promised. "And the band wants this to work. They'll try anything to keep it going forward."

She shook her head, backing away from him as if he were stalking her.

Dillon's grin transformed his face. He looked boyish, charming, altogether irresistible. "Want to go for a walk with me?"

It was late, already dark outside. She had been away from the twins for a long while but the temptation of spending more time alone with him was too much to resist. She nodded her head.

"There's a door over here." He picked up one of the sweaters he'd thrown aside days earlier and dragged it over her head. Shrugging into his jacket, Dillon opened the door and stepped back to allow her to go first. He whistled softly and the German shepherd who had greeted Jessica and twins so rudely when they had arrived, came running to them, a blur of dark fur.

The night was crisp, cold, the air coming off the ocean, misty with salt and tendrils of fog. They found a narrow path winding through the trees and took it, side by side, their hands occasionally brushing. Jessica didn't know how it happened but somehow her hand ended up snugly in his.

She glanced up at him, drawing in her breath, her heart fluttering, racing. Happy. But it was now or never. She either cleared the air between them or he would be lost to her. "How did you happen to end up with Vivian? She didn't seem to fit you."

For a long moment she thought he wouldn't answer her. They walked in silence for several yards and then he let out his breath in a long, slow exhale.

"Vivian." Dillon swept his free hand through his black hair and glanced down at her. "Why did I marry Vivian? That's a good question, Jess, and one I've asked myself hundreds of times."

They walked together beneath the canopy of trees, surrounded by thick forest and heavy brush. The wind rustled through the leaves gently, softly, a light breeze that seemed to follow them as they followed a deer path through the timber. "Dillon, I never understood how you chose her, you two were so different."

"I knew Vivian all of my life, we grew up in the same trailer park. We had nothing. None of us did, not Brian, or Robert, or Paul. Certainly not Viv. We all hung out together, playing our music and dreaming big dreams. She had a hard life, she and Brenda both. Their mother was a drunk with a new man every week. You can imagine what life was like for two little girls living unprotected in that environment."

"You felt sorry for her." Jessica made it a statement.

Dillon winced. "No, that would make me appear noble. I'm not noble in this, Jess, no matter how much you want me to be. I cared a great deal for her, I thought I loved her. Hell, I was eighteen when we got together. I certainly wanted to protect her, to take care of her. I knew she didn't want kids. She and Brenda were terrified of losing their figures and being left behind. Their mother drilled it into them that it was their fault the men always left because they had ruined her figure. She even told them, when her boyfriends came on to them, that it was their fault, that of course the men preferred them to her." He raked his hand through his hair again, a quick, impatient gesture. "I'd heard it from the time we were kids. I heard Vivian say she would never have a baby, but I guess I didn't listen."

They continued along the deer path for several more minutes in silence. Jessica realized they were moving toward the cliffs almost by mutual consent. "So many old ghosts," she observed, "and neither one of us has managed to lay them to rest."

Dillon brought her hand to the warmth of his chest, right over his heart. "You didn't have the kind of life we lived, Jess, you can't understand. She never had a childhood. I was all Vivian had—me and the band and Brenda, when she wasn't fighting her own demons. When Vivian found out she was pregnant, she freaked. Totally freaked. Couldn't handle it. She begged me to give her permission to get rid of them, but I wanted a family. I thought she'd come around after they were born. I married her and promised we'd hire a nanny to take care of the kids while we worked the band."

Dillon led the way out of the timberline onto the bare cliffs overlooking the sea. At once the wind whipped his hair across his face. Instinctively he turned so that his larger body sheltered hers. "I hired Rita to take care of the children and we left. We just left." He stared down at her, his blue eyes brooding as he brought her hand to the warmth of his mouth. His teeth scraped gently, his tongue swirled over her skin.

Jessica shivered in response, her body clenching, molten fire suddenly pooling low in her belly. She could hear the guilt in his voice, the regret, and she forced herself to stay focused. "The band was making it big."

"Not right away, but we were on the upswing." He reached out, because he couldn't stop himself, and crushed strands of bright red-gold hair in his fist. "I wanted it so bad, Jess, the money, the good life. I never wanted to have to worry about a roof over our heads or where the next meal was coming from. We worked hard over the next three years. When we would go home, Vivian would bring the twins bags of presents but she would never touch them, or talk to them." He allowed the silky strands to slide through his fingers. "By the time the twins were four, the band was a wild success but we were all falling apart." Abruptly he let go of her.

"I remember her coming in with gifts," Jessica acknowledged, shivering a little as the wind blew in from the sea. All at once she felt alone. Bereft. "Vivian stayed away from us, away from the twins. She didn't come home very often." Dillon had visited without her, but Vivian had preferred to stay in the city most of the time with the other band members.

A peculiar fog was drifting in on the wind from the sea. It was heavy, almost oppressive. The dog looked out toward the pounding waves and a growl rumbled low in his throat. The sound sent a chill down Jessica's spine but Dillon snapped his fingers and the animal fell silent.

"No, she didn't." Dillon shrugged out of his jacket and helped her into it. "She was always so fragile, so susceptible to fanatical thinking. I knew she was drinking. Hell, we were all drinking. Partying was a way of life back then. Brian was into some strange practices, not devil worship, but calling on spirits and gods and mother earth. You know how he can be, he runs a line of bull all the time. The problem was, he had Vivian believing all of it. I didn't pay attention, I just laughed at them. I didn't realize then that she was seriously ill. Later, the doctors told me she was bipolar, but at the time, I just thought it was all part of the business we were in. The drinking, even the drugs, I thought she'd tame down when she got it out of her system. I didn't realize she was self-medicating. But I should have, Jess, I should have seen it. She had the signs, the intense mood swings, the highs and lows and the abrupt changes in her thinking and behavior. I should have known."

His hands suddenly framed her face, holding her still. "I laughed, Jess, and while I was laughing about their silly ceremonies, she was going downhill, straight into madness. The drugs pushed her over the edge and she had a schizophrenic break. By the time I realized just how bad she really was, it was too late and she tried to hurt you."

"You put her in rehabs—how could you have known what bipolar even was?" She remembered that clearly. "No one told you that last year while you were on the world tour just how bad she'd gotten. You were in Europe. I heard them all discussing it; the decision was made not to say anything to you because you would have thrown it all away. The band knew. Paul, Robert, especially Brian, he called several times to talk to her. Your manager, Eddie Malone, was adamant that everyone stay quiet. He arranged for her to stay here, on the island. He thought with all the security she would be safe."

Dillon let go of her again, his blue gaze sliding out to sea. "I knew, Jess. I knew she had slipped past sanity, but I was so wrapped up in the tour, in the music, in myself, I didn't check on her. I left it to Eddie. When I'd talk to her on the phone she was always so hysterical, so demanding. She'd sob and threaten me. I was a thousand miles away and feeling so much pressure, and I was tired of her tantrums. At the time I listened to everyone telling me she would pull out of it. I let her down. My God, she trusted me to take care of her and I let her down."

"You were barely twenty-seven, Dillon—cut yourself some slack."

He laughed softly, bitterly. "You always persist in thinking the best of me. Do you think she started out the way she ended up? She was far too fragile for the life I took her into. I wanted everything. The family. The success. My music. It was all about what I wanted, not what she needed." He shook his head. "I did try to understand her at first, but she was so needy and my time was stretched so thin. And the kids. I blamed her for not wanting them, not wanting to be with them."

"That's natural, Dillon," Jessica said softly. She tucked her hand into the crook of his arm, wanting to connect herself to him, wanting the terrible pain, the utter loneliness etched so deeply into his face, to be gone.

The fog thickened, a heavy blanket that carried within it the whisper of something moving, of muffled sounds and veiled memories. It bothered her that the dog stared at the fog as if it held an enemy within its midst. She tried to ignore the animal's occasional growl. Dillon, too engrossed in their conversation, didn't appear to notice.

"Is it natural, Jess?" His eyebrow shot up as he looked down into her wide green eyes. "You're so willing to forgive my mistakes. I left the kids. I put my career first, my own needs first, what I wanted, first. Why was it okay for me, but unforgivable for her? She was ill. She knew she had something wrong with her; she was terrified of hurting the kids. She didn't need rehab, she needed help with mental illness." He rubbed his hand over his face, his breath coming in hard gasps. "I didn't come home much that year because of you, Jessica. Because I was feeling things for you I shouldn't have been feeling. Rita knew, God help me. I talked to her about it and we agreed the best thing to do was for me to stay away from you. It wasn't sex, Jess, I swear to you, it was never about sex."

There was so much pain in his voice her heart was breaking. She looked up at him and saw tears shimmering in his eyes. At once she put her arms around his waist, laid her head on his chest, holding him to her without words, seeking to comfort him. He had never touched her, never said a word that might be deemed improper to her, nor had she to him. But it was true they'd sought each other's company, talked endlessly, *needed* to be close. She could feel his body tremble, with emotion rising like a long dormant volcano come to life.

Dillon was all about responsibility; he always had been. She had always known that. His failure was eating him from the inside out. Jessica felt helpless to stop it. She drew back cautiously, putting a step between them so she could look up at his face. "Did you know she was into séances and calling up demons?" She had to ask him and her heart pounded in time to the rhythm of the sea as she waited for his answer.

"She and Brian would burn candles to spirits but there had been nothing remotely like devil worship, sacrifices, or the occult. I didn't know she had hooked up with some lunatic who preached orgies and drugs and demon gods. I had no idea until I walked into that room and saw you." He closed his eyes, his fist clenching.

"You got me out of there, Dillon," she reminded gently.

Rage. He tasted it again, just as it had swirled up in him that night, a violence he hadn't known himself capable of. He had wanted to destroy them all. Every single person in that room. He had beat Vivian's lover to a bloody pulp, satisfying some of his rage in that direction. He had vented on Vivian, his wrath nearly out of control, calling her every name he could think of, allowing her to see his disgust, ordering her out of his home. He had sworn she would never see the children, never be allowed into his life again. Vivian had stood there, naked, sobbing, and hanging on him, the musty smell of other men clinging to her as she begged him not to send her away.

Dillon looked down to meet Jessica's vivid gaze. They both recalled the scene clearly. How could they not remember every detail? The heavy fog carried a strange phosphorescence within, a shimmering of color that floated inland.

Dillon looked away from the innocence on Jessica's face. Staring at the white breakers he made his confession. "I wanted to kill her. I didn't feel pity, Jessica. I wanted to break her neck. And I wanted to kill her friends. Every last one of them."

There was honesty in his voice. Truth. She heard the echo of rage in his voice, and the memories washed over her, shook her. He had learned there was a demon hidden deep within him and Jessica had certainly witnessed it.

"You didn't kill them, Dillon." She said it with complete conviction.

"How do you know, Jess? How can you be so certain I didn't go back into that room after I carried you upstairs? How can you be so certain, after I laid you on the bed with your heart torn out, after I knew that she had encouraged some lecherous pervert to put his hands on you, to write symbols of evil all over your body? When I saw you like that, so frightened—" His fist clenched tightly. "You were everything good and innocent that they weren't. They wanted to destroy you. Why would you believe that I didn't walk back up the stairs, shoot both of them, lock them all in that room, start the fire, and leave the house?"

"Because I know you. Because the twins, the band members, my mother, and I were all in that house."

"Everyone is capable of murder, Jess, and believe me, I wanted them dead." He sighed heavily. "You need to know the truth. I did go back into the house that night."

A silence fell between them, stretching out endlessly while the wind rose on a moan and shrieked eerily out to sea. Jessica stood on the cliffs and stared down into the dark foaming waves. So beautiful, so deadly. She remembered vividly the feeling of the water closing over her head as she went after Tara who had tumbled down the steep embankment. She felt exactly the same way now, as if she were being submersed in ice-cold water and dragged down to the very bottom of the sea. Jessica looked up at the moon. The clouds, heavy with moisture, were sliding through the sky to streak the silver orb with shades of gray. The fog formed tendrils, long thin arms that stretched out as greedily as the waves leapt and crashed against the rocky shore.

"Everyone knows you went back. The house was on fire and you ran in." Her voice was very low. There was sudden awareness, a knowledge growing inside of her.

Dillon caught her chin, looked into her eyes, forcing her to meet his gaze, to see the truth. "After I left your room I went outside. Everyone saw me. Everyone knew I was furious at Vivian. I was crying, Jess, after seeing you like that, knowing what you'd been through. I couldn't stop ranting, couldn't hide the tears. The band thought I'd caught Viv with a lover. I stalked out, huddled in the forest, walked around the house a couple of times. But then I went to find your mother. I felt she ought to know what Vivian, her friends, and that madman had done to you."

"She never said a word to me."

"I told her what happened. All of it. How I found you with them. What they were doing. I was crazy that night," he admitted. "Rita was the only person I could talk to and I knew you wouldn't tell her about it, you kept begging me not to, you couldn't bear for her to know." He raked a hand through his hair again in agitation, the memories choking him. "Rita blamed herself. She knew what Vivian was doing, had known for some time. I yelled at her when she admitted it, I was so angry, so out of control, wanting vengeance for what had happened to you. Looking back, I can see that it was my fault, all of it. I blamed everyone else for what happened to you, and I hated them and wanted them dead, but I was the one that allowed it to happen."

Dillon studied her face as she stared up at him with her wide eyes. He reached out, brushed her face with his gloved hand, his touch lingering long after he dropped his hand. "I went back into the house, angry and determined to avenge you. Rita knew I went back. Your mother believed I murdered Vivian and her lover. She thought the fire was an accident, caused by the candles being knocked over while we were fighting. She knew I went back into the house and she believed I shot them but she never told anyone."

Jessica's green gaze jumped to his face. "She didn't believe you killed them." She shook her head adamantly. "Mom would never believe that of you."

"She knew my state of mind. There was so much rage

in me that night. I didn't even recognize myself. I had no idea I was capable of such violence. It consumed me. I couldn't even think straight."

Jessica shook her head. "I won't listen to this. I won't believe you." She turned away from him, away from the pounding sea and the heartache, away from the thick, beckoning fog, back toward the safety of the house.

Dillon caught her arms, held her still, his blue eyes raking her face. "You have to know the truth. You have to know why I stayed away all those years. Why your mother came to see me."

"I don't care what you say to me, Dillon, I'm not going to believe this. Seven people died in that fire. *Seven*. My mother may have kept quiet to save you because of what Vivian did to me, but she would never stay quiet if she thought you'd killed seven people."

"But then, if the fire was an accident, it wouldn't have been murder, and those seven people who died were having an orgy upstairs in my home, using Rita's daughter as the virginal sacrifice for their priests to enjoy." He said it harshly, his face a mask of anger. "Believe me, honey, she understood hatred and rage. She felt it herself."

Jessica stared up at him for a long while. "Dillon." She reached up to lay her hand along his shadowed jaw. "You will never get me to believe you shot Vivian. Never. I know your soul. I've always known it. You can't hide who you are from me. It's there each time you write a song." Her arms slid around his neck, her fingers twining in the silk of his hair. "You were different enough at first that I was afraid of who you had become, but you can't hide yourself from me when you compose music."

Dillon's arms stole around her. It was amazing to him, a miracle that she could believe in him the way she did. He held her tightly, burying his face in her soft hair, stealing moments of pleasure and comfort that didn't belong to him.

"My mother never said a word to me, Dillon, about what happened to me that night. Why didn't she talk to me about it all those years? The nightmares. I wanted someone to talk to." She had wanted him.

"She told me she waited for you to come to her, but you never did."

Jessica sighed softly as she pulled away from him. "I could never bring myself to tell her what happened. I felt guilty. I still go over every move I made, wondering what I should have done differently to avoid the situation." Her hand rubbed up and down his arms. She felt the raised ridges of his scars beneath her palm, the evidence of his heroism. A badge of love and honor he hid from the world. "How could Mom have thought you were guilty?"

"I told her what went on and the entire time I was breaking things, threatening them, swearing like a madman. She was sobbing; she sat on the floor in the kitchen with her hands over her face, sobbing. I went back upstairs. I didn't know what I was going to do. I think I was going to physically throw Vivian and her friends out of the house, one by one, into the ocean. Your mother saw me go up the stairs. I stood on the landing and could hear Vivian weeping, shrieking to the others to get out, and I knew I couldn't look at her again. I just couldn't. I went back downstairs and out through the courtyard. I didn't want to face your mother, or the band. I needed to be alone. I walked into the forest and sat down and cried."

She could breathe again. Really breathe again. He wasn't going to do anything silly such as try to convince her that he had actually shot Vivian. "I've always known you were innocent, Dillon. And I still don't think my mother believed you killed them."

"Oh, she believed it, Jessica. She stayed silent at the trial, but she made it abundantly clear that I wasn't to go near you or the children. I owed her that much. For what happened to you, I owed her my life if she asked for it."

Jessica felt as if he'd knocked her legs out from under her. "She never said anything but good things about you, Dillon."

"She knew I wanted you, Jess. There was no way I would ever be able to be around you and not make you mine." He admitted it without looking at her.

His tone was so casual, so matter-of-fact, she wasn't certain she heard him correctly. He was looking out to sea, into the thick veil of mist, not at her.

"And I would have let you." She confessed it in the same casual tone, following his example, looking out at the crashing waves.

His throat worked convulsively; a muscle jerked along his jaw at her honest admission. He waited a heartbeat. Two. Struggled for control of his emotions. "Someone has been attempting to blackmail me. They sent a threatening letter, telling me that they knew I had gone back into the house that night and that if I didn't give them ten thousand dollars a month, they would go to the police. I was supposed to transfer the money to a Swiss account on a certain day each month. They used words cut out of a newspaper and pasted onto paper. To my knowledge Rita was the only person who saw me go back into the house that night before the shots were fired. That was the reason I asked her to come here, to discuss the matter with me."

"You thought my mother was blackmailing you?" Jessica was shocked.

"No, of course not, but I thought she may have seen someone else that night, someone who saw me go back into the house."

"You mean one of the security people? The staff? One of the groundskeepers? There were so many people around back then. Do you think it was one of them?"

"It had to be someone familiar with the inside of the house, Jessie." He raked a hand through his hair, his gloved fingers tunneling deep, tousling the strands in his wake.

Jessica glanced back toward the house. "Then it has to be one of them. A member of the band. They lived there on and off. They all survived the fire. Robert? He and Brenda need the cash and it's a plan she's capable of coming up with. I doubt if blackmailing someone would bother her in the least."

Dillon had to laugh. "That's true—Brenda would think she was perfectly within her rights." His smile faded, leaving his blue eyes bleak. "But they all need money, every last one of them."

"Then it's possible one of the band members killed my mother. She must have seen someone, maybe she confronted them about it."

Dillon shook his head. "That's just not possible. I thought about it until I thought I'd go out of my mind—it just isn't possible. I've known them all, with the exception of Don, all of my life. We were babies together, went through school, went through hard times together. We were family, more than family."

Her hand went to her throat, a curiously vulnerable gesture. "I can't imagine someone we know killing Mom."

"Maybe it really was an accident, Jessie," he said softly.

She just stood there looking up at him with that look of utter fragility on her face, tugging at his heartstrings. Unable to stop himself, Dillon reached out, pulled her to him and bent his dark head to hers. There was time for a single heartbeat before his lips drifted over hers. Tasting. Coaxing. Tempting. Kissing Jessica seemed as natural to him as breathing. The moment he touched her, he was lost.

Dillon drew her into his arms and she fit perfectly, her body molding to his. Soft. Pliant. Made for him. His tongue skimmed gently along the seam of her lips, asking for entrance. His teeth tugged at her lower lip, a teasing nip, causing her to gasp. At once he took possession, sweeping inside, claiming her, exploring the heated magic of her. Where she might have wanted to be cautious, with him she was all passion, a sweet eruption of hunger that built with his insistence.

Her mouth was addicting and he fed there while the wind whipped their hair around them and tugged at their clothing. The sea breeze cooled the heat of their skin as the temperature rose. His body was full, heavy and painful. The hunger raged through his body for her, a dark craving he dared not satisfy. Abruptly he lifted his head, a soft curse escaping him.

"You don't have an ounce of self-preservation in you," he snapped at her, his blue eyes hot with an emotion she dared not name.

Jessica stared up at his beloved face. "And you have too much of it," she told him softly, her mouth curving into a teasing smile.

He swore again. She looked bemused, her eyes cloudy, sensual, her mouth sexy, provocative. Kissable. Dillon shook his head, determined to break free of her spell. She was so beautiful to him. So innocent of the vicious things people were capable of doing to one another. "Never, Jess. I'm not doing this with you. If you have some crazy idea of saving the pitiful musician, you can think again." He sounded fierce, angry even.

Jessica lifted her chin. "Do I look the type of woman who would feel pity for a man who has so much? You don't need pity, Dillon, you never have. I didn't run away from life, you did. You had a choice. No matter what my mother said to you about staying away from me and the children, you still had a choice to come back to us." She couldn't quite keep the hurt out of her voice.

His expression hardened perceptibly. "It was my choices that brought us all to this point, Jess. My wants. My needs. That isn't going to happen again. Have you forgotten what they did to you? Because if you haven't, I can tell you in vivid detail. I remember everything. It's etched into my memories, burned into my soul. When I close my eyes at night I see you lying there helpless and frightened. Damn it, we aren't doing this!" Abruptly he turned his back on her, turned away from the turbulent sea and stalked back toward the house.

Jessica stared after him, her heart pounding in rhythm with the foaming waves, the memories crowding so close that for a moment madness swirled up to consume her. The fog slid between them, thick and dangerous, obscuring her vision of Dillon. She swayed, heard chanting carried on the ocean breeze. Beside her, the German shepherd snarled, his growl rumbling low and ominous as he stared at the moving vapor.

"Jess!" Dillon's impatient tone cut through the strange illusion, dispelling it instantly. "Hurry up, I'm not leaving you out here alone."

Jessica found herself smiling. He sounded gruff, but she heard the inadvertent tenderness he tried so hard to keep from her, to keep from himself. She went to him without a word, the dog racing with her. There was time. It wasn't Christmas yet and miracles always happened on Christmas.

"COME ON, JESSIE," Trevor wheedled, stuffing a third pancake in his mouth. "We've been here a week. Nothing's happened to us. There's no weird stuff happening and we haven't even had a chance to explore the island."

Jessica shook her head adamantly. "If you two want to explore, I'll go with you. It's dangerous."

"What's dangerous?" Trevor glared at her as he picked up a huge glass of orange juice. "If Tara and I are in any danger, it's of being sucked into one of those video games we're playing so much. Come on, you and the others have been locked in the studio and we're always alone. We can only watch so many movies and play so many games. We're living like zombies, sleeping all day and staying up all night."

"No." Jessica didn't dare look at the band members. She knew they thought she was overly protective when it came to the twins.

Brenda snickered. "It's none of my business but if you ask me, they're old enough to go outside all by themselves."

"I have to agree with her," Brian seconded, "and that's plain scary. Trevor's a responsible kid, he's not going to do anything silly."

Tara glared at Brian. "I am *very* responsible. I said we'd *look* for a Christmas tree. Trevor wants to find one and chop it down."

Jessica paled visibly. "*Trevor!* Chopping involves an axe. You certainly aren't going to go chopping down trees." The thought was truly frightening.

"They aren't babies," Brenda sounded bored with the entire conversation. "Why shouldn't they go outside to play? All that fresh air is supposed to be good for kiddies, isn't it?"

Jessica glared at the twins' aunt as she sipped her morning coffee. "Stop calling them kiddies, Brenda," she snapped irritably. "They have names and like it or not you are related to them."

Brenda slowly lowered her coffee mug and peered intently at Jessica. "Do us all a favor, hon, just have sex with him. Get it over with and out of your system so we can all live in peace around here. Dillon's walking around like a bear with a sore tooth and you're so edgy you exhaust me."

Trevor spewed orange juice across the counter, nearly choking. Tara gasped audibly, spinning around to glare accusingly at Jessica.

"Oh dear," Brenda sighed dramatically. "Another huge gaffe. I suppose I shouldn't have said 'sex' in front of them. One must learn to censor oneself around kid . . ." she paused, rolled her eyes and continued. "*Children.*"

"Don't worry, Brenda," Trevor said good-naturedly,

"we *kiddies* learn all about sex at an early age nowadays. I think we were a little more shocked at your mentioning Jessica and our dad doing the a . . ." he glanced at his sister.

"Dastardly deed," Tara supplied without missing a beat.

Brian mopped up the orange juice with a wet cloth, winking at Jessica. "It would be dastardly if you decided to hop in the sack with Dillon. All his wonderful angst and creativity might evaporate in a single night."

"Shut up," Jessica snapped, placing her hands on her hips. "This conversation is not appropriate and it never will be. And we aren't doing anything, dastardly or otherwise, not that it's any of your business."

Tara tugged at the pocket of Jessica's jeans. "You're blushing, Jessie, is that why you're irritable all the time?"

"I am certainly *not* irritable." Jessica was outraged at the suggestion. "I've been working my you-know-what off with a madman perfectionist and his group of comedy club wannabes. If I've been a teensy little bit *edgy,* that would be the reason."

"Teensy?" Brenda sniffed disdainfully. "That doesn't begin to describe you, dear. Robert, rub my shoulders. Having to watch my every word is making me tense."

Robert obediently massaged his wife's shoulders while Brian circled around Jessica completely, peering at her with discerning eyes. "Your you-know-what is definitely intact and looking delicious, Jess, no need to worry about that."

"Thank you very much, you pervert," Jessica replied, trying not to laugh.

Dillon paused in the doorway to watch her with hungry eyes. To drink in the sight of her. The sound of her laughter and her natural warmth drew him like a magnet.

He had spent the last week avoiding brushing up against her soft skin, avoiding looking at her, but he couldn't avoid the scent of her or the sound of her voice. He couldn't avoid the way his blood surged hotly and little jackhammers pounded fiercely in his head when she was in the same room with him. He couldn't stop the urgent demands of his body. The relentless craving. She haunted his dreams and when he was awake she became an obsession he had no way to combat.

Thoughtfully, Dillon leaned one hip against the door. The intensity of his sexual hunger surprised him. He had always felt that Jessica was a part of him, even in the old days when it was simply companionship he had sought from her. They merged minds. Her voice blended perfectly with his. Her quick wit always brought him out of his brooding introspections and pulled him into passionate battles in every aspect of music. Jessica was well versed in music history and had strong opinions about composers and musicians. His conversations with her inspired him, animated him.

There was so much more. He felt alive again after a long interminable prison sentence. It wasn't at all comfortable, but along with bringing him to life, Jessica was putting the soul back into his music. He swore to himself, each time the moment he opened his eyes that he wouldn't give in to the whispers of temptation, but it seemed to him that he had gone from a barren, frozen existence straight into the fires of hell.

He couldn't help loving his children, being proud of

them. He couldn't help seeing the way Jessica loved them and the way they loved her back. And he couldn't help the desperate longing to be part of that bond, that intense love. Dillon had no idea how much longer he could keep his hands to himself, how much longer he could resist the lure of a family. Or even if he wanted to resist. Did he have the right to allow them into his world? He had failed once and it had changed the course of so many people's lives. Death and destruction had followed him. Did he dare reach out again, risk harming the ones he loved? He swept a hand through his thick hair and Jessica immediately turned, her vivid eyes meeting his.

Jessica could feel her heart thundering at the sight of him. A faint blush stole into her face as she wondered if he had overheard the conversation. She could only imagine what he must be thinking. Looking at him nearly took her breath away. There had always been such a casual masculine beauty to Dillon. Now, it seemed more careless, a sensual allure against which she had no resistance. One look from his smoldering eyes sent her body into meltdown. He was looking at her now, his blue eyes burning over her, intense, hungry, beyond her ability to resist.

Jessica tilted her chin at him in challenge. She had no reason to resist the strong pull between them. She wanted him to belong to her, body and soul. She saw no reason to deny it. As if knowing her thoughts, he lowered his gaze which drifted over her body, nearly a physical touch that left her aching and restless and all too aware of his presence.

"Dad?" Tara's voice instantly stopped all conversation

in the room. It was the first time she had addressed Dillon that way. "Trevor and I want to go looking for a Christmas tree." She glared at Jessica. "We aren't going to chop one down, only look for one."

Dillon smiled unexpectedly, looking like a mischievous, charming boy, so much like Trevor. "Is Mama Tiger showing her fangs?"

"Her claws anyway," Brenda muttered into her coffee mug.

"The weather's good, so we'll be perfectly safe," Trevor added, a glimmer of hope in his eyes. "Someone has to get this Christmas thing off the ground. We have less than two weeks to go. You're busy, we don't have that much time left, so Tara and I can handle the decorations while you work."

Dillon didn't look at Jessica. He *couldn't* look at her. The boy's face was hopeful and eager and trusting. Tara had called him 'Dad'. It tugged at his heartstrings as nothing else could have. His gaze shifted to his daughter's face. She wore an expression identical to her brother's. Trust was a delicate thing. It was the first time he'd come close to believing in miracles, that there might be second chances given out in life, even when he didn't deserve it. "You think you can find the perfect tree? Do you know how to choose one?"

Jessica blinked, her teeth sinking into her lower lip to keep from protesting. Dillon's tone had been casual, but there was nothing casual in the vivid blue of his eyes, or the set of his mouth. His gloved hand rubbed along his denim-clad thigh, betraying his uncharacteristic show of nerves. The gesture disarmed her, stole her heart. She wanted to put her arms around him, hold him close, protectively, to her.

Tara nodded eagerly. She grinned at Trevor. "I have a long list of requirements. I know exactly what we want."

Don had been sitting quietly in a chair by the window but he turned with a quick frown. "You don't just arbitrarily chop down trees because you want a momentary pleasure. In case you're not aware of it, when you chop the tree down, it dies." The frown deepened into a fierce scowl when Dillon turned to face him. "Hey, it's just my opinion, but then that doesn't count for much around here, does it?"

"I'm well aware of your environmentalist concerns, Don," Dillon said gently. "I share your views, but there's no harm in topping a tree or taking one that's growing too close to another and has no chance of survival."

"We're supposed to be working here, Dillon, not celebrating some commercialized holiday so the privileged little rich kids can get a bunch of presents from their rich daddy." There was unexpected venom in Don's voice.

Tara slid close to Jessica for comfort. Immediately Jessica pulled the girl into her arms, stroking the dark, wavy hair with gentle fingers. Beside her, Trevor shifted, but Jessica caught his wrist in a silent signal and he remained silent. His arms went around both Jessica and Tara, holding them close to him. The silence stretched to apprehension.

Dillon stirred then, straightening from where he had been leaning lazily against the doorframe. Dillon walked over to stand in front of his children. Very gently he caught Tara's chin in the palm of his gloved hand and lifted her face so that her blue eyes met his. "I'm looking forward to Christmas this year, Tara, it's been far too long for me without laughter and fun. Thank you for giving the holiday back to me." He bent his head and kissed her forehead. "I apologize for my friend's rudeness. He's obviously forgotten, in his old age, how fun holidays can be."

He touched his son then, his hand on the boy's shoulder. "I would greatly appreciate it if you and your sister would go out this evening before it gets too dark and find us the best tree you can. If we weren't in the middle of working this song I'd go with you. You find it and we'll go together to get it tomorrow evening." His fingers tightened momentarily as his heart leapt with joy. His son. His daughter. The terrible darkness that had consumed him for so long was slowly receding. His body actually trembled with the intensity of his emotions. He had never dared to dream of the two beloved faces staring up at him with such confidence and faith. "I'm trusting you to take care of your sister, Trevor."

Trevor swelled visibly. He glanced at Jessica, a tremor running through him, his hands tightening until his fingers dug into Jessica's arm. She smiled up at him with reassurance. With understanding. She could not allow her fears to take the pleasure from all of them. Especially when she didn't even know if her fears were grounded in reality. When she looked back at Dillon her feelings were naked on her face.

Dillon's breath caught in his chest. There was raw love on Jessica's face, in her eyes. She looked up at him as no other in his life ever had. Complete confidence, unconditional love. There was never a hidden agenda with Jessica. She loved his children completely, fiercely, protectively. And she was beginning to love him the same way. "You and Tara go now before it gets dark. I have some business matters to discuss."

Trevor nodded his understanding, grinning triumphantly at Don. He led Tara out of the room, urging her to hurry to get her jacket so they wouldn't lose the light they needed.

Dillon reached down and took Jessica's hand, raised it to the warmth of his mouth. His blue gaze burned into her green one. Mesmerizing her. Holding her captive with his sensual spell, in front of all the band members, he slowly pressed a kiss into the exact center of her palm, blatantly branding her. Staking his claim.

Jessica could feel hot tears burning behind her eyes, clogging her throat. Dillon. Her Dillon. He was coming back to life. The miracle of Christmas. The story her mother had so often told her at night. There was a special power at Christmas, a shimmering, translucent, positive, force that flowed steadily, that was there for the taking. One had only to believe in it, to reach for it. Jessica reached with both hands, with her heart and soul. Dillon needed her, needed his children. He had only to open his heart again and believe with her.

Dillon tugged on her hand, drew her to him so that her soft curves fit against the hard strength of his body. Then he turned his head above hers toward Don, pinning the man with a gaze of icy cold fury. "Don't you ever speak that way to my children again. Not ever, Don. If you have a gripe with me, feel free to tear into me, but never try to get to me through my children." There was a promise of swift and brutal retaliation in his voice.

Jessica looked up into his face and shivered. Dillon was different now, no matter how many glimpses she caught of the person she had once known.

"You want me out, don't you, Wentworth? You've always wanted me out. It's always been about 'Precious Paul' with you. You're loyal to him no matter what he does," Don snarled. "I worked hard, but I never got the recognition. You've always resented me being in the band. Paul," he gestured toward the man sitting ramrod stiff in the chair by the window. "He can do anything and you forgive him."

"You're not so innocent, Don." Brenda yawned and lazily waved a dismissing hand. "You musicians are so dramatic. Who cares who loves whom best? At least Paul didn't use his lover to get him into the band."

Dillon's head snapped up, his eyes glittering. "What the hell are you talking about, Brenda?"

Jessica glanced around the room. Everyone had gone still, looking nervous, guilty, even Paul. Don flushed a dull red. His eyes shifted away from Dillon.

Brenda winced. "Ouch. How was I to know you were kept in the dark?" Dillon's relentless blue gaze continued to bore into her. "Fine, blame me, I'm always in trouble. I thought you knew; everyone else certainly knew."

Dillon's fingers tightened around Jessica's hand. She could feel the tension running through his body. He was trembling slightly. She shifted closer to him, silently offering support.

"Tell me now, Brenda."

For the first time, Jessica saw Brenda hesitate. For a moment she looked uncertain and vulnerable. Then her expression changed and she shrugged her shoulders carelessly, her tinkling laugh a little forced. "Oh for heaven's sake, what's the big deal? It was a million years ago. It's not as if you thought Vivian had been faithful."

Jessica felt him take the blow in his heart. It was a gutwrenching jolt that shook him, turned his stomach so that for a moment he had to fight to breathe, to keep from being sick. She felt his struggle as clearly as if she were experiencing it herself. Dillon's face never changed expression, he didn't so much as blink. He could have been carved from stone, but Jessica felt the turmoil raging in him.

"So Viv had an affair with Don, no big deal," Brenda shrugged again. "She got him into the band. You needed a bass player—it all worked out."

"Viv and I weren't having problems when Don joined the band," Dillon said. His voice held no expression and he didn't look at Don.

Brenda inspected her long nails. "You know Viv, she had problems, she always had to be with someone. You were working on songs for the band, trying to help Paul. If you weren't with her every minute, she felt neglected."

Dillon waited a heartbeat of time. A second. A third. He was aware of Jessica, of her hand, of her body, but there was a strange roaring in his head. His gaze shifted, settled on Don. "You were sleeping with my wife and playing in my band, allowing me to believe you were my friend?" He remembered how hard he had tried to make Don feel a part of the band.

Don's mouth tightened perceptibly. "You knew, everyone knew. It was no secret Viv liked to pick up a man now and then. And you got what you wanted. A bass player to kick around, someone to put up with your wife's tantrums when you didn't have the time or inclination to put up with her yourself. I won't even mention the extra money you saved because she was always wanting me to buy her things. I'd say we were more than even."

Dillon remained silent, only a muscle jerked along his jaw, betraying his inner turmoil.

"She was a bloodsucker," Don continued, looking around the room for support.

"She was ill," Dillon corrected softly.

"She had no loyalty and she was as cold as ice," Don insisted. "Damn it, Dillon, you had to have known about us."

When Dillon continued to look at him, Don dropped his gaze again. "I thought that was why you didn't want me in the band."

"Your own guilt made you think I didn't want you in the band." Dillon's voice was very soft, yet deep inside he was screaming at Jessica to help him. To stop him from saying or doing anything crazy. To save him. There had been such a surge of hope in him. A spreading warmth, a belief that he might reclaim his life. In a blink it was gone. He felt ice-cold inside. Emotionless. His heart and soul had been torn out. Everything he had built or cared about had been destroyed. He thought it had all been taken from him, but there was more, gouging old wounds to deepen them, to reopen them. He was shattering, crumbling, piece by piece until there was nothing left of who he had been.

"Damn it, Dillon, you had to have known," Don was almost pleading.

Dillon shook his head slowly. "I can't discuss this right now. No, I didn't know, I had no idea. I always thought of you as my friend. I did my best to understand you. I trusted you. I thought our friendship was genuine."

Jessica reached up and touched his face. Gently. Lovingly. "Take me out of here, Dillon. Right now. I want to be away from here." More than anything she wanted to get him away from treachery and betrayal. He had just begun to emerge into the sun after a long, bleak, cold winter. She could feel hands pulling him away from her, back into the deeper shadows. She kept her voice soft, persuasive. Her hands stroked his jaw, the pad of her thumb caressed his lips, a brush of a caress that centered his attention on her. His vivid blue gaze met hers. She saw the dangerous emotions swirling in the depths of his eyes.

Jessica tugged at him, forced him to move away from the others, out of the kitchen. She guided him through the house up to his private floor. He went with her willingly enough, but she could still feel the edge of violence in him, roiling and swirling all too close to the surface.

"I learned a lot of things about myself when I was at the burn center," Dillon said, as he pushed open the door to his study and stepped back to allow her to precede him. "There's so much pain, Jess, unbelievable pain. You think you can't bear any more, but there's always more.

Every minute, every second, it's a matter of endurance. You have no choice but to endure it because it never goes away. There's no way to sleep through it, you have to persevere."

The room was dark with the shadows of the late afternoon but he didn't turn on the light. Outside, the wind set the tree branches in motion so that they brushed gently against the sides of the house, producing an eerie music. Inside the room the silence stretched between them as they faced one another. Jessica could feel the turbulence of his emotions, wild, chaotic, yet on the surface he was as still as a hunter. She knew his strength of will, knew why he had survived such a terrible injury. Dillon was a man of deep passions. He sounded as if he was describing his physical pain, but she knew he was telling her about the other kinds of pain he'd also endured. The emotional scars were every bit as painful and deep as the physical ones.

"Don't look at me like that, Jess, it's too dangerous." He warned her softly, even as he moved to close the distance between them. "I don't want to hurt you. You can't look at me with your beautiful eyes so damn trusting. I'm not the man you think I am and I never will be." Even as he uttered the words aloud, meaning every one of them, his hands, of their own volition, were framing her face.

Electricity arced and crackled, a sizzling whip dancing with white-hot heat through their blood. The heat from his body seeped into hers, warming her, drawing her like a magnet. His head was bending toward her, his dark silky hair spilling around his angel's face like a cloud. Jessica's breath caught in her lungs. There was no air to breathe, no life other than his perfectly sculpted lips. His mouth settled over hers, velvet soft and firm. The touch was tantalizing. She opened her mouth as his teeth tugged teasingly at her lips to give him entrance to her sweetness, to the dark secrets of passion and promise.

Dillon closed his eyes to savor the taste of her, the hot silk of her. There was sheer magic in Jessica's kiss. It was madness to indulge his craving for her, but he couldn't stop, taking his time, leisurely exploring, swept away from the gray bleakness of his nightmare world into one of vivid colorful fireworks, bursting around him, in him. The need was instantaneous and elemental, the hunger, voracious. His body was all at once savagely alive, thick and hard and pounding with an edgy, greedy lust that shook him to the foundations of his soul. He'd never experienced it before, but now, it surged through his body, primitive and hot, demanding that he make her his.

Jessica felt his mouth harden, change, felt the passion flair between them, hot and exciting, a rush that dazzled her every sense. Her body melted into his, pliant and soft and inviting. His mouth raged with hunger, devoured hers, dominating and persuasive and commanding her response. She gave herself up to the blazing world of sheer sensation, allowed him to take her far from reality.

The earth seemed to shift and move out from under her feet as his palms slid over her back, down to her bottom, where they settled to align her body more firmly with his. His touch was slow and languorous, at odds with his assaulting mouth. His tongue plundered, his hands coaxed. His mouth was aggressive, his hands gentle.

Dillon's body was a hard, painful ache, his jeans

stretched tight, cutting into him. The feel of her, so soft and pliant, was driving him slowly out of his mind. There was a strange roaring in his head; his blood felt thick and molten like lava. She tasted hot and sweet. He couldn't get close enough to her, wanting her clothes gone so that he could press himself against her, skin to skin.

His mouth left hers to travel along her throat, with playful little kisses and bites, his tongue swirling to find shadows and hollows, to reach little trigger points of sheer pleasure. When he found them, she rewarded him with a little gasp of bliss. The sound was music to him, a soft note that drowned out his every sane thought. He didn't want sanity, he didn't want to know that what he was doing was wrong. He wanted to bury his body deep inside of her, to lose himself forever in a firestorm of mindless feeling.

His mouth found the hollow of her throat, the pulse beating so frantically there. He nudged aside the neckline of her blouse to find the swell of her breasts. She was soft, a miracle of satin skin. His hand closed over her breast, her taut nipple pushing into his palm through her blouse, through his glove. Beckoning. Urging him on. He bent his head to temptation.

The door to Dillon's study burst open and Tara stood there, her face white, her hair wildly disheveled. There was sheer panic on her face. "You have to come right now. *Right now!* Jessica! Hurry, oh, God, I think he's crushed under the logs and dirt. Hurry, you have to hurry!"

chapter

8

 PANIC SENT ADRENALINE coursing through Jessica's body. She looked up at Dillon, sheer terror in her eyes. His eyes mirrored her fear. He circled Jessica's waist with one strong arm, pulling her tight against him so that, briefly, they leaned into one another, comforting them both.

"Take a deep breath, Tara, we need to know what happened." Dillon's voice was calm and authoritative. He pulled the child into the circle of his arms, up against Jessica where she felt safe.

Tara gulped back her tears, buried her face against Jessica's shoulder. "I don't know what happened. One minute we were walking along and then Trevor said something weird, it didn't make sense, something about a magic circle and he ran ahead of me. I heard him yell and then there was a huge noise. The side of a hill gave way, rocks and dirt and logs rolling down. His yell was cut off and when I got to where I thought he was, the air was all dirty and cloudy. I couldn't find him and when I called and called, he didn't answer me. I think he was buried under all of it. The dog started digging and barking and growling and I ran to get you."

"Show me, Tara," Dillon commanded. "Jessica, you'll have to find the others, tell Paul we'll need shovels just in case." He was already pushing his daughter ahead of him.

They ran down the stairs, Dillon calling for the band members. As he jerked open the front door and raced across the front verandah, he nearly knocked Brian back down the front steps. They steadied one another. "It's Trevor. It sounds bad, Brian, come with me," Dillon said.

Brian nodded. "Where are the others?"

"Jess is rounding them up," Dillon replied. Tara ran ahead of him, but he kept pace easily, swearing under his breath. Night was falling all too fast and it would be very dark in a matter of minutes. He prayed his daughter didn't get lost, that she could lead them straight to his son.

Tara ran fast, keeping to the main path, her heart pounding loudly in her ears, but terror had subsided now that her father was taking command. He seemed so calm, so completely in control, that she felt her panic fading. She was afraid she wouldn't be able to find the exact location in the dark so she ran as fast as she could in an attempt to outrun the nightfall. It was even more of a relief when the large German shepherd came bounding out of the timberline to pace beside her. He knew the way to Trevor.

Jessica took several deep breaths as she hurried through the large house calling for the others. She found

Brenda outside the kitchen, in the courtyard, smoking. "What is it now? I swear there's no rest for the wicked around this place."

"Where are the others?" Jessica demanded. Brenda's chic hiking boots were covered in mud. Pine needles were stuck to the bottom and Brenda was trying to remove them without getting her fingernails dirty. "There's been an accident and we need everyone to help."

"Oh good heavens, it's those kids again, isn't it?" Brenda sounded annoyed. She backed up a step holding up a placating hand as Jessica advanced on her. "Really, darling, you wear me out with your agonizing over those *children*. See? I'm learning. Tell me what's wrong and I'll do my part to help, although I hope you send them both to their rooms and punish them suitably for disrupting my day."

"Where are the others?" Jessica spit each word out distinctly. "This is an emergency, Brenda. I think Trevor is trapped under a landslide, under dirt and rocks. We need to dig him out fast."

"Surely not!" Brenda's hand fluttered to her throat and she paled visibly. Her throat worked as if she was struggling to speak but no words would come. When they did, it was a choked whisper. "This place really is cursed, or maybe just Dillon is."

Jessica was surprised to see the woman was close to tears. "Brenda," she said desperately. "Help me!"

"I'm sorry, of course." Brenda straightened her shoulders. "I'll find Robert, he'll know what to do. Paul's around back playing horseshoes, at least he was when I walked up. I think Don was going to the beach, but I'm not certain. You get Paul and I'll find the others and send them to you. Which way did they go?"

"Thanks." Jessica put a hand on Brenda's arm, touching her to offer comfort. There was something very vulnerable on Brenda's face when her mask slipped. "I think they took the main trail heading into the forest."

"I just came back from that way," Brenda frowned, "I didn't see the kids."

Jessica didn't wait to hear any more; she raced around to the back of the house. Paul was idly tossing horseshoes. He paused in mid-swing when he spotted her. "What is it?" He tossed the horseshoe aside and hurried to her.

Feeling desperate, Jessica blurted out what she knew. Time seemed to be going by while she was getting nowhere. She wanted to race to Trevor, dig him out with her bare hands, not rely on the others.

"I'll get the lights," Paul told her, pulling open the door to a small shed. "There are shovels in here. I'll meet you around in the front." He was gone quickly.

Jessica pressed a hand to her churning stomach as she looked frantically through the potting shed for the shovels. All the larger tools were at the back of the shed. She felt sick, *sick* with fear for Trevor. How many minutes had gone by? Not many, her conversation with Brenda had taken only seconds, but it seemed an eternity. It was dark in the shed, the waning light insufficient to light the interior. She felt her way to the back, placing her hand on first a rake, a pry bar, and two sharper tools before she found the shovels. Triumphantly she caught up all three and rushed out of the small building.

Don was waiting impatiently for her. "Paul's gone on ahead." He grabbed the shovels from her, frowning as he did so. "What the hell did you do to your hand?"

Jessica blinked in surprise. Her palm was muddy and a single long slash in the center mingled blood with the dirt. A few stray pine needles stuck in the mixture as if it were artwork. "It doesn't matter," she muttered and hurried past him to take the trail.

Darkness had fallen in the forest, the heavier canopy blocking out what little light remained. Jessica ran fast, uncaring of her burning lungs. She had to get to Trevor and Tara. To Dillon. It couldn't be that bad. She consoled herself with the thought that someone would have come for her if the news were the worst. She could hear Don running beside her, and was vaguely aware of her throbbing palm. She wiped it on her thigh as they spotted lights off to her left.

Tara threw herself at Jessica, nearly knocking her over. "He's under all those big rocks and dirt. That big log fell on him, too! Dad's been trying to dig him out with his bare hands and Robert's been helping."

"They'll get him out quickly," Jessica reassured, holding the little girl close, "the soil is soft enough for them to dig him out very fast."

"Take her up there, out of the way," Dillon directed. His gaze met Jessica's over Tara's head as he caught in midair the shovel that Don tossed to him. "It's going to be okay, baby, I promise. He's talking, so he's alive and conscious. He's got air to breathe, we just have to get him out to see the damage."

Jessica nodded. Hugging Tara closer to her, she bent

down to the child's ear. "Let's move out of the way, honey. We'll go up there." She pointed to a small embankment off to the side but up above where the men were frantically digging.

The dog nudged her legs as she walked and Jessica absently patted his head. "Are you all right, Tara?" The girl was trembling.

Tara shook her head. "I shouldn't have insisted we keep looking. We found two trees we thought you and Dad might like, but I wanted to keep looking. Trevor said it was getting dark and wanted to go back to the house." She rubbed her face against Jessica's jacket. "I knew if I hadn't been with him he would have kept looking. I hate that, the way he always treats me like I'm a baby."

"Trevor looks out for you," Jessica corrected gently. "That's a good thing, Tara. He loves you very much. And this wasn't your fault." She stroked the girl's hair soothingly. "It just happened. Sometimes things just happen."

Tara shivered again. She looked up at Jessica, her eyes too large for her face. "I saw something," she whispered softly and looked around quickly. "I saw a shadow back in the trees, over there," she pointed toward the left in the deeper timber. "It looked like someone with a long cape and hood, very dark. I couldn't see the face, but he was watching us; he watched it all happen. I know he was there, it wasn't my imagination."

If it was possible, Jessica's heart began to pound even harder. "He was watching you while the rocks and dirt crumbled down on Trevor?" Jessica struggled to get the timing right. She believed Tara, she'd seen a cloaked figure in the woods the night they'd arrived, but she couldn't imagine any of the band members not rushing to aid the twins. Whoever had been in that cloak really might want to cause harm to one of them. Could someone other than the band members be on the island? The groundskeeper was an older, kindly man. The island was large enough that someone could hide out, camping, but surely the dog would have alerted the children to a stranger's presence. The twins had been spending time with the animal and she knew the German shepherd had guard instincts.

Tara nodded. "I yelled and yelled for help. I couldn't see Trev, he was buried under everything and when I looked back, the person was gone." She wiped her face, smearing dirt across her chin and cheek. "I'm telling the truth, Jessie."

Jessica brushed the top of the girl's head with a kiss. "I know you are, honey. I can't imagine why whoever it was didn't come to help you." She was determined to find out, though. She had been lulled into a false sense of security, but if the cloaked figure was a band member, and it had to be, then one of them was behind the accidents and the death of her mother. Which one? "Stay here, honey, away from the edge."

She couldn't stand still, pacing back and forth restlessly, her fist jammed in her mouth to keep from screaming at them to hurry. Don and Robert pried a rather large rock loose and it took all of the men to move it carefully away from the site.

Brenda joined Tara a little hesitantly. "He'll be all right, honey," she offered, placing her hand on her niece's shoulder in an attempt to offer comfort.

"He hasn't moved," Tara told her tearfully. "He hasn't moved at all."

"He's breathing though," Brenda encouraged. "Robert said Trevor told them he dove into a small space, a depression against the hillside."

"He was talking? Dillon said he spoke, but I haven't heard anything." And Jessica wanted the reassurance of the sound of his voice. She continued to pace, rubbing her arms as she did so, shivering in the night air. "Are you certain he spoke?"

"I'm pretty sure," Brenda answered.

Jessica stared up at the sky. She could hear the pounding of the sea in the distance. The wind rustling through the trees. The chink of the shovels against rock. Even the heavy breathing of the men as they worked. She could not hear Trevor's voice. She listened. She prayed. There was not even a murmur.

"He'll be all right," Brenda tried again to be reassuring. She tapped her foot, drawing Jessica's attention to the muddy ground strewn with pine needles and vegetation. A few fallen trees crisscrossed the area from the violent storm. Most had been there for some time but two smaller ones were fairly fresh.

She couldn't help the terrible suspicion that slid into her mind. Another accident. Could it have been rigged? Almost without even being aware of it, she examined the ground, the position of the logs, searching for clues, searching for anything that might provide an answer for what had happened. There was nothing she could see, nothing that would make Dillon listen to her that something wasn't quite right. Maybe she was paranoid, she didn't know, only that she had to find a way to make the children safe.

"I won't be able to take it if anything's happened to him," Jessica murmured to no one in particular. She meant it. Her heart was breaking. She was white-faced, sick to her stomach and moving to keep from being sick in front of everyone. "I shouldn't have let him go off like that. I should have been with him."

"Jessica, you couldn't have prevented this," Brenda said firmly. "They'll get him out." Awkwardly she hugged Tara to her as a muffled sob escaped the child. "Neither one of you could have stopped this. After a storm, sometimes the land is soft and it just shifts. You both would have been hurt had you been with him."

Jessica crouched down, peering at the men as they frantically dug away the dirt and rocks to free Trevor. She could see his legs and part of one shoe. "Dillon?" Her voice wavered. Trevor wasn't moving. "Why is he so still?" She could barely breathe, her lungs burning for air.

"Don't go getting all sappy," Trevor's disembodied voice floated up to her. He sounded thin and reedy, but it was his usual cocky humor. "You'll just be mad at me later if everyone sees you all teary-eyed."

Jessica slowly attempted to stand, her body trembling with relief. Her legs felt rubbery, and for a moment she was afraid she might faint. Brenda shoved her head down, held her there until the earth stopped spinning so crazily. Robert came up on the other side of her, holding her arm as she swayed. Jessica bit down hard on her fist to keep from crying as she straightened. Tears glittered in her eyes, on her lashes. Her gaze met Dillon's in complete understanding. For a moment there was no one else, just the two of them and the sheer relief only a parent could feel after such a frightening experience.

Tara hugged her, relief in the vivid blue of her eyes. Jessica barely registered it. She couldn't remember ever being so shaky but she managed a tentative smile at Brenda and Robert. "Thanks for keeping me from landing on my face in the dirt."

Brenda shrugged with her casual eloquence. "I can't let anything happen to you. I'd be stuck with the kiddies." She winked at Tara even as she went into her husband's arms. She seemed to fit there, to belong.

Tara grinned back at her. "We grow on you."

"No they don't," Jessica replied firmly, "they take years off your life. I think you have the right idea, Brenda, no kiddies or animals." Her eyes remained on Trevor as they slowly freed him. He was stretching his legs cautiously. She could hear him talking with Dillon. His voice was still shaking, but he was holding his own, laughing softly at something his father said to him.

"Brenda, would you mind taking Tara back to the house? It's already so dark. She should take a hot bath, and when I come in I'll fix hot chocolate. She's muddy and wet and shaking whether she knows it or not," Jessica said.

"So are you," Brenda pointed out with unexpected gentleness.

"I'll be right in," Jessica promised. She squeezed Tara's hand. "Thank you for getting everyone here so quickly, honey, you were wonderful."

"We'll get her to the house safely," Robert assured

Jessica, and with an arm around Brenda and one around Tara, he started back toward the house.

Jessica had to touch Trevor, to make certain he had not suffered a single injury. She made her way down to the site and knelt beside Dillon next to Trevor. Dillon examined every inch of the boy, testing for broken bones, lacerations, even bruises. His hands were unbelievably gentle as he ran them over his son.

Trevor was filthy, but grinning at them. "It's a good thing I'm skinny," he quipped, patting Jessica's shoulder, knowing if he hugged her she'd burst into tears in front of everyone and then he'd really be in trouble.

"He's fine, a few bumps and bruises. Tomorrow he's going to be sore," Dillon announced to the others. "Thank you all for helping." He sat back, wiped his hand across his forehead, leaving behind a smear of dirt. His hand was trembling. "You took a couple of years off my life, son. I can't afford it."

Paul gathered up the shovels. "None of us can afford it."

"Don't feel alone," Trevor said, "It felt like the entire hillside came down on top of me. For a few minutes there, all I could think about was being buried alive. Not a pleasant thought."

Jessica stepped back to allow Paul room. Dillon and Paul lifted Trevor to his feet. The boy swayed slightly but stood upright, his familiar grin on his face. "Jess, I'm really okay, you know?"

Dillon watched her face crumble, her composure gone as she circled Trevor's neck with her slender arms and hugged him fiercely, protectively, to her. There was no awkwardness in the boy's manner as he tightened his arms around her and buried his face on her shoulder. They were easy, natural, loving with one another. Dillon felt a burning in his chest, behind his eyes, as he watched them. A terrible longing welled up, nearly blindsided him. The layers of insulation were being stripped away, exposing his heart, so that he was raw and vulnerable.

Part of him wanted to lash out at them like a wounded animal. Part of him wanted to embrace them, to hold them safely to him. *Safe.* The word shimmered bitterly in his mind. He tasted bitterness in his mouth. For a heartbeat of time he stared at them, his heart pounding, adrenaline surging. His blue eyes glittered with the violence that always seemed to be swirling just below the surface.

Before Dillon could turn away from them, Jessica lifted her head, her gaze colliding with his. At once he was lost in the joy on her face. Her smile was radiant, like a burst of sunshine. She held out her hand to him. An invitation to a place he couldn't go. He stared down at her hand. Delicate. Small. A bridge back to living.

He didn't move. Dillon later swore to himself he hadn't moved, but there he was, taking her hand in his. His gloves were filthy but she didn't seem to notice, her fingers tightening around his. Touching her, he was lost in her spell, a web of enchantment, losing all touch with reality, with sanity. He found himself drawn up against the soft invitation of her body. Her head nuzzled his chest, her silky hair catching in the shadow along his jaw.

Without thought, without hesitation, his hand circled her vulnerable throat, tipping her head back. Her green eyes were large, haunting, cloudy with emotion. He swore softly, a surrender, a defeat, as he bent his dark head to hers. Her mouth was perfection, velvet soft, yielding, hot and moist and filled with tenderness. With the taste of love. The smoldering ember buried deep in his gut flared to life, flooded his system with such craving he fed on her, devoured her, swept away by the addicting taste of her. By the rich promise of passion, of laughter, of life itself.

She found a way past his every barricade, past his every defense. She wrapped herself around his heart, his soul, until he couldn't breathe without her. The loneliness that had consumed him for so long, and the bleak endless existence, vanished when she was near him. Need slammed into his body, hard and urgent, a demand that threatened to steal his control. The sheer force of their chemistry alarmed him. His body trembled, his mouth hardened, his tongue thrusting and probing, a hot mating dance his body desperately needed to perform.

Trevor cleared his throat loudly, dragging Dillon back to reality. Startled, he lifted his head and blinked, slowly coming back into his own scarred body and soul.

Trevor grinned up at him. "Don't look so shell-shocked, Dad, it's kind of embarrassing when I had this image of you all suave with the ladies."

"Suave isn't the word for it," Don muttered acidly under his breath.

Dillon heard him and turned the weight of his stare in Don's direction. The others attacked from all directions, diverting him.

"Boyo," Brian let out his breath in a slow whistle. "What the hell was that?"

"I'd like to see that on rewind," Paul said, nudging

Dillon with his elbow. "A little vicarious experience goes a long way around here."

Jessica hid her scarlet face against Dillon's shoulder. "All of you go away."

"We don't dare, Jessie girl, no telling what you might do to our beloved leader," Brian teased. "We want the boyo suffering angst and melancholy. Haven't you heard that makes for the best songs?"

"Frustration's good for that, too," Paul chimed in.

Jessica reached up to frame Dillon's face with her hand. "I don't think it matters what state he's in," she objected, "he manages to compose beautiful music."

Dillon caught her hand and turned up her palm, his eyes narrowing. "What the hell did you do to your hand? It's bleeding."

He sounded so accusatory Jessica couldn't help smiling. "I was feeling around in the tool shed for the shovels and cut my hand on something sharp." Now that he'd pointed it out, the wound was beginning to burn.

"We have to wash that. I don't want you picking up an infection." Dillon indicated the path, retaining possession of Jessica's hand. "Are you steady enough to walk back, Trevor?"

Trevor nodded, hiding his smile as he turned onto the trail, following Paul closely. Don and Brian gathered up the lights. Dillon brought Jessica's hand up for another, much closer inspection. "I don't like the look of this, honey—you clean it the moment you get to the house." He was fighting to breathe, to stay sane. What the hell was he doing? He raked a hand through his hair, breathing hard, feeling as if he'd run miles. Emotions were crowding in so fast, so overwhelming he couldn't sort them out.

Jessica couldn't suppress the small surge of joy rushing through her. Dillon sounded so worried about such a trivial cut. They walked close together, his hand holding hers. Above their heads the stars tried valiantly to shine for them despite the gray clouds stretching out into thin veils covering the tiny lights.

Dillon deliberately slowed his pace to allow the others to get ahead of them. "I'm sorry, Jess, I shouldn't have kissed you like that in front of the others."

"Because they're going to tease us? They've already been doing that," she pointed out. She tilted her chin at him, a clear challenge to deny what was between them.

He sighed. "Because I wanted to tear your clothes off and take you right there, right then. I think I made it damned obvious to the band. You aren't some groupie and I don't want them looking at you that way—to ever see you in that light. You always think the best of everyone. Has it occurred to you, that their seeing me kissing you like that, they might consider you fair game?"

Jessica shrugged her shoulders, feigning a casualness she didn't feel. A heat wave spread through her body at his words. The thought of Dillon so out of control left her breathless. She managed to keep her voice even. "I doubt that I'll faint if one of them makes an attempt. This might shock you, Dillon, but other men have actually found me attractive and some of them have even asked me out. Believe it or not, you're not the only man who has ever kissed me." She felt him stiffen, felt the sudden tension in him.

A hint of danger crept into the deep blue of his eyes. "I don't think now is the best time to talk to me about other men, Jess." His voice was rougher than she'd ever heard it, that smoky, edgy tone very much in evidence. He halted abruptly, dragging her into the deeper shelter of the trees. "Do you have any idea what you're doing to me? Any idea at all?" He pulled her uninjured hand between his legs, rubbed her palm along the front of his jeans where the material was stretched taut, where he was thick and hard and she could feel heat right through the fabric. "I haven't been with a woman in a very long time, honey, and if you keep this up, you're going to get a hell of a lot more than you bargained for. I'm not some teenager looking for a quick feel. You keep looking at me the way you've been doing and I'm going to take you up on the invitation."

For one moment Jessica thought about slapping his handsome face, outraged that he would try to reduce her to a teen with a crush. That he would try to frighten her, or that he would think that he ever could frighten her. If there was one man on earth she trusted implicitly with her body, it was Dillon Wentworth. It took a heartbeat to realize he had captured her uninjured palm, that he was still cradling her wounded hand against his chest. Carefully. Tenderly. The pad of his thumb was rubbing gently along the edge of her hand and he wasn't even aware of it. But she was.

Deliberately provocative, she rubbed the stretched material at the front of his jeans. "You aren't very well suited to the roll of big bad wolf, Dillon, but if it's some fantasy you have, I guess I can play along." Her tone was seductive, an invitation. Her fingers danced and teased, stroking and caressing, feeling him respond, thicken more, harden more.

His eyes glittered down at her like two burning gemstones. "You don't have a clue about fantasies, Jessie."

"You're in the wrong century, Dillon." Her tongue slid provocatively along her lush bottom lip and, damn her, she was laughing at him. "I certainly wouldn't mind unzipping your jeans and wrapping my hand around you, feeling you, *watching* you grow even harder. And I did consider not wearing my bra so that the next time you kissed me and started working your way along my throat, you would feel my body is ready for you. The thought of your mouth on . . ."

"Damn it." A little desperately he bent his head and stopped her nonsense the only way he could think of. He took possession of her mouth and instantly was lost in her answering hunger. She was too sexy, too hot, too everything. Magic. Jessica was sheer magic. He caught her shoulders and resolutely set her away from him before he lost his mind completely.

She smiled up at him. "Are you ever going to kiss me without swearing first?"

"Are you ever going to learn self-preservation?" he countered.

"I don't have to learn," Jessica pointed out, "you watch out for me very nicely."

chapter
9

JESSICA TOOK HER TIME in the shower,
allowing the hot water to soak into her skin.
Dillon. He filled her thoughts and kept her
mind from dwelling on the possibility that she could have
lost Trevor. She had never experienced such a powerful
attraction. They had always belonged together. Always.
Best friends when it hadn't made sense. She had always
found him magnetic, but it had never occurred to her
that one day the sexual chemistry between them would
be so explosive. She shook with her need for him.

She closed her eyes as she dried her body with a thick
towel, the material sliding over her sensitive skin, height-
ening her awareness of unfamiliar sexual hunger. She
didn't feel like herself at all around him. His blue gaze
burned over her and made her feel a wanton seductress.
Jessica shook her head as she dressed with care. She
wanted to look her best to face him.

By the time she was back downstairs, everyone was
already in the kitchen ahead of her. Dillon looked handsome in clean black jeans and a long-sleeved sweater. It

bothered her that he still felt the need to wear gloves in front of his family and friends, in front of her. His hair was still damp from his shower, curling in unruly waves to his shoulders. As always he was barefoot, and for some strange reason, it made her blush. She found it amazingly sexy and intimate. He looked up the moment she appeared in the doorway as if he had built-in radar where she was concerned.

Dillon almost groaned when he turned his head. He knew she was there, how could he not know the moment she was close to him? She was so beautiful she took his breath away. Her jeans rode low on her hips showing a little too much skin for his liking. Her top was an inch too short, and the material lovingly hugged her full breasts the way his hands might. Her red-gold hair looked wine-red, still wet from her shower and pulled back away from her face, exposing the column of her neck. He blinked, looking closer. She damn well had better be wearing a bra under that thin almost nonexistent top. When she moved, he thought he saw the darker outline of her nipples, but then, he wasn't certain.

Just looking at her made him so hard he didn't want to take a step. "Did you put something on that cut?" His voice was harsh enough that even he winced at his tone.

Brian caught her wrist as she swept past him and turned up her palm for his inspection, halting her before she could make her way to Dillon's side. "It's still bleeding a bit, Jessie girl," he observed. "She needs to cover it with a bandage, Dillon," he added helpfully, tugging until Jessica followed him around the counter.

Dillon grit his teeth together, watching them. Brian

was a large bear of a man and Jessica looked small and delicate beside him. His scowl deepened as he watched the drummer span her waist and lift her onto the counter, wedging himself between her legs as he bent forward to examine her palm. His forehead nearly brushed her breasts. Brian said something that made Jessica laugh.

"What the hell are you doing?" Dillon burst out, stalking around the counter to jerk the bandage out of Brian's hand. "It doesn't take a rocket scientist to put a Band-Aid on her hand." He just managed to restrain himself from pushing Brian out of the way. Her thighs were open and she looked sexy as hell sitting there with her large green eyes silently reprimanding him. "Move," he said rudely.

Grinning broadly, Brian held his hands up in surrender and strode back around to the other side of the counter. "The man's like a bear with a sore tooth," he confided to Trevor in an overloud whisper.

"I noticed," Trevor replied in the same exaggerated whisper.

Dillon didn't care. He slipped into the spot Brian had vacated, nudging Jessica's thighs apart and moving close enough to catch that fresh elusive scent that stirred his senses. At once the heat of her body beckoned. And damn her, she wasn't wearing a bra, he was certain of it. He bent over her palm, examining the laceration.

The smile faded from Jessica's mouth. She nearly snatched her hand back. His breath was warm on the center of her palm sending tiny whips of lightning dancing up her arm. His hips were wedged tight between her legs. The smallest movement caused a heated friction along the inside of her thighs and spread fire to her deepest core. Her body clenched unexpectedly as he moved closer, his head brushing her breasts. She bit down on her lip to keep a small moan from escaping. Her breasts were achy and tender, so sensitive she could barely stand the lightest touch. He moved again, his forehead skimming against her blouse as he examined her palm. Right over her taut nipple. Tongues of fire lapped at her breasts, her body clenched again, throbbed and burned for release. All he had to do was turn his head slightly to pull her aching flesh into his hot, moist mouth. Her breath hitched in her throat.

His blue gaze found hers. Both of them stopped breathing.

"Well, is she going to live?" Paul asked, breaking the web of sexual tension between them. "Because if you don't finish up over there, the rest of us might not make it through the night."

"Holy cow, Jess," Trevor began.

"You don't need to say a word, young man," Jessica stopped him. She kept her eyes averted from Dillon; it was the only safe thing to do. She noticed it was awkward for him to manipulate the bandage into place. The brush of his fingers was like a caress against her skin, the glove stroked across her hand as he worked. Her body clenched more with each graze. She trembled. His hand tightened around hers, brought her injured palm to his chest, right over his heart.

"I think that should protect it, baby," he said gently. He caught her waist, only his gloves preventing him from touching her bare skin as he helped her to the floor. "It doesn't hurt, does it?"

She shook her head. "Thanks, Dillon, I appreciate it."

"How long is the darned thing going to take to heal?" Don demanded. "We need her to play. We're not nearly finished."

"I laid down several different guitar tracks earlier today, before you were up," Jessica said, "I wanted to try a few things, so at least you have something to work with." She moved cautiously around Dillon's large frame, careful not to touch his body with hers. She curled her fingers in Trevor's hair, needing to touch him, but not wanting to injure his boyish pride by making too big a fuss now that he was safe.

"What things?" Robert asked curiously, a hint of eagerness in his voice. "I thought bringing in the sax was a perfect touch. The orchestral background worked like magic. You have some great ideas, Jess."

Jessica gave him a quick grin of thanks. "I wanted to record a few different guitar sounds. I used the progression we started with yesterday but enhanced it with some melodic embellishments. I wanted an edgy sound to go with the lyrics so I used the *Les Paul* for rhythm. I still would like to do a little more layering. You should listen to it, Robert, and see what you think. I thought we might use the *Strat* for lead over the rhythm. The different sounds layered might really add to the piece."

"Or make it too busy," Don objected. "Dillon has a hell of voice, we can't just blast over the top of him."

"But that's the beauty of it, Don," Jessica countered. "We're still sticking to basic sounds. Very simple. Layering allows us to do that."

Brenda slumped over the tabletop dramatically. "Just

one night I'd like to talk about something other than music."

"I thought they were talking in a foreign language," Tara said. She pulled out the chair beside her aunt. "Boring."

Jessica laughed at her. "You just want that hot chocolate I promised you. I'll get it for you. Trevor? Anyone else?"

"You shouldn't be so careless, Jessie," Don reprimanded. "We only have a short time to get this together. You can't afford to damage your hands."

She paused in the act of removing mugs from the cupboard. "I don't honestly remember you being such a jerk, Don. Have you always been this way, or just recently?" If he took one more potshot at Dillon she was afraid she might throw a mug at his head. She didn't look at Dillon as she took the milk and chocolate from the refrigerator. There were wounds that went deep and Don seemed to want to rake at them. Jessica set everything very carefully on the counter and smiled sweetly, expectantly, at Don.

Trevor and Tara exchanged a long, amused glance. They'd heard Jessica use that tone before and it didn't bode well for Don. Tara nudged Brenda to include her, and was rewarded with a small smirk and a raised eyebrow.

"I didn't mean anything by it, Jess—everyone's too sensitive," Don replied defensively.

"I suppose we'll all overlook it this time but you need to work on your social skills. Some things are acceptable and some things aren't." Without turning her head she raised her voice. "You'd better not be mimicking me, Trev."

The twins exchanged another quick grin. Trevor had been mouthing the words, having heard them said numerous times. "Wouldn't think of it," he said cheekily.

"Dillon, would you like me to make you a cup of hot chocolate?" Jessica offered.

Dillon shook his head adamantly, shuddering at the mere thought of it. "I can't bear to look at the stuff. I had enough of that at the burn center."

"Why do you keep it then?" Jessica asked curiously.

"For Paul, of course," Dillon grinned boyishly at his friend. "He practically lives on the stuff. I think it's his one vice."

Jessica held up a mug. "How about you then, Paul?"

"Not tonight, I've had enough excitement. It might keep me up." He ruffled Tara's hair. "I figure we can share it until Christmas, then I expect it to be replaced by gift certificates and Hershey bonuses."

"I write lovely I.O.U.'s," Tara announced. "Just ask Trev."

"And you'll be old before you can cash them in," Trevor warned Paul. "But her handwriting is beautiful."

"So true, I'm vain about my handwriting. I need to be famous so I can sign autographs." Tara took a sip of the chocolate. "Why did you have too much chocolate at the burn center, Dad?"

There was a small silence. Brenda casually draped her arm around Tara. "Good question. What did they do, make you live on the stuff?"

"Actually, yes." Dillon looked across the room at Paul,

a vulnerable, almost helpless look on his handsome face. It was so at odds with his usual commanding presence, his expression tugged at Jessica's heartstrings.

It was Paul who answered very matter-of-factly. "Burn patients need calories, Tara, lots and lots of calories. Where your father was, they made drinks using chocolate. You'd think they would taste good, but they didn't—the mixture was awful, and he was forced to drink them all the time."

"They ruined chocolate for you?" Tara was outraged. "That's terrible."

Dillon gave her his heart-stopping, lopsided grin. "I guess it was a small price to pay for surviving."

"Chocolate is my comfort drink," Tara admitted. "What's yours?"

"I never really thought about it," he admitted. His blue gaze was drawn to Jessica. There had been no comfort in his life since he'd lost his family, lost his music, lost everything that mattered to him. Until Jessica. He felt a sense of peace when he was with her. In spite of the overwhelming emotions, the explosive chemistry, in spite of all of it, when she was near him, he felt comforted. He could hardly say that to his thirteen-year-old daughter. If he didn't understand it, how could anyone else?

"I like that thought, Tara," Paul said, "I use chocolate for my comfort drink, too."

"Coffee, black as can be," Brenda chimed in. "Robert likes a martini." She smiled up at him. "I drive him to drink."

"You drive everyone to drink," Brian pointed out.

"You were swilling six-packs of beer long before I ever

came on the scene," Brenda said, looking bored. "Your sins are all your own."

"We went to kindergarten together," Brian reminded everyone.

"And you were already beyond salvation."

"Give it a rest," Don begged.

Jessica thought it a perfect time to change the subject. "By the way, who owns the long, hooded cape?" She asked with feigned indifference. "It's quite dramatic."

"I have one," Dillon said. "I used it onstage years ago. I haven't thought of it in years. What in the world made you ask?"

"I've seen it a couple of times," Jessica said, her eyes meeting Tara's as they sipped their chocolate. "It was so different, I wanted to get a look at it up close."

"It has to be here somewhere," Dillon said, "I'll look around for it."

A chill seemed to creep into the room with her question. Jessica shivered. Once again the terrible suspicion found its way into her mind. Had someone deliberately lured Trevor to that exact spot? It wasn't possible. No one could actually predict a rockslide closely enough to set a trap. She was really becoming paranoid. Dillon couldn't have been the one wearing the cape when the rockslide had buried Trevor because Dillon had been with her. She glanced around the room surreptitiously, realizing she really knew very little about the other band members.

"I remember that cape!" Brenda sat up very straight with a wide smile. "Do you remember, Robert? Viv loved it. She was always swirling it around her and pretending to be a vampire. Dillon, we borrowed it from you for that

Hollywood Halloween thing, Robert wore it, remember hon?" She looked up at her husband, patting his hands as he gently massaged her shoulders.

"I remember it," Paul said. "It was hanging in your closet, Dillon, at least it was a month ago. I hung your shirts up when they came back from the laundry service. Viv thought vampire and you thought magician."

"I thought women," Brian said. "You know how many women wanted to see me in that cape and nothing else?" He puffed out his chest.

"Ugh," Tara wrinkled her nose. "That's totally gross."

"That's beyond gross, Brian," Brenda protested, "I'll never get the picture out of my mind." She covered her face with her hands.

"You loved it," Brian pounced immediately. "You begged me."

"Way too much information," Jessica cautioned.

"I did not, you idiot!" Brenda was outraged. "I may be many things, Brian, but I have taste. Seeing you prance around naked in a vampire cape is not my idea of sexy."

"You know, Brian," Robert said conversationally, "I actually like you. But I may have to shove your teeth down your throat if you aren't more careful in the way you choose to taunt my wife."

"Wow! That's so cool," Tara said, her blue eyes shining up at him. "He's pretty cool, after all, Brenda."

Brenda grinned at her in complete agreement. "He is, isn't he?"

Dillon leaned against Jessica, trapping her body between his large frame and the counter. "That cape might have possibilities," he whispered wickedly against her bare neck. His teeth skimmed very close to her pulse as if he might bite into her exposed skin.

"Not with knowing what Brian was doing in it," she whispered back. She pushed back against him, resting her bottom very casually against him. With the counter between their bodies and the rest of the room, no one could see her blatantly tempting him. She ached for him, her body heavy and needful. She wanted to turn into his arms, be held by him, and lie beside him, under him. She wanted to see his blue eyes blazing, burning for her alone.

Dillon savored the feel of her small, curved bottom pressed tightly against him. He was becoming used to walking around in a continual state of arousal. At least, he knew he was alive. She had the softest skin, and smelled so enticing he couldn't think of too much else when she was near. He cleared his throat, trying to pull his mind away from the thought of her body.

"Are you going to tell us about your Christmas trees?" Dillon wanted to find a way to connect with the children. They always seemed just out of his grasp. He reached around Jessica to remove the mug of chocolate from her hand. The smell was making him feel slightly sick and he wanted to inhale her delicate scent. To think about the possibility of a future, not remember the agony of where he had been. Jessica gave him such hope. His arms caged her, brought his chest in contact with the sweeping line of her back. She was the bridge between Dillon and the children. She was the bridge that led from merely existing to living life.

"We found two that might work," Trevor said, "but neither was perfect."

"Does a Christmas tree have to be perfect?" Don asked.

"Perfect for us," Trevor answered before Jessica could draw a breath and breathe fire. "We know what we're looking for, don't we, Tara?"

"Well, next time you'd better be a little more careful and stay on the trails," Dillon cautioned, using his most authoritative voice.

"There isn't going to be a next time," Jessica muttered rebelliously, "my heart couldn't stand it."

Trevor looked mutinous. "I knew you were going to be like that, Jess. It could have happened to anybody. You always get so crazy, even when we fall off a bike."

"Watch your tone," Dillon's mouth settled in an ominous line. "I think Jessica and the rest of us are entitled to feel protective. You were completely buried, Trevor, we didn't know if you were alive or dead or whether you were able to breathe or were broken into a million pieces." His arms tightened around Jessica, holding her close, feeling the tremor go through her body. His chin nuzzled the top of her head in sympathy. "Have the decency to let us be shaken up. But don't worry, we'll get a Christmas tree."

Jessica wanted to protest. She didn't want Trevor going anywhere outside, but Dillon was his father. There was no sense in dissenting, but she was *not* letting the twins go anywhere outside by themselves, father or no father.

Dillon felt her instant reaction, her body stiffening, but she remained silent. He pressed a quick kiss against the tempting nape of her neck. "Good girl." Her skin was so soft he wanted to rub his face against her. His palms itched to hold the soft weight of her breasts. His mind was becoming cloudy with erotic fantasies right there in the kitchen with everyone standing around.

"Sorry, Jessie," Trevor mumbled. "I saw that circle. The one with two rings, one inside of the other. The one you said was used to invoke spirits or something. It was drawn on a flat rock. It was really bright. I went off the trail to check it out."

There was a sudden silence in the room. Only the wind outside could be heard, a low mournful howl through the trees. A chill went down Jessica's spine. She felt the difference in Dillon immediately. His body was nearly blanketing hers as they both leaned against the counter, so it was impossible to miss the sudden tension in him. His body actually trembled with some sudden overwhelming emotion.

"Are you certain you saw a double circle, Trevor?" Dillon's face was an expressionless mask, but his eyes were blazing.

"Yes, sir," Trevor answered, "it was very distinct. I didn't get close enough to see what it was made out of before everything came down on me. It wasn't drawn or painted onto the rock. The circles were made of something and set on the rock. That's all I saw before I tripped on a log and everything crashed on top of me. I fit into the little opening against the hill so I wasn't crushed. I covered my mouth and nose and as soon as everything settled, I breathed shallowly, hoping you'd hurry. I knew Tara would get you fast."

Dillon continued to look at his son. "Brian, have you brought that filth into my home? Did you dare to do that after all that happened?"

No one moved. No one spoke. No one looked at the drummer. Brian sighed softly. "Dillon, I have my faith and I practice it, yes, wherever I am."

Dillon turned his head slowly to pin Brian with his steely glare. "You are practicing that garbage here? In my home?" He straightened up unhurriedly and there was something very dangerous, very lethal in his body posture as he rose to his full height.

Dillon was vaguely aware of Jessica laying a restraining hand very gently on his arm, but he didn't even glance down at her. The anger always simmering far too close to the surface rose in a vicious surge. The memories, dark and hideous, welled up to devour him. Screams. Chanting. The smell of incense mingled with the musty smell of sexual lust. Jessica's terror-stricken face. Her nude body painted with disgusting symbols. A man's hand violating her innocent curves while others crowded around her breathing heavily, obscenely. Watching. Stroking and pumping to bring their own bodies to a fever pitch of excitement while they urged their leader on.

Bile rose, threatening to choke him. Dillon suppressed the urge to coil his hands around Brian's throat and squeeze. Instead he held himself utterly still, curling his fingers into fists. "You dared to bring that abomination back to my home after all the damage that was done here?" His tone was soft, menacing, a spine-chilling threat.

"Trevor and Tara go upstairs right now," Jessica stood up straight, too, very afraid of what might happen. "Go, right now and don't argue with me."

Jessica rarely used that particular tone of voice. The

twins looked from their father to Brian and obediently left the room. Trevor glanced back once, worried about Jessica, but she wasn't looking at him and he had no choice but to go with Tara.

"I want you off this island, Brian, and don't ever come back," Dillon bit out each word distinctly.

"I'll go, Dillon," Brian's dark eyes betrayed his own rising anger, "but you're going to listen to me first. I do not now, nor have I ever had anything to do with the occult. I don't worship the devil. I never turned Viv on to that scene, someone else did. I did my best to talk to her, to influence her away from it."

Jessica rubbed her hand soothingly up and down Dillon's stiff arm, feeling the ridges of his skin, the raised scars, reminders of that horror-filled night that were forever etched into his flesh.

"Go on," Dillon said, his voice rough.

"My religion is old, yes, but it is the worshiping of things of the earth, spirits that live in harmony with the earth. I use the magic circles, but I don't invoke evil. That would be against everything I believe. I did my best with Viv to make her understand the difference. She was so vulnerable to anything destructive." Tears glittered in his eyes, his mouth trembled slightly. "You aren't the only one who loved her, we all did. And we all lost her. I watched her go downhill just like you did. I did my best to stop her, I really did, the minute I found out she was involved with that Satanic crowd."

Dillon raked a hand through his hair. "They weren't even the real thing," he said softly, sighing heavily.

"She went nuts when she hooked up with Phillip

Trent," Brian said. "She listened to everything he said as if it was gospel. I swear to you, Dillon, I tried to stop her, but I couldn't counteract his influence." He looked as if he were breaking apart, his face crumbling under the memories.

Dillon felt his rage subsiding. He had known Brian nearly all of his life. He knew the truth when he heard it. "Trent dragged her down into a world of drugs and manic delusion so fast I don't think any of us could have stopped her. I had him investigated. He had his own little religious practices, looking for money, drugs, and sex, kicks maybe, but not based on anything he didn't make up."

Jessica stepped away from him, her lungs burning. She needed to be alone. Away from them all. Even Dillon. The memories were crowding far too close. None of the others knew what had happened to her and the discussion was skimming the edges of where she did not want to go.

"I'm sorry, Brian, I guess it just seems so much easier to blame someone else. I thought I'd gotten over that. I should have tried harder to put her into a hospital."

"I don't worship in your house," Brian said. "I know how you feel. I know you keep battery-powered lights rather than candles in case your generator breaks down because you can't stand to see an open flame. I know you don't want incense or any reminders of the occult here and I don't blame you, so I take it outside away from your home. I'm sorry—I didn't mean to upset you, Dillon."

"I shouldn't have accused you. Next time, get rid of the circle so the kids don't get curious. I don't want to have to explain all that to them."

Brian looked confused. "I didn't set up for a ceremony

anywhere near the trail, or that area." His protest was a low murmur.

Dillon's gaze and attention was on Jessica. She was very pale. Her hands were trembling and she put them behind her as she backed toward the door. "Jess." It was a protest.

She shook her head, her eyes begging him for understanding. "I'm turning in, I want to spend some time with the twins."

Dillon let her go, watched her take his heart with her as she hurried out of the room.

chapter
10

TARA HELD THE COVERS back to allow Jessica to leap beneath the quilt. Clad in her drawstring pajama bottoms and a spaghetti strap top, Jessica's hair spilled loosely down her back in preparation for bed. She hopped over Trevor's makeshift bed and slid in beside Tara. "Why is the room so cold?"

"Your mysterious window-opener has struck in Tara's room," Trevor said. "It was wide open and the curtains were wet from the rain. The room was all foggy, Jess." He deliberately didn't tell her about the magic circle made of incense ash on the floor beside the bed which both he and Tara had worked to clean. She would never let them out of her sight if she found out about it.

Jessica sighed. "How silly. Someone has a fetish for open windows. How about your room, Trev, anything out of place?"

"No, but then I set up the video camera in my room," he said with a cheeky grin. "I thought someone had come in and gone through my things so I wanted to catch them in the act if they came back." He wiggled his eyebrows at her.

"And just who did you suspect and what did you think they were looking for?" Jessica demanded.

"I figured I'd catch Brenda looking for the cash," he admitted.

"Brenda's nice now," Tara objected. "She's not going to go through your smelly old socks looking for the money everyone knows you stash in them."

"Only you know that," Trevor glared at her.

"Now I do," Jessica pointed out with an evil smirk.

Tara wrinkled her nose. "He puts the money in his dirtiest, smelliest pair."

"That is so disgusting, Trevor. Put your dirty socks in the clothes hamper," Jessica lectured, "they aren't a money bank."

"So are you going to tell us whether or not Dad killed Brian?" Trevor tried to sound very casual, but there was an underlying hint of worry in his voice. "The suspense is doing me in."

"Of course he didn't. Brian's religion is a very old one, the worshipping of the earth and deities that are in harmony with the earth. He does not worship the devil, nor is he into the occult." She hesitated, looked at the two identical faces. "Your mother followed his example for a while but during the last year of her life, when she became so ill, she met a man named Phillip Trent. He was truly evil." Just saying his name sickened her. She felt it then, that terrible coldness that could creep into a room. Unnatural. Unbidden. Beneath the covers she pressed her hand to her stomach, terrified she would be sick.

"What's wrong, Jess?" Trevor sat up very straight.

She shook her head. It was a long time ago. A different house. That evil man was dead and nothing that he had brought to life remained behind. It was impossible. Everything had burnt to the ground, reduced to a pile of ashes. It was only her imagination that the curtain stirred slightly on a cold air current when the window was closed. It was only her imagination that she felt eyes watching her. Listening. To think that if she spoke of that time, something evil would triumph, would be set free.

"Your father knows the difference. Brian explained that he worships outside, rather than in the house, out of respect for Dillon's feelings. I didn't ask him about the circle in my room because I want to ask him about it in private. Dillon is protective of all of us. They're good friends and they've talked it out." Jessica shivered again, her gaze darting around the room to the corners hidden in shadows. She felt uneasy. Memories were far too close to the surface. She knotted her fist in the quilt.

Tara leaned close to her, studying her face. She glanced at her brother, and then put her hand over Jessica's, rubbing lovingly. "Tell us the Christmas story, Jessie. It always makes us feel better."

Jessica slipped deeper into the bed, snuggling into the pillow, wanting to hide beneath the covers like a frightened child. "I'm not certain I remember it exactly."

Trevor snorted his disbelief but gamely opened the familiar tale. "Once upon a time there were two beautiful children. Twins, a boy and a girl. The boy was smart and handsome and everyone loved him, especially all the girls in the neighborhood, and the girl was a punky little thing but he generously tolerated her."

"The true story is just the opposite," Tara declared with a sniff.

"The true story is, they were both wonderful," Jessica corrected, falling in with their all too obvious ploy. "The children were good and kind and very loving, and they deserved much happiness. Alas, they both suffered broken hearts. They hid it well, but the evil, wicked Sorcerer had stolen their father. The Sorcerer had locked him away in a tower far from the children, in a bitter, cold land where there was no sun, where he never saw the light of day. He had no laughter, no love, and no music. His world was bleak and his suffering great. He missed his children and his one true love."

"You know, Jess," Trevor piped up, "that whole one true love thing used to make me gag when I was little, but I think I like it now."

"That's the best part," Tara objected, appalled at her brother's lack of romance. "If you can't see that, Trev, there's no hope you're ever going to get the girl."

He laughed softly. "It's all in the genes, little sister."

Tara rolled her eyes. "He's so weird, Jessie, is there hope for him? Don't answer, just tell us why the evil Sorcerer took him away and put him in the tower."

"He was a beautiful man with an angel's face and a poet's heart. He sang with a voice like a gift from the gods and wherever he went, people loved him. He was kind and good and did his best to help everyone. He brought joy to their hard lives with his music and his wonderful voice. The Sorcerer grew jealous because the people loved him so very much. The Sorcerer didn't want him to be happy. He wanted the father to be ugly and mean inside, to be cruel the way he was. So the Sorcerer took away everything that the father loved. His children. His music. His one true love. The Sorcerer wanted him to be bitter and to grow hateful and twisted. He had the father tortured, a painful, hideous cruelty in the dungeons of the tower. The Sorcerer's evil minions hurt him, disfigured him and then they threw him in the tower, sentenced to an eternity of darkness. He was left alone without anyone to talk to, to comfort him, and his heart wept."

There was a catch in Jessica's voice. They would never know completely what life had done to him, taken from him. The twins had been five at the time of the fire and they had only vague memories of Dillon as he was in the old days, the charismatic, joyful poet who brought such happiness to everyone with his very existence.

"The children, Jess," Trevor prompted, "tell us about them."

"They loved their father dearly, so much so that they cried so many tears the river swelled and flooded the banks. Their father's one true love comforted them and reminded them that he would want his children to be strong, to be examples of how he had always lived his life. Helping people. Loving people. Taking responsibility when others would not. And the children carried on his legacy of service to the people, of loyalty and love even as their hearts wept in tune with his."

"One night, when it was cold and the rain poured down, when it was dark and the stars couldn't shine, a white dove landed on their windowsill. It was tired and hungry. The children immediately fed it their bread and gave it their water. The father's one true love warmed the shivering bird in her hands. To their amazement the dove spoke to them saying that Christmas was near. That they should find the perfect tree and bring it into their home, and decorate it with small symbols of love. Because of their kindness, a miracle would be granted them. The dove said they could have riches untold, they could have life immortal. But the children and the father's one true love said they wanted only one thing. They wanted their father returned to them."

"The dove said he wouldn't be the same, that he would be different," Tara chimed in eagerly with the detail.

"Yes, that's true, but the children and the father's one true love didn't care, they wanted him back any way they could have him. They knew that what was in his heart would never be changed."

Outside Tara's room, Dillon leaned against the door, listening to the sound of Jessica's beautiful voice telling her Christmas tale. He had come looking for her, hating the sorrow he'd seen on her face, needing to remove the swirling nightmares from her eyes. He should have known she would be with the twins. His children. His family. They were on the other side of the door. Waiting for him. Waiting for a miracle. Tears burned in his eyes, ran down his cheeks unchecked, and clogged his throat, threatening to choke him as he listened to the story of his life.

"Did they find the perfect tree?" Tara prompted. There was such a hopeful note in her voice that Dillon closed his eyes against another fresh flood of tears. They were wrenched from the deepest gouge in his soul. Enough to overflow the banks of the mythical river.

"At first they thought the dove meant perfection, as in physical beauty," Jessica's voice was so low he had to strain to hear. "But eventually, as they looked through the forest, they realized it was something far different. They found a small, bushy tree in the shadow of much larger ones. The branches were straggly and there were gaps but they knew at once it was the perfect giving tree. Everyone else had overlooked it. They asked the tree if it would like to celebrate Christmas with them and the tree agreed. They made wonderful ornaments and carefully decorated the tree and the three of them sat up on Christmas Eve waiting for the miracle. They knew they had chosen the perfect tree when the dove settled happily in the branches."

There was a long silence. The bed creaked as someone turned over. "Jessie. Aren't you going to tell us the end of the story?" Trevor asked.

"I don't know the end of the story yet," Jessica answered. Was she crying? Dillon couldn't bear it if she were crying.

"Of course you do," Tara complained.

"Leave her alone, Tara," Trevor advised. "Let's just go to sleep."

"I'll tell you on Christmas morning," Jessica promised.

Dillon listened to the sound of silence in the next room. The tightness in his chest was agony. He stumbled away from the pain, back up the stairs, back into the darkness of his lonely tower.

Jessica lay listening to the sounds of the twins sleeping.

It was comforting to hear the steady breathing. Outside the house, the wind was knocking at the windows like a giant hand, shaking the sills until the panes rattled alarmingly. The rain hit the glass with force, a steady rhythm that was soothing. She loved the rain, the fresh clean scent it brought, the way it cleared the air of any lingering smell of smoke. She inhaled, drifting, half in and half out of sleep. Fog poured into the room carrying with it an odor she recognized. She smelled incense and a frown flitted across her face. She tried to move. Her arms and legs were too heavy to lift. Alarmed, she fought to wake herself, recognizing she had moved beyond drifting, past dreams to her all too familiar nightmare.

She wouldn't look at them. Any of them. She had gone beyond terror to someplace numb. She tried not to breathe. She didn't want to smell them, or the incense, or hear the chanting, or to think about what was happening to her body. She felt the hand on her, deliberately rough, cruelly touching her while she lay helplessly under the assault. She had fought until she had no strength. Nothing would stop this demented behavior and she would endure it because she had no other choice.

The hand squeezed her hard, probed in tender, secret places. She would not feel, would not scream again. She couldn't stop the tears; they ran down her face and fell onto the floor. Without warning the door burst open, kicked in so that it splintered and hung at an angle from broken hinges. He looked like an avenging angel, his face twisted with fury, his blue eyes blazing with rage.

She cringed when he looked at her, when he saw the obscenity of what they were doing to her. She didn't want him to see her naked and painted with something evil touching her body. He moved so fast she wasn't certain he was real, ripping Phillip Trent away from her. There was the sound of fist meeting flesh, the spray of blood in the air. She was helpless, unable to move, unable to see what was happening. There were screams, grunts, a bone cracked. Shouted obscenities. The smell of alcohol. She was certain she would never be able to bear the odor again.

And then he was wrapping her in his shirt, loosening the ties that bound her hands and feet. He lifted her, with tears streaming down his face. "I'm sorry, baby, I'm sorry," he whispered against her neck as he carried her from the room. She caught glimpses of broken furniture, of glass and scattered objects. Bodies writhing and moaning on the floor as he carried her out. His hands were bloody but gentle as he placed her in her bed, rocked her gently while she cried and wept until both their hearts were broken. She begged him not to tell anyone how he found her.

She had no idea how much time passed. He was filled with fury, his rage was still lethal. He was arguing she needed her mother, stalking from her room to cool off outside where he couldn't hurt anyone. She scrubbed herself in the shower until her skin was raw, until there were no tears left. She was dressing, her hands shaking so badly she couldn't button her blouse, when she heard the volley of shots ring out. The sound of the gun was distinctive. The smell of smoke was overwhelming. It took a few moments to realize it wasn't steam from the bathroom that was making the room hazy, it was clouds of thick smoke. She had to crawl through the hall to the twins' room. They were crying, hiding under the bed. Flames ate greedily at the hall, up the curtains. There was no getting to the others.

She dragged the children to the large window, shoved them through, following, dropping to earth, skidding on the slick dirt. Tara crawled forward blindly, tears streaming from her swollen eyes that prevented her from seeing. She screamed as she slipped over the edge. Jessica lunged after her. They rolled, bounced, sliding all the way to the sea. Tara disappeared beneath the waves, Jessica hurtled after her. Down. Into darkness. The salt water stung. It was icy cold. Her fingers brushed the child's shirt, slipped off, she grabbed again, caught a handful of material and held on. Kicking strongly. Surfacing. Struggling through the pounding waves with her burden. They lay together on the rocks, gasping for breath, the child in her arms. Her world in ruins.

Black smoke. Noise. Orange flames reaching the clouds. Screams. Wearily she pulled Trevor into her arms when he joined them. Together they slowly made their way back up the path leading to the front of the house. She saw Dillon lying there. He was motionless. His body was black, his arms outstretched. He was utterly silent but his eyes were screaming as he looked down in shock at the blackened ruin of his body. He looked up at her. Looked past her to the children. She understood then. Understood why he had entered a burning inferno. His gaze met hers as he stared helplessly up at her, in much the same way she must have stared up at him when he'd rescued her. As long as she lived, she would never forget the look on his face, the horror in his eyes. Jessica watched his blackened fingers turn to ash, watched the ash fall to the ground. She heard herself screaming in denial. Over and over. The sound was pure anguish.

"Jessie," Trevor called her name softly, his arm around Tara. They helplessly watched as Jessica pressed herself against the wall near the window and screamed and screamed, her face a mask of terror. Her eyes were open, but they knew she wasn't seeing them, but something else, something vivid and real to her, that they couldn't see. Night terrors were eerie. Jessica was caught up in the web of a nightmare and anything they did often made it worse.

The door to the bedroom was flung open and their father rushed in, still buttoning his jeans. He wore no shirt, he was barefoot. His hair was wild and disheveled, falling around his perfectly sculpted face like dark silk. His chest and arms were a mass of rigid scars and whorls of raised red skin. The scars streaked down his arms and spread down his chest to his belly fading into normal skin.

"What the hell is going on?" Dillon demanded but his frantic gaze had already found Jessica pressed against the wall. He glanced at his children. "Are you all right?"

Tara was staring at the mass of scars. She pulled her gaze up to his face with an effort. "Yes, she has nightmares. This is a bad one."

"I'm sorry, I forgot my shirt," Dillon told her softly before turning his attention back to Jessica. "Wake up, baby, it's over," he crooned softly. His voice was low and compelling, almost hypnotic. "It's me, sweetheart, you're safe here. I'm not going to let anyone hurt you."

Tara turned her head as more people crowded into the doorway of her room. She had to blink tears out of her eyes in order to focus on them. Trevor put his arm around her, offering comfort, and she took it.

"Good heavens," Brenda said, "what happened now?"

"Get them out of here, Trevor," Dillon ordered, "get out and close the door."

Trevor acted at once. He didn't want anyone staring at Jessica, seeing her in such a vulnerable state. And he didn't like the way they were staring at his father's body, either. He took Tara with him, pushing through the group, closing the door firmly and leaving Dillon alone with Jessica. "Show's over," he said gruffly, "you all might as well go back to bed."

Brenda glared at him. "I was actually trying to be helpful. If Jessie needs me, I don't mind sitting up with her."

To everyone's astonishment, Tara wrapped her arms around Brenda's waist and looked up at her. "I need you," she confided. "I hurt him again."

Trevor cleared his throat. "No you didn't, Tara." He was happy to see the band members dispersing, leaving only Brenda and Robert behind.

"Yes I did, I was staring at his scars and he noticed," Tara confessed, looking up at Brenda. "Even with Jessie screaming and how much he wanted to help her, he noticed. And he said he was sorry." Tears welled up and spilled over. "I didn't mean to stare at him, I should have looked away. It must have hurt him so much."

It was Robert who dropped his hand on her head in a clumsy effort to comfort her. "We couldn't stop him. The house was completely engulfed in flames. He was calling for you and your brother, for Jessica. He ran toward the house. I caught him, so did Paul. He knocked us both down." There was sorrow in his voice, guilt, a ragged edge. Robert paused, rubbed the bridge of his nose, frowning slightly.

Brenda put her hand on his arm. Casually. As if it didn't matter, but Trevor saw that it did. That it steadied Robert. Robert smiled down at Brenda's hand and leaned forward to kiss her fingertips. "He ran inside the house, right through a wall of flames. Paul tried to go in after him, but Brian and I tackled him and held him down. We should have done that to Dillon. We should have." He shook his head at the memories.

Trevor found himself reaching out to his uncle, touching him for the first time. "No one could have stopped him. If I know anything about my father, it's that no one could have stopped him from trying to get to us." He glanced back at the closed door. Jessica's screams had stopped. He could hear the soft murmur of Dillon's voice. "No one could have stopped him from trying to get to Jess."

Robert blinked and focused on Trevor. "You're so like him, like he was back in the old days. Tara, what I'm trying to say to you is, don't be afraid of looking at your father's scars. Don't ever be ashamed of the way he looks. Those scars are evidence of how much he loves you, what you mean to him. He's a great man, someone you should be proud of, and he'll always put you first. Few people have that and I think it's important for you to know that you do have it. I could never have entered that house, none of the rest of us could go in, even when we heard the screams."

"Don't, Robert," Brenda said sharply. "No one could

have saved those people. You didn't even know they were up there."

"I know, I know." He rubbed a hand over his face, wiping away old horrors and determinedly forcing a smile to his face, needing to change the subject. "Anyone up for one of Brenda's silly board games? She's obsessed with them."

"I always win," Brenda pointed out smugly.

Trevor glanced at the closed door anxiously then switched his attention back to his aunt. "I always win," he countered.

Tara slipped her hand into Robert's. "He does," she confided.

"Then it's all-out war," Brenda decided, leading the way back to her rooms. "I detest losing at *anything.*"

"Do you really have an insurance policy on us?" Trevor asked curiously as he followed her down the hall.

"Of course, silly, you're a boy, the odds are much higher that you'll do something stupid," Brenda remarked complacently. "All that lovely lollie," she added, grinning back at him over her shoulder.

Trevor shook his head. "I'm not buying your act any more, *Auntie.* You're not the bad girl you want the world to believe you are."

Brenda flinched visibly. "Don't even say that, it's sacrilegious. And by the way, your cute little pranks aren't scaring me in the least, so you may as well stop."

"I don't pull cute little pranks," Trevor objected strenuously to her choice of words. "If I was pulling off a prank, it wouldn't be cute or little. And it would scare you. I'm a master at practical jokes."

Brenda pushed open the door to her room, raising one

eyebrow artfully as he preceded her into the suite. "Oh, really? So what is with the hooded face appearing in the window, and the mysterious messages written on my makeup mirror? *Get out while there's still time.*" She rolled her eyes. "Really! Perfectly childish. And just how do you explain the water running in the bathtub with the stopper in the drain and the room always filled with steam? If I didn't know it was you, it would give me the creeps. The open window and Brian's magic circle is such a clever touch, throwing suspicion his way. We've all talked about it, we know it's you two. Even that motley dog is in cahoots with you, growling at the steam and staring at nothing just to scare us."

There was a small silence. Tara and Trevor exchanged a long look. "Is your window open when you come into your room?" Tara ventured, her voice tight. "And fog or steam all through the room?"

Robert looked at her sharply. "Are you saying you kids haven't been pulling these pranks?" He poured them both a soda from the small ice chest they had stashed in their room.

Trevor shook his head, took a long grateful drink of the cold liquid, nearly draining the glass. He hadn't realized how thirsty he was. "No, sir, we haven't. And Jessica's window is open all the time." A chill crept into the room with his denial. "Tara's window was open this evening. And there was burned incense and one of those circles on the floor of both Jessie's and Tara's rooms. Jess didn't tell Dillon because she was afraid he would quit recording with everyone, and she thinks it's important for him and everyone else to make the music."

Robert and Brenda exchanged a long look. "If you kids have been playing tricks, it's all right to say so," Robert persisted. "We know kids do that sort of thing." He pulled a *Clue* game from the closet, carried it to the table.

"How perfectly apropos, a murder game on a dark and stormy night just when we're discussing mysterious occurrences," Brenda quipped as they spread the game board out on the small table.

"We didn't do any of those things," Trevor insisted. "I don't know who it is or why, but something wants us out of here."

"Why do you say that?" Robert asked sharply as he separated the cards.

Trevor noticed his clue sheet was filled and he crumpled it, looking around for a wastebasket. He couldn't toss it, practicing his technique, because the basket was filled with newspaper. With a sigh he got up and walked over to it. For some reason his stomach was beginning to cramp uncomfortably and his skin felt clammy. The conversation was bothering him a lot more than he realized. "I don't know, I always feel like something's watching us. We've been letting the dog in and sometimes we're in a room alone and it starts growling, looking at the door. All the hair rises up on its back. It's freaky. But when I go look, no one's there."

"I'd think you were making it up," Robert said, "but there have been some strange things happening in here, too. We thought it was you kids, so we didn't say anything either, but I don't like the sound of that. Have you told Jessie?"

Trevor bent down to press the sheet of paper into the wastebasket. The newspaper caught his eye. It had tiny little holes in it where words were cut out. He glanced back at his aunt and uncle. They were putting the game pieces on the board. Tara looked pale, a frown on her face. She was holding her stomach as if she had cramps, too. Trevor lifted the newspaper slightly. It reminded him of movies where ransom notes had been concocted from printed words pasted on paper. The glass in front of Tara was empty. A frisson of fear went down his spine. Very slowly he straightened, moved casually away from the evidence in the wastebasket.

"No, I haven't told Jessie much at all. She's been busy with the recording and she's so darned overprotective." He looked directly at his aunt. "I'm feeling a little sick. It wasn't the soda, was it?"

"I'm not feeling very well either," Tara admitted.

Brenda bent over Tara solicitously. "Is it the flu?"

"You tell me," Trevor challenged. A wave of nausea hit him. "We need Jessie."

Brenda sniffed. "I think I'm quite capable of taking care of a couple of little kiddies with the flu."

"I hope so," Tara said, "because I'm going to throw up." She ran to the bathroom, holding her stomach.

Brenda looked harassed for a moment, then rushed after her.

chapter
11

"JESS, BABY, CAN YOU hear me now? Do you know who I am?" Dillon used his voice shamelessly, a velvet blend of heat and smoke. He didn't make the mistake of trying to approach her, knowing he could become part of her frightening world. Instead, he flicked on the light, bathing the room in a soft glow. He hunkered down across from her, his movements slow and graceful. "Honey, come back to me now. You don't need to be in that place, you don't belong there."

She was staring, focused on something beyond his shoulder. There was so much terror and horror in her eyes that he actually turned his head, expecting to see something. It was icy cold in the room. The window behind her was fully open, the curtains fluttering like twin white flags. It made him uneasy. She was pressed up against the wall, her hands restlessly searching the surface, seeking a place of refuge. His breath hitched in his throat when her fingers skimmed the windowsill and she inched toward it.

"Jess, it's Dillon. See me, baby, know I'm here with you." He slowly straightened, shifted to the balls of his feet. His heart was hammering out his own fright. Her screams had stopped but she was staring at something he couldn't see, couldn't fight.

With a small moan of terror, Jessica flung herself at the open window, crawling out as quickly as she could pull herself through. Dillon was on top of her in an instant, his hands wrapping securely around her waist, dragging her backward into the room. She fought like a wild thing, tearing at the windowsill, the curtains, her fingernails digging into wood as she desperately tried to make her escape.

"You're two stories up, Jess," Dillon said, twisting to avoid her scissoring legs. He managed to wrestle her to the floor without hurting her, holding her down, straddling her, pinning her there so she couldn't harm herself. "Wake up. Look at me."

Her gaze persisted in going beyond him, caught in a web he couldn't break through. When she stopped fighting, he pulled her onto his lap, his arms still holding her tightly there on the floor, and he sang softly to her. It had been her favorite song as long as he could remember. His voice filled the room with a warmth, a soothing comfort, a promise of love and commitment. He had written it in the days of hope and belief, when he believed in love and miracles. When he believed in himself.

Jessica blinked, looked around her, focused on Dillon's angel's face. It took a few moments to realize she was on his lap, his arms binding her tightly to him. She turned her head to search for the twins. The room was empty.

She shivered, relaxed completely into Dillon, allowing his voice to drive away the remnants of terror.

"Are you back, baby?" His voice was a wealth of tenderness. "Look at me." He brought both of her hands to his mouth, kissed her fingers. "Tell me you know who I am. I swear I won't let anything happen to you." With Jessica on his lap, only thin cloth separated them, and the knowledge was awakening his body. Her breasts were spilling out of her thin top giving him a generous view of soft skin. The temptation to lean down and taste her was strong.

A small smile managed to find its way to her trembling mouth. "I know that, Dillon. I've always known that. Did I frighten Tara and Trevor?"

"Tara and Trevor?" he echoed, astonished. "You frightened *me*." He brought her palm to his bare chest, straight over his pounding heart. "I can't take much more of this. I really can't." He traced her trembling lips with a scarred fingertip. The raised whorls rasped sensually over her soft mouth. "What in the hell am I supposed to do with you? If I had a heart left, I'd have to tell you, you're breaking it." He had been so afraid for her that he had left his room with his body uncovered. He had turned on the light to help dispel her dream world, not thinking what it would reveal of him. He held her in his lap, his scarred body exposed to her gaze when it was the last thing he ever intended.

"I'm sorry, Dillon." Tears shimmered in her vivid green eyes, threatened to spill over onto her long lashes. Her lips were still trembling, tearing at his heart even more. "I didn't mean for this to happen. I didn't know it would be like this."

He groaned, a sound of surrender. The last thing he wanted was for her to be sorry. He helped her from his lap, rose and hauled her up beside him, his arm curling around her waist, clamping her to his side. "Don't cry, Jess, I swear to God if you cry you'll destroy me."

She buried her face against his chest, against the scars of his past life. She didn't wince, she didn't even stare in utter disgust. His Jessica. His one light in the darkness. He could feel her tears wet against his skin. With an oath he lifted her, cradled her slight weight to him. There was only one place to take her, the only place she belonged. He took the stairs fast, climbing to the third story, his refuge, his sanctuary, the lair of the wounded beast. He kicked the door closed behind him.

"Are you afraid of me, Jess?" he asked softly. "Tell me if you're afraid of how I look." He strode to the large bed and laid her down on his sheets. "Tell me if you're afraid I went back into that house and did what most people think I did."

She rested her head on the pillow, met the hypnotic blue of his eyes, was lost instantly, drowning in the deep turbulent sea. "I've never been afraid of you, Dillon," she answered honestly. "You know I don't believe you shot anyone that night. I've never believed it. Knowing you went back into the house before the gun was fired doesn't change what I know about you." She reached up, framed his face with one hand while the other skimmed lightly over his chest. How could he ever think his scars would repulse her? He had gone into a burning inferno to save his children. The scars were as much a part of him now as his angel's face. Her fingertips traced a whorl of ridged flesh. His badge of courage, of love—she could never think of his scars any other way. "And you've always been beautiful to me. Always. You were the one who kept me away from you. I tried so many times to see you in the burn center and you wouldn't give your consent." There was hurt in her voice, pain in her eyes. "You cut yourself off from me and you left me struggling on my own. For so long I couldn't breathe without you. I couldn't talk to anyone. I didn't know how to go on."

"You deserve something better than this, Jess," he said grimly.

"What's better, Dillon? Being without you? The pain doesn't go away. Neither does the loneliness, not for me or the children."

"I always knew exactly what I was doing, what I was worth." Confusion slipped across his face. "My music was my measure of who I was, what I could offer. Now I don't know what I can give you. But you have to be certain being with me is what you really want. I can't have you and then lose you. I have to know it means the same thing to you as it does to me."

Jessica smiled at him as she stood up. Deliberately she moved in front of the large sliding glass door leading to the balcony. She wanted what light there was to fall on her, so there would be no mistake. For her answer, she simply caught the hem of her tank top and pulled it over her head.

Standing there, facing him with the glass framing her, she looked like an exotic beauty, ethereal, out of reach. Her skin gleamed at him, a satin sheen, beckoning his touch. Her breasts were full, firm, jutting toward him, so perfect he felt his heart slam hard in his chest and his mouth go dry. His body tightened painfully, his need so urgent his body was straining against the fabric of his jeans.

He reached out to the offering, his palm skimming along her soft skin. She felt exactly as she looked and the texture was mesmerizing. Jessica's breath hitched in her throat, her body trembled as he cupped her breasts in his hands. His thumbs found taut buds and stroked as he leaned into her to settle his mouth over hers.

Jessica was aware of so many sensations. Her breasts achingly alive, wanting his touch, his thumbs sending bolts of lightning whipping through her bloodstream until her lower body was heavy and needy. Every nerve ending was alive, so that his silken hair brushing her skin sent tiny darts of pleasure coursing through her. His mouth was hard and dominant, moving over and into hers with male expertise and hot, silken passion.

Outside the wind began to moan, shifting back from the sea, rattling at the glass doors as if seeking entrance. Dillon's mouth left hers to follow the line of her shoulder, the hollow of her throat, to close, hot and hungry, around her breast. Jessica's body jerked with reaction, her arms coming up to cradle his head. His mouth was fiery hot, suckling strongly, a starving man let loose on a feast. His hands skimmed her narrow rib cage, tugged impatiently at the drawstring of her pajamas.

Her body wound tighter and tighter, a spiral of heat she couldn't hope to control. The pajama bottoms dropped to the floor and she kicked them aside, reveling in the way his hands glided possessively over her.

"I've wanted you for so long," he breathed the words against her satin skin, moving to her other breast, his fingers stroking the curve of her bottom, finding every intriguing indentation, every shadow. "I can't believe you're really here with me."

"I can't believe it either," she admitted, closing her eyes, throwing back her head to arch more fully into his greedy mouth. She felt a wildness rising in him, skating the edge of his control. It gave her a sense of power that she might not have had otherwise. He wanted her with the same force of need as she did him which allowed her a boldness she might never have managed. Her hands found the waistband of his jeans. She deliberately rubbed her palm over his bulging hardness, just as she'd done in the woods. She felt the breath slam out of his lungs. He lifted his head, his blue gaze burning into her like a brand.

Jessica smiled at him as she unfastened his jeans. "I've wanted to do this," she confided as he burst free. Thick and long and ready for her, pulsing with heat and life. Her fingers wrapped around the length of him, a proprietary gesture. Her thumb stroked the velvet head until he groaned aloud.

Very gently he exerted pressure on her, forcing her back toward the bed. "I don't want to wait any longer, I don't think I can."

Jessica knelt on the bed, still stroking him, leaning forward to kiss his sculpted mouth, loving the hunger in his gaze. He was more intimidating than she had expected so she took her time getting used to the feel and size of him. She fed on his mouth, trailed kisses over his scarred chest, experimentally swirled her tongue over the head of his shaft. He jumped beneath her ministrations, sucked in his breath audibly.

"Not yet, baby, I'll explode if you do that. Lie back for me." His hands were already assisting her, pushing her into the mattress so she lay naked and waiting for his touch. His hand stroked a caress down her body, over her breast, lingering for a moment until she shivered, over her belly, down to the thatch of curls, glided to her thighs.

He sat up, his blue eyes moving over every inch of her. She was so beautiful, moving restlessly on the bed beneath him. Wanting him. Needing him. Hungry for him alone. He loved the way the muted light skimmed lovingly over her body, touching her here and there along the curves and shadows he was familiarizing himself with.

"Dillon," it was a soft protest, that he had stopped when she was burning for him, her body heavy and throbbing with need.

"I love to look at you, Jess." His hands parted her thighs just a little wider, his fingers stroking a long caress in the damp folds between her legs. She jumped when he touched her, pushed forward against his palm, a small cry of pleasure escaping her. Dillon smiled at her, leaned down to swirl his tongue around her intriguing belly button. Those little tops she wore that didn't quite cover her flat belly were enough to drive him mad. His hair brushed her sensitive skin and he pushed his finger slowly, deep inside her tight, hot sheath. At once her muscles clenched around him, velvet soft, firm, moist, and hot. His own body throbbed and swelled in response.

Her hips pushed forward wantonly. Jessica had no inhibitions with Dillon. She wanted his body, wanted every single erotic dance with him. She had no intention of holding back; she was determined to get every last gasp of pleasure she could. She had learned the hard way that life is precarious and she wasn't going to let an opportunity slip by because of modesty, pride, or shyness. Jessica lifted her hips to meet the thrusting of his finger, the friction triggering a rippling effect deep in her hottest core.

Dillon nipped her flat belly with a string of teasing kisses, distracting her while he stretched her a little more, sinking two fingers into her soft, hot body. More than anything else, her pleasure mattered to him. He was large and thick and he could tell she was small. Her velvet folds pulsed for him, wanting, and he fed that hunger, pushing deep, retreating, entering again so that her hips followed his lead. "That's what I want, honey, just like that. I want you ready for me."

"I am ready for you," she pleaded softly, her fingers tangling in his hair.

"Not yet, you're not," he answered. His breath was warm against the curve of her hip. She felt his tongue stroke a caress in the crease along her thigh. His mouth found the triangle of fiery curls at the junction of her legs. Her breath hissed out of her as his tongue tasted her moist heat. His name was a whispered plea. He lifted his head to look at her face. Very slowly he withdrew his fingers to bring them to his mouth. She shivered, her gaze fascinated as he licked her juices from his hand. "Open your thighs wider, baby." It was a whispered enticement. "Give yourself to me."

She was lost in the pulsing hunger; the fire was racing through her body. She opened her legs wider to him, a clear invitation. She was hot and wet and slick with her passion. Dillon pressed his palm once against her heated entrance, so that she shivered in anticipation. Then he slowly lowered his head once more.

She nearly screamed, drowning in the sensation of pure pleasure. His tongue caressed, probed deep, stabbed into hot folds, swirled and teased and sucked at her until she was mindlessly sobbing his name, writhing beneath him, her hips thrusting helplessly for the relief only he could bring her. He took her up the path several times, pushing higher each time so that her body shuddered and rippled with pleasure over and over. Until he knew she was hot and slick and needed him enough to accept him buried deep within her body.

Dillon knelt between her legs, and watched his body probe desperately for the slick entrance to hers. He wanted to see them come together, in a miracle of passion. His engorged head pushed into her. At once he felt her sheath, tight and hot, grip him, close around him. The sensation shook him so that he had to hang on to his control. "Jess," her name burst from between his teeth. He slid in another inch, pushing his way through the tight folds. If it was possible, she grew even hotter. His hands tightened on her hips. "Tell me you're okay, baby."

"Yes, more," she gasped. He was invading her body, a thick, hard fullness, stretching her immeasurably, but at the same time, the craving for him grew and grew.

His hands tightened and he surged forward, past her barrier, and buried himself deeper. Sweat broke out on his forehead. He had never felt such a sensation of pure ecstasy. It was difficult to keep from plunging his body madly into hers. "Tell me what it feels like." He bit the words out huskily, and lowered his head to flick his tongue over her taut nipple. The action tightened her body even more around his.

"It's everything, Dillon. You're big and you're stretching me so it burns a little, but at the same time, I want more, I want all of you deep inside me," she answered honestly. "More than anything, that's what I want right now."

"Me, too," he admitted and surged forward. The sensation shook him. Her muscles were slick and hot and velvet soft, so tight he could barely stand it. He buried himself deep, withdrew, and thrust hard again. He watched her face carefully for signs of discomfort, but her body was flushed, her eyes glazed, her breath coming in little needy pants.

Satisfied that she was feeling the same pleasure he was feeling, Dillon began to move in a gentle rhythm. Long and slow, gliding in and out of her, stretching, pushing deeper with each stroke. He tilted her hips, held her body so he could thrust even deeper, wanting her to accept every last inch of him, almost as if her body could accept his, she would see who he really was and love him anyway. He buried himself to the hilt, sliding so deep he felt her womb, felt her contractions beginning, a spiraling that began to increase in strength. "Jess, I've never felt like this. Never." He wanted her to know what she meant, how much a part of him she was.

His rhythm became faster, harder, his hips surging forward into her, his body beyond any pretense of control. Jessica cried out softly as her body fragmented, as the room rocked and the earth simply melted away. Dillon could feel how strong her muscles were, milking him, gripping him in the strength of her orgasm, taking him with her right over the edge. He pumped into her frantically, helplessly, unable to control the wildness in him, the explosion ripping through his body from his toes up to the top of his head.

Dillon didn't have enough energy to roll over, so he lay on top of her, his body still locked to hers. His heart was beating hard. He buried his face against her breast, tears burning at the back of his eyes and throat. He had never been so emotional in the old days. He had never felt like this, sated and at peace. He had never thought it possible.

Jessica wrapped her arms around Dillon, holding him close, feeling the emotions swirling so deeply in him. She knew he was struggling. Part of him wanted to remain a recluse, hidden from the past and the future, and part of him desperately wanted what she was holding out to him. It was all tied up in his music. In his perception that he had failed everyone he loved. He wanted her to love him as he saw himself, a man without anything to offer. She didn't see him that way and never could. She could only offer him what she had, her honesty, her belief in him, her trust.

She felt his tongue flick her nipple, a lazy back and forth swirl that sent shock waves through her body. Her muscles rippled with the aftershock and gripped his. He exhaled, his breath warm against her skin.

"Tell me I didn't hurt you, Jess," he asked. He lifted himself up to his elbows, his hands framing her face.

"Dillon! I was practically yelling your name shamelessly for the entire household to hear." She smiled as he leaned down to kiss her. The touch of his mouth sent a series of shocks through her body so that she once more rippled with pleasure. "I think I'm hypersensitive to you," she admitted.

His eyebrow shot up. "That appeals to me on a purely primitive level," he said as he buried his face in the valley between her breasts. "I love how you smell, especially now after we've made love." His mouth nuzzled her skin, his tongue teasing along her ribs. He allowed his sated body to slide away from hers, but his hand slipped along the path of her belly to rest in her triangle of curls. "I want to just explore every inch of you for the rest of the night. I want to know you, what brings you pleasure, what gets you hot fast and what takes a little longer. Mostly, I just want to be with you." His silky hair played over her aching breasts as he lifted his head high enough to look at her. "Do you mind?"

There was a curious vulnerability about him. Jessica stretched languidly beneath him, offering up her body to him. "I want to be with you, too."

She lay listening to the rain on the roof while his hands skimmed her body, framed every curve, touched every inch of her with tenderness. She felt as if she were drifting in a sea of pure pleasure. He made love to her a second time, a slow, leisurely joining that stole her heart along with her breath.

Jessica realized she must have fallen asleep a while

ago when she woke to feel Dillon's hands gliding over her once again. She lay in the dark, smiling as he brought her body to life. His hands and mouth were skillful, teasing, tempting. He shifted to pull her closer to him, his knowledge of her body growing with every exploration.

His tongue was busy at her nipple, his mouth hot with passion and Jessica closed her eyes, willing to give herself up to the incredible sensation. Her hands in his hair, she tried to relax, tried to ignore the shiver of awareness moving down her spine. She felt eyes on them. Watching them. Watching Dillon suckling at her breast, his fingers delving deeply into her wet core. Her eyes flew open and she looked wildly around the room, trying to see into every shadow.

Dillon felt her sudden resistance. "What is it, baby?" he asked, his mouth still busy between words. "Have I made you sore?"

"Someone is outside the door, Dillon," Jessica whispered against his ear, "listening to us." It was difficult to think when his mouth was pulling so strongly at her breast, sending white-hot streaks of lightning dancing through her bloodstream. When he pushed two fingers deep and stroked her with such expertise.

Dillon's body was hard and hot and wanting hers. His tongue flicked over the tight bud of her nipple, did a long, slow lazy swirl. He lifted his head away from the lush pleasures of her body when she tugged at his hair. His blue eyes burned over her face hungrily. "I didn't hear anything."

"I'm not kidding, Dillon," Jessica insisted, "someone is

listening to us, or watching us. I can feel them." She stiffened, pushing at him, looking toward the glass balcony half expecting to see a hooded figure standing there.

Sighing with regret, Dillon left the pleasures of her body and looked around for his jeans. She had already slipped into his robe, cinching it around her slender body. Her face was pale and her red-gold hair spilled around her like a waterfall of silk. He didn't understand her. She was always a miracle of good sense, but when it came to certain things, she lost every bit of it, she was so positive that forces were conspiring to harm those she loved. He couldn't really blame her for worrying. Dillon stalked to the door and jerked it open wide to show her no one was there.

His heart nearly stopped when he came face-to-face with his bass player. They stood so close their noses were nearly touching.

Don stared for a moment at Dillon's exposed chest, then glanced past him to see Jessica huddled in Dillon's robe. Dillon stepped instantly to block Don's view of her. "What the hell are you doing, Don?" Dillon snapped, angrily.

Don flushed, glanced past him to Jessica's pale face, and half turned to leave. "Forget it, I didn't realize you were busy. I saw the light and knew you were up."

Dillon swallowed his annoyance. Don never sought him out. It was a rare chance to clear the air between them, even if it was untimely. "No, don't go, it must have been something important that brought you here this late." He raked a hand through his thick black hair, tossed Jessica a pleading smile. She responded exactly the way he knew she would, nodding slightly and drawing his robe more closely around her. "Hell, it must be close to five in the morning." He stepped back and gestured for Don to enter. "Whatever it is, let's deal with it." Don looked rumpled and Dillon smelled alcohol on his breath.

Don took a deep breath, stepped inside. "I'm sorry Jessie." His gaze found her, then slid away. "I didn't know you were here."

She shrugged. It was far too late to hide anything that had been going on. The bed was rumpled, the pillows on the floor. Her hair was disheveled and she wore nothing under Dillon's robe. "Would you like me to leave?" She asked it politely. Don seemed terribly nervous, his apprehension adding to her own discomfort. Her stomach rolled ominously, a wave of nausea swamping her for a moment.

"I don't know if I have the courage to say to Dillon what I need to say, let alone in front of anyone, but on the other hand, you're always a calming influence." He paced across the room several times while they waited.

"Have you been drinking?" Dillon asked, curious. "I've never seen you drink, Don, not more than one beer."

"I thought it would give me courage." Don gave him a half hearted humorless grin. "You need to call the police and have me arrested." The words tumbled out fast, in a single rushed breath. The moment he said them, he looked for a place to collapse.

Dillon led him to one of the two chairs positioned on either side of a small reading table. "Would you like a glass of water?"

Jessica had already hurried to get a glass from the large master bathroom. "Here, Don, drink this."

He took the glass, gulped the water down, wiped his mouth with the back of his hand, and looked up at Dillon. "I swear to God I thought you knew about Vivian and me. All this time I thought you were waiting for a chance to get rid of me and replace me with Paul. I kept waiting for it to happen. I tried so hard never to give you a reason."

"Before anything else, Don, I'm a musician. I love Paul. He's my best friend. We've stood together through the best and worst of times, but he doesn't have your talent. I *wanted* you in the band. From the first time I heard you play, I knew you were right. Paul doesn't have your versatility. He helped start the band, and I had no intention of leaving him along the wayside, but once you signed on with us, you were as much a part of the band as I was." Dillon shook his head regretfully. "I'm sorry you thought differently, that I never told you how valuable you were to me."

"Great. I didn't need to hear you say that." Don heaved a sigh. "This isn't easy, Dillon. I don't deserve you to be civil to me."

"I'll admit I was shocked and upset about you and Vivian," Dillon said. He reached for Jessica, unable to help himself, needing to touch her. Needing her real and solid beside him. At once she was there, her small body fitting beneath his shoulder, her arm slipping around his waist. "It was a rotten thing to do, Don, but it hardly warrants calling the police."

"I tried to blackmail you." Don didn't look at either of

them as he made the confession. He stared down at his hands, a lost expression on his face. "I saw you go into the forest that night. We all heard the yelling upstairs, and the pounding. We figured you caught Viv with one of her lovers. No one wanted to embarrass you so they all went to the studio to be out of the way, but I went to the kitchen for something to drink and I saw you go out. You had tears on your face and you were so shaken, I followed you, thinking I could offer to help. But you were more distraught than anyone I'd ever seen before and I figured, since it involved Vivian, you wouldn't want to talk to me. I walked around, undecided, and then just when I was going back, I saw you go in through the kitchen. Rita was in there and I heard you talking, telling her what happened. You were so angry, you were wrecking the place. I didn't dare approach you or Rita. I saw you start up the stairs and I headed for the studio. Then I heard the shots." As proof of his crime he pulled a plain sheet of paper from his pocket. Words cut from the headline of a newspaper were pasted on it. "This was one I was going to send you."

"Why didn't you testify to that at the trial?" Dillon's voice was very low, impossible to read. He snatched the paper from Don's hand and crumpled it without glancing at it.

"Because I was already on the basement staircase, looking out through the glass doors, and I saw you when the shots were fired. I knew you didn't do it. You had gone back outside a second time and you were heading toward the forest."

"Yet you decided blackmail was a good alternative?"

"I don't know why. I don't know why I did any of the things I've done since then," Don admitted. "All I cared about was the band. I wanted it back. You sat up here in this house with Paul, no one else could get near you. You had all that talent just going to waste, a musical genius, and you locked yourself up with Paul as the warden. He never wanted me anywhere near the place. I had this stupid idea that if you had to pay out a lot of money, you'd have go back to work and we'd all be back on the ride."

"Why didn't you just talk to me?" Dillon asked in the same quiet voice.

"Who could talk to you?" Don demanded bitterly. "Your watchdog wouldn't let anyone near you. You have him so well trained he practically has the Great Wall of China surrounding the island." He held up his hand to prevent Dillon from speaking. "You don't have to defend him, I know he's protective and even why. I needed the band back and I felt hopeless so I sent you a stupid letter and followed it with a couple of others. Obviously you weren't very worried because you didn't respond."

"I didn't give a damn," Dillon admitted.

"There's no excuse for what I've done," Don announced, "so I'm ready to go to jail. I'll confess everything to the cops."

Dillon looked so helpless, Jessica put her arms around him. "Did you talk to my mother about this?" She couldn't see Don sneaking around her mother's car, fraying the brake lines. Nothing seemed to make sense anymore. If she felt so lost, with the ground shifting out from under her, how must Dillon feel?

"Hell no, she would have boxed my ears," Don said emphatically. "Why would I do a dumb thing like that?"

"You're drunker than you think you are, Don," Dillon said, "go sleep it off. We'll talk about this later." He had absolutely no idea what he was going to say when they talked. He almost felt like laughing hysterically.

Jessica pressed her hand to her stomach as Dillon closed the door. "I feel sick," she announced before he could speak and raced for the bathroom.

chapter

12

"COME ON, BRENDA, you have to come with us," Tara wheedled. "It will be fun."

"Are you certain you're feeling better? You were so sick this morning. I almost made Robert get Paul to bring in a helicopter to transport you to the hospital. And now you're jumping around like nothing happened."

Jessica looked up alertly. Everyone had gathered in the kitchen, sleeping late as usual so that it was early evening. "Tara was sick this morning? Why didn't someone come and get me?"

"*Both* the children were sick this morning and I handled it just fine, thank you very much," Brenda announced. "Some kind of stomach flu. You know, Jessie, you aren't the only one with maternal instinct. I was a miracle of comfort to them. Not to mention I was being wonderfully helpful and discreet to give you and Dillon time to . . . er . . . work things out."

Trevor made a rude noise, somewhere between a raspberry and a choking cough. "A miracle of comfort? Brenda, you were hanging out the window gagging and calling for smelling salts. Robert didn't know whether to run to you, Tara, or me. The poor guy was cleaning up the floor half the day."

"Robert, you are a true prince," Jessica flashed him a grateful smile. "Thank you for cleaning up after them."

"Just remember it was my good sense to notice him," Brenda took the credit.

Don made a face. "I thought we were working today. I want to finish the recording and see what we have. Do we have to do this now?"

"We're staying up all night working," Paul pointed out. "By the time we get up, most the day is gone and we lose the light we need hunting for the Christmas tree. I say we go now."

Don muttered softly beneath his breath, his gaze studiously avoiding Dillon's.

Jessica frowned, studying the twins. "You *both* had the stomach flu? I was feeling a bit queasy this morning myself. Did anyone else? Maybe we all ate something bad."

"Brian's pancakes," Brenda said instantly, "ghastly things designed to drive us all mad with monotony. Devoid of all nutrition and basically the worst meal on the face of the earth. And if you ask me, he's trying to poison me." She blew him a kiss, pure glee on her face. "The heinous plot won't work, genius though it might be, because I have a cast-iron stomach."

Brian leapt up out of his chair, nearly knocking it over. "I make pancakes that are works of art, Brenda," he snapped, as if goaded beyond endurance. "I don't see you slaving away in the kitchen for all of us."

"And you won't ever, darling—the very idea makes me shudder," she said complacently. "Trivial things should be left to trivial people."

"The children are fighting again," Jessica pointed out with a soft sigh, leaning into the comfort of Dillon's body. "And as usual, it isn't the twins."

"Tara, are you certain you're feeling well enough to go traipsing around in the woods? It's cold out and the wind is really blowing. There's another storm on the way. If you'd rather curl up here where it's warm, we'll go look and bring you back a tree," Dillon offered. He wrapped his arms around Jessica, uncaring that anyone saw them.

For the first time in years, he felt at peace with himself. There was hope in his life, a reason for his existence. "Jess and Trevor can stay with you, if you'd like."

"No way," Trevor objected. "I'm feeling fine. No one else can pick our tree. We know what we're looking for, don't we, Tara?"

Tara nodded solemnly, wrapping her arm around her brother's waist, her eyes on Jessica. All three smiled in perfect understanding. "We all go," she announced. "We'll know the right tree."

Dillon shrugged. "Sounds fine to me—let's do it then. Anyone who would like to find the tree with us is welcome to come. We can get the tools out of the shed and meet you on the trail." He tugged at Jessica, determined to take her with him. A few minutes alone in the shed was looking good. He hadn't had two minutes to steal a kiss from her.

"Whoa there," Trevor held up his hand. "I'm not

sure how safe it is to let our Jessica go to a *shed* with you, Dad. You have a certain reputation as a Casanova type."

Dillon's eyebrow shot up. "And where would I get a rep like that?"

"Well, for one thing, look at this house. I've been meaning to talk to you about this place. You have weird carvings and things hanging off the eaves. What's that all about? This place looks like something out of an Edgar Allen Poe novel. The men in those books were always up to no good with the ladies." He wriggled his eyebrows suggestively.

"Weird carvings?" Dillon was horrified. "This house is a perfect example of early Gothic and Renaissance architecture combined. You, son, are a cretin. It's a *perfect* house. Look at the carvings on the corners: winged gargoyles scaling the south side, lions clawing their way up the east side. The detail is fantastic. And every true Gothic and Renaissance man has his secret passageways and moving walls. Where's the fun in a stately mansion? Everyone has one."

"Dad," Tara stated firmly, "it's creepy. Have you ever looked at it at night from the outside? It looks haunted and it looks as if it's staring at you. You're a little bit out there, even if you are my father."

"Treacherous children," Dillon said. "You've been spending far too much time with your aunt. She shares your opinion of my home."

Brenda rolled her eyes heavenward. "Dillon you have things crawling up your house and watching every move one makes outside. I shudder every time I'm in the garden or walking through the grounds. I look up and there something is, staring at me."

"Technically," Brian interrupted, "they watch over the house and the people in it. If you're afraid, it's probably because you have good reason to be." He hitched closer. "Like maybe you're harboring ill will toward those inside."

Jessica crumbled a napkin and pitched it at Brian. "Back off, drummer boy, since Brenda was such a miracle of comfort to my babies, I can't very well let you spout your nonsense. I've always loved Gothic architecture, too. We used to look at all the books together and Dillon would bring home photos from Europe." She winked at Trevor. "I would think those hidden passageways would intrigue you."

Dillon captured her hand and pulled her toward the double doors leading toward the courtyard. "Dress warm you two—we'll meet you on the trail."

Jessica followed him out into the courtyard, ignoring Trevor's taunting whistle. "I don't like it that both of the kids were sick this morning, Dillon," she said. "Yesterday, Tara saw someone watching them when the landslide occurred. She couldn't tell who it was, he or she was wearing a long hooded cape. I saw the same person the night we arrived."

Dillon slowed his pace, pulling her closer to him so that she was beneath the protection of his shoulder. "What are you saying, Jess?" He was very careful to keep his tone without expression. "Do you think the landslide was rigged in some way? And the kids didn't have the flu, that someone somehow poisoned them?"

When he said the words, they did sound absurd. Oil on a staircase anyone could slip on. How could one rig a landslide and know the children would be in that exact spot? And she had been sick, too. People got the flu all the time. She sighed. How could she explain the uneasiness she felt? The continual worry that never went away? "Why wouldn't the person wearing the hooded cape help them? Clearly they were in trouble, Tara was screaming her head off."

"I don't know the answer to that, baby, but we'll find out," he assured. "Everyone certainly pitched in and helped to free Trevor. I didn't notice anyone holding back, not even Don."

"Don." Jessica shook her head. "It's hard to like that man. Even after last night, and I did feel sorry for him, I've been struggling to find something good about him."

"I did like him," Dillon answered, frowning slightly. "He was always reserved with me but he always worked hard. There was no looking around for him at the end of the night; he pulled his share of the work and then some. He was steady and I counted on him heavily at times. I had no idea he disliked me so intensely. And I sure didn't know Vivian was sleeping with him. She suggested I go hear him play, but I brought him into the band because he's so talented, not because she asked me." He sighed, raked his hand through his hair. "I don't know anymore, Jess. In the old days, it was all so easy. I never opened my eyes. I just lived my life in blissful ignorance until it all came crashing down." He looked at her, his fingers tightening around hers. "I was so arrogant, so sure that I could make it all work out. The truth is, how can I condemn Don when I've made so many mistakes myself?"

"Do you think it was a member of the band who killed Vivian and Phillip?" she asked carefully.

"No, of course not. They had five nutcases up there with them that night. All of them were mixing drugs and alcohol. For all I know, one of them brought a gun in. Someone shot Viv and Trent and maybe the others jumped the shooter, tried to wrestle the gun away and knocked over the drinks and candles. I hope it happened that way. I hope the fire didn't start while I was beating up Trent. It was pretty wild. We knocked tables and lamps over. Maybe a candle hit the floor and no one noticed. I'll never know. The band had no idea what was going on up there. We'd just arrived."

"Why did you come upstairs?" she asked curiously.

"I wanted to check on the kids. Tara was asleep but she didn't have her blanket. I hadn't seen you in so long and I knew you must have gone looking for the thing. I was looking for you," he admitted. "I couldn't wait until morning to see you."

Pleasure rushed through her at his words. "I'm grateful you came looking for me, Dillon," she said softly.

Dillon threw open the door to the shed, flicked on a switch to flood the room with light. "So am I, honey." He couldn't look at her, knowing the fury of that moment was etched into his face. He couldn't look back and not feel it.

Jessica laughed, the sound of her joy dispelling old memories. "I would like to have known about the lights in here yesterday."

"Really," his eyebrow shot up. His voice softened into seduction. "I was just thinking it would have been smarter to keep it dark."

Jessica quirked an eyebrow at him and took a step backward. "You have that wicked look on your face like you're up to something." His expression alone sent heat coursing through her body.

"Wicked? I like that." His hand curled around the nape of her neck, drew her to him. He bent his head to claim her mouth. His lips were firm, soft, tempting. His tongue teased her lower lip, tracing the outline, probing and dancing until she opened to him.

His hand slipped under her jacket and blouse to find bare skin. Her breast pushed into his palm. He tasted the same hunger in her mouth. "Take off your jacket, Jess," he whispered as he reached once more for the light switch, plunging the shed into a murky gray. "Hurry, baby, we don't have much time."

"You can't think we're doing anything in this little shed, outdoors where anyone could find us," she said, but she was shedding her jacket, tossing it aside, wanting the searing heat of his mouth on her breast. Wanting her hands on him. It already seemed far too long.

Dillon watched her unbutton her blouse with breathless anticipation. He watched the richness of her breasts spill into his sight and he slowly let out his breath, his lungs burning for air. She did that to him with her exquisite skin and haunting eyes. "I thought about you while I showered this evening," he confided. "You should have been there with me. I thought about how you tasted and how you feel and how you sound when

I'm inside of you." He bent his head to draw her breast into his mouth.

Her body rippled with instant need, with hunger. She laughed softly. "I was with you. As I recall, you did a lot of tasting."

"Are you certain? It wasn't enough, I need more." His hands slipped over her jeans, fumbled with the zipper. "Get rid of these things, you need them off." His teeth nipped at the underside of her breast, returned to the heat of her mouth, kissing her senseless. "I need them off."

"Do you think we have time?" She was already complying, wanting him so much that the stolen moments were as precious as the long all-night session of lovemaking.

"Not for all the things I want to do with you," he whispered against her ear, his tongue probing her frantic pulse. "But enough for what I have in mind. Push my jeans off my hips." The instant his body was free of the confining cloth he breathed a sigh of relief. "Much better. I'm going to lift you up. Put your arms around my neck and wrap your legs around my waist. Are you ready for me?" His fingers were already seeking his answer, probing deep, slipping into her body to find her damp with need.

He buried his face in her neck. "You are so hot, Jess. I love how you want me the same way I want you." Just feeling her dampness hardened his body even more. He took her weight as she put her arms around his neck and lifted her legs to wrap them around his waist. The engorged head of his shaft was pressed tightly to her. Very slowly he lowered her body over his. There was the familiar resistance, her body stretching to receive his fullness. The impression of sliding a sword into a tight sheath left every nerve ending raw. The sensation was building like a firestorm, spreading wilder, hotter, more explosive than ever. It roared through his body like a freight train, through his mind, a crescendo of notes and promises, of half-formed thoughts and needs.

He loved the little anxious sounds escaping her throat, the way she moved her hips to meet his, in a perfect rhythm. Jessica, the completion of his heart.

Jessica lost herself in the hard thrusts of his body into hers, in the fiery heat and sizzling passion that rose up and engulfed her entirely. She threw her head back, riding fast, tightening her muscles around him, gripping and sliding with a friction designed to drive them both up and over the edge quickly.

She couldn't believe herself, the wild wanton ride she took, there in the shed with their disheveled clothes half on and half off. But it didn't matter, nothing mattered but the burst of light and color as she broke into fragments and dissolved, her body rippling with a life of its own. She hung on tightly to Dillon as he thrust hard, repeatedly, his hoarse cry muffled by her shoulder.

They clung, their laughter coming together, a soft, pleased melding as their heart rates slowed to normal and Dillon slowly lowered her feet to the floor. The stolen moments were as precious as gold to both of them. It took a little scrambling and fumbling to adjust their clothing. Jessica couldn't find her slip-on shoes. Dillon distracted her often while she searched, kissing her neck, her fingers, swirling his tongue in her ear. She found one shoe among the pots and the other upside down on top of a bag of potting soil. She picked it up and idly picked out the seaweed caught in the sole.

"I haven't worn these shoes anywhere near the ocean bank. Where did I pick up seaweed?" She slipped the shoes back on her feet and went back into his arms again, turning up her mouth for his kiss. There was a long silence, while they simply got lost in each other. Dillon trailed kisses down her chin to her throat.

Jessica tilted her head to give him better access and caught a movement outside the small window.

"What's wrong?" Dillon asked, lifting his head reluctantly as he felt her stiffen. "Your neck is so perfect to nibble on—soft and tempting. I could stay here forever. Are you certain we have to get the Christmas tree today?"

"Something moved out there. I think someone is watching us," Jessica whispered. A shiver crept down her spine. Looking through the small window, she strained to see but couldn't spot anyone. It didn't matter. Someone watched them.

Dillon groaned. "Not again. Don had better not make another confession or I might pitch him off the cliff." He stepped past her to the small square window, looked around carefully. "I don't see anyone, baby, maybe it's the gargoyles on the roof."

Jessica could hear the amusement in his voice. Soft, gentle, teasing. She tried to respond, going into his arms, but she couldn't shake the feeling of something sinister staring at them.

"Come on, Jessie," Trevor shouted, breaking them

apart immediately. "You two better not be doing anything I don't want to know about, because I'm coming in." There was the briefest of hesitations and then the door was thrust open. Trevor glared at them. "Everyone else was too chicken to come see what you were up to."

"We're looking for the axe," Jessica improvised lamely.

"Oh, really?" Trevor's eyebrow went up, in just the same way as his father's did sometimes. He fit the role of the chastising father figure perfectly. "Do you think this might help?" He flicked the switch so that light permeated every inch of the small building. He glared at his father in disapproval. "In a tool shed?"

"Trevor!" Blushing, Jessica hurried to the back of the shed where she knew the larger tools were kept. As she reached for the axe, she knocked over the large pry bar. Muttering, she picked it up and started to replace it. The dried mud and pine needles stuck on the edge of it caught her eye. She frowned at the tool.

Trevor took up the axe. "Come on, Jessie, everyone's waiting. Stop mooning around, it's embarrassing. At least you have the good sense to fall for my dad."

"You don't mind?" Dillon asked, his eyes very serious as he studied his son's face.

"Who else would we want for Jessie?" Trevor asked matter-of-factly. "She's our family. We don't want someone else stealing her away from us."

"As if that could happen," Jessica leaned over to kiss his cheek. "Come on, we'd better hurry or the others will be looking for us." She led the way out of the shed.

"And, by the way, we had kitchen duty this afternoon," Trevor added righteously.

She turned to look at him skeptically. "*You* cleaned up or your sister did? I can't imagine you remembering."

"Well, Brenda remembered and I would have cleaned up but Tara's mothering me again because I suffered trauma yesterday." He put on his most pathetic face.

"Trauma?" Dillon interrupted. "*We* suffered the trauma, Jess, your sister, and I, not you. You ate it up. Don't think we didn't notice your sister waiting on you hand and foot. Is that a normal, everyday thing?"

"Absolutely," Trevor was grinning with unabashed glee. "And I love it, too!"

"He has no shame," Jessica pointed out to Dillon.

"Not when it comes to *domestic* chores," Trevor admitted. "Hey! I'm beginning to sound like Brenda and that's scary!" He waved to Tara and the group huddled together under the trees waiting for them. "I told you I'd get them," he called.

There was no time for anything but finding the all-important Christmas tree. Tara and Trevor had an idea where to look and they set off immediately. Paul kept pace with them, laughing, punching Trevor's arm good-naturedly and occasionally tousling Tara's hair. Brenda and Robert walked together at a much more sedate pace, whispering with their heads together. Brian and Don argued loudly over the best way to save the rain forest and the ozone layer and whether or not the taking of one small Christmas tree was going to have global effects.

Dillon walked along the trail, his hand firmly anchored in Jessica's. His life had changed dramatically. Everyone who was important to him was with him, sharing his home. He glanced down at the woman walking so close to him. Jessica had somehow changed his entire world in the blink of an eye. His children were with him, trust was slowly beginning to develop among them. He could see such potential, his mind awakening to all the possibilities of life. It was exhilarating, yet frightening.

Dillon knew his self-esteem had always been wrapped up in his music, in his ability to shoulder enormous responsibility. His childhood had been difficult, a struggle just to feel as if he counted for something. What did he have to offer them all if he could no longer play the music pounding in his head?

The fine mist began to turn into a steady drizzle as they walked along the trail. The band members pointed out tree after tree, big fir trees with full branches. The twins adamantly shook their heads, looking to Jessica for support. She agreed and followed them to the small, thin tree with gaps between the branches they had chosen the night before. The tree was growing at a strange angle out from under two larger trees at the edge of a bluff overlooking a smaller hill. The rain was making the ground slick.

"Stay away from that edge, Tara," Dillon commanded, scowling as he walked around the sad little tree. "This is your perfect Christmas tree?"

Trevor and Tara exchanged a grin. "That's the one. It wants to come home with us. We asked it," Tara said solemnly.

"I tramped through the forest in the pouring rain for that little mongrel of a tree?" Brenda demanded. "Good heavens, look around, there are fantastic trees everywhere."

"I like it," Don said, clapping his hands on the twins' shoulders. "It hasn't a hope of surviving here—I say we take it in, show it a good time, and let it have some fun."

Jessica nodded. "It looks perfect to me." She skirted the forlorn little tree, touched one of the longer branches that reached out toward the sea. "This is the one."

Dillon raised his eyebrow at Robert, who shrugged helplessly. "Whatever makes them happy, I guess."

Brian stepped forward to take the axe out of Dillon's hands. "I like the darned thing—it needs a home and some cheering up." He sent the axe sweeping toward the narrow trunk. He was strong and the first bite cut deep.

Tara hugged her brother, her eyes shining. "This is *exactly* how I imagined it, Dad." She wrapped her other arm around her father.

Dillon stood very still while pleasure coursed through him at his daughter's affectionate gesture.

Paul laughed and began removing his jacket. "Did you imagine the rain, too, Tara? We could have done without that."

The gray drizzle was beginning to fall a little faster. Brian took another swipe at the tree trunk, sinking the blade in solidly. He repeated the action again and again with a steady rhythm that matched the drone of the rain. Robert put his arm around his wife to help protect her from the rising wind. The tree shivered, beginning to tilt.

"Hey!" Paul was shaking out his jacket, reaching across Jessica, holding it out toward Tara. "Put this on."

Tara grinned happily at him through the gray mist. "Thanks, Paul." Her fingers closed around the material just as there was an ominous crack.

The branches wavered, then rushed at them. Paul yelled a warning, stepping back in an attempt to stay out of reach. His elbow cracked into Jessica's shoulder, sending her flying backward as his feet slipped out from under him in the thick mud.

Dillon shoved Tara hard, sending her sprawling into Trevor's arms, even as he dove across the muddy ground for Jessica. To his horror, Jessica went down hard, skidding precariously close to the edge of the bluff. He saw her make a grab for the wavering tree branches but Paul's larger frame crashed into hers in a tangle of arms and legs. They both went sliding over the edge of the crumbling cliff. Paul's fingers made thick tracks in the mud as he attempted to find a purchase.

Dillon skidded in the mud, lying flat out on the ground, catching Jessica's ankle as she plummeted over the edge. He realized he was yelling hoarsely, a mind-numbing terror invading him. The Christmas tree lay beside him, inches to his left. Don threw himself across Dillon's legs, pinning him to the ground to prevent him sliding over the edge after Jessica and Robert leapt to catch Paul's wrists as he clung to the rocks. There was a moment of silence broken only by the moaning wind, the pounding sea, the sound of rain, and heavy breathing.

"Daddy?" Tara's voice was thin and frightened.

Trevor dropped into the mud beside his father, looking down over the edge at Jessica. She was upside down, straining to turn her head to look up at them. Other than her head, she was very still, aware that the only thing preventing her from falling was Dillon's fingers circling her

After the Music 221

ankle. Trevor reached out with both hands and caught her calf. Together they began to pull her up.

"It's all right, honey," Dillon soothed his daughter. "Jess is fine, aren't you, baby?" He could pretend his hands weren't shaking and his mind wasn't numb with terror. "Robert, can you hold Paul?"

"I've got him." Robert was straining back. Brenda and Tara caught his belt and pulled as hard as they could. Brian simply reached past them and added his strength to Robert's, pulling Paul straight up. He immediately turned his attention to helping Trevor and Dillon with Jessica.

All of them sat in the mud, Dillon, Tara, and Trevor holding Jessica tight. The rain poured down harder. Jessica could hear her heart thundering in her chest. Dillon's face was buried against her throbbing shoulder. Tara and Trevor clung to her, their grip so tight she thought they might break her in two. She looked at the others. Paul looked absolutely stunned, his face a mask of shock. Brenda's face was white. Robert, Don, and Brian looked frightened.

Another accident. This time Jessica was in the middle of it. She couldn't imagine that it had been anything other than an accident. Had all of the other accidents that had occurred recently really just been flukes and coincidence? Had she become paranoid after her mother's death? Certainly with Trevor's accident, she had carefully examined the ground, yet she had seen no signs that the landslide had been anything more than a natural shift in the land after a storm. But what about the hooded figure Trevor and Tara had seen yesterday and the one she'd seen the night they'd arrived on the island? Who could that be? Perhaps it was the groundskeeper and his eyesight was so poor he didn't notice anyone or anything around him. It was a poor explanation, but other than someone hiding on the island, she couldn't think of anything else.

"I saved your jacket, Paul," Tara said in a small voice, holding up the precious item for everyone to see.

Everyone burst out laughing in relief. Except Paul. He shook his head, the stunned disbelief still on his face. Jessica was certain it was on her face, too.

"Let's get back to the house," Dillon suggested. "In case no one's noticed, it's really raining out here. Are you okay, Paul?"

Paul didn't answer, his body shaking in reaction, but he allowed Brian and Dillon to help him to his feet.

Jessica mulled the idea over that she could be wrong about the accidents. Even about the brakes on her mother's car being tampered with. About her own car. All the other trivial things could be something altogether different. She swept a shaky hand through her hair. She just didn't know.

chapter 13

IT TOOK A SURPRISINGLY short time for everyone to reconvene in the kitchen, freshly showered and once more warm after the outdoor adventures. Upset by another near tragedy, Jessica kept a close eye on the twins. The string of accidents was just too much for her to believe they were all coincidences. Yet nothing ever added up.

She looked around the room at the other occupants of the house. She liked them. That was the problem. She really liked them. Some more than others, but she couldn't conceive of any of them deliberately harming the twins.

"Jessie, you aren't listening to me," Tara's voice penetrated her thoughts. "I don't know what kinds of ornaments we can make." Tara added sadly, "Mama Rita had beautiful ornaments for our trees." She stood very close to her brother, her gaze seeking reassurance from Jessica. Obviously she was as shaken by the accident as Jessica was.

"We're supposed to *make* them, Tara," Trevor pointed out. "That's the way it works, right, Jessie?"

Jessica nodded. "I have a great recipe for a dough. We can roll it out, cut out whatever shapes we want, bake them and then paint them. It will be fun." She set two mugs of chocolate in front of the twins and held up a third mug toward Paul. He shook his head and she set it down in front of her, reaching for a towel to clean the counter.

Brenda yawned. "Susie Homemaker strikes again. Do you know how to do *everything*, dear? Have you any idea how utterly tiring that can be?"

Jessica threw the wadded up tea towel at her, hitting the perfectly fashionable head and draping the Kelly green towel over the chic chignon. "No one believes your little heartless wench act, Brenda—you've blown it, so start thinking up ideas. And I didn't say I was going to do the mixing and baking. I'm the *supervisor*. You and the twins are the worker bees."

"Robert, are you going to let her get away with throwing things at me?" Brenda complained. She wadded the towel into a tight little ball, looking for a target. "Surely you could exact some sort of revenge for me. I'd do it myself but I've just been endangering my life, tramping through mosquito-infested waters and through alligator-ridden swamps to find the perfect Christmas tree for two ungrateful little chits. And the perfect tree turned out to be some straggly, misshapen bush!"

"There aren't alligators here," Trevor pointed out, "so technically your life wasn't really in danger. It's your duty as our aunt to do these things and *enjoy* them, isn't that right, Dad? So buck up, babe. We'll let you sing the first Christmas carol."

The tea towel hit Trevor's face dead center. "You *horrid* little boy!"

"Ouch, ouch," Trevor clutched at his chest, feigning a heart attack. "She spears with me with her unkind words." He drained the mug of hot chocolate. "More?" he asked hopefully, holding up the cup.

"No, you're going to bed soon," Jessica objected. "I swear, you're becoming a bottomless pit."

"He can have mine," Tara said, pushing the mug toward her brother. "I don't want any more."

Jessica intercepted it, catching it up before Trevor could snatch it out of her reach. "What if she still has the flu, Trev? Don't drink from the same mug," she chided. "Tara, do you feel sick? You've gone so pale."

"I think I still have the flu," Tara admitted, "or maybe I'm just still scared. I didn't like seeing you and Paul falling off the cliff."

"We didn't like it much either," Jessica exchanged a small smile with Paul.

"Hey, paper chains," Don said suddenly. "When I was a kid we used to make paper chains and hang them on the tree. I think I remember how to do it."

"I remember that," Robert agreed. "We should take all those musical notations we've thrown away and use them. We all love music. Does that work, Jessie? Brenda, we made a chain one year. We didn't have a tree so we made a chain of love."

Jessica grinned at Brenda as the woman visibly winced, horrified to be found out. "A love chain, Brenda? You're really a mushy girl after all, aren't you?"

"She's all sappy like you are, Jessie," Trevor was wearing an identical grin. "Brenda, you little romantic you. A *luv* chain."

"Why, Brenda," Dillon was outright smirking. "You've truly amazed me. I had no idea you were a marshmallow under all that sophistication."

"Don't start. Robert is making it all up as you know perfectly well," Brenda looked haughty, her nose in the air.

Brian wagged his finger at her. "Robert doesn't have the imagination to make something like that up, Brenda. You *did* make a love chain with him."

Tara protectively flung her arms around Brenda, glaring at everyone. "Leave her alone, all of you!" She pressed a kiss against Brenda's chin. "We can make as many chains as you want. Don't let them bother you."

Jessica met Brenda's gaze across the room. Tears glistened in the depths of Brenda's eyes. She sat very still, not moving a muscle. The two women simply stared at one another, caught in the moment. Brenda nuzzled the top of Tara's head briefly, her eyes still locked with Jessica's. "Thank you," she mouthed, blinking rapidly to rid herself of unwanted emotion.

"You're welcome," Jessica mouthed back with a watery smile.

Dillon felt his throat close, his heart swelling with pride at observing the exchange. Jessica brought her light to everyone. She could so easily have turned the twins against Brenda, against him. The children loved her beyond any other. Their loyalty to Jessica was strong. A single word from Jessica would have prevented the twins from even trying to work with all the different personalities around them. Jessica had been so generous in sharing them and she had instilled her giving nature in both of them. He knew, better than most, how Brenda often appeared cold and uncaring to others. He was proud of his children, that they saw beyond the barrier she presented to world to the real woman.

"There's always strings of popcorn," Paul pointed out. "Those are easy enough to make. We used to make those in your basement, Brian."

"We ate most of them," Dillon pointed out, laughing at the memory.

The next two hours were spent companionably, baking and coloring ornaments and stringing paper chains and popcorn. Dillon managed to lead them in Christmas carols that Paul and Brian turned into other much more ribald ballads. Brenda and Brian got into a popcorn fight until Trevor and Tara took their aunt's side and Brian was forced to cry uncle.

When Jessica could see that both Tara and Trevor were overtired and too flushed, she called a halt and took them both upstairs. She was surprised that both teenagers went without a murmur of protest.

Tara clutched her stomach. "I really don't feel very well, but I didn't want to ruin the fun," she admitted.

Little warning bells began going off in Jessica's head despite her determination not to worry. She rubbed at her temples, annoyed with herself for being so protective. Everyone got the flu, even she still felt sick.

"I wish we had played all those tricks on everyone," Trevor said suddenly to Tara. "Didn't that make you mad that they were blaming us for all those pranks while we were waiting for Jessica and Dad? It's so typical for adults to always blame kids for everything." He suddenly lunged for the bathroom.

"What do you mean they were blaming you for pranks?" Jessica tucked the blankets around Tara and smoothed back her hair. "Are you feeling any better, honey? I can get your father and we can take you to a doctor."

"I'm the one throwing my guts up," Trevor yelled from the bathroom.

"Sweetie, I'll be happy to take you to the doctor. It's just that I know you'd rather be boiled in oil than see the doc," Jessica said sympathetically.

They could hear Trevor noisily rinsing his mouth for the third time. "And it sucks that they thought we were going into their rooms. I wonder if someone's been going into Dad's room and he thinks it's us, too. Just because we're teenagers doesn't mean we don't have respect for other people's things," he said indignantly. He stumbled from the bathroom back to them, crossing the floor with an aggravated frown on his face. "I asked Brian point blank if he was in your room, Jessie, and if he'd burned incense and created one of his magic circles there, and he said no. And then he had the gall to tell me to stay out of his room."

"To stay the *hell* out of his room," Tara corrected. "He was really mad at us. I never went into his stupid room."

"Wait a minute," Jessica held up her hand. "What are you talking about? The others accused you of going into their rooms?"

Tara nodded. "Even Brenda and Robert thought we were playing pranks on them. I guess it's happened to everyone since we've been here and I don't think they believed us when we told them it was happening to us, too."

"What pranks?" Jessica wanted to know. "And where have I been?"

Trevor and Tara exchanged a slow grin. "With Dad," they said in unison.

Jessica blushed as she sat on the edge of Tara's bed. "I guess I deserved that. I'm sorry I've been in the studio working so much and that I've been going off with Dillon. I'll talk to Brian. He shouldn't have accused you. What do they think you've been doing?"

Trevor shrugged. "The usual teen-in-the-spooky-old-mansion stuff. Opening windows, leaving water running in the bathtub, moving things, writing weird leave-before-it's-too-late messages on mirrors. That sort of thing."

"Brian said no one else would be so childish." Tara was clearly offended. "Like I would want to find a stupid secret passageway and sneak into his dumb room!" Her gaze slid to her twin's face. "Well, Trevor and I did look for secret passageways, but just because it was fun. If we were going to try to convince everyone there was a ghost here, we'd have done a *much* better job," she declared. "At least Brenda and Robert said they believed us. Do you think Dad believes we're sneaking into people's rooms?" She sounded a little forlorn.

"Of course not, Tara. If your father thought you were doing such a thing, he would have spoken to you about it immediately. I'm sorry they accused you of such childish behavior. You're right, oftentimes an adult who isn't used to teenagers has a false idea of the things they do." Jessica stroked Tara's hair. "I noticed our resident ghost forgot to open the window tonight."

"Could there be a real ghost in the house?" Tara asked hopefully.

"The house isn't old enough," Trevor protested knowledgably. He'd read a lot on the subject. "Dad had it built after the fire. The contractor finished it while he was still in the burn center." When his sister and Jessica looked at him he shrugged with a sheepish grin. "Paul told me. I ask him questions about Dad. Sometimes he doesn't mind and other times he just sort of ignores me. You don't learn anything if you don't ask questions. A house has to be really old to have a ghost."

"Or there has to have been a murder in it," Tara agreed.

A chill went down Jessica's spine at Tara's words. She remembered the sound of the gunshots, the crackle of the flames, the heat and smoke. Standing up, she walked to the window, not wanting the twins to see the expression on her face. *Murder.* The word shimmered in her mind. Both children were watching her closely. Not wanting them to know what she was thinking, she changed the subject. "Did Brenda really take care of you and Tara this morning when you were sick? That amazes me."

Trevor laughed immediately. "She tried. She was as white as a sheet. The funny thing was, Robert wanted to go get you but she said no, they could handle it. I think she really wanted to, not only to give you and Dad time to work things out, but because she wanted to be the one to help us. The crazy part was, while she was being so nice, I was thinking Robert and Brenda might have tried to poison us."

Jessica looked at him sharply. "Why would you think something like that?"

"Well, we both drank a soda in their room and then we were sick. And I found a newspaper in their wastebasket with words cut out of it like for a ransom note. I had this wild idea they were going to hold us hostage or something until you paid them money. Or kill us and collect the insurance on us." He grinned, looking sheepish.

"I was sick *before* I drank the soda, that's why I drank it so fast." Tara scowled at her brother indignantly. "Brenda and Robert weren't trying to poison us!"

"I know that *now*," Trevor flung himself on his makeshift bed.

"You found *what* in Brenda's room?" Jessica tripped over Trevor's shoes and nearly fell on the bed. Don had confessed to attempting to blackmail Dillon. Why would Brenda and Robert have the remnants of a cut up newspaper in their room? What would be the point of Don's confessing and then trying to cast blame on someone else? Jessica could feel the strange shiver of apprehension snake down her spine. Unless someone else was involved. Someone far more sinister than Don. Jessica didn't like the implications of it at all.

"It was just an old newspaper," Trevor said, shrugging it off. "Some of the words had been cut out of it, but I didn't really have time to look at it closely."

Jessica sat down on the edge of the bed. Outside the rain had started again, pounding at the window and rattling branches against the house. "What is it you two used to call me?" she asked softly. The raindrops matched the rhythm in her heart.

"Magical girl," Tara's voice was drowsy. "You're our magical girl."

Jessica leaned over her to kiss her again. "Thank you, honey, I think I need to be magical girl again. I'm going down to the studio. If you need me, come get me." She needed to go somewhere and think and it always helped when she had a guitar in her hands. Her shoulder was aching, a reminder of the day's events, as she noiselessly crept down the hall to the wide staircase. The lights were off and the house had grown silent.

Dillon would be waiting for her to come to him. If she was too long he might go looking. She didn't want to be with him while she sorted things out. He distracted her, made her lose confidence in herself. *Magical girl.* Even her mother had used that name for her because she knew things. She knew things instinctively. Things like when what appeared to be an accident was really something much more sinister. Since coming here she had been relying on Dillon. Expecting Dillon to solve the mystery, to make it all better.

Lightning zigzagged across the sky and lit up the courtyard as she paused on the landing to look out through the glass doors. She could see the fir trees as they jerked in a macabre dance like wooden marionettes. Dillon didn't believe anyone was trying to hurt the children. Jessica believed it and if she was going to find the truth, she needed to rely on herself and her own judgment.

The sound room was empty, strangely eerie with the glass and instruments in the dark. She idly picked up one of Dillon's acoustic guitars, a *Martin* he particularly loved. She ran her fingers over the strings, heard the small jarring note not quite in tune. That was what the accidents were like, a note not quite in tune. She had to sort it all out just as she so efficiently tuned the guitar. She played there in the darkness, sitting on the edge of the instrument panel, her mind compiling the data for her. She closed her eyes and allowed the music, *Dillon's* music, to soothe her as she played.

She slipped a few random notes into the melody. Notes off-key, off-kilter, like the accidents that could have happened to anyone. Anyone. The word repeated like a refrain in her head. Random accidents. Secret passageways. Blackmail. Pieces of a puzzle like musical notations written on paper. Move them around, put them together differently, and she would have a masterpiece. Or a key.

Thunder crashed all too close, the clash of cymbals, the exclamation point after the melody. She opened her eyes just as another bolt of lightning lit up the world. A figure loomed up right in front of her, a dark shadow of terror. Jessica lunged to her feet, gripping the expensive guitar like a weapon.

Brenda stumbled backward with a frightened shriek. "Jess! It's me! Brenda!"

Her heart pounding too loudly, Jessica slowly lowered the guitar. "What in the world are you doing here?"

"Looking for you. Trevor told me where to find you. You're the only one who might believe me. I don't know who else to talk to." Brenda's hand shot out, prevented Jessica from turning on the light. "Don't, I can't look at you and say this." She took a deep calming breath. "I wanted to believe the kids were behind the pranks, but I don't think so. I think it's Vivian."

A chill went down Jessica's spine. Her eyes strained in the darkness to see Brenda's face, to read her expression.

"I'm not crazy, Jessie. I feel her at times." Brenda pressed a trembling hand to her mouth. "I think the kids or Dillon or maybe me, are in danger and she's trying to warn us. Vivian wasn't a bad person, and she believed in spirits. If she could come back to help set things right, she would. I've been afraid something was wrong for a while and the minute I came to the island, I was certain of it."

"You think Vivian is opening windows and drawing magic circles on the floor? Why, why would she do that, knowing how Dillon feels?" Jessica kept her voice very even. She didn't know if Brenda was attempting to frighten her, or if she really believed what she was saying.

"To protect you. To protect me. Dillon, the children. All of us. It was the only religion she knew." Brenda leaned closer to her, pleading with her. "Do you feel it, too? Tell me I haven't completely lost my mind. I don't want to end up like Viv."

Jessica carefully leaned the guitar against the wall. She didn't know if Vivian's presence was in the house helping her or if the next flash of lightning merely illuminated her brain. Like the notes blending into harmony, the pieces clicked into place.

"Since we came here, the accidents have all been random. I was trying to mold them, fit them into my idea that someone wanted to harm Trevor and Tara. But all the accidents could have hurt any of us. Anyone in the house. Do you see it, Brenda, the pattern?"

Brenda shook her head. "No, but you're chilling me to the bone."

"And the cape. The hooded figure. The dog didn't bark."

"You've lost me. Bark when?"

"When Trevor was buried under the landslide, Tara saw a hooded figure, but the dog didn't bark. So it wasn't a stranger hiding on the island, it was someone the dog knew." Jessica knew she was on the verge of discovery. It was all there for her to see. The pattern in the discordant notes. "Why were only the three of us sick? Why Tara and Trevor and me? None of you were sick." She pressed a hand to her mouth, her eyes wide. "It's the chocolate. My God, he poisoned the chocolate. He did everything. He shot Vivian, he must have, and he covered his tracks with the fire."

"What do you mean, he poisoned the chocolate? Dillon? You think Dillon tried to poison the twins?" Brenda sounded shocked.

"Not Dillon. Of course not Dillon. You can't believe he shot Vivian! It was never Dillon," Jessica was impatient. "You'll have to call the helicopter, have them pick up the kids and take them to the hospital and tell them to bring the police." She had to get to the twins, hold them in her arms, make certain they were alive and well.

The next flash of lightning revealed the dark, hooded figure standing so silently in the corner. Jessica saw him clearly, saw the ugly little gun in his hand. The light faded away, but she knew he was there. Real. Solid. A sinister demented being bent on murder. Brenda gave a frightened cry and Jessica thrust the woman behind her. She felt her way along the instrument panel for the switch to turn on the recorder.

There was a moment of silence while the rain came down and the wind howled and tugged at the house. While the gargoyles watched silently from the eaves.

Jessica forced a small smile, forced a calmness she didn't feel. "I knew it was you. It's going to break his heart all over again." There was deep regret in her voice. The knowledge of such a betrayal would hurt Dillon immensely. Some part of Jessica had known all along, but she hadn't wanted to see it. For Dillon's sake.

"You didn't know," Paul denied, his face so deep inside the hood they couldn't see him. He presented a frightening image, the grim reaper. All he needed was a long-handled scythe to complete the persona of death.

"Of course it had to be you. No one but you would know that someone was trying to blackmail Dillon."

"Your mother," he spat, "was so greedy. The money he gave her to care for the children wasn't enough. I wrote the checks out to her—she had enough."

"Not my mother," Jessica snarled back. "Don was blackmailing Dillon. She came here at Dillon's request to discuss it with him."

"I don't understand," Brenda said. "Paul, what are you doing? Why are you standing in that stupid cape with a gun pointed at us? And you'd better not be naked under that thing! Everyone's being so melodramatic! What are you talking about? Why would anyone want to blackmail Dillon?"

Jessica ignored her. She didn't dare take her eyes off of Paul. He was unstable and she had no idea what could set him off. But she knew he was perfectly capable of killing. He had done so numerous times. "You were the only one it could be, Paul. You had access to all the rooms through the passageways. You're the only one who has been here on a regular basis. Once I realized the accidents were random, directed toward everyone here, I knew they were designed to send everyone away. The landslide, the Christmas tree, the oil on the stairs. Even the chocolate. You thought if enough things happened, we'd all go away. That's what you wanted, wasn't it? You just wanted everyone to stay away from here." Her voice was soothing, the voice she had used for years on the children, a blend of sweetness and understanding.

"But you wouldn't go away," he said. "You brought them back here. *Her* children. Vivian was evil, an evil disgusting seductress who wouldn't leave us all alone."

Jessica's heart thudded. She heard it in his voice, the guilt, the seething hatred. It always came back to Vivian. She knew then. Her heart bled for Dillon. So much treachery, how did one survive it? She wanted to weep for them all. There wasn't going to be any miracle for the twins or Dillon this Christmas, only more heartache, more tragedy.

"You loved her." She said it simply, starkly, saying the words in the dark to the man who had calmly walked up the stairs, shot Vivian and her lover in cold blood and locked the other occupants in the room after ensuring the fire was raging.

"I *hated* her! I *despised* her!" Paul hissed the words. "She seduced me. I begged her to leave me alone, but she would crawl into my bed and I could never stop myself. She laughed at me, and she threatened to tell Dillon. He was the only friend, the only family I ever had. I wasn't going to let her destroy me. Or him. Phillip deserved to die, he used her to get at Dillon. He thought Dillon would pay him to leave Vivian alone."

"Where would he get an idea like that?" Brenda was far too quiet and that worried Jessica. She glanced at the other woman but couldn't see her clearly in the dark.

"What does it matter? None of it matters. He chose you. When I knocked you off the bluff and slipped myself, he saved you, not me. I couldn't believe it. He was never worth it. All these wasted years. His genius. I served his greatness, cared for him, *protected* him, *killed* for him, and he fell for another harlot." Paul shook his head so that the hooded cloak moved as if alive. "I gave him everything, and he chose you." He snarled the last words at her, like a rabid dog wanting to strike out.

Jessica forced a derisive laugh. She was inching her fingers along the wall seeking the guitar, her only weapon. "Is that how you lie to yourself at night in order to sleep, Paul? You betrayed him by sleeping with his wife. You probably brought Phillip Trent into Vivian's life. You let Dillon go through a trial, knew everyone believed he committed murder and yet you could have stopped it by telling the truth. You were responsible for the fire that burned him. You murdered my mother thinking she was blackmailing him. You left him open to blackmail and you arranged accidents that could have killed his children just to frighten them away from him. How in the world is that giving him everything? You made him a prisoner in this house and when it looked as if he might break free you started all over again to try to isolate him from the rest of the world."

"Shut up!" Pure venom dripped from Paul's voice. "Just shut up!"

"The biggest mistake you made was going after the children. Your plan backfired. You must have intercepted my letter telling him the children should be with him. You didn't want them here, did you? They were a threat to you. You wanted me to think Dillon was trying to hurt them, didn't you?" She looked at him steadily. "But, you see, I know Dillon. I knew he would *never* have killed Vivian or my mother or done harm to his children. So I brought the children here, knowing he would try to protect them."

"And delivered them right to me," Paul snarled.

"Put the gun down, Paul." Dillon's voice was weary and sad, a melody of smoke and blues. "It's over. We have to figure out how best to handle this." Dillon moved through the doorway.

While Dillon was so calm, Jessica wanted to scream. Were the children writhing in agony upstairs, while they talked to a madman with a gun? Her fingers found the neck of the guitar, circled, and gripped hard.

"There is only one way to handle it, Dillon," Paul said just as calmly. "I'm not about to be locked up for the rest of my life. I couldn't stand being interviewed behind bars while the band makes it to the top again."

Jessica knew. She always knew before things happened, even though she had doubted herself. There in the darkness with the rain coming down, she knew the precise moment Paul shifted the gun. She knew he was finished talking and that his finger was squeezing the trigger. Without hesitation, Jessica stepped solidly in front of Dillon and swung the guitar toward Paul with every ounce of strength she possessed.

She heard the bark of the gun, the simultaneous crack of the guitar as she hit Paul hard, and Dillon's husky cry of denial even as something knocked her legs out from under her. Jessica hit her head hard on the floor. She lay still, staring up at the figure in the hooded cloak. He was bent over, twisted. She blinked to clear her vision. Everything seemed hazy, a weird phosphorescent light was seeping into the room, a mist of colors and cold. The draft was icy, so that she could see the air as a foggy vapor. It seemed to slide between Paul and the other occupants of the room.

Paul screamed, a hoarse dark cry of rage and fear. For one moment the colors shifted and moved, formed the shimmering, translucent image of a woman in a flowing gown reaching out a long thin arm beckoning toward Paul. Dillon moved then, covering Jessica's body with his own, blocking her view of the strange apparition, so that she only heard the gun as it went off a second time.

"Vivian, don't leave me again!" Brenda's cry was anguished and she stumbled forward, her arms outstretched. Dillon caught her, dragging her down to the safety of the floor.

Jessica heard the body fall with a soft thud to the floor, and she found herself staring into Paul's wide-open eyes. She knew he was dead, with the life already drained from his body before he hit the floor. In the end, he had been determined to take Dillon with him, and she had been just as determined he would not.

Brenda's weeping was soft and brokenhearted. "Did you see her, Jessica? I told you I wasn't crazy. Did you see her?"

Dillon kicked the gun away from Paul's hand. "Call the doctor, Brenda, right now!" His voice was pure authority, snapping Brenda out of her sorrow. "Check on Tara and Trevor—make certain they're all right. And then call the police." His hands were running over Jessica's legs, searching for a wound, searching for the bullet hole that had knocked her to the floor.

There was no blood, no gaping wound, only a huge dark bruise already forming on her left thigh. The area was tender, painful, but neither Dillon nor Jessica knew who had struck her hard enough to knock her legs out from under her. Brenda had stood frozen, unable to move. They both stared at the strange mark, two circles, one inside the other, the center circle much darker. A circle of protection.

"I have to see to Paul," he said and she heard the heartbreak in his voice.

"He's beyond help, Dillon. Don't touch anything,"

Jessica cautioned gently. Now that it was over she began to shake almost uncontrollably. Her need to get to the children was paramount. Her need to comfort Dillon was just as great. More than anything else she was afraid for him. This time the truth had to be plain. "Wait for the police."

chapter
14

THE WHITE BIRD WINGED its way across the wet sky. Far below, waves crashed against rock, foamed and sprayed, reaching toward the heavens, toward the small white dove as it flew with a glittering object in its beak.

"Jessie, get out of bed," Tara insisted, jarring Jessica right out of her happy dream. "It's Christmas Eve, you can't just stay in bed!"

Jessica turned over with a small groan and pulled the blanket firmly over her head. "Go away, I'm never getting up again."

She wasn't going to face Christmas Eve. She didn't want to see the disappointment on the faces of the twins. She didn't want to face Dillon. She had seen him when the police took Paul's body away, when he told the truth about what had happened. Dillon looked like a man lost, with his heart and soul torn out. Reporters had been brutal, swarming to the hospital, nearly rioting at the police station. So many pictures, so many microphones thrust at him. It had to have been a nightmare for him. It had been for her. The police had the recording Jessica had made as well as Brenda's and Jessica's statements to back up Dillon's. The crime scene people had come and gone. Paul was dead by his own hand. They all said so. By mutual consent, they kept their knowledge of the apparition to themselves. There was no need to complicate the story to the police or the newspapers. And who would ever believe them?

"Jessie, really, get up," Tara dragged at the covers.

"I'll get her up," Dillon told his daughter gently. "You go play hostess, Tara. Tell everyone your Christmas story. They all need a feel-good story tonight. And Brian's made a special Christmas Eve feast. I believe he made pancakes."

Tara giggled as her father walked her to the door. "Not his famous pancakes! What a shocker." She leaned over to kiss his forehead as she went out.

Jessica heard the door close firmly and the lock turn. There was a mysterious rustle and then the room was flooded with music. Soft, beautiful strains of music. The swelling passion of the song she and Dillon had worked on so hard. She blinked back tears and sat up as he crossed the room to sit on the edge of her bed. The light was off and the room was dark, only the sliver of moon providing them with a streak of a silvery glow.

Jessica drew up her knees, rested her chin on them. "So what now, Dillon?" She asked it quietly, facing the worst, prepared for his rejection. He hadn't talked with her, hadn't come near her in days. He'd spent most of the time on the mainland.

Dillon reached out to her, his palm cupping her chin,

skin to skin. She realized then, that he wasn't wearing his gloves. "It's Christmas Eve, we wait for our miracle," he told her gently. "Don't tell me after believing all this time, you've suddenly had a crisis of faith." His thumb brushed along her chin, a slow sensual movement that made her shiver with awareness of him.

Jessica swept a trembling hand through her hair as it tumbled around her face. "I don't know what I think anymore, Dillon. I feel numb right now." It wasn't altogether true. When she looked at him, every part of her came alive. Heat coursed through her body, while her heart did a somersault and a multitude of butterfly wings brushed at the pit of her stomach. "I thought, with all that has happened, that . . ." she trailed off miserably. No matter what she said, it would be hurtful to him. How could she admit she thought he would retreat from her, from Trevor and Tara?

Dillon's smile was incredibly tender. "You didn't really think I would be so incredibly stupid as to send you and the children away again, did you? I wouldn't deserve you, Jess, if I'd been thinking of doing something that thick-skulled. I don't know that I deserve you now, but you offered and I'm holding on tight with both hands." He rubbed the bridge of his nose, suddenly looking vulnerable. "I thought about things, sitting up in my room, about treachery and betrayal and about letting life pass me by. I thought about courage and what it means. Courage was Don coming to me when he didn't have to and telling me how idiotic he had been. Courage was him willing to be kicked out of the band or even prosecuted. Courage is Brenda and Robert learning how to be an aunt and uncle to two children they are secretly terrified of. Courage is Brian standing in that kitchen and telling me his beliefs."

His hands framed her face. "Courage is a woman stepping between a man and death. You fought for me, Jess, even when I wouldn't do it myself. I'm not walking away from that. I'll never play the guitar again like I did, but I still have my voice and I still can write and produce songs. I have two children you gave back to me and God willing, I hope we have more. Tell me I still have you."

She melted into him, a long slow kiss that stole her breath and took her heart, that told him everything he wanted to know.

"Everyone's waiting for you," he whispered against her mouth.

Jessica hugged him hard, leapt out of bed, rushed for the bathroom. "Ten minutes," she called over her shoulder, "I have to shower." She peeled off her pajama top and flung it toward a chair.

Dillon's breath hitched in his throat as he saw her drawstring pants slide over the tempting curve of her bottom just as she disappeared into the other room. He stood up, a slow smile softening the edge of his mouth as he tossed his own shirt aside. He padded on bare feet to the bathroom door to watch her as she stepped under the cascade of hot water. She turned her head toward him just as he slowly pushed his jeans away from his hardened body. At once her gaze was on his heavy erection. Knowing she was looking hardened him more so that the ache grew and his need was instant and urgent.

"You missed me," she greeted, her smile pure invitation. The moment he stepped into the large compartment, she wrapped her hand around his thickness, warm and tight. "I missed you."

His hands moved over every inch of her he could touch, marveling that she could want him the way she did. Dillon caught the nape of her neck and turned up her head to fasten his mouth to hers. He wasn't gentle. He didn't feel gentle. He wanted to devour her. He fed there, his hands cupping her breasts, his thumbs circling her nipples.

She was driving him crazy with her bold caresses, stroking him even as her mouth was mating with his. Hot silken kisses; the earth spinning madly. The water running over their bodies and the steam rising around them. She was soft and pliant, as her body moved against his. One leg slid up to the curve of his hip, she pressed close, as wild as he was.

Dillon bent his head to the terrible bruise on her shoulder where Paul's elbow had cracked her hard enough to send her flying toward the edge of a cliff. His tongue eased the throbbing ache, and traveled lower to trace the outline of her breast. He felt her tremble in reaction. His mouth closed over her hard nipple, his teeth teasing gently before he suckled strongly. She gasped in reaction, arcing more fully into him. His hand shaped her every curve, slid lower to push into her body. She was wet and pulsing with her own need and he wanted all the time in the world to love her. To just lie beside her and bring her so much pleasure so she would know what she meant to him.

Jessica leaned forward to catch a little drop of water that ran from his shoulder to the muscles of his chest. She wasn't fast enough. Her tongue followed the little bead of moisture as it traveled across the ridges over his heart. She couldn't quite catch up and her arms slipped around his waist as she ducked her head to lap at the droplet, racing it over his flat belly. Her hand was still wrapped proprietarily around his heavy erection. She felt him swell more, thick, and hard, as she breathed warm air over him, as her tongue lapped at the droplets on his most sensitive tip.

Dillon went rigid, his body shuddering with pleasure as she took him into the heat of her mouth. The water cascaded down, sensitizing his skin. The roar started in his brain, the fire burned in his gut, a sweet ecstasy that shook him. Strains of their music penetrated into the shower, and fired his blood even more with the driving, impassioned beat. Her hips moved against his hand, her muscles were tight and clenching around his fingers.

"Jess." He said her name. Called to her. A pleading. A promise. "I need you now, this minute." Because there was nowhere else he would rather be than in her, with her, a part of her.

Her green gaze slid over him as she straightened. Took in every inch of him, the perfection of his face, the scars on his body, his heavy, thick evidence of his need for her. And she smiled in welcome. In happiness. Deliberately she turned and placed her hands carefully on the small half bench in the corner, presenting her rounded bottom and the smooth line of her back.

His hands went to her hips as he pulsed against her. She was more than ready for him, slick and hot and as eager as he was. Even as he pushed into her tight sheath, she pushed back, so that he filled her with a single surge. Molten lava raced through her, through him. He groaned, began to move hard and fast, thrusting deeply, wildly, a frenzy of white-hot pleasure for both of them. She was meeting every stroke, demanding more, her body gripping his, clenching and building a fiery friction that shook him all the way to his soul. And then she was rippling around him, milking him of his seed, so that his own orgasm ripped through him with such intensity her name was torn from his throat.

She always managed to surprise him. His Jessica, so unafraid of life, of passion, of showing her true feelings. She cried out with her release, her body spiraling out of control and she gave herself up to the pleasure, embraced it the way she did everything. It seemed to last forever. It seemed over far too fast. They collapsed together, holding each other, kissing each other, their hands greedy for the feel of each other's body.

Dillon caught her hair in his hand. "I can't get enough of kissing you." His mouth devoured her ravenously. "More, I need more."

"I thought you said everyone was waiting for us. It's been a lot longer than ten minutes," Jessica pointed out. "They'll send the twins."

"Promise me when you marry me, which will be very, very soon, I can spend a couple of weeks in bed with you. Just touching you. I love the way you feel." He reached past her to turn off the water.

Jessica stilled, stared up at him with the water running off her lashes. "You never mentioned marriage."

Dillon blinked down at her, managed to look boyishly

vulnerable. "I'm old-fashioned, I thought you knew I meant for life." He looked around, saw his jeans carelessly discarded on the floor. "I have a ring." He said it like a bribe.

"Dillon!" Flustered, Jessica wrapped her hair in a towel, staring at him wide-eyed. "You have a ring?"

She looked so beautiful with the confusion on her face, with the water beading on her petal soft skin and her large eyes bright with happiness, Dillon wanted to start all over again. He found the ring in his pocket and caught her hand. "I want us to be forever, Jess, forever."

The diamond sparkled at her as she smiled down at it. Then he was catching her up, throwing her on the bed in a tangle of sheets and arms and legs, his tongue lapping at every bead of water on her skin.

It was considerably longer than either of them expected before they were dressed and ready to join the others. Jessica's face was slightly red from the shadow on Dillon's jaw and the insides of her thighs held matching abrasions. She went with him willingly, confidently. Together they could manage to bring off Christmas.

She stopped in the doorway of the large room where the tree had been set up. Hundreds of tiny lights were woven in and out of the branches, highlighting the ornaments they had all made.

"So this is what you've been doing all this time," Jessica whispered, joy coursing through her as she looked at the lights on the Christmas tree, at the mound of brightly wrapped presents beneath the branches. "You've been playing Santa Claus."

He grinned at her, with his boyish, mischievous grin.

"I'm into the miracle business in a big way these days. I couldn't let Tara and Trevor be disappointed. They wanted their father back, didn't they?"

Jessica wrapped her arms around his neck and claimed his oh-so-beautiful mouth. Happiness blossomed inside of her. She had thought Paul's betrayal would have been the last straw, that it would have broken Dillon's spirit totally. Instead he had emerged to the other side, whole once more.

His kiss was gentle, relaxed, tasting of passion and hunger. Behind them Trevor groaned. "Are you two going to be doing that all night, because there are other rooms where you can be alone, in case you hadn't noticed."

"Don't tell them that," Brian slapped Trevor on the back. "We'll never have Christmas if you give them any ideas."

Dillon took his time, kissing Jessica. It mattered, kissing did, and he made a thorough job of it while the twins tapped their feet and the band members nudged one another. He lifted his head slowly, and smiled down into her upturned face. "I love you, Jessica, more than I can ever express, I love you."

She touched his mouth with a trembling fingertip. "Surprise! I love you right back." She would count that as her Christmas miracle. Dillon. Her other half.

"Dad!" Tara squeaked impatiently. "We all know what's going on here, so don't keep us in suspense. Are you or aren't you?"

Dillon and Jessica turned to look at the expectant faces gathered around them. "What are you talking about?" He put his arm around Jessica's shoulders, drawing her into the shelter of his body.

Trevor threw his hands up in the air. "So much for being suave. Jeeze, Dad, get a clue here. A little action on your part, you know?"

Don shook his head. "You disappoint me, Wentworth."

"Boyo," Brian slumped against the wall, a hand to his head. "You've destroyed my faith in true love."

Brenda stepped forward, caught Jessica's wrist and yanked her left hand up to their faces. "Oh, for heaven's sake, you are the most unobservant group on the face of the earth!" The ring glittered beneath the light.

"Holy cow, Dad," Trevor grinned from ear to ear. "You're amazing. I apologize. Profusely."

Jessica was kissed and hugged until Dillon rescued her, pulling her to him and waving the others off with a good-natured scowl. He turned off the overhead lights so that only the twinkling Christmas lights shone. A multitude of colors sparkled and glowed. "It's midnight. We should sing Christmas in," he announced, leaning down to steal another kiss.

Brenda settled close to Robert, resting her head on his chest. Brian sat across from the couple, on the floor, stretching out his long legs toward the tree. Don followed suit, dropping to the floor, his back against the couch, sprawling out, leaning back to look at the lights.

Dillon laced his fingers through Jessica's as he sat in the large armchair and pulled her beside him. Tara and Trevor immediately found a place on the floor close to their father and Jessica. Robert reached behind the chair where he was sitting and casually pulled out an acoustic guitar. Dillon's oldest, not expensive, but one he had carried with him for years. Robert handed it across the floor to Trevor who held it out to his father.

"Play for us tonight, Dad," Trevor said.

Jessica could feel Dillon stiffen beside her. He shook his head, took the guitar out of his son's hand and tried to give it to Jessica. "You play. I don't play anymore."

"Yes, you do," Jessica said, ignoring the instrument, "you just don't play for large crowds. We're family. All of us here together tonight. We're you're family, Dillon, and it's okay to be imperfect. Just play, don't be great, just play for us."

Dillon looked into her eyes. Green eyes. Guileless. Sincere. He glanced at the others watching him while he made his decision. The lights flickered and shimmied, winking at him as if in encouragement. He didn't have to do it all himself, he didn't have to be perfect. Sometimes people did get second chances. With a small sigh, he capitulated, bringing the guitar to him, cradling it in his arms like a lost lover. His longtime companion. His childhood friend when he was lonely. A small smile curved his mouth as he felt the familiar texture, the grain of the wood, the wide neck.

His fingers found the strings; his ear listened to the sound. He made the adjustments automatically, without thinking. He lived and breathed music: the notes that took on a life in his head. He still had that, a gift beyond comparison. He had his voice. It spilled out of him, his signature, a blend of edgy smoke and husky blues. He sang of hope and joy, love found, and families together. While he sang, his fingers found the familiar chords, moved over the strings with a remembered love. He didn't have the dexterity to play the fast riffs and the intricate melodies he often heard in his mind and composed, but he could do this, play for his family, and take pleasure in the gift of love.

They sang with him, all those he loved. Jessica's voice blended with his, in a perfect melding. Brenda was slightly out of tune, but he loved her all the more for it. Tara's voice held promise and Trevor's held enthusiasm. The pleasure of sitting in his home, surrounded by his family on Christmas Eve, was incomparable. His miracle.

A slight noise at the window distracted Jessica from the music and she frowned, looking beyond the glass pane to the darkened, wild storm. There was a small fluttering of white that settled on the outside windowsill. A storm-tossed bird, perhaps lost in the dark of night and the violence of the squall.

"There's a bird at the window," Jessica said softly, afraid if she spoke too loudly the white dove would vanish before anyone else saw it. She made her way with caution across the room while the others stayed motionless. "Birds aren't out at this time of night. Did it fly into the window?"

The bird looked bedraggled—a wet, unhappy, shivering dove. Jessica carefully opened the window, crooning to the creature, not wanting to frighten it away. To her astonishment, it waited calmly on the windowsill while she struggled to push one side of the window out against the fierce wind. Almost at once, the bird hopped onto her arm. She could feel it shaking, and immediately cupped its body in the warmth of her palms. It was carrying something in its beak. She could just make out the glint of gold between her hands. There was something else: a band on its leg. Jessica felt it drop into her palm as the bird rose, flapped its wings, and launched itself into the air. It flew around the room. As the bird passed over the twins, it opened its beak and dropped something between the twins. The bird made another fast circuit of the room while the lights played over its white feathers in a prism of colors that was mesmerizing and beautiful. The dove flew out the window, back into the night, winging its way toward some other shelter.

"What is it, Tara?" Trevor leaned in close as his sister lifted a gold chain for all of them to see. "It's a locket." It was small, heart-shaped, and intricately etched on the outside.

"I think it's real gold," Trevor said, lifting it up to peer at it more closely.

"Is it for me? Did someone get this for me? Where did this come from?" Tara looked around the room at the band members who had fallen silent as she held up the necklace. "Who gave it to me?"

Dillon leaned forward to get a closer look. Brenda's hand went to her throat in a curiously vulnerable gesture. Her gaze met Dillon's across the small space and she quickly shook her head. "I didn't, Dillon, I swear I didn't."

"It opens, doesn't it?" Trevor wrapped his arm around his sister's shoulder and peered at the delicate locket. "What's inside?"

Tara pressed the tiny catch and the locket popped open. There were two smiling faces, a two-year-old girl and an identical two-year-old boy. Both children were smiling. Their black, wavy hair framing their faces.

"Dad?" Tara looked at her father. "It's us, isn't it?"

Dillon nodded solemnly. "Your mother never took that necklace off. I didn't even know the pictures were inside of it."

Tara turned to Jessica, an awkward, uncertain expression on her young face. She didn't know what to think or feel about such a gift. Everyone was stunned, and had shocked looks on their faces. She didn't know whether to hug the locket to her, or to throw it away and cry a river of tears.

Jessica immediately hugged her. "What a beautiful gift. It is a day of miracles. Every child should know their mother wanted and loved them. I remember how precious that locket was to your mother. She wore it always, even when she had much more expensive jewelry. I think the necklace is proof of what she felt for you, even when she was too ill to show you."

Brenda caught Jessica's hand and squeezed it tightly. "Vivian always wore it, Tara—I teased her about her preferring it to diamonds. She said she had her reasons." Tears glittered in her eyes. "I know why now. I would never have taken it off either."

Tara kissed her aunt. "I'm glad you're here, Aunt Brenda," she confided. "I love you." She handed her the necklace. "Will you put it on me?"

Brenda nodded, her heart overflowing. "Absolutely I will."

"It was for both of us, Trev," Tara said. "She loved both of us after all. We'll share it." She leaned over to kiss her brother on the cheek.

Jessica settled in Dillon's lap, waited until the others were crowded around the twins, and she slowly opened her hand to show him what lay in her palm. The small ring was a mother's ring with two identical birthstones in it. They looked from the ring to one another without speaking.

Jessica closed her fingers around the precious gift the dove had left behind. It was better than diamonds. The most important gift ever given. Dillon's scarred fingers settled over hers, guarding the treasure, holding it close to their hearts. Trevor and Tara were theirs. They had their Christmas miracle and it was exactly what they needed.

LADY
OF THE
LOCKET

Melanie George

chapter

1

THE CASTLE ROSE OUT of the heavy mist like a phoenix emerging from the ashes, a looming monolith seemingly born of its craggy foundation, perched on the uppermost edge of the earth for the purpose of lording over the village in the distance.

A trio of crenellated towers reached for the sky, where slim fingers of scarlet-tinted sunlight endeavored to wedge through the damp December fog that enshrouded the entire jagged coast of Inverness, Scotland.

To Rachel Hudson, who had stopped her rental car in the long gravel-strewn driveway leading to the front steps of Glengarren, the castle echoed of things past, of secrets long held—imposing, yet somehow tragic.

The sight left her breathless as she pushed open the car door and got out, letting the brisk winter air sting her cheeks and whip at her long hair.

An acute sense of isolation struck her, an almost palpable aura that warned people to stay away, to turn around and hasten from its unhallowed grounds.

Rachel could picture a tormented Heathcliff ranging its windswept moors, or imagine that she caught a glimpse of a woman's ghostly figure disappearing among the ramparts, as in *Rebecca*, Rachel's favorite novel, by Daphne du Maurier.

"'When the leaves rustle, they sound very much like the stealthy movement of a woman in evening dress,'" she softly recited. "'And when they shiver suddenly and fall, and scatter away along the ground, they might be the pitter-patter of a woman's hurrying footsteps, and the mark in the gravel the imprint of a high-heeled satin shoe.'"

Rachel felt as though she finally understood what her parents had found so fascinating about this place, its mien of romance mingled with bittersweet despair.

Her mother and father had met here thirty-one years ago. Her mother had come to spend Christmas with relatives, and her father had been visiting his old college friend, Ian MacGregor of Glengarren.

Her parents' paths had crossed and they fell in love during that magical holiday. The following year, they returned to Scotland together, marrying twelve months to the day after they had met.

They had planned to return this year to celebrate their thirtieth wedding anniversary, but it wasn't to be. In June, six months after her mother had been diagnosed with end-stage breast cancer, she had died. Five months after that, and two weeks before Thanksgiving, her father had passed away. A massive heart attack, the doctors said.

Rachel didn't believe a heart attack had been the cause of her father's death, but rather a broken heart. He had not been the same after his wife had died. Her passing had ravaged him. Now, they were together again. And soon Rachel would carry out her parents' last request.

She did her best to shake off the pall of sorrow threatening to overcome her, and climbed back in the car. Windows that resembled lifeless eyes glittered out at her as she proceeded up the sloped and pitted driveway, a coil of disquiet settling in the base of her stomach.

No one came out to greet her as she drew to a stop at the front door, but she didn't expect anyone to. The castle and grounds would be hers alone to explore, courtesy of the current owner of Glengarren, the son of her father's friend.

She had met the elder Lord MacGregor once when he had come to America to visit her father some ten years earlier, but she had never met his son. Yet it was his son who occupied Rachel's thoughts at that moment, as she remembered his condolence letter, filled with compassion, his words reaching across the distance to console her.

Perhaps he understood her grief so well because his own father was now ill, removed to Edinburgh, to a nursing facility that could monitor his health, and the devastating effects of his decline from Alzheimer's disease.

Troubled by thoughts of illness and death, Rachel sought a familiar comfort, taking hold of the locket around her neck—a very special keepsake that had once belonged to her mother. The pendant gave her strength, infused her with courage when her own faltered, as it did now.

She prayed she would find what she was looking for here, the solace she so desperately needed to ease her sore heart . . . and the closure that would help her move forward.

She removed her luggage from the trunk of the car, but hesitated, glancing toward the cliff. Over the crest, she could just make out the faintest glimmer of the River Ness, curving like a serpent's gray back, whitecapped by the lashing winds as it flowed toward the sea.

Through a break in the mist stood a rowan tree, balanced precariously at the edge of a three-hundred-foot precipice, its gnarled limbs reaching toward the heavens, as if seeking surcease from the air of tragedy bending its branches.

That was the spot, Rachel thought, the place where she would fulfill her parents' last wish and sprinkle their ashes, letting them drift out to sea on their anniversary, together forever.

With a lump in her throat, Rachel turned away and lugged her suitcase to the front door, pausing to reach under an upturned clay pot, locating the key exactly where Lord MacGregor had told her it would be.

After unlocking the heavy wooden portal with its intricate carvings, she pushed it open. The hinges creaked, as if oiling had been long forgotten and rust had become a familiar friend.

A rush of cold air swept through the mostly shadowed room, stirring her hair, causing her flesh to shiver and a sense of foreboding to tap at her subconscious.

Ridiculous, of course. While there was reported to be more ghosts haunting these aging premises than any other place in the world, she had never been one to believe in such Poe-esque tales—things that go bump in the night had never sent her fleeing into her parents' arms or caused her to hide, trembling, under her blankets.

Again the air moved. A haze of dust motes danced and collided in the stream of dim light filtering through the heavy drapes on the windows, and with this stirring came a hint of mustiness—a certain indication that the castle had been unoccupied for a while.

Rachel glimpsed a movement out of the corner of her eye; something scurrying into the gathering shadows by the far wall. A rat? A cat? Or simply a figment of her imagination brought on by the gloom of her surroundings?

A prickling of unease raised goose bumps on her arms as she fanned away the dust that lingered in front of her face. With a deep, nervous breath, she stepped over the threshold.

There she stopped in her tracks, her bag dropping to the floor with a dull thud that resonated through the cavernous space like a gunshot and rattled loose windowpanes.

It was as though she had crossed a portal into another era, a time when harried servants in tattered clothes scampered over rush-strewn floors to do their master's bidding, and kilted Highlanders restlessly paced its armament-laden hallways, preparing for some skirmish against a rival clan.

A huge, circular foyer with a vaulted, buttressed ceiling surrounded her, and a U-shaped staircase ascended to the second floor. In darkened corners, snarling stone gargoyles peered down at her from their lofty perches.

On the walls hung Flemish tapestries, yellowed by age and moth-eaten, detailed yet fading, dating back—she suspected—hundreds of years or more.

Her eye then followed a ribbon of nebulous light to a spot between the arms of the staircase, and there, her heart gave an unexpected stutter.

Bathed in the hazy illumination and braced upon the wall, an enormous oil painting of a virile Highland warrior stared down at her—eyes of the most penetrating shade of blue burning straight through her, seemingly alive as they regarded her from that rugged face, tracking her every move as she walked across the foyer, as if pulled by some invisible force.

The man forever captured on the canvas had a commanding presence, a combination of arrogance and confidence that was clearly delineated on his chiseled features.

He was rigged out in full regalia, one hand resting on the jewel-encrusted hilt of the sword sheathed at his hip, the words *GRACE ME GOD* etched into the glittering blade. His kilt barely covered heavily muscled thighs and his linen shirt spread taut across a firm chest and broad shoulders.

Against a backdrop of cliff's edge and sky, the artist had imbued an aura of wind into the portrait, blowing the warrior's wild skein of jet-black hair over his shoulders, hair that looked raked by impatient hands. Rachel could almost feel its texture between her fingertips, and shivered as a chill breath of air glided over her skin.

"It's just a painting," she chided herself, then forced her gaze away, letting it drift downward to the brass plaque at the bottom of the ornate gilt frame. "Duncan MacGregor, 1745. A mighty Scotsman who battled a kingdom for the House of Stuart." Her eyes lifted and locked with his. He looked every inch the hero, she thought—and every inch the epitome of women's fantasies.

"I see ye've met the master."

With a startled gasp, Rachel whirled around to find a stooped old man lingering in the shadows behind her. His face grizzled, he peered at her with one eye squinted, the right side of his mouth frozen in a grimace. She took a step backward, her heart climbing into her throat.

"Frightened ye, have I?" He shook his head and shuffled toward her, dragging his right leg while his right arm dangled uselessly at his side. "Must learn tae announce myself," he said in a voice made breathless by his efforts to walk. "The missus is always tellin' me I creep up on folks like Hamlet's ghost."

Encircled with an air of stale smoke, he stopped before her. "Name's Fergus Osgood. I'm the caretaker of Glengarren." He glanced around and gave a grunt of disapproval. "Not that I'm up tae much caretakin' these days—not since my stroke." Cutting his gaze back to hers, he said, "Ye must be Mistress Hudson."

Rachel managed a weak nod, as unnerved by the man's frightening aspect as she was by his sudden appearance.

He gestured toward the painting. "Fine lookin' man was our Duncan." He tugged a rag from his back pocket and whisked away a layer of dust that had settled along the frame.

"Who is he?" she asked, her attention diverted.

"The man who built Glengarren."

Rachel's curiosity about Duncan MacGregor momentarily eclipsed her discomfort, and she wondered if the old tome she had discovered in a small bookstore the day before would have more information about him.

The book was a detailed history of the MacGregor clan. She had bought it, thinking to familiarize herself with her host's ancestors. The story, however, only went as far as 1965, and would give her no information about the current lord of the castle.

Fergus tucked the rag back into his pocket, then turned his attention on Rachel again, his expression somber, his good eye regarding her with an intensity that made her acutely uncomfortable.

"Is there a problem, Mr. Osgood?"

He squinted and ran his hand over his mouth. "Aye," he admitted, nodding. "I told the young MacGregor when he called tae tell me ye was comin' that this ain't no place for a woman alone. House is too damn queer. Local folks don't come 'round here—least those with good sense, anyways. Too much history, ye see. Too much woe."

Rachel glanced around the vast chamber, dark and looming, and fresh shivers raced up her spine. "Are you saying the place is haunted?"

"If ever there was a place that had a right tae be, 'tis this one." He shuffled closer. "Ye look like an intelligent woman, and bein' from America, yer no doubt accustomed tae comfort. Ye'll find no comfort here.

"Half the bloody time the electricity don't work—comes and goes as it pleases, and even when it's workin', it don't warm this place or light it worth a spit. Ain't nothin' of this good earth that can help dispel this cold and gloom. If ye've got any smarts at all, ye'll climb back in yer car and take ye a room in the village. Leave these dreary walls and lonely shadows tae the souls who've occupied Glengarren for the last centuries."

Rachel tamped down her growing apprehension and forced a light smile to her face. "I'm accustomed to being alone, Mr. Osgood, and I don't believe in ghosts. I'll stay, thank you."

A moment of silence passed as he regarded her, not exactly with an expression of disfavor, she noted, but more of concern, which bothered her even more.

"Suit yerself," he finally said with a shrug, reaching for her suitcase and starting toward the stairs, a corner of her bag dragging on the floor, the sound like a whisper as it shifted along the walls.

Rachel had no choice but to follow, her gaze darting about, awed by the sheer size and magnitude of the castle as they reached the second floor.

Here the cold bit at her, teeth-sharp and marrow-chilling, making her bones ache and her skin quiver. She hugged herself, endeavoring not to think about how she would soon be alone in these empty, rambling corridors.

She cast a nervous glance over her shoulder, as if expecting to find someone lurking there—a figure, ghostly pale and still as death.

Yet nothing but endless shifting shadows greeted her. Still, she couldn't shake the sensation of being watched, as though eyes followed her through slits in one of the paintings. Obviously, she was allowing Fergus's moni-tions to bother her more than she should.

Fergus rattled off details as they headed down the long corridor. "Twenty-two rooms there are," he said. "Most of the castle is original and in middlin' shape, but I warn ye now tae keep out of the east wing."

"What's the matter with the east wing?"

"Ain't nothin' but ruins. Burnt down somewheres in the eighteenth century. The current master's great-great-great-grandfather, or some such, tried tae restore it, but none of the workers hired tae do the job would stay beyond the first few days."

"Why?"

"Can't rightly say." His head turned, one steely eye peering at her over his shoulder. "Though there's them as say that somethin' don't want that section rebuilt."

"Something? As in a ghost?"

He shrugged and looked away. "Don't know. Only repeatin' what I heard."

Rachel refused to be intimidated by Fergus's claims of spooks, though she hurried to catch up to him when he got a few paces ahead of her.

"Keep an eye about ye when dark weather rolls in," he said then. "Stay indoors."

"What kind of weather?" she asked.

"Lightning, mostly. Place is famous for it, sittin' as it is on the highest rise above the river. Those bloody tow-ers invite trouble, thrust so defiantly toward heaven as they are. Almost as if Glengarren is shakin' its fist at God."

Was the man purposely trying to scare her? Or was his

perpetual voice of gloom and doom merely a facet of his personality?

He motioned down the long corridor. "Most of the rooms is closed off, as there ain't nobody stayin' here since the master's father took ill. But I had a room cleaned for ye. On a clear day, ye can see all the way down tae Culloden Moor." He stopped and pushed open one of the doors with his foot. "This is it."

"Oh, my . . ." Rachel murmured, her eyes widening as she scanned the murk-stricken room, a single ray of gray light filtering through the dark burgundy drapes that swallowed the floor-to-ceiling windows.

An enormous four-poster bed commanded attention in the center of the room, swathed in a canopy that matched the drapes. A massive fireplace dominated the length of one wall, the hearth charred by eons of soot that lent an acrid smell to the air.

"Ye'll be needin' that tae warm yerself on cold nights," Fergus said when she moved to stand in front of the empty grate. "And we have plenty of them—cold nights, I mean. I stacked up some logs and kindlin' for ye."

"Thank you." Rachel rubbed her arms for warmth, but the chill went deeper, and felt as if it had become a permanent part of her.

Fergus deposited her suitcase on the bed while she drifted to the window, parting the curtains to look out at the view, or what little she could see of it, cloaked as it was in a mist that crept across the landscape like a living entity.

Though nearly noon, the sky had darkened severely. Beyond the patches of descending fog, the black clouds roiled just above the treetops. The air felt ominously still, and heavy.

Fergus scuffled up beside her, his gaze wandering the moors, his wizened face creased with worry. "Looks like we're in for it. Gets this way now and again—cold collidin' with heat. They're comin' late this year—the storms, I mean. The missus says it's 'cause of that El Niño. Maybe." He shrugged. "Maybe not. Weather 'round here been strange for a while. Damn air feels electrified half the time. Hard to breathe. More so here at Glengarren," he added, sliding a wary glance in her direction, to which she tried to show no reaction, even though that look chilled her.

He shifted his gaze, bringing her attention to the octagonal dovecote by the west side of the house. "Six-hundred-forty nesting boxes it has," he told her. "Though there ain't no doves in there now—nor any mongrels in the kennel. Haven't been none of either since the old master's son lived here. He's a fancy lawyer in Edinburgh now. Reckon he finds the gloom of this old place depressin' compared tae the glitter of the city. Good lad, though. Came tae see his father whenever he could. That's his room there across the hall."

Rachel glanced over her shoulder at the closed door across from hers, then looked at Fergus. "So is that where he is now? In Edinburgh?"

"Aye. Brought his father there tae keep the old gent close by." Fergus shook his head. "Sad it is, all comin' tae an end like this. First the elder gettin' ill, and now the castle passin' from the family. Ye're the last guest. The master is givin' it tae the town of Inverness as an historical land-mark, which it rightly is, mind ye.

"'Tis said Bonnie Prince Charles once stayed here for two days shortly afore the ragin' battle of Culloden Moor." Fergus pointed toward a tall cairn in the distance. "Many a restless Scottish spirit resides beneath the soil of Culloden. Brave men who fought and died for what they believed in. It's them very souls who roam these grounds . . . accordin' tae some."

A chill washed over Rachel, as did a pang of sadness as she thought about all the lost souls interred in a mass grave, outnumbered nearly two to one in that bloody bat-tle, if she recalled correctly.

"'Tis a shame, I tell ye. Glengarren has been owned by one MacGregor or the other for over two-hundred-fifty years. His lordship—a right handsome lad, if I say so m'self—still don't have himself a missus. No MacGregor heir tae carry on the family name." Fergus sighed. "'Tis a shame indeed."

It seemed a shame to Rachel as well, and infinitely bit-tersweet, like something coming to an end that shouldn't be. Now, more than ever, she was glad she had taken the trip to Scotland. This was Glengarren's last Christmas, and Rachel would, in some way, be able to share this with her parents.

"What are those?" she asked, gesturing to a ring of mist-shrouded stones standing erect near the bluff.

Fergus's cheeks drained of color, and he backed away from the window. "Those be the Destiny Stones," he said in a muted voice.

Destiny Stones. The name conjured up images as dark

and mysterious as everything else she had encountered thus far. "How long have they been there?"

"'Tis claimed they were erected in the time of the druids."

Rachel had read about such stones. Supposedly, prophets and sorcerers used them during sacred rituals, the circle possessing some sort of mythical symbolism.

"'Twas near that very spot Duncan MacGregor was cut down. Story is, he was laid tae rest amid that ring of stones. His survivin' army buried him there in the hopes the magic of them rocks would bring him back—in spirit, if not in body—so he could lead them into the fray against stinkin' Willy, the Hanoverian king."

An image arose in Rachel's mind of the magnificent Highland warrior depicted on the canvas downstairs. How tragic to have been killed in the very shadow of his home.

For a moment, she allowed her romantic heart to overcome her practical mind and wonder what it would have been like to know such a man, someone fierce and brave, who fought for the things he believed in, and who would give his life for those he loved.

Rachel suspected he would love just as fiercely as he had lived, though he would not give his heart lightly. But when he finally did, he would bestow it fully, without restrictions or reservations.

What might it feel like to be loved in such a way? To be so completely a part of another person? To know a soul-deep devotion, like the kind her parents had once shared?

She was twenty-seven now, and had begun to doubt

she would ever find someone she could trust with her heart. There had always been something missing in the men she had dated, few and far between as they were.

Or perhaps the problem lay with her. Perhaps she simply wanted too much—her expectations of what the man of her dreams would be like too high. As yet, no man had come close.

"Well, I'll leave ye tae yer unpacking," Fergus said, breaking into Rachel's musing. "But first I'll get a fire goin' for ye."

With surprising efficiency, he had the hearth ablaze in minutes, and Rachel eagerly warmed her hands in front of the crackling flames.

"I'll come by and check on ye in a day or so and see how ye're farin'. The larder's been filled, so ye need not worry about that. I only live about a mile down the road, if ye need me." He eyed her for a long moment, as if hesitant to leave. Then finally he turned, giving her one more uneasy glance over his shoulder before shuffling out, the door groaning shut behind him.

Rachel shook off the disturbing feeling Fergus's look had left her with and regarded her suitcase with ambivalence. As if compelled, her gaze drifted back to the view outside the window, to the ominous ring of standing stones.

She shivered as strange sounds carried to her on the wind, raising the hair on the back of her neck. She admonished herself, certain Fergus's dire statements had played tricks on her mind.

And yet, she felt as though she could really hear the muted clash of steel against steel, the distant shouts of men, of chaos, of a battle to the bitter end . . . and the bellowing war cry of a solitary male voice.

A man fighting savagely to save all he held dear.

WITH MIDNIGHT CAME THE WINDS, moaning through the eaves and battering the ramparts with frigid fists, chilled air seeping through cracks.

Rachel lay bundled beneath the down comforter, shivering, too cold to focus on the old book she had purchased the day before. It lay forgotten on her lap as thoughts of her parents occupied her, remembering how they had once embraced these primitive surroundings.

Certainly, there was a romance about the place that intrigued her as well, filling her with an odd restlessness, an inexplicable eagerness to traipse the winding hallways and snoop through the dusty alcoves.

Still, the prospect of exploration did not alleviate the nagging sense of disquiet she felt in that moment. The import of her staying here, alone, sunk into her every nerve ending as soon as Fergus had departed.

Again came the wind, slamming against the windows. Then a sound . . .

Swallowing, Rachel jerked upright against the pillows, starting violently when the banging sounded once more.

Sliding from the bed, her feet landing gently upon the cold floor, she crept toward the closed bedroom door, one hand clutching her flannel pajama top, the other shaking slightly as she tugged at the tarnished knob that clicked and creaked as she turned it.

Darkness loomed. A scurry of wind rushed at her

from nowhere and crept up her pajama legs like damp, icy talons, making her tremble.

Afraid to breathe, she moved down the corridor, apprehension curling around her. The noise came again, intermingling with the rattle of the wind, lifting the hair on her nape and brushing her face.

Soon the foyer opened up around her, lit by a solitary iron lamp on the wall, a twisted multipronged girandole that had been renovated to burn flame-shaped bulbs as opposed to tallow candles.

Bang!

Rachel jumped, but caught herself before she spun around and retreated on winged feet back to her room. Her gaze locked on a distant window, where the drapes billowed from the walls like restless spirits in the throes of eternal damnation.

The shutters rapped against the outside wall, the wind whistling through a broken pane. With a sigh of relief and a nervous laugh, Rachel quickly padded over to the window, shoved it open, and then secured the shutter, locking it in place with a rusty hook.

"See, there's a logical explanation for everything," she murmured, forcing herself to relax.

It was then the first rumbling of thunder rolled through the house, growling like the distant beat of bass drums, vibrating the floor and reverberating through her body.

Beyond the wall of midnight, a burst of lightning briefly illuminated the churning clouds that shifted through the treetops like cloaked marauders.

Fergus had been correct on one count. The air felt

charged, as if tiny electrical currents were pulsing on her nerve endings. Breathing in that moment was difficult, as if she were trying to inhale through a wet wool blanket.

Panicked, she turned . . . and froze, her heart climbing up her throat, the air leaving her in a rush as her eyes locked with those of the warrior in the portrait, blue eyes shining with the girandole's light.

The painting appeared to float in the semidarkness, or perhaps it was she who moved as the Highlander's gaze drew her in. She stood before him, slightly hypnotized by his presence, a strange longing rising within her.

He was beautiful. A perfect example of pure, unadulterated male. That such a man had once thrived within these walls filled her with a heat that supplanted the ache of cold in her bones. To have known him. Touched him. Loved him, perhaps.

The fact that he no longer existed stirred a forlornness inside her, a sense of desperate loss, and a need that, until that moment, had gone unacknowledged in her mind . . . and in her heart.

"Duncan," she whispered, the sound of her voice a haunting echo in the dark, seeping out into the cold night where a wild tempest brewed, swirling with the wind . . . and beyond.

chapter 2

No doubt it was her strange reaction to the portrait that prompted Rachel to return to the tattered history book on her bedside table and huddle deeply beneath the down comforter to read, doing her best to tune out the wind whipping against the windows and the growl of thunder; its inimical force resonated just beneath her skin and entrenched itself within her every fiber.

Something about the painting had caused a tendril of desperation to blossom in her heart, a need to know as much as possible about the virile man who had once roamed these dark halls; to understand what things had moved him, what battles he felt were worth fighting and why. Had Glengarren always emanated such a bleak and unforgiving aspect? Or had there once been laughter? Even love?

Rachel glanced toward the dying fire. The sputtering flames danced with invisible gusts of air, while the unsettling howl and groan of the elements pounded relentlessly against the house.

A log crackled and shifted, expelling a vivid blue flame from the embers, the color reminding her of Duncan MacGregor's eyes.

Opening the book on her lap, her gaze skimmed much as she searched for tidbits about the man whose face had surfaced in her mind for much of the day.

She was not surprised to discover that he had been a heroic figure and a leader of men. His clan's fiercest enemies had been the Gordons, whose lands bordered the MacGregor's. Many conflicts had arisen from the Gordons reiving MacGregor livestock.

One of their bloodiest skirmishes occurred when the Gordons instigated a sneak attack on Glengarren in the middle of the night . . . the twenty-fifth of December, 1745.

"Christmas Day," Rachel murmured, her heart increasing in tempo as she read the passage.

From the characteristic bravery of the MacGregors, and their disdain of death, it is reasoned that those who perished on the field of battle did not yield their lives without a desperate struggle.

But history has preserved one case of individual valor in the person of Duncan MacGregor, which deserves to be recorded in every history book relating to Scotland and the Highlanders.

This man, who is represented to have been of the enormous stature of six feet four inches and a half, was beset by Gordon and his men.

Fierce combat between the two chiefs ultimately found Gordon mortally wounded. Legend has it that, as Gordon lay dying, he vowed revenge against his foe, and with his last bit of strength, he stumbled toward Glengarren, torch in hand, setting the east wing ablaze.

MacGregor, who had charged back into the fray, fought with his target and claymore against the onslaught of warriors who crowded upon him, enraged by his killing of their laird and the widespread destruction he had wrought among their comrades, twelve of whom lay slain at his feet.

Though the Gordons were bested that night, Glengarren was partially destroyed, and MacGregor had neither the funds nor the time to begin rebuilding before he was called upon by Charles Stuart to rally the Highland chiefs to fight against "The Butcher," William Augustus, son of King George II.

MacGregor was instrumental in gaining the support of the clans, and fought tirelessly to restore a Stuart to the throne, though neither the cause, nor MacGregor's life, would accomplish this feat.

At the Battle of Culloden Moor, he was overtaken by a group of the king's men, who had targeted him specifically. MacGregor was cut down, though not before taking a few of the soldiers with him. He fought to the end, but finally died from his wounds in the early morning hours on the seventeenth of April, 1746.

Tears blurred Rachel's vision, and she could read no more. Her heart filled with despair for a man she never knew, a man who had died in the very prime of his life.

A single, scalding tear dropped from her lashes as she laid her head back on the pillow, gazing once more into the waning fire, images of Duncan MacGregor stalking her mind as her eyelids slowly began to droop, the potent elixir of sleep tugging her down beneath its intoxicating weight . . . down into a world of dark and disturbing dreams.

RACHEL AWOKE WITH A VIOLENT START. Thunder rolled from colliding clouds and crashed against the house with such force that she covered her ears and sank against the pillows, certain the walls were caving in on her.

The bed vibrated. The window glass shook. Lit by the sudden fire of lightning bolts, the room gyrated with specters of three-dimensional shadows.

It was then she heard the cries.

Shouts of fear and anger. Clashing steel. The plaintive wail of a solitary bagpipe. All interspersed with the crack of thunder and howl of wind that rang out like the unearthly keening of a soul newly damned.

Again the cries . . . louder, harsher. The screams sluiced through her heart like a knife blade.

Flinging back her blankets, she hit the floor running, mindless of the frigid wood beneath her bare feet and the biting air that struck her pajama-clad body. Someone was in trouble. In pain.

In terror.

She swiped at the light switch—nothing. She stumbled into the pitch-black corridor, the draft of cold air like an ice fist against her face.

Again the shouts—more distinct, before drowning in another onslaught of crashing thunder that made her duck and cover her head, crouching against the wall, shivering in fear of an unknown threat, a force that pulsed in the very air, thick and menacing . . . and drawing nearer.

A jagged bolt of lightning flashed through the window, propelling Rachel to her feet and into a wild flight down the hall.

Confused by the dark and the ear-shattering cacophony, she turned round and round, frantically groping for a stronghold as the night closed in on her in suffocating blackness.

Blindly, she stumbled forward, falling to her knees, pushing on, racing toward the staircase, her ears burning with the intermittent cries that floated to her upon waves of pummeling thunder and blasts of wind.

Halfway down the staircase, she froze, Fergus's warnings suddenly blazing as brilliantly in her mind as the lightning electrifying the sky.

Leave these dreary walls and lonely shadows to the souls who've occupied Glengarren for the last centuries.

Panic surged. Rachel's gaze swept the darkness, eyes aching and body rigid as she expected to discover herself besieged by wailing poltergeists—white mists of formless shapes easing in through the jagged fissures and age-old chinks in the stone, no force on earth able to keep them out.

No! The shouts were not coming from inside the house, but from outside. Someone had gotten caught up in the storm. Perhaps the river had flooded—or worse.

By the sounds of the agonized howls, surely every resident of the nearby village must have fled for Glengarren's higher grounds.

Throwing open the front door, Rachel staggered back, bludgeoned by a tunnel of wind—warm and cold, exploding into the house with the force of a tidal wave.

The shouts drummed against her ears like a radio blasting, swirling around her like an orchestra of screeching, tuneless instruments, wrenching from her what little coherent thought she had clung to in the last horrifying moments.

The night boiled. Above her. Around her. Crawling over her skin like needles—painful and burning as she fought her way toward the melee, her path illuminated by sporadic bursts of crimson-hued lightning, unnatural and terrifying.

The tumult rose to a crescendo, as ear-shattering as the explosions overhead. She ran and stumbled and ran again, fear mounting inside her to a hysterical pitch, building with the fervor of the beast raging around her.

The cries in the night surrounded her; no longer the frightened clamor of hapless, flooded villagers, but the enraged shouts of men, the bloodcurdling screams of horses and pounding hooves, the clash of honed steel and the groans of agony, culminating in the palpable, unequivocal sounds of death.

Dear God, what was happening?

Rachel swung in a circle, desperate to find the source of the havoc, panic roaring through her veins, chewing away at her insides like acid. Fear closed off her throat and beat at her chest as the shrieks hammered her eardrums and reality became a blur.

Surely this was a bad dream—a nightmare. She would awaken at any moment, shivering in her bed, the old history book open on her lap where she had been reading of warring clans and bloodletting battles—of Duncan MacGregor, who had cut down his most hated rival on these very grounds.

But no. No dream. No nightmare. Nothing in her wildest imagination could have contrived the bedlam erupting around her, some preternatural force focusing its combined strength on this high precipice.

As if the sky had swallowed her, the clouds swirled around her body in ever-tightening coils—hot and ice-cold, burning and freezing and electrified, making her flesh quiver as if every ion in the universe was exploding beneath her skin.

Again came the lightning, blindingly brilliant, illuminating her surroundings. Rachel gasped at what was revealed.

She stood within the Destiny Stones!

They surrounded her, towered above her—massive black monuments whose very peaks appeared to scrape the low, churning clouds.

Along their weather-eroded peaks danced odd flashes of light—like a thousand fireflies blinking red-gold fire. For an instant Rachel stared, hypnotized, oblivious to the escalating chaos that swarmed around her.

She could only gaze up at the pillar of stone, the breath wrung from her throat and her eyes fixed upon what appeared to be the etching of a name . . . *MacGregor.*

A sizzling bolt of lightning pierced the sky in that

moment, ripping through the clouds like a god-spear, driving into the heart of the monolith with shattering force, sending sharp bullets of stone in every direction, the explosion flinging Rachel backward onto the ground, her eyes momentarily blinded by the glare and her ears deafened by an odd, shrill whine that made her cry out in pain.

Then a horse—black as onyx, frothing, teeth bared—exploded through the incarnate lightning like evil from Pandora's box. Rearing, its forelegs slashed the air, while vapor streamed from its nostrils like smoke from a dragon's snout.

Rachel scrambled back as the beast's mighty hooves crashed to the earth. Then her gaze locked on the huge man astride the stallion's bare back, his bloodied sword raised as if preparing to lop off her head.

A roar of rage tore from his lips as his eyes, flashing with the lightning's fire, focused first on her; then, with a snatch of his reins against the horse's neck, he and the snorting, pawing beast spun round, dirt flying and the lightning appearing to dance on his broad shoulders.

"To arms!" he bellowed into the turbulent night—oddly silent now of the shouts that had lured Rachel into this aberrant tempest. "I did not give ye orders tae retreat!" The thunder responded with a rebellious growl.

In one swift move, the man leapt from the horse, which dashed away into the dark, its reins flying and its hoofbeats jarring the ground as resoundingly as Rachel's heart rapped in her chest.

"To arms!" he roared again. Then, suddenly, he turned on his heels, facing her.

His teeth showed white in his dark countenance and his midnight hair whipped wildly in the wind. But it was his eyes . . . they burned with fire, pinning her against the cold stone within whose black embrace she hovered, praying the night would cloak her.

"What the hell have ye done with my men?" he demanded. "Speak now, or I'll cut your heart out and spike it on yonder rise."

Rachel could not utter a sound. Could not move. Terror held her immobile.

Again the lightning flashed, turning night into day. And in that momentary dance of illumination, their eyes met.

"Sweet Jesus." The words hissed through his teeth as his expression shifted from fury to confusion, then to enlightenment, which was as frightening as his anger. "Who the hell are ye?"

Rachel swallowed and searched for her voice. "W-who . . . who the hell are you?"

"Ye dare speak back tae me?" he boomed.

Rachel tried to tell herself that what she was seeing could not possibly be real, that she must wake from this nightmare, but no amount of coaxing, or blinking, on her part would make the image dissipate.

He loomed over her, wearing a kilt that barely covered his massive thighs. A shorn linen shirt hung in ribbons from his shoulders, revealing enormous arms whose muscles flexed with every move.

"Answer me, damn ye! Where is Gordon? And my

men? What evil work have ye done here, sorceress? And I issue ye fair warning—'tis best advised not tae rile me when blood lust is racing through my veins."

Fear and confusion blotted out good sense, and Rachel snapped, "I don't know what you're talking about!"

If she had thought he couldn't appear any fiercer than he already did, she was sadly mistaken. "Do not think ye can fool me," he said in a voice that was deceptive in its calmness. "None of your evil tricks will keep me from killing that whoreson. Is that why ye're here? Has he bade ye tae put a curse on me?"

"A curse? No."

"Then ye must be a spy for that Hanoverian bastard."

"A spy?"

"Aye. For the king. Come here tae find out what plots are being planned against him."

Before Rachel could utter a vehement denial, the sky opened up, throwing down daggers of rain that stabbed at her face as she struggled to rise, solid ground quickly turning to mud beneath her feet.

Without a word, the warrior snatched her up by the arm and propelled her toward the castle, his hold sending hot pain and pressure into her shoulder, and though she resisted, her efforts proved useless.

With one mighty kick, he sent a side door flying open and shoved her into the house, where the electricity flickered as inconsistently as candlelight. Then he slammed the door behind him, effectively trapping her.

He stalked her. She backed away, glancing wildly about her, thoughts of escape thwarted by his hulking form as the rain slashed against the house, battering the roof as if hurtling hailstones, a barbed pike of lightning slicing into a tree just outside the window, sending sparks in every direction.

"Stay away from me!"

"Silence!" he barked, his voice reverberating off the walls as explosively as the thunder overhead. "When I invite ye tae speak, then ye'll speak. Not before."

Rachel quickly closed her mouth, her outrage dampened by the threat in the man's eyes. Undoubtedly he was deranged. Why else would he be running around in the middle of the storm, bellowing for a nonexistent army and brandishing a sword?

Yes, he was mad; that had to explain his erratic behavior. But it was criminally unfair that the rest of the package wasn't equally as distorted. Not even remotely close. The man, for all his insanity, was heart-stoppingly gorgeous.

Rachel suddenly felt as mesmerized by his presence as she was petrified of his menacing demeanor. He towered over her, more than six plus feet of him, his long dark hair plastered to his head and shoulders by the rain.

"I'll ask ye one last time, woman; what have ye done with Gordon and my men? Where are ye hiding them?"

She returned his glare and set her shoulders mutinously, the old, defiant Rachel returning, refusing to cower any longer, no matter how sulfurous his regard.

"Answer me," he commanded.

"Make up your mind. First you order me to silence, then—"

He loomed over her. "I'm in no mood for insolence, witch," he cautioned, a muscle working in his jaw. "Be forewarned that rebellion will be treated accordingly. Should ye not wish tae find yourself shackled in the dungeon, 'twould be wise tae tread carefully."

Shackled in the dungeon? Now he was pushing it. "I don't know who you think you are—"

In one swift move, he withdrew his sword and leveled it before her eyes. The gleaming razor-edged blade glimmered with deadly purpose and appeared stained with something dark—something that looked disconcertingly . . . like blood. Rachel swallowed.

"At last I had him," he growled through clenched teeth, his power and presence charging the air as keenly as the lightning flitting over the treetops. "Sliced my blade across his hide, and yet he mocked me with his laughter." He edged closer, his eyes narrowing. "Tell me what ye've done with him, and I'll go easy on ye. Ye have my word that your punishment will not be severe."

Punishment? Rachel forced back the trepidation his threat caused, knowing that if she showed any fear, he would only use it against her.

Squaring her shoulders, she stared into those bluer-than-blue eyes, and said with far more bravado than she felt, "I'm giving you to the count of ten to get off this property or I'm calling the police."

"This is *my* property, wench, and the only one who will be departing . . . is you." His gaze then raked her body, once, twice, the burn of anger in his eyes slowly refashioning into something else—something less fierce . . . though far more disturbing to her peace of mind.

As much as she tried not to, she couldn't keep her eyes from wandering over the rippling arm muscles exposed by his sleeveless shirt, or take note of his large, strong hands . . . hands that could easily snap her neck.

Forcing air into her constricted lungs, she said with as much authority as she could muster, "I want you to leave."

Ignoring her, he took a step closer, less than a foot now separating them. His gaze, blue and hot as the heart of a flame, studied her face, and then slid downward again, narrowing as they focused on her breasts, which felt absurdly conspicuous beneath her sodden pajama top.

His voice, so harsh and cold, changed to a husky rumble as he said, "Remember my name, lady, for I'll not tell ye it again. 'Tis Duncan MacGregor, Laird of Glengarren . . . and master of all who dwell within its confines."

No. Not possible. This darkly disturbing stranger was not some mythic warrior from the past, even though his resemblance to the man in the portrait was uncanny.

Rachel took a step back and found herself against the wall. "No man is my master . . . and you're trespassing."

"A person cannot trespass on his own property."

"Look . . . I don't know where you came from or what you're doing here. All I know is that I'm the only one who is supposed to be in this house."

Thunder crashed in that moment, and lightning lit the

dim room. The explosion diverted the man's attention. He frowned and looked away, toward the window where the play of light flickered and the slash of driving rain pummeled the panes.

He turned from her, confusion creasing his brow, as though he had just noticed something he hadn't before. He moved through the shadows to the window to stare out into the darkness.

"There was no rain," he said in a troubled voice. "No thunder and lightning." He shook his head, and raked a hand through his hair. "And this place . . ." His gaze swept the room. "'Tis my home . . . and yet not." He turned, pinning her with his blue stare. "What manner of madness is this?"

As he searched her face for answers she did not have, Rachel was almost tempted to believe his claim. The hectic, frightening moments preceding his sudden appearance rushed back to her—the shouts of men, discovering she had stumbled into the circle of stones, the erupting of lightning, and the strange energy that had turned reality into a surreal nightmare.

Again, Fergus's warnings about the stones tapped at her subconscious. She tried to shake off her misgivings, but she couldn't. The man was obviously as upset as she. More so, in fact.

He paced in front of the window, then around the room, his expression of distress growing with each second, making the hair stand up on the back of her neck. And yet, something akin to sympathy stirred in her chest. If he was, by some freak act of nature . . .

No, if she allowed herself to believe such a thing even for a moment, she would be as crazy as he.

He stopped abruptly, legs planted apart, and clutched at his shoulder. Pulling his hand back, he stared at something that, to Rachel's horror, appeared to be blood.

He groaned. Just slightly. And as he unsteadily swiveled toward her, she watched the dark bloom spread over the tattered cloth of his shirt. She bit back a cry of alarm.

His blue eyes raised to hers, and the anger was back in force. "Damn that bastard Gordon," he hissed, his rugged face a shadow of frustration and pain. "He's cut me—but not so badly that I intend tae die before I've seen his limbs scattered for the damned crows." He started toward her, grim determination in the set line of his jaw. "I'll give ye one last chance tae confess where ye've hidden him. If ye refuse . . ." He swayed suddenly, his face leaching pale as his shirt.

Concern assailed Rachel. Lunatic or no, the man was injured and in pain. Quickly, she crossed the room, forgetting the fact that his presence endangered her.

He stepped back, his gaze cutting to his sword, as if to warn her away. Then the last thread of energy drained from him and the weapon clattered to the floor, the sound echoing off the old beams overhead.

His head bowed forward, and his bloodied hand gripped his shoulder again. "God's teeth," he moaned. "My strength at last fails me."

Rachel took a deep breath and reached out to peel back his shirt. "Please, let me take a look at your wound."

"Nay," he growled, his massive hand snatching her

wrist, twisting in a way that dragged her against his hard body, his fingers digging into her arm so forcefully she bit back a whimper.

Hot pain sluiced through her, as did the musky scent of his flesh. She felt the defined muscles of his chest against her damp breasts.

As his body heat radiated through her every pore, her legs grew weak. Not from fear, she realized as she threw back her head and glared defiantly up into his piercing blue eyes . . . but from desire.

"Witch," he whispered against her cheek, his warm breath stirring the hair at her temple. "Do ye think me a fool? Shall I allow ye tae touch me so that ye may hex me further? Finish what Gordon began?"

Words of contempt lodged in her throat as her gaze dropped to his lips, wondering what they would feel like against her own, wanting to know the answer with an almost desperate fervor, a need she barely understood yet felt compelled to surrender to. Her body seemed to melt into his.

Suddenly, a fierce blast of wind, ice-cold and razor sharp, swirled around them, raking over their faces and groaning like an anguished soul.

The man heaved backward, as if jerked, clawing at his neck, his eyes showing white in shock. Horrified, Rachel watched him fall to the floor, his arms thrashing as if to fight back at some invisible force.

As quickly as the terrifying ordeal had begun, it was over. He lay sprawled across the floor, gasping for breath, his bloodied hand pressed to his throat and his glazed eyes fixed on her in disbelief.

Dropping to her knees beside him, she placed her hand over his in a beseeching gesture. "Please. You're injured—"

"What powers are these?" he snarled, knocking her hand away. "'Tis no witch ye are, but the devil."

"I only want to help."

"By trying tae kill me?"

Rachel gaped at him. "Kill you? That's not only ridiculous, but would have been impossible, considering you had hold of my arm."

"'Tis your black magic."

Exasperated by his irrational accusations, she glared down at his scowling face. "If I were a witch, I wouldn't stop with choking you. I'd skewer you with your own sword, not just for behaving like an ass but for luring me out of my bed and into that horrid storm. If I were a witch, I'd twitch my nose and gladly send you up in a puff of smoke. Now"—she metered the words—"you are bleeding badly. If we don't get it stopped, you might very well bleed to death. Is that what you want?"

He regarded her warily, still clutching his shoulder. "Nay," he begrudgingly admitted.

"Fine." Standing, she offered her hand. "Then come with me. We'll clean the wound and bind it."

His gaze shifted to her hand, then back to her face, and he grunted. "'Twill be a cold day in hell before Duncan MacGregor allows a woman tae heft him as if he were a helpless babe."

Rolling away, he unsteadily shoved himself to one knee, then staggered to his feet before righting himself to his full, imposing height.

Nervously, Rachel regarded him, wondering if she knew what she was doing as she pointed toward the distant corridor. "The kitchen is that way."

He made an inarticulate sound. "I'll remind ye again, 'tis my house and I know where my own bloody kitchen is."

With that declaration, he pivoted on his heels and stalked from the room, disappearing through the shadows.

chapter
3

COLLECTING HER FRAZZLED WITS, Rachel cautiously followed the beautiful giant down the long, dark corridor, the air growing colder and damper and even more biting with each step she took. A veil of foreboding whispered over her shoulders and twined around her nerves.

While the chill had been noticeably uncomfortable before, there was a keenness to it now, an almost tactile quality to the air as it stirred around her ankles, slowly easing up her body to her thighs, her belly, breathing across her breasts, drifting through her hair and brushing her face with wraith-like fingers, as if . . .

No, she wasn't going there. She had enough to deal with. She didn't believe in ghosts . . . or Highland warriors plucked from another century and zapped into her life by a lightning bolt.

Yet she could not deny that there was something different about her surroundings, even the very space she occupied, as if a sphere of quintessence was keeping pace with her. Something almost . . . malevolent.

Rachel forced herself to concentrate on moving forward, or she would surely turn on her heels and run from the house. Storm or no storm.

She found the mysterious stranger slumped against an old, rough-hewn table in the middle of the kitchen, one hand pressed against his shoulder, his gaze shifting around the room, renewed bewilderment etching his brow. Odd, how he suited the massive chamber.

With a fortifying breath, Rachel moved across the room, her steps slowing as he elevated riveting blue eyes in her direction. Never had she encountered such forcefulness in a glance. No insanity lurked behind those eyes—just weariness and confusion.

"I'd better take a look at that wound," she said, only to hesitate under the intensity of his regard, his expression having grown suspicious, guarded, as though he expected her to do something to him, as if she could possibly harm this hulk of a man.

Yet that look moved her, revealing the barest suggestion of vulnerability. Of despair.

"I won't hurt you," she murmured. "I just want to see how badly you're injured."

He scowled a moment longer, then nodded, eyeing her the way a hawk eyes its prey as she eased back his shirt. She gasped when she saw the ragged four-inch cut running just below the front of his shoulder toward his left arm.

Gently, she probed the inflamed area around the wound. "How did this happen?"

When he didn't answer, she looked up and found him scrutinizing her. A ripple of anticipation flowed through her, an unfamiliar ache, like a thousand warm butterflies taking flight in her stomach.

"'Tis as I told ye," he said in a rumbling burr. "'Twas a gift from that swine Gordon."

Gordon, again. Rachel was beginning to greatly dislike this invisible threat. "Remove your shirt, please." She expected him to balk, perhaps refuse completely. Surprisingly, he did neither.

She forced herself to turn away as he shed his stained garment, rummaging through the old cupboards until she collected enough supplies to attend to the wound: a clean cloth and the first aid kit she had spotted earlier, which contained ointment and self-adhesive gauze bandages.

She filled a basin with water and returned to the table with her supplies, doing her best to keep from looking at the sculpted contours of his chest.

"This might sting a bit," she said, thankful her voice sounded normal—and that she had spoken before facing him. Her enraptured gaze traveled over perfect pectorals and washboard abs. Everything inside her liquefied in that single glance.

She was suddenly, and acutely, aware of just how long it had been since she had felt anything even remotely close to desire. And she had certainly never experienced anything like this—a yearning to explore the chiseled planes of him, the rugged line of his jaw, ease the tension from around his eyes. Madness. Pure madness.

Gently, she began bathing the wound, becoming absorbed in the task, not realizing that she stood rather intimately between his thighs until she felt his legs press against hers.

Her gaze jumped to his, and what she saw there took her breath away. His eyes had darkened to a velvety midnight blue. With the lightest of touches, he brushed a lock of her hair off her shoulder, his fingers leaving a path of warmth in their wake.

Dear Lord, what was it about this man that made her want to lean into his touch? She had known him so short a time . . . and yet, it seemed as if she had known him an eternity.

"You really should get to a doctor," she managed to say, though her voice held a slight quaver. "This is deep. You'll need stitches."

"And are ye concerned about me, sweet witch?" A hint of sensuous amusement laced his words, the corners of his full lips slanting upward.

Rachel scoffed. "Don't flatter yourself. I'd simply prefer you didn't bleed to death in my company."

Anger she could take from this man. Arrogance. Even brooding. But that smile she was entirely defenseless against, and it had the power to string her nerves tighter than a bow.

He chuckled low in his throat, the sound vibrating across her skin in the strangest way. "Ye have a sharp tongue, but I like a wench with spirit."

Disconcerted, Rachel flung the bloody rag into the bowl. "Look, if you call me wench again, I'll punch you in the nose."

Her bout of temper made him slant a black brow at her. "And what manner of name would ye like tae be called, lass?"

"By my given one. Rachel."

He pondered her request for a moment, then murmured, "As ye wish . . . Rachel." Her name rolled off his tongue in a growling caress, like the sound made by a hungry lion.

Rachel had to mentally shake herself to diffuse the honeyed languor that had taken hold of her body. She busied herself by putting the supplies away.

When she had her equilibrium in hand, she turned back to him—and found his gaze sketching down her body with far too much suggestive intimacy.

"What raiment are these ye wear?" he asked, gesturing to her legs.

"Jeans," she replied, sounding out of breath.

"I like them greatly. They cling tae your body like a second skin and cup your woman's mound."

Heat rose fast and furiously to Rachel's cheeks, leaving her mouth hanging open, but no words forthcoming.

He canted his head, his expression contemplative. "Though your hips are a bit narrow."

That remark untied her tongue. "What have my hips to do with anything?"

"'Tis not that I do not like the sweet curves outlined in those odd breeks ye sport. Aye, they sorely tempt me tae forget your interference with Gordon. But Highland women are more buxom, wider-boned for the birthing of large bairns."

Rachel waited for the indignation to come, and was surprised when all she felt was an unexpected heat tugging low in her belly.

His comment brought her reluctant gaze to his attire, or lack thereof. A light dusting of dark hair disappeared behind the waistband of his kilt, and she wondered, with an almost indecent sense of curiosity, if he wore anything underneath.

As if reading her mind, he said, "'Tis bare-assed I am. And should ye continue tae stare at me with those hot sea-green eyes, I may be tempted tae show ye what your lustful looks have wrought."

Rachel's cheeks burned. "I didn't . . . I mean, I wasn't—"

"Aye. Ye were, lass." He reached for her, his hand encircling her wrist, tugging her closer, his male scent enveloping her, his heat making her nearly melt into his embrace. "Though I have no love of witches, ye beckon me and test my control tae its very limit. 'Tis too long since I last pleasured a woman."

His chest was right in front of her, and it was all Rachel could do not to run a finger down the stretch of bare skin, to lightly score the musculature, and confirm that he was truly flesh and blood and bone.

He drew her closer. "I sense your desire for me. Your body quivers for my touch." Those big fingers splayed against her pajama top as his voice dropped to a husky tone. "Ye bewitch me, lass, and make me forget your treachery in denying me my revenge against Gordon. But if ye're good, and promise tae fix what your wicked actions have wrought, I'll pleasure ye. And I vow ye have never known such pleasure as I can give."

His arrogance infuriated her—about as much as his nearness enflamed her. She needed to distance herself, or be consumed in the conflagration. "You rate your appeal too highly."

A muscle worked in his jaw. "With your vexsome ways, I suspect ye have no man."

Rachel glared at him, more hurt than she should be by his remark. "If you mean do I have a boyfriend, then the answer is no. Not every woman will die for want of a man's company. In fact, some of us are pretty darn happy without one!"

"But not you," he said, his voice softening, his knuckles brushing across her cheek, making her shiver beneath his touch. "Ye need a man. Someone who will tame the hellion in ye and turn the heat of your anger into passion. A man who will make love tae ye and drive the devil from your soul."

His words took all the fight and anger out of her. Never had a man tempted her so, made her forget the kind of woman she was—one who never acted precipitously and wouldn't dream of bedding a man she hardly knew.

And yet . . . it felt as if she *did* know him, that perhaps there had been a time she had once burned beneath his hungry kisses, her hands whispering over his hard flesh, feeling muscles ripple and flex beneath her palms, their bodies merging . . . as well as their souls.

It was crazy. Insane.

Rachel backed away, out of his reach. "No."

"Ye deny me?" he said, sounding incredulous, as if a woman's refusal was something that had never happened before, which she suspected was the case.

"I do."

Those haunting bedroom eyes abruptly changed into hot, angry flames. "Blast ye, then!" he boomed and slammed one big fist on the table, shoving himself from the chair to tower over her, intimidating her, making her jump back. "I need no reluctant witch in my bed. I'll take my leave of ye now, and good riddance."

"Ditto!" she shouted back at him, surprised by her bravado in the face of his black glower.

He leaned over her, his eyes narrowing on her face. "I order ye tae lift whatever conjuring ye have put upon my head and send me back tae my men."

"If snapping my fingers would make you disappear, I'd do it in a second." *Liar,* her inner voice refuted.

He growled. "Lift this wretched curse, witch, or ye'll sorely regret it."

Rachel backed away, her buttocks coming up against the table. "Stay away from me."

"There is nowhere for ye tae run. Surrender."

"Never." Fear had not immobilized her in the past, but had instead galvanized her to action—as it did now. She lunged for the meat mallet on the counter and waved it at him.

He stopped in his tracks and raised a single eyebrow, as if daring her to go for it, which only brought home the utter foolishness of her actions. The man had blundered into her life wielding a sword, for Pete's sake. He was hardly going to cringe with dread over a kitchen implement.

"Please," she begged, dropping the mallet. "Won't you just leave?"

His expression changed, hardened, a muscle worked in his jaw as he inclined his head with a quick jerk. "So be it."

Then he turned on his heel and strode from the room,

flinging open the kitchen door, sending a blast of wet, icy wind scudding over the floor as he dissolved into the darkness as if he'd never existed.

For several minutes, Rachel remained rooted to the spot, her sense of disconcertment and fear not alleviating with his departure . . . but mounting instead.

Everything inside her clamored that she go after him, her mind tumbling over a slew of logical reasons why she should. He was hurt. Confused. Lost. The night was cold and wet. Whatever demons plagued him, she should have tried to help him, get him to a doctor, if nothing else.

But more than that, his very presence had shifted something within her, something she didn't completely understand, igniting a flame—of need, of attraction, a pull so strong her heart felt torn knowing that he might simply disappear from her life, as suddenly and strangely as he had appeared.

She had to go after him, had to find him. She couldn't let him go. Not yet.

Not yet.

She raced into the night, her eyes scanning the moonless dark. Although the rain had stopped, the icy wind slashed at her face and whipped her long hair into flying banners around her head.

"Duncan!" she cried, and stumbled forward, cold air stinging her eyes, causing tears to momentarily blind her.

She tripped and fell to her knees before clawing herself upright and pressing forward, disoriented by the cloaking darkness, fear building inside her like a dawning tempest. Some instinct clamored that she would find him at the stones.

But where were they?

The grounds yawned before her, unfamiliar and frighteningly alien. Skeletal trees loomed through the shadows.

She turned one way, then another, running wildly, her internal compass spinning as she called his name again and again, only to have her voice drowned amid the roar of the wind and something else . . . something powerful, growling like the belly of some Goliath beast.

"Duncan!" she cried again. "Please . . . come back!"

One moment the ground was there, and then she was hovering for an infinitesimal heartbeat, suspended, the earth beneath her becoming as insubstantial as the fog whirling around her. With a strangled cry, she began to fall.

Then, out of nowhere, he was beside her, his strong arms wrapping around her waist and hauling her back against a hard chest.

"God's teeth, lady," he hissed in her ear, "is it your wish tae get killed?"

Rachel stiffened, hating the leap of her pulse that happened whenever he touched her and the relief that coursed through her, having found him.

He swung her around to face him. "Do ye not hear that sound?"

She listened, trying to discern the source of the noise over the harsh rasp of her breathing. Then she heard it.

The crash of waves against the cliff.

Her body went cold. She had been running headlong toward the precipice—and a sheer, jagged drop of nearly three hundred feet.

She began shaking uncontrollably, her mind whirling with thoughts of how close she had come to dying, of how she would have plunged to a watery grave had he not saved her.

Suddenly her knees buckled and she sank into him. Without a word, he swept her up into his arms, stalking silently through the dark.

She clung to him with desperate fervor, her tear-streaked face buried against his broad shoulder, her hands clutching what was left of his shirt.

Not for the first time had his scent infused her with an unsettling heat that vanquished the chill and fear that numbed her. The warmth of his flesh against hers made her blood ripple with a slow-building fire.

He shoved open the front door and with a quick stride, carried her over the threshold and into the house. Carefully, as if she were precious and fragile, he set her on her feet. Yet when she gazed up at him, he wore a dark scowl.

With a grunt and a muttered curse, he distanced himself from her. "Damnation, wench, what am I tae do with ye? First ye bewitch me from the battlefield and thrust me into this odd place that is my home and yet not, then ye tantalize me with your strange clothes and saucy mouth, only tae tell me tae be gone from ye, and then nearly get yourself killed trying tae find me. Ye make no sense, woman!"

Rachel said nothing. There was no rationale for her to fall back on, no specific logic to her actions. Only a feeling. How could she explain something even *she* didn't understand? Make sense of an emotion that had no solid basis? Reason away a situation that *had* no reason?

She watched him pace like a caged animal, raking his disheveled hair back with one hand, his brow creased with anger . . . perhaps even desperation. Stopping in his tracks, he whirled on her again, drew himself up to his full, towering height, and glared.

It was in that instant that the irrefutable truth of this whole unbelievable situation struck Rachel as her gaze slowly moved from his face, beyond him to the portrait.

"Dear God," she whispered in a raw voice.

"What are ye babbling about?" he grumbled.

"You're him." Her astonished gaze slid back to him.

"Him?"

"Duncan MacGregor." She raised a shaky arm and pointed at the painting. "*That* Duncan MacGregor."

The sound of the grandfather clock tolling in some distant part of the castle intensified the silence as he turned his head and stared up at the portrait, then back at her.

"Aye," he said wearily. "'Tis as I told ye." No triumph lit his eyes, but rather an emotion far more disturbing. Anguish. "Where am I?" he asked, his voice a tortured rasp, his gaze searching her face as though she had suddenly become his bedrock in a wildly unstable universe. "I had thought ye had simply made Gordon and my men vanish, but this . . ." He gestured around him. "I am out of place."

Rachel trembled, shaken to the core by his words as well as the truth she had consciously denied. Seeing the living version of Duncan MacGregor, in all his brooding, darkly beautiful glory, and then looking at the portrait behind him, was a shock that made her legs weaken beneath her.

She sank down into the only available chair, a high-backed affair of worm-eaten wood and musty, fraying tapestry, the arms carved into the likeness of lion paws.

Jaundiced light from the girandole cast eerie claw-like shapes on the floor and obscured Duncan in half-formed shadows, making him look like a brooding Lucifer, devising the downfall of mankind.

He raked a hand through his wind-whipped hair and glanced around his home, seeking something familiar, perhaps—something more than old stones now slowly eroding with decay.

The shadows shifted as he turned once more to regard her, darkness appearing to settle over his face like a shroud. "Why have ye brought me tae this place?"

Rachel's fingers convulsed around the carved paws on the chair arms as his piercing blue gaze drove through her as keenly as the sword on his hip.

She shook her head. "I have no explanation for you. I only wish I did."

He curled his fingers into his palms and abruptly pivoted on his heel, stalking to the window. He braced one hand against the moldering stone to stare out into the moonless night.

The wind whistled through the eaves, skeletal branches scraping over the thick panes, lending a sense of loneliness to his solitary silhouette.

He stood so still he might have been a statue, suspended in time and space, as mournful as the groaning drafts of wind that shuffled along the floor and swirled at her feet, coiling around her frayed nerves.

A long moment passed in silence. Then his words, soft

and edged with despair, whispered hauntingly through the air, "I am lost."

His confession tore at her, whittled down to the deepest part of her being and lodged itself there.

Collecting her courage, Rachel stood, her legs unsteady as she moved across the foyer toward him, through the cold shadows, her steps silent on the mist-strewn floor as she came to stand beside him at the window.

Her heart went out to him, this confused and distraught warrior whose greatest battle in that moment was against an invisible enemy, struggling to save the only thing he still possessed.

His soul.

How would *she* feel if she had been transported to another time? A time far different from her own, with nothing familiar, all friends and family left behind?

Was he thinking about the men who would surely die without his leadership? Or was the pain etched on his face caused by something else? A woman, perhaps? A lovely Scottish girl who was now pining over his loss? Rachel did not want to face the thought.

"My clan . . . what will they think became of me? That I fled from Gordon? Ran away like some piffling coward instead of facing him?" His jaw tensed, the hand resting against the wall curling into a fist. "Or will they never know what happened tae me?"

Rachel had no answer for him. She did not know what tomorrow would bring, if time would right itself and he would return to his own world as suddenly as he had appeared in hers.

She longed to offer him some measure of hope, some

solace, to smooth away the pain stamped on his desolate profile. Yet she knew that he would not accept her offer. He was too strong, too fearless to admit any weakness.

"What year is it?" he asked, his voice barely audible.

She searched for some way to preface her reply, ease the blow, but there was nothing, except the truth. "2001."

His gaze slashed to hers, disbelief standing out in stark counterpoint in his dark eyes. "'Tis a lie."

For his sake, she wished it were a lie. And yet, at that moment, with him standing so close and the warmth from his body drawing her like a moth to a potent, dangerous flame, she wanted him to be part of her century, to be part of the present and not the past.

"It's true," she murmured.

He closed his eyes and bowed his head, his fingers scraping against the cold stone and a shuddering breath shaking his frame as he said bleakly, "I am truly lost then."

chapter
4

ETERNAL NIGHT. Remote and endless and black as a raven's wing.

Shivering from the escalating cold, Rachel lay in her bed, hunched beneath the comforter, listening to each tick of the clock, the wind howling and scratching on the window with dire fingers, as if seeking entrance.

Yet her mind was elsewhere, imagining Duncan pacing his room, haunted by whatever odd force of nature had wrenched him from his existence and deposited him within the realm of hers.

How tempted she was to rap upon his door and assure herself he was not a dream. Yet she didn't dare. She felt too disconcerted by his presence. He skewed her priorities, not to mention her emotions. She had come to Glengarren for one purpose: to fulfill her parents' request to scatter their ashes on their anniversary, a day that was all too quickly approaching.

A sad smile touched Rachel's lips as she looked toward the matching urns she had placed on the mantle. She could imagine her father's thrill over this strange and unexplainable occurrence with Duncan.

Her father had been a history buff, and loved the mystique of rambling old castles and the families who had once dwelt within them.

With each journey to Scotland, he had lugged home kilts and bagpipes and rusty battle swords, turning their house in Connecticut into, as her mother had termed with a sentimental smile, a maudlin old museum.

Her father would not have been the least bit intimidated by Duncan MacGregor. Instead, he would have planted himself at the warrior's side and drained him of every last detail of his life.

Rachel, on the other hand, wasn't nearly as concerned over Duncan's life story as she was over the effect he had on her physically—and emotionally.

She stared up at the ceiling, watching the light and shadows cast by the flickering fire, reasoning with herself that it was Duncan's despair that called to her, brought out this need to protect him, shelter him from things he didn't understand, the perils that lurked in a world he no longer recognized. There could be no other explanation for the feelings he evoked in her.

And yet, deep down, in a place she would not consciously acknowledge, she knew she lied. Duncan filled her with a yearning of the soul ... and of the body, leaving her weak and on fire for him.

Even now, as she sank deeper into the down mattress, listening to the wind buffet the walls and mourn hauntingly through the eaves, it wasn't the cold that made her limbs ache and her insides knot painfully, but pure, undiluted desire. She burned with it.

She shivered from the mental pictures of Duncan's mouth fused to hers, his skin against her own, sleek, moist, and hard, his powerful thighs between hers ...

Rachel drew in an unsteady breath, stunned by the direction in which her thoughts were traveling, willing back the erotic visions until they were safely tucked away.

A sound arose out in the hallway, bringing her fully alert and upright. Her breath suspended in her throat as she strained to listen, picking out the familiar creaks and moans made by the house, trying to reassure herself that whatever she heard had only been a product of the wind.

Then the noise came again—and it was not the wind, but a low, eerie moan, a whisper of a voice that sent a shiver up her spine. Duncan? Could he be in pain? Had his injury worsened?

Despite the alarms clamoring in her head, Rachel slid from the bed, tugged on her robe, and crept to the door, pressing her ear against the wood to listen.

Cautiously, she opened the door and peered out. The hallway was dim, lit only by a few sconces scattered intermittently on the walls, their hazy yellow light glowing through an odd, diaphanous mist that appeared to shift in the shadows and coalesce gradually along the floor, lingering outside Duncan's door.

The lament drifted to her on a draft of wind, making her want to turn tail and fly back into her room, barricading the door until gauzy morning light filtered through the drapes. She had to remind herself that she was fearless, and that Duncan might need her.

Taking a deep breath, Rachel eased across the corridor, her gaze focused on the gray mist that sprawled over the bare floor like a rug, slowly seeping along the knotted and pitted old wood to crawl around her ankles and slide up her calves.

She tried to reason away the strange and creepy mist as a result of the equally strange and creepy weather; the low-lying fog sweeping across the moors had somehow found its way into the house, slithering over the front doorsill and through cracks in the windowpanes.

Still, there was something disquieting about the smoky vapor, a tangible element. A pulse. As though it possessed a life of its own, inching along her skin, making the hair rise on her arms and her heart pound in her throat, hastening her steps toward Duncan's room.

Reaching his room, she stared at the closed portal for only a moment before turning the knob and easing open the door, wanting to escape the mist even as she justified her actions by telling herself she was simply checking on an injured man.

She found him sitting silent and unmoving before the hearth, slouched in a enormous black leather chair, gazing into the blazing fire, his face and body painted by the flickering gold light.

His head slowly turned, and his troubled blue gaze collided with hers. Her heart faltered at the certain despair in those eyes, and she was forced to check her need to rush across the room and comfort him.

"I thought I heard voices," she said, remaining motionless in the doorway.

He made no remark, but continued to regard her from that brooding countenance, shadows obscuring all but his eyes—piercing as a dagger and deepened to ebony by his surroundings.

She glanced away from him, needing to compose herself and the riot of emotions that tumbled through her whenever she was in his presence.

She looked around the bedroom, which—unlike the rest of the house—she had not explored the day before, feeling as if it were somehow sacrosanct, off-limits. Now she allowed her gaze to roam.

The room had yet to be cleared out, nor had the furnishings been covered over with sheets, as many of the other rooms had. It still held the masculine appeal of its normal occupant: dark furniture, deep wine-colored bedding and draperies, bookshelves flanking one entire wall, leather-bound novels crammed into every conceivable crevice, and the faintest hint of smoke and brandy.

Rachel wondered if the current lord of Glengarren was anything like the man now watching her from across the room. The same blood ran through their veins, after all.

Even so, would she feel the inexplicable pull that drew her to Duncan with another MacGregor? Would she ever feel this way with *any* man?

She forced the thought aside, and quietly asked, "Are you all right?"

"Aye," he said, sounding weary. Then he motioned toward the bed. "I could not sleep in that. 'Tis like a rock, and too small." He sighed. "It matters not. There is too much tae think about anyway." He looked again into the fire, his profile as perfect as a Greek coin.

"Are you still worried about your men?"

He nodded and glanced around the room. "This place . . . it discomfits me. I have looked many an enemy in the eye and cursed his name and have not felt the disquietude that this air gives me. 'Tis as if I am not alone."

"You aren't alone," she told him, though she well understood the sensation he referred to—the feeling of something being just out of sight, inches beyond reach—but she pushed her unease to the back of her mind. It was not a path she wanted to traverse at that moment. "I'm only across the hall if you need to talk."

His gaze captured hers, the look in his eyes bringing a rush of heat to her cheeks. "'Tis more than talk I crave, lass." His meaning was readily apparent, and yet he had not acted on his urges. Rachel didn't know whether to be glad he had controlled himself, or if she should give free rein to the disappointment swirling inside her. "Come and sit with me by the fire." It was a request, not a command, and the first he had issued, though it didn't make her decision any easier.

She knew what would happen to her if she got too close to him, the onslaught of physical symptoms, as though she were running a high fever that only one thing could cure.

Duncan beckoned her—with words. And without. Yet even knowing the danger he posed—no longer to her well-being but to her heart—she still wanted to be near him.

Shaking slightly, from nerves this time rather than cold or fear, she padded across the room and sat down in front of the hearth, her back to the flames and Duncan before her, regarding her from beneath drowsy lids.

"How is your shoulder?" she asked.

"It vexes me little. 'Tis the ache here that bothers me more." He placed a hand on his heart. "My men will believe that I deserted them."

"No," she said, shaking her head. "They won't think that."

"And what makes ye so certain?"

"Because you wouldn't abandon them. They know it . . . and I know it." Rachel couldn't say *how* she knew what Duncan would or would not do, what things his honor commanded of him. Yet she felt as if she knew him as well as she knew herself.

"And what else is it that ye think ye know about me, lass?"

His gaze was hooded, so Rachel couldn't tell if he was mocking her, or if he was truly interested in hearing what she thought. Regardless, she told him.

"For one, I think you're not as tough as you look."

A dark scowl clouded his face. "Are ye saying that I'm a coward?"

"No. Of course not. I'm simply saying that somewhere beneath that hard shell resides a compassionate heart."

He grunted, appearing moderately satisfied with her answer, the fierceness slowly easing from his face. "What else?"

"Well, you fight for what you believe in. You care

deeply for your people. And I suspect you're very honorable, though something tells me you don't readily show that side of yourself."

"Honorable, am I?" His gaze bore into hers, transfusing heat into her very soul, before dipping to her lips, that lone glance making them tingle. "And might ye know what honorable thoughts I'm thinking right now, sweet witch? That my mind turns over with visions of being less honorable at this moment. That, in fact, I wish tae be very, *very* dishonorable and tae take what I desire, tae seek heaven where I know it can be found, a tunnel of slick warmth tae sheath me and loving arms tae hold me close."

Rachel's flesh felt as though it was on fire. The very spot he so boldly spoke of began to ache, her body wanting him to do exactly as he wished. But perhaps any warm body would do just then, any female to help him forget the turmoil of his life for a few desperate, pleasure-filled hours.

"You're just lost," she said, staring down at her hands, not wanting him to see what was in her eyes.

He tipped her chin up. "I am not lost at this moment, lady." His eyes conveyed all she had wanted to see but was afraid to look for. Then, the tension returned to his body, the hand beneath her chin moving to clutch his shoulder, a black scowl marring his face as he sat back. "Bloody Gordon," he hissed beneath his breath. "The man is the bane of my existence."

Rachel was growing to dislike this Gordon almost as much as Duncan did. The name seemed familiar, yet she couldn't remember why. Something elusive tugged at the back of her mind, but at that moment, her thoughts were too focused on Duncan. He looked ready to shatter.

Wanting to comfort him, she placed her hand on top of his. The contact was electric. Jolting. As if something inside her had merged with something inside him . . . their hopes and desires, fears and joys . . . their very souls.

Frightened, she attempted to pull away, but his hand closed around hers. "Don't," he whispered, tugging her closer until she knelt between his thighs.

His large, warm hand cupped her cheek, searing her. She could not resist, or perhaps she simply didn't want to. Instead, she gave in to the need inside her, closing her eyes and leaning into his touch as she had ached to do.

Odd how such a short time ago this huge warrior had sent tremors of fear through her. No more. For the first time in a long while, everything seemed right with the world, as if she had come home at long last.

Was it selfish, she wondered, to want to hold on to that feeling, to wish to steal time and hold it close? Christmas was said to be the season of miracles. Perhaps this man, this haunted, beautiful man, was her miracle?

Or perhaps he would disappear as suddenly as he arrived, leaving her emptier and more desolate than she had been before.

The thought chilled Rachel, and she forced herself to pull away from him, drawing her resolve around her like a cloak, striving for some semblance of rationality before she did something foolish.

Something that couldn't be undone.

She searched for something to say, and noticed he still wore his stained clothing. "There might be something you can wear to bed in one of the bureaus."

He regarded her with those dark, unfathomable eyes—eyes that had the power to unravel her. "I wear nothing tae bed," he stated, watching her reaction, which was immediate, heat prickling her skin and warming her face.

The image of Duncan's naked body sliding beneath the sheets was a powerful one. Evocative. Unnerving. Rachel knew she had to put distance between them—or risk the chance of answering the desire in his eyes with her own.

"This is where I say good night."

It wasn't until that moment that she realized her hand was still clasped within Duncan's, the contact seemed so natural, so . . . right.

He was reluctant to release her, and she, reluctant to be released. Yet, slowly, she eased her hand from his, wondering why the chill air assailed her the moment they were no longer touching.

"Don't leave me, lass," he whispered in a heated voice, the request beguiling, beseeching, and terribly hard to resist—but resist she must.

"Good night," she murmured, rising unsteadily to her feet, trying not to run for the door and across the corridor that separated them, even though far more separated them than the width of the hallway, and she had to remember that. Hundreds of years stood squarely between them.

The last thing she saw as she closed her bedroom door was Duncan's large frame silhouetted in front of the fire, blue eyes cutting through the shadows and delving into her soul, the darkly haunting whisper of a single word reaching out to her.

Rachel . . .

chapter
5

 THE MORNING DAWNED gray and cloudy, with a steady drizzle of rain that hinted of snow.

As Rachel stood shivering at the cliff's edge, she gazed out at the silver-limned water of the River Ness, willing back the rise of emotion within her as she thought about her parents and how they had loved this place.

She tried to see it as they had, and not as the desolate, tragic shell it had become. It must have been grand once, must have possessed a certain magic, when the grounds stirred with men and women and children. The thrum of life.

Those days were gone now. But they had once existed . . . back in Duncan's time.

Would he ever return to where he belonged? And would she be able to forget him once he was gone?

Rachel forced the thought aside, knowing such questions were unproductive. What would be would be, and she could not change that, no matter what she wanted.

Though she closed one door in the passageway of her

mind, another opened, full of poignant memories—visions of her parents, of what they would be doing right now had they still been alive. They had found such joy during the holidays. They had known such love.

Sadness took hold of Rachel, enclosing her in its relentless web. Soon she would have to say good-bye to them, and the sorrow of that moment made an ache unfurl and expand inside her, like an old wound newly lanced. She was not yet ready to let them go.

She closed her eyes tightly and tipped her face up to the sky, allowing the drizzle to bead upon her chilled face and run like tears down her cheeks—replacing the real tears that longed to flow. But she was too afraid she would drown in her grief should she allow them to fall freely.

What irony, she thought. *What cursed fate.* That in this very place where her parents had found love, she had, by some skewed miracle, conjured up a man who epitomized her most secret fantasies, her most longed-for wishes, and the wretched reality was . . . he could never belong to her.

No doubt Duncan was pacing Glengarren's shadowed corridors, despairing over his circumstances, a spirit and soul wrenched from his existence by the whims of fate, his mind consumed with thoughts of how he would find his way back to his own century—while she wondered if she really wanted him to find the answer.

A gust of frigid air whipped up from the gorge below, bringing her back to the moment—and banishing dreams that she would be foolish to hold out hope might be granted.

Rachel opened her eyes to find the first flurries of snowflakes brushing against her cheeks as lightly as ghostly kisses.

The sight reminded her that Christmas was nearly upon her. Families the world around were decorating trees and wrapping presents to the familiar strains of *"Deck the Halls"* and *"Silent Night."* Soon they would be drinking eggnog and eating fruitcake . . . while visions of new toys and games danced in children's heads.

Rachel's gaze shifted to the castle that jutted out of the earth like a gray mountain, her thoughts once more returning to Duncan—and where they would both be on Christmas Day. Perhaps it was best not to know.

The temperature suddenly plummeted, and she trembled as the cold cut through her layered clothing like a dull knife and began to numb her gloved hands and booted feet.

Bundling her coat close around her, she hastened toward the house. As she stepped through the front door, shaking the snow from her hair, she paused, noting that the foyer felt surprisingly warm.

Slowly, she closed the heavy portal behind her, her gaze sliding to the library, where a glowing light spilled out over the threshold, burnishing the floor with a golden hue.

A roaring fire burned in the hearth, the flames licking greedily against the long-unused grate, making wild shapes dance over the walls and floor like writhing apparitions.

Rachel started as the lights suddenly flicked on and off. On and off. On and off. A moment later she heard a distinctive male grumble and a curse. She turned to find Duncan flipping the light switch on the wall up and down, his face a mixture of confounded amazement.

She smiled at the sight he made. He looked so beautifully perplexed and utterly disgruntled over his new discovery that her heart did a little flip. This warrior, who lived in a time of bloody combat, was held captive . . . by the power of electricity.

"Having a good time?" she asked, shrugging out of her coat and hanging it up on a peg near the door.

With a fiercely concentrated scowl, Duncan's gaze snapped to hers. "My home is full of witch's magic."

Rachel sighed and removed her wet boots. "It's not witch's magic. It's simply modernization. A lot of years have passed since you lived here."

Duncan grumbled something under his breath that sounded suspiciously like "sorcery" as he regarded the light switch and bulb dubiously, his expression conveying that he was decidedly wary of this artificial illumination as he gave the switch another flick.

At last he grew tired of the marvels of modern science and turned to face her, moving out of the shadows that had partially cloaked him.

Rachel's eyes widened and her mouth dropped open as she got her first full glimpse of him—clad only in a pair of faded jeans.

Sweet heaven, there was something awe-inspiring about the way God had created a man's body—particularly a man at the height of his sexual peak.

He gestured to his crotch. "This . . . *thing*"—he tugged on the zipper—"it sorely vexes me. I pull and I pull and yet it remains steadfast, mocking me. God's teeth! How do men in this century have time for such nonsense?"

The answer to that question eluded Rachel. She had never been particularly concerned with men's dressing habits. Then again, very few looked as this man did.

"It's probably stuck," she said, hoping he didn't notice that she sounded slightly out of breath. "Wiggle it a little bit."

He scowled and tugged at the zipper, demanding that it obey. To her great relief, the zipper finally complied.

Then he looked at her . . . really looked, his gaze drifting down her body, the barest hint of a smile tilting up the corners of his lips.

"'Tis quite a sight ye make this morn, sweet witch." His voice was a husky rumble that did strange things to her insides.

"I was cold," she said, trying to explain away her bulky and decidedly unappealing layers of clothing, which she had not merely donned for protection against the pervasive chill, but against hot blue eyes that seemed to bore into her as though seeing into her soul.

"Had ye stayed in my bed last night, such a thing 'twould not have been an issue." The remark was not an accusation, but rather an observation, one she had little doubt would have proven all too accurate.

She had spent a good portion of the night thinking about him. Imagining herself lying beneath his solid frame, enveloped in his heat, staring up into those hypnotic eyes and getting lost—as she was doing at that very moment, which might explain why she nearly jumped out of her skin at the sudden banging on the front door.

Her gaze shot to the door, where someone waited for her to answer the summons—someone she couldn't allow to get a glimpse of Duncan, especially with his portrait looming directly behind him.

"Hide." She rushed out.

He scowled. "I hide from no man."

"Think about it," she said, trying to reason with him. "How would I explain you? I'm supposed to be here alone." When he made no move to depart, she softly beseeched, "Please, Duncan."

He hesitated, looking none too happy. Then he nodded curtly and stepped away, blending into the deeply shadowed corridor.

Rachel breathed a sigh of relief as she turned to the door, hoping she appeared at ease as she opened it, relieved when she saw who it was. "Good morning, Fergus."

"Mornin'," he replied brusquely, his shoulders slumped against the cold and falling snow as he scrutinized her with squinted eyes that seemed to know she hid something. "Is there aught amiss?"

"No," she said a bit too quickly. "Why?"

"Yer lookin' peaked."

"I'm just a bit tired."

"Guess ye ain't slept much, eh?"

"The storm kept me awake."

"Told ye they was bad."

An *understatement*, Rachel thought, hugging herself as the cold, blustery wind blew around her, scattering snow at her feet.

"I brought somethin' for ye." He stepped away and then reappeared with a lush pine tree.

She blinked. "What's that for?"

"'Tis Christmas," he said gruffly. "Thought ye should have yourself a tree. Cut it m'self right from Glengarren's woods."

Despite Fergus's somewhat intimidating personality, obviously there was a gentleness buried beneath his austere demeanor.

Rachel knew she should be thanking him instead of staring at the tree with something akin to despondency, the words to tell him she didn't want it on the tip of her tongue.

But she couldn't hurt his feelings like that. He had been making a nice gesture, and it would be wrong of her to throw his thoughtfulness back at him.

"Thank you, Fergus," she murmured. "That's very sweet of you." She moved back in the doorway and motioned him inside.

The smell of pine and brisk air followed him into the house, little green needles dusting the foyer floor as he struggled with his burden.

"I'll just put it there in the library."

Rachel nodded and watched him walk away, glancing cautiously toward the shadows where Duncan had disappeared, unable to catch even the slightest glimpse of him in the gloom of the corridor. Was he still there?

With a strange sense of unease, Rachel headed into the library, where Fergus was propping up the tree, his movements surprisingly efficient for a man with his disabilities.

"Is this spot all right for ye?" he asked, glancing over his shoulder at her.

"It should be fine."

Fergus nodded and then brushed his hands off on his pants. "There should be some geegaws up in the attic. Them sparkly lights and hangin' doodads—and also one of them things that holds up the tree."

"Do you have your tree up yet?"

"Nope. Don't got one. Most folks 'round here don't celebrate Christmas. The Scots' time for celebratin' is Hogmanay, which is at the end of the month. But his lordship's mother, ye see, was American, like yerself, and she wanted her children tae take part in the holiday, so she got all the fixin's and would do the place up fancy every year."

Rachel could only imagine how festive the castle must have once been, all decorated for Christmas, twinkling lights whisking away the shadows, brightly colored ornaments banishing the gray pall, red and white poinsettias enlivening the gloom of the foyer stairs, fresh garland twining around the sadly worn banister, the smell of pine and spices eclipsing the odor of damp mustiness, and a wreath with a big red velvet bow on the front door welcoming all visitors. It would have been a sight to behold.

"The family used tae make a big deal outta it," Fergus went on. "Stringin' up rows of popcorn and them berries, and the kiddies would hang candy canes and dangle beribboned cookies from the tree limbs. 'Twas quite a fetchin' picture, if I say so m'self."

"It sounds lovely." And just hearing about it made Rachel's heart ache for days that were gone forever.

Fergus's gaze dropped from hers then, and he shrugged. "I have me own selfish reasons for bringin' ye the tree, what with this bein' Glengarren's last Christmas and all. It just seemed kinda like the thing tae do, if ye know what I mean."

Rachel essayed a gentle smile. "You did the right thing, Fergus," she reassured him. And though it was the right thing for Glengarren, she didn't know if it was the right thing for her.

He gave her a quick nod. "Well, I'll be goin' then." He shuffled toward the door, but then paused on the threshold, eyeing her. "Ye sure everything's all right? Ain't nothin' strange happened tae ye since I left ye here alone?"

More things than she cared to confide, Rachel thought. "No. I'm fine."

He made a low grunt. "Well, don't say as I didn't warn ye. There's things about this old place that just ain't right. No, not right a'tall. Ain't seen nothin' with me eyes, mind ye. 'Tis just a feelin' I get, here, in the pit of me belly."

Rachel well understood that feeling. She rubbed her arms as a chill suddenly assailed her, her mind replaying the night before, hearing whispers, seeing the odd mist in the hallway.

"Thanks for the warning," she said. "I promise you'll be the first to know if I encounter any problems."

"Well, all right, then. Good day tae ye." He doffed his dusty hat and scuffled out the door, closing it soundly enough that the bang echoed in the far-reaching corridors.

Rachel sighed, her gaze straying to the pine tree leaning against the wall next to the bay window, filling the room with its scent—a scent that brought back poignant memories of Christmases past, of long-ago days when she, like the MacGregor children, had strung popcorn for the tree.

Closing her eyes, she backed out of the room, standing motionless in the hallway until the rise of emotion subsided. Then she glanced about, expecting Duncan to reappear; disgruntled, of course, because he had been forced to keep out of sight. But no sound came to her, no shadows shifted to reveal his brooding, beautiful face.

Where was he?

Rachel moved through the foyer, her feet whispering across the cold surface as she headed toward the darkened corridor where Duncan had retreated. Her eyes strained to see through the murky gloom. She called his name; the sound rebounded like a cry down a well.

With faltering steps she continued on, the darkness swallowing her, as did the cold. She moved cautiously down the unfamiliar hall that meandered like a maze, long-undisturbed dust rising with each step she took.

Here the surroundings appeared older, the air mustier, cobwebs clinging tenaciously in the corners and along rotted moldings, jagged pieces of wood and broken sections of stone scattered on the floor, sad remnants of neglect and age. Clearly, no repairs had been done in this part of the house in generations.

Rachel stopped abruptly as the air stirred against her. No draft. No place for air to get in. Yet it crept up her body inch by inch, touching her flesh here, there, crawling over her face . . . and then slowly, inescapably, shifting around her throat.

Her hand flew to her neck, panic driving through her blood like an ice spike, as freezing and brutal as the air. Her rational mind was eclipsed by fear, by the certain knowledge that something threatened her—and that something was tightening around her throat.

Rachel began to run blindly through the shadows, desperate to escape the terrifying presence that followed her. "Duncan!" she cried as the gloom of her ancient surroundings intensified, his name reverberating off the vaulted ceiling.

She froze in her tracks, her heart slamming against her ribs and cold sweat rising to her face. The echo that had come back to her had not been her voice . . . but a deep masculine knell—as jeering as it was menacing.

Rachel forced her rigid legs to move, then move faster, every nerve in her body standing on end as the pressure around her throat increased.

She struggled to breathe—stumbling forward, all her attention centered on the dim rays of light that suddenly appeared ahead.

Frantic, she burst from the corridor and into the cavernous, charred ruin of the decimated east wing, with its blackened walls and rafters that yawned around her and above her like the exposed bones of some mammoth beast.

She spotted him then—Duncan, standing amid the rubble of what had once been part of his home. The pressure increased around her throat, leaving her unable to call his name.

She dropped to her knees, struggling for air, trying to pry away unseen hands, her eyes widening as a funnel of wind and odd white vapor whirled before her, whipping up dust that appeared to take form.

Duncan turned then, his eyes shockingly blue against his blanched face. For an instant their gazes locked through the roiling haze—then a roar—howling, ear-splitting, coming from nowhere and everywhere—ripped through the air, the force hurling Duncan backward into the wall, the sound of her name on his lips the last thing she heard before unconsciousness engulfed her.

chapter
6

HE CARRIED HER TO THE library, to the fireplace, where the flames banished the cold. Still, he held her secure in his arms as he sat down in front of the hearth, smoothing the hair from her brow. His fingers trembled, and he released a shaky breath.

"Lady," he whispered. "How do ye fare?"

Gazing into his concerned eyes, Rachel did her best to shake off the icy shock and fear that had numbed her the last few minutes.

"I'm fine," she murmured, her voice sounding raspy. "What about you?" She reached up to smooth her fingers over a cut along his cheek.

He took her hand in his and gently kissed her palm. "'Tis a scratch." His eyes held hers, somber, sorrowful. "Had anything happened tae ye, lass . . ."

She gave him a gentle smile. "Don't worry. I'm stronger than I look." Her vow did not seem to appease him. She could feel the tension in his body, his distress almost palpable. Never had a man looked at her in such a way, as if his very world would collapse if she had been hurt. "What happened in there?"

He shook his head. "I know not."

"Duncan . . ."

"Aye, lass. I sense what troubles ye."

"Then I didn't imagine it? There was something—"

"Aye."

"But it can't be. I don't believe in spirits, malevolent or otherwise."

"Nor I. But neither would I have believed that this thing that has transpired with me could have happened."

Rachel didn't want to think that Duncan's appearance and whatever had just taken place could be connected, though strange, frightening things had begun happening shortly after his arrival.

"Perhaps it was a freak wind?" she said, searching for an explanation. "Like the voice I heard. The wind through the corridors and rafters often sounds human."

"Perhaps," he said without conviction, tension bracketing his mouth.

He stood up and carried her over to the couch, where he laid her down, his gentleness bordering on reverence, touching a place in Rachel she long believed cold and remote.

He began to pace, and in moments his anger was back, swirling around him as turbulently as the wind that had brought them both to their knees.

As she watched him rake a hand through his hair, his face stamped by frustration, she tried desperately to convince herself that what had transpired in the east wing had been brought on by fear when she couldn't find him, panic closing off her throat rather than an invisible hand.

And perhaps Duncan had stumbled back into the wall instead of some force throwing him into it. Fear could easily shroud the truth, blur the mind.

And she *had* been afraid . . . afraid of losing him. When he had not appeared after she called his name repeatedly, she began to think that he was gone—disappeared into the mist, never to be seen again—that perhaps everything she had experienced thus far had not been real but rather her unconscious mind wanting something so desperately it was willing to bring her fantasies to life.

Yet she couldn't quite dispel the feeling that strange forces were at work here. The same forces that had brought Duncan to her. Hadn't Fergus told her that Glengarren was more than it appeared to be?

"There is much that confuses me," Duncan said, moving to stand in front of the fire, his troubled gaze fixed on the lapping flames.

Rachel rose unsteadily to her feet, her knees still weak and her head aching. She longed to console Duncan. But, more than that, she wanted him to hold her again. Those few minutes his arms had been around her, comforting and warm, had infused her with a sense of security she had not felt in a long time.

This blue-eyed Highlander, whose starkly beautiful mien now resembled more a lost child than a heroic warrior, had filled an empty space in her heart.

He released a burdened sigh and ran a hand over his brow. "I am weary."

Instinctively, Rachel touched his cheek. His flesh was chilled, though the fire in the hearth cast enough heat into the room to make her clothing feeling uncomfortably warm.

A fresh surge of fear assailed her. Something was different. She couldn't put her finger on the variance, but something had changed, some alteration in his appearance, as if a vivid oil painting, like the one of him in the foyer, had diffused to watercolor.

He turned his cheek into her hand, and closed his eyes. "I am glad ye were not hurt. 'Twould grieve me much were ye tae suffer."

Rachel's heart missed a beat at the gentleness she detected in his voice, and the sincerity in his words. "Duncan . . ." His name was a plea.

He opened his eyes, and a gasp lodged in her throat. His piercing blue eyes were as faded as a winter sky, the color nearly drained from them.

Then he blinked, and his eyes appeared normal again. Rachel stood rooted to the spot, stunned and shaken. Could what she had seen been a trick of the light? A temporal illusion brought about by the flickering flames and her overstressed mind?

Her questions drifted to the background as Duncan ever so lightly touched his fingertip to her bottom lip, gently smoothing the callused pad across her suddenly sensitive mouth.

The contact was as jarring as it was seductive; that this battle-scarred warrior, whose very presence denoted power and danger, could evoke such tenderness in a touch, left her weak . . . and aching for him.

His mouth curved into a sensual invitation, a promise of pleasure she could only imagine. To feel those lips on her own. To experience the full measure of that soul-melding she knew only with him, a heightened awareness that dug into every fiber of her being, would be bliss.

The need to press her mouth to his nearly overwhelmed her. Made her tremble. She felt her lids grow slumberous, her body languid.

"Rachel," he whispered, his breath fanning her cheek, teasing a tendril of hair, blowing into her very heart and lodging there.

Everything inside her focused on him, tunneled solely on this moment, a second of eternity that seemed to have been building for a lifetime, waiting ... waiting.

Then, without warning, he stepped away, leaving a cold chill in his wake, and a haunting despair to take up residence inside her.

She opened her eyes to find him standing with his back to her, his head bowed, his body rigid. For long moments they stayed frozen in time, silent, torn, grief and need clashing in an inner battle before pieces of her began to quietly shatter.

She turned away from him—and from the turmoil in her heart, fleeing on silent feet back to the sanctuary of her room, back to the familiar demon of loneliness.

THE BLIZZARD STARTED that afternoon.

Rachel hugged herself as she stared out her window into ever-darkening skies, watching the snow that had continued unabated for most of the day, covering the ground in a thick blanket of white, weighing down tree limbs and layering the rooftops of the sleepy town in the distance, the inhabitants oblivious to the turmoil and despair residing on its very perimeter.

The snow collected in deep drifts along the castle walls and painted the windowpanes in a complex veil of ice crystals as the wind moaned its plaintive song.

Rachel sighed wearily and sat down before her bedroom hearth, the logs crackling, spewing orange and blue flames, black wisps of ash ascending the chimney.

She was dressed for bed; flannel pajamas she was glad to have packed. Though her body was tired, her heart was too sore and her mind too involved in troubling thoughts for sleep to come easily this night.

She wrapped a hand around her mother's antique locket, having not removed it from around her neck since her mother's death. The locket was Rachel's solitary comfort, her last vestige of the life she had once known.

The metal warmed in her palm, and she could almost imagine it was her mother's hand within hers, giving a reassuring squeeze, bidding her to be strong, that the future would again hold all that Rachel had once hoped for.

She wanted to believe, but was too afraid of that future, of what she had seen when she closed her eyes at night, images of a life with Duncan.

And a life without him.

Like a dream, he had suddenly appeared in her world, making her hope again, taunting her with glimpses of a love she knew was meant to be, a love that had struggled across time, obstacles, chasms, to find its other half. Its completion.

Her feelings for him were more than just passion,

though the ache was there, burning stronger than the fire in the hearth. She could feel Duncan's own desire, it seared her, and yet he had denied her, leaving her ashamed of the strength of her yearning for him.

What would he do were she to slip into his bed and press her flesh against his? Take him inside her body, sheath him, rock him, fulfill her fantasy to make them one, to bring their joining, their fate, full circle?

She tried to shake free of the thought, yet it would not release her. She had to get away, outdistance the talons of despair seeking to sink into her.

She pushed to her feet and hastened to her bedroom door, opening it and gazing warily out into the dark corridor, her attention shifting against her will to Duncan's room, wondering what he was doing. If he was thinking of her as she was of him. If he was hoping she would come to him. She felt as if he called her, silently beckoning.

But what if all she heard was her own need? What if he was fast asleep? What if she slipped beneath his sheets and he rejected her? She simply couldn't bear it.

Run, her mind clamored. *Run as fast as you can. Get away from here.*

She did not question the command. Instead she fled down the hallway, not knowing where she was going, simply wanting to feel her breath rasping through her lungs, to remember she was alive and this was real and that somehow she must deal with whatever came next.

She shut out the chill racing over her, keeping pace with her, the brush of air upon her cheeks, the increasing groan of the wind. She ran, faster, her senses expanding and her heart racing, her breath a vapor in the cold.

Her chest was heaving by the time she descended the massive staircase and stumbled into the foyer, her breath coming out in short pants.

She closed her eyes and inhaled deeply, calming her body, easing back into her skin, feeling the sedative affect the exertion had given her.

A hint of wood smoke wafted to her, and she opened her eyes, seeing the door ajar to the library, the orange glow of a fire blazing in the hearth.

Her body and mind were immediately alert, the perspiration growing chill on her brow. Hadn't Duncan extinguished the fire before he had come up to bed?

Or had someone else rekindled it?

With trepidation, Rachel moved quietly across the foyer and hesitated on the threshold to the library, the warmth of the fire enveloping her even from a distance, the flames chasing the shadows into the corners to gather and grow, threatening, cloaking whatever chose to hide within its blackened folds.

Tentatively, she entered the room, a gasp breaking from her lips at the sight that greeted her, her incredulous gaze taking in the Christmas tree in front of the bay window, the tree that had been barren only a few hours before but was now fully decorated.

Baubles glistened in the firelight, and the red, green, and gold lights woven amid the lush boughs lent a fairy-like shimmer in the dark.

A moth-eaten Santa perched in a chair, his hat slanted on his head, his cheeks blooming with faded color. Beside him sat Rudolf, staring up at her with one black button eye, the other missing.

How? she wondered. *Who had done this?*

"I found the boxes in the storage area," came a deep voice from the darkness.

With a startled cry, Rachel whirled around to find Duncan lounging in a wing chair in the shadows across the room. The pulse of fear immediately dissolved into a sense of anticipation, a thrumming of her blood at the very sight of him.

"I frightened ye," he said, shaking his head in regret. "'Twas not my intention."

"W-what are you doing here?"

"I could not sleep." She heard something in his voice, a yearning that struck a chord within her. Yet his face was cloaked in shadows, denying her a glimpse of his expression.

"Did you do all this?" she asked, gesturing to the tree and the decorations.

"Aye," he said, rising from his seat and walking through the flickering light toward her, causing a sensation akin to bottled lightning to sizzle down Rachel's spine, his male beauty riveting her.

Then he stood before her, his dark eyes drinking her in, her own gaze eagerly reciprocating. Never had she enjoyed the simple marvel of looking at someone.

Her lips tingled and her nipples tautened, her entire body quickened, and he had not yet touched her, not uttered a single seductive word. That look alone had undone her every good intention.

She moistened her dry lips, and his eyes followed the path of her tongue. "I don't understand. How did you know how to decorate the tree?"

"I found this." He reached into the pocket of the soft blue chambray shirt he wore and pulled out a photo. "It was in the box."

Rachel glanced at the old picture, the color having lost a shade of distinction with age. But there was no mistaking the family gathered in front of a beautiful Christmas tree situated before the library's bay window.

The MacGregors, when their children were still young. Rachel's gaze focused on the oldest boy, who appeared to be about twelve, but his bluer-than-blue eyes were unmistakable, clearly marking him as one of Duncan's descendants.

Rachel glanced up at him. "This is your family."

He nodded, his gaze fastened on the picture, an emotion on his face that made her want to weep. "We lived on," he said in a raw voice.

"Yes," she murmured. "The MacGregors lived on." Rachel could not bear to think of what life held in store for Duncan back in his own time, an era of unrest, of constant warring. She didn't want to recall what she already knew. Not tonight. "Everything looks beautiful."

His gaze slid to hers. "I did it for you."

"Me?" she whispered.

"Aye."

"Why?"

"Tae take the sadness from your eyes."

Rachel averted her gaze. "I'm not sad."

"Aye, lass, ye are." He cupped her chin, turning her back to face him. "Tell me why."

Rachel stepped back out of his reach and slipped around him, moving toward the fireplace to warm her suddenly cold hands in front of the crackling flames.

He followed, standing so close she had no choice but to look up at him. She had to fight to keep from closing her eyes and pressing her cheek against his chest.

"What hurts ye so?" The tenderness in his eyes was nearly her undoing.

Tears pricked the back of her eyes and she turned from him, feeling as though she was slowly unraveling as she focused her gaze on the flames.

"This is my first Christmas without my parents," she managed in a barely audible voice. "They both died this year."

How often had she, as a child, crept from her bed to spy on her parents who, after tucking her between the sheets, had spent the evening cuddled together before the tree, soft Christmas carols whispering from the stereo as they shared hot chocolate and an occasional kiss.

As a child she had not appreciated their special bond. As an adult, she had dreamed, even craved to spend her Christmases in an identical manner—wrapped up in the security and love of a man who worshipped her.

Duncan moved behind her, his body close—so close. The warmth of it suffused her, seeped beneath her skin and twined inside her. "Your heart is breaking, is it not?"

Grief instantly clogged her throat. "You would think that I was too old to allow the sight of a Christmas tree to make me weep," she said, her voice crumbling.

"'Tis not the tree that makes ye weep, lass. 'Tis your sadness. But I do not think your parents would wish for ye tae suffer such sorrow on their behalf."

He was right. Her parents would have wanted her to

be happy, to remember the good times, and there had been so many, she thought.

Her mind drifted back to all the wonderful Christmases in Connecticut, precious memories invading, making her smile even as her chest ached with despair.

"Every year, on Christmas Eve, my father and I built a snowman on our front lawn. We would dress him up like Santa in his red suit and hat. He called it our holiday tradition." She shook her head and stared down at her hands. "I stopped doing it when I turned fifteen, thinking it was too childish."

"If ye love something, ye are never too old tae enjoy it."

"I know that now." Now, when it was too late to go back. "I guess I always believed my parents would be around forever, and that they would see that I carried on the tradition with my own children."

Duncan was quiet for a moment, and then he asked in a low, deep voice, "Do ye have any bairns?" He placed his hands on her shoulders and gently turned her around to face him, his expression solemn, his blue eyes delving into hers.

"No," she murmured. "I don't have any children. That would require a husband."

"And why have ye no husband? Ye are as comely a female as I've ever clapped eyes on." He lifted a piece of her hair, fanning the strands through his fingers. "With hair like midnight silk, spillin' down over your shoulders, making a man itch tae comb his fingers through it." His gaze elevated to hers. "And eyes the color of ferns, soft and green. Ye are a temptation, lass. A woman any man would be proud tae call his own—a woman any parent would be proud tae call their daughter."

The tears Rachel had so carefully held in check slipped from her eyes then, and emotions she had kept bottled up inside for so long began pouring forth. She had had no one with whom to share her pain. No one who truly cared.

Duncan pulled her into his arms. She did not resist. It felt good to be held, too right to lay her head against his shoulder and simply let go.

Words spilled from her. She told him of the loss of her parents, how much they had meant to her and how desperately she missed them, and all the while he held her, understanding her sorrow.

When at last her tears subsided and her grief had all poured forth, he tipped her chin up and gazed deeply into her eyes. "Ye are a brave and beautiful woman. Don't ever forget that."

His full, sensuous lips were only a hairbreadth from hers. The kiss was inevitable . . . and so long overdue. A lifetime it seemed.

"Rachel . . ." Her name whispered from his lips like a benediction, a sweet prayer for salvation, and every lonely, yearning place inside her responded.

His mouth descended, plundered, tasted her desire for him, which he amply returned. His hands swept down her sides to cup her buttocks, pulling her harder against his erection, his chest abrading her nipples.

Then those large, beautiful hands slid between their bodies, his thumbs sweeping across her turgid peaks, sending honeyed bliss spiking through Rachel. She moaned into his mouth, the sound wanton and wicked.

He pulled back and stared down at her, conflict and confusion battling in his eyes, even as his gaze continued to devour her, bringing heat to all her most sensitive spots. She didn't want it to end. Why did he stop?

Perhaps, she thought painfully, because he was being the sensible one, realizing that theirs was a temporary relationship and that the scales of life and time might very well tip at any moment, righting those things that were out of kilter.

Or perhaps his reticence to take what she willingly offered had nothing to do with the fact that some twisted fate had set them worlds apart, but something far more cruel.

A wife. Children.

A life that did not include her.

Was he thinking about another woman when he kissed her? Yearning to hold another body close?

She wanted to ask him, but wondered if she really desired to hear the answer. Perhaps it was better not to know.

"What's the matter, lass?" he quietly asked.

Did he not see what was in her eyes? Could he possibly not know how she felt?

"Tell me," he gently commanded, cupping her cheek, raising her eyes to his. "We keep no secrets between us."

No secrets. No lies. Not when time was so very precious. "I . . . I want to know . . . if you have a wife."

He regarded her for a long moment, and with each second that ticked past, her heart began to crumble, piece by devastated piece. She could not blame him for loving another woman.

No matter what she thought, true love did not translate through time, through barriers that no human could breach; their souls had not been searching through eternity to find each other. Such thoughts belonged to other realms. Not theirs.

Rachel turned away from him, not wanting him to see what his silence had wrought, the pain so clear on her face.

He came up behind her, sliding his hands around her waist, his pelvis nestling against her bottom, and in an instant, her despair ebbed, her loneliness waned, replaced by a merging of something earthy, a connection unable to be explained. It simply . . . was.

She wanted to hold him close, feel his heart beating in tempo to hers, rub like a cat over the sweet hardness pressing against her, feel him tense, hear him groan with desire. For her. Only for her.

Never had a man made her feel so wild, so wicked, yearning with the need to release all her inhibitions and revel in her sexuality.

His hands fisted in her hair, gently tugging her head back to rest against his chest as he whispered in her ear, "There is no other woman, lass. Only you."

Relief and a sweet ache poured through her veins. This was madness. They were worlds apart, centuries apart, and yet not apart at all.

His fingers splayed across her stomach, his lips tracing her jawline. "God, lady . . . ye make me forget myself. 'Tis as if all the years of honing my skills on the battlefield and learning the necessity of control were for naught. With a winsome smile, a sultry glance, ye bring me tae my knees. I yield tae ye, lady. Ye are a force far greater than I."

His words sent a delicious thrill through her. To think she made this beautiful pagan wild with desire for her was bone-melting, divine. Pure heaven.

Rachel tipped back her head and closed her eyes, simply wanting to feel the warm press of Duncan's hands on her body, imprint his every touch in her mind.

She turned her head up for his kiss, his tongue thrusting into her mouth in a rhythm she longed for him to do with his body. She throbbed, heat pooling at the juncture of her thighs.

"I want tae touch ye," he whispered against her lips, asking her permission instead of simply taking what he wanted.

"Please . . ." she begged, curling into him as his hand cupped her breast, her body dissolving under his sensual demand.

She gave in to her need and rubbed her bottom across his erection, reveling in the soft groans her actions elicited.

"Ye are indeed a witch tae have enticed me so. Heaven help me, lass, ye make me want . . ." He stopped abruptly, his hands stilling.

Rachel could feel his withdrawal, and she very nearly cried out her despair. "What?" she begged. "What do I make you want?"

When he didn't answer, she turned in his arms, looking into those haunting eyes, knowing she could lose herself in them, in him.

"What, Duncan . . . please tell me."

"Ye make me want tae forget that my life is not here," he said, his words laced with anguish, lancing her heart.

"But you're here with me now. We could—"

He pressed a finger to her lips, stopping her from saying something that she could not, should not. He smoothed a tendril of hair from her face, his fingers lingering, a bittersweet smile on his face.

"Ye know as well as I that I must find a way tae get back tae where I belong. There are people who depend on me, who even now may be struggling with my disappearance." He paused, and then made a startling confession, "I have a son."

His admission stilled everything inside her. "But you said—"

"I have no wife," he reassured her. "But I cannot deny that I've had mistresses." His words wounded when they should not, when they had not been meant as weapons.

Rachel tried to pull away from him, not wanting to hear whatever was coming next. Though he held her to him without force, his grip was unrelenting. He would not let her run away.

"Nay, lass," he rumbled in a voice meant to soothe. "Listen tae me."

Rachel shook her head. "I don't want to hear that you loved another woman."

He took hold of her chin and forced her head up. "I did not love another woman. There has been no one who has captured my heart, and yet I fear . . ." He stopped, his gaze roaming her face as if to memorize what he saw.

"What do you fear?" she whispered.

His smile was almost grim as he looked into her eyes once more. "I fear, sweet witch, that I could very well lose my heart tae ye. Truth . . . but I think I already have. 'Tis as if my heart, and all I am, has always belonged tae ye."

Rachel's heart soared, and she felt as if her entire life had been building toward this very moment, as if she had simply been biding time until the emptiness inside her was filled by the only thing missing.

This man.

She had felt a connection with him from the start, and though she had not known him, her soul had recognized him, seen what her eyes had not.

"I feel the same way."

"Ye do?"

"I do." She smiled gently and said, "Now, tell me about your son."

He looked uncertain about where to begin. "I have only known the lad these past six months. I knew naught of his existence for fourteen years, and then his mother died of the pox and he sought me out. He is a fine boy." His words rang with pride. "Strapping. Fierce. A warrior at heart. And the next MacGregor laird."

How Rachel wished that his child had been part of her, that fate hadn't played a terrible joke and set them lifetimes apart, only allowing them this one fleeting glimpse of how they could have been together.

A frown settled on his brow. "I worry, though, that he shall take up arms against the Gordons if I do not return."

The thought shocked Rachel. "But he's only a boy! Certainly he can't go into battle."

"Aye, he can. Already he trains with my men-at-arms. He says he will take up the MacGregor cause against the king and help rally the clans for the Young Pretender. I have bid him tae stay at Glengarren and see tae my people while I am gone on the Stuart crusade. This does not sit well with him. But he will do as his laird commands, unless . . ." He stopped.

Rachel knew what he did not say. His son would fight in his stead should he not return. She did not want to think about the bloody battles a child might be forced to engage in to defend the MacGregor land and honor.

"Do not fret, lass," he said then, tugging her back into

his arms, a place she longed to be. "Things will work out as they should."

She wanted to believe him, desperately. She longed to wake up and discover that Duncan was not a warrior from another century, but of hers. That what they shared was real, and strong, and indomitable. And that no force—not time, not duty, not even death—could separate them.

"Ye have not asked me why I was here in the library when ye came down," he said then, diverting the wild flight of her thoughts with the lazy sensuality etched on his handsome face.

"You said you couldn't sleep."

"But you have not queried me as tae *why* I couldn't sleep."

"Why?" she breathed.

"I was lonely for ye."

His admission weakened her knees and sent a thrill spiraling through her.

"I thought 'twas best for me tae stay down here . . . or else risk knocking upon your bedroom door and beseeching ye tae heal the wound within me, tae allow me to find succor within the sweetness of your lips."

He had felt as she had, known that longing, that aching despair that sought only one relief: merging—of hearts, of bodies. Minds and souls.

"Duncan . . ." she murmured, sliding her hands up his chest, her fingers twining in his hair. She lifted on her toes to drop kisses along his jaw. "Love me . . ."

His hands tightened at her waist, and when she looked into his eyes, they burned with desire held barely in check. One kiss. One touch. And she prayed she would break his control.

She brought his head down and fused her mouth to his, heard his low groan and knew she had won, knew she stood victorious against this larger-than-life Highlander, and the defeat was all she could have ever hoped for.

His hands slipped beneath her pajama top, and the feel of his large, hot fingers against her flesh was almost more than she could stand. She moaned into his mouth as his fingers flicked across her sensitive nipples.

"I must taste these," he said in a husky rasp, as his lips trailed a hot path down her throat. "They have haunted my dreams and taunted my waking hours."

With deft, expert fingers, he made quick work of the buttons and pushed the pajama top off her shoulders. He looked at her, a flush rising to her skin under that heated regard.

"Ye are beautiful, lady."

His words humbled her, made the feelings she had for him redouble—let her know, without a doubt, that what was about to happen between the two of them was right.

He dropped to his knees before her, his posture almost reverent as he pressed his mouth to her stomach, feathering kisses across her skin, not missing a spot, being more than thorough . . . and driving her mad as he slowly worked his way up to the underside of her breasts, first one, then the other.

"Bend over, sweet."

Rachel willingly obliged, her breasts dangling like ripe fruit in front of his mouth.

Her womb contracted as his mouth closed around her

nipple, suckling her, gently tugging, drawing the peak farther into his mouth as his hand worked on her other
breast, rolling the aching peak between thumb and fore-
finger. She had to place her hands on his shoulders to
remain upright.

"Now," he said, glancing up at her through a fringe of
thick, black lashes, "I must taste the very heart of ye."

Then he tugged down her pajama bottoms.

Like a willing puppet, she let him do as he pleased,
barely cognizant as his large hands gripped her thighs
and spread her legs, his thumbs opening her folds . . . the
tip of his warm tongue sliding into the cleft to flick the
engorged pulse point.

Everything inside Rachel dissolved in an onslaught of
divine, exquisite, erotic pleasure. And when his hands slid
up her sides to cup her breasts and resume his sensual
ministrations, she knew she had truly found heaven.

She tossed her head back as he brought her to an
explosive climax, the first she had ever experienced, the
convulsions going on and on, sheathing his finger when
he slipped it inside her, a groan breaking from his lips,
bringing her gaze down to his bowed head.

She combed her fingers through his silky, dark hair.
He looked up, taking hold of her arms, easing her slowly
to her knees before him.

No words passed between them as he coiled an arm
around her waist and took her down to the carpet in
front of the fireplace. No words were needed. What they
had to say was in their eyes, was communicated with
their hands, their mouths.

He spread her legs and slid his hard length into her wet

and waiting heat, her body tightening around him, accepting him, sighing into him.

He stroked in and out of her in a slow, steady rhythm, keeping himself poised above her, making her watch what he was doing to her, the muscles in his arms standing out as he strained to hold back, to draw out her pleasure until another orgasm, deeper and more intense than the first, pulled everything from her, culminating in a sweet flood where their bodies merged.

Then he took her hands in his, lifting them above her head, his lips coming down hard on hers, his tongue driving into her mouth as his shaft drove into her body, pumping away, harder and faster, sweat beading on their flesh as she moaned his name.

His endurance was unending, and he kept up the divine torture until she convulsed around him one more time. Then, and only then, did he pour his love into her, her name a rumbling exultation on his lips.

He rolled to his side, drawing her back against his chest, his body spooning along hers as he wrapped his arms tightly around her. Together they watched the fire flicker and dance, the flames ebbing with the night.

And as her eyes slowly drifted shut, her body enfolded within his protective embrace, Rachel knew, no matter what happened, whatever tomorrow brought, she would never be the same again.

Love had forever changed her.

chapter 8

SNOW BLANKETED THE MOORS and the town nestled peacefully in the valley below the castle the next morning; the image one of picture-perfect serenity.

A cold wind whipped snowflakes loose from the ground, making them swirl in little funnels as Rachel stood shivering beneath the rowan tree.

Never had the cold affected her so, made her blood feel sluggish and her mind grow numb. Or perhaps it was simply sorrow, deep in the heart of her, for what she was preparing to do.

She glanced up and saw gray clouds churning, ominous black streaks rolling through their centers, telling her the break in the weather was only temporary, and that the storm was rebuilding its strength to barrage the land once more.

Already the wind had begun to increase, the smell of new snow stinging her nostrils as sharply as the bite of cold air upon her face. She had to get started. This might be her only opportunity.

Rachel briefly closed her eyes, snowflakes dusting her eyelids as her mind drifted back to the night before, thoughts of Duncan's lovemaking taking the edge off her chill, a sweet ache of remembered pleasure gathering at the juncture of her thighs.

He had loved her all night long—by the Christmas tree, again in front of the fireplace, on the couch, then carrying her up to his bedroom and laying her down there, on the cloud-soft comforter, his whispered adoration and caresses keeping the dark secrets and menace at bay.

He had filled her in every way a man could fill a woman, emotionally and physically, and Rachel knew beyond a shadow of a doubt that she would never regret giving Duncan her body, or her heart.

But now it was time to honor her obligation and do what she had come to Glengarren to do. Release her parents' spirits into this barren, beautiful place and let them drift together on the wind, float through the sky, sail on to heaven.

She had slipped out of the house without Duncan, knowing she had to do this by herself, but never had anything been harder, more wrenching, and she could have used his strength to help her through this ordeal.

Once she spread her parents' ashes, they truly would be gone from her forever, and she just didn't know if she was ready. In her heart, she knew she had to let go, that she could never hope to move forward unless she did this one last thing for them.

Her hands trembling, Rachel lifted the urns in front of her, a tear spilling down her cheek as she thought about what life could be reduced to, the vital essence burnt away until only ounces of ash were left to mark a person's existence.

"But what a life you had, Mom and Dad," she whispered, her words borne on the wind, a flurry of snow spiraling in the air like a winged angel. "You found one another. You were one of the few, the blessed, to have experienced a love that knew no bounds, a love that included me. And for that, I, too, was blessed."

The tears rolled in earnest now. "I love you both, and I will always carry the wonderful memories in a special place inside me, a place that neither time nor separation can ever change, or erase. Someday we will all be together again. Until then, I want you to take my love with you . . . and know that I hold your love in my heart."

Tears blurring her eyes, Rachel removed the caps from both urns, choking back the silent sobs threatening to stop her, emotions that made her want to hold fast to her parents, turn back time, tell them again how much they had meant to her, say all the things she thought she would have more time to say.

Hold Infinity in the palm of your hand, and Eternity in an hour, a cherished voice whispered—her father's voice, reciting the words of his favorite poem by William Blake.

Recalling the quote was a comfort in that moment, and made Rachel feel as if her parents were there with her, giving her the fortitude to tip the urns . . . and let the breeze lift the ashes.

"Mom . . . Dad . . ." she wept, reaching out for something solid to hold on to, and finding nothing there but a fistful of emptiness.

They were gone.

Rachel bowed her head and cried, her shoulders shaking and grief knotting in her stomach, her despair nearly overwhelming at times.

The crunch of snow sounded behind her a few minutes later. She didn't need to look to know it was Duncan. She could feel his presence, his strength that she so desperately needed, enfolding her, comforting her, even from a distance. It had been that way from the start.

Then his voice, deep and solemn and steadfast, rang out in a bittersweet tribute to her parents.

> *In the gloaming,*
> *oh, my darling,*
> *when the lights are soft and low*
> *and the quiet shadows falling,*
> *softly come and softly go.*
>
> *When the trees are*
> *sobbing faintly*
> *with a gentle unknown woe,*
> *will ye think of me and love me*
> *as ye did once, long ago.*
>
> *In the gloaming,*
> *oh, my darling,*
> *think not bitterly of me,*
> *though I passed away in silence,*
> *left ye lonely, set ye*
> *free.*

For my heart was
tossed with longing,
what had been could never be.
It was best tae leave ye thus, dear,
best for ye and best for me.

In the gloaming,
oh, my darling,
when the lights are soft and low,
will ye think of me and love me
as ye did once, long ago.

Fresh tears filled Rachel's eyes at the beauty of his words as she slowly turned to face him, knowing that no matter what tomorrow brought, she would never love a man as much, or as deeply, or as forever, as she loved this man.

Snow dusted his dark hair and cold torched his cheeks. His eyes were blue pools of sympathy, and it was all she could do not to throw herself against him and cling to the strength that would bolster her.

"That was beautiful," she murmured, her voice choked with emotion. "Thank you."

He came to her then, silent, solid, indomitable, wrapping his strong arms around her and holding her close—so close that she ached to remain in that spot forever, feeling cherished. Loved.

"I knew ye needed me," he said, his words so gentle, new pain sluiced through her.

She nodded against his chest, her cheek pressing against the thick wool of his coat. "I did. So desperately."

"I'll always come when ye need me."

Will you? Rachel silently asked, too afraid to speak the words out loud, not wanting to hear the answer as she crowded closer to him, deeper against his coat, holding on to him as if her very life depended on it—and in all the ways that mattered, it did.

He was her other half. If she lost him . . . what would become of her? It was as if he offered her a new life just as the old one had ended.

He put a finger beneath her chin, tilting her face up. "Your tears are like daggers tae my heart, lass. Tell me what I can do tae comfort ye."

"Hold me, Duncan. Hold me tight and don't let go."

"Aye, lass. That I will. Always."

Rachel didn't know how long they stood there, huddled close together, snow dusting their shoulders, painting their hair. But she did not feel the cold. Duncan kept it at bay.

At last, he slipped his hand into her gloved one, dropping a kiss against her forehead as he led her back to the house, the world around them enshrouded in silence and the billowy drifts that shifted shape with each subtle movement of the frigid air.

The few treasured moments of sunlight quickly faded, chased away by building clouds that scraped against Glengarren's spires. The castle's dark windows reflected like somber, watchful eyes.

As though she were a child, he removed her coat when they entered the house and hung it up on a peg for her near the door. Then he rubbed his hands up and down her arms when a shiver overtook her.

"I've got the fire going in the library. Go warm yourself in front of it. I'll pour ye a glass of brandy tae take the chill away."

Rachel almost told him that the only thing she needed to chase away the chill was him, but she wanted to tell him with her body instead.

"That sounds heavenly," she murmured. "I'll fix us some food."

He studied her for a moment, concern in his eyes, as if still worried over her state of mind. She gave him a gentle, reassuring smile, which seemed to appease him.

"Hurry back tae me," he said softly, brushing a tender kiss across her lips, gracing her with the hint of a wicked smile that told her he wanted her just as badly as she wanted him. Then he headed across the foyer and disappeared among the flickering shadows of the library.

Rachel's feet did not touch the floor as she turned toward the kitchen, feeling as if she floated on a cloud of contentment, her thoughts consumed with Duncan, her body yearning for his touch, her mind turning over with images of their first time together, how he had laid her down in front of the fireplace and loved her with reckless abandon.

She could almost feel his hard, silky length sliding in and out of her, his warm lips suckling her nipples, the liquid pleasure building inside her as he brought her to that bright, spiraling place she had only experienced in his arms.

Her body began to quicken in anticipation, knowing there could be nothing better in the world than spending the day and night in Duncan's arms, living moment by moment, and not allowing themselves to think beyond that.

Upon reaching the kitchen, Rachel turned on the radio nestled between an old breadbox and a tea cozy, flipping through several stations until deciding on light music, sighing with pleasure as the golden voice of Frank Sinatra filled the room.

She rummaged through the well-stocked refrigerator, spotting a fat wedge of smoked ham, some turkey and cheese, mayonnaise, hot mustard, sweet peppers, pickles.

She wondered what Duncan would prefer to eat. Then she shrugged, deciding she would bring a little bit of everything—have a smorgasbord picnic on the library floor.

With a smile, she loaded up her arms and turned toward the table. Then she froze, her food spilling to the floor, glass jars shattering and spewing condiments in white and yellow blotches at her feet, as she heard a roar of unearthly anguish echo through the corridors, ramming a spike of dread down her spine.

Oh, God, Duncan! He was in trouble.

Her heart slammed against her ribs as she whirled around and headed out of the kitchen, the howl of pain and rage rushing over her like an avalanche, her eyes assaulted by the sudden darkness of the hallway.

She ran blindly, straining to see, the shadows playing tricks on her eyes, clouding her vision, confusing her until at last she caught the hazy dance of dust motes filtering through a shaft of light in the foyer.

"Ye bloody whoreson!" came Duncan's bellow, followed by a grunt of pain.

Oh, God. Oh, God. The words beat a tattoo in her mind as she raced across the foyer and into the library, freezing at the threshold, fear rising up her throat.

Near the Christmas tree, Duncan had fallen to his knees, body rigid, his breath rasping in his lungs as he gasped for air.

Her head snapped up as a glimmer of something caught the corner of her eye. She thought it was simply the light glittering off one of the numerous Christmas ornaments on the tree.

Her breath lodged in her throat as a shaft of winter light shone through the bay window, highlighting a man's hazy figure standing in front of it . . . black eyes staring at her, epitomizing all that was dark and malevolent in that single unwavering glare. He seemed to be there and yet not, as if he was half in and half out of their world.

In horror, she watched him begin to take on more substance, more form, a flesh-colored hue that was almost human coming into his face as Duncan grew weaker and paler.

Then the man sank to the ground before Duncan, locking that malevolent stare on Duncan and baring his teeth in a feral snarl, a growl of rage issuing from his lips, rebounding through the room like evil personified.

In that instant, Rachel realized that some kind of internal struggle was going on, a force whose very power enclosed a barrier around the two men, pushing her back.

She could feel a palpable force center squarely on Duncan, a violent charge of crackling sparks and shimmering illumination. Around them the lamp lights flickered and dimmed, the colored tree globes winked and sputtered. Rachel knew this man—this *thing*—meant to kill Duncan.

Her panic mounting, she watched Duncan's form begin to dwindle, fading to a diaphanous veil, while the unholy apparition before him grew more distinct by the second.

The man's energy expanded, became more vibrant and powerful—an energy that made the air move wildly, whipping the limbs of the Christmas tree so that the glass balls began to crash to the floor.

"Leave him alone!" she cried, fighting to get to Duncan, only to be driven back.

Her gaze flew around the room, her eyes alighting on a vase situated on a table near the door. Frantically, she reached for it, and with all the power she could muster, she hurled it toward the man . . . only to see it sail right through him with no effect and smash resoundingly against the wall behind him.

Dear God, what madness was this? Her world was spinning out of control and she was helpless to stop it, helpless to save Duncan. He was dying right in front of her, and she could do nothing but watch.

No! She wouldn't stand by and allow that to happen.

"In the name of God Almighty, go back to hell where you belong!" she shouted.

The man's head jerked up, shock momentarily limning his face before changing to undiluted rage. "Harlot!" he roared, his eyes blazing. "I'll see ye suffer for your interference!"

In the next moment he began to dim, his image fading, until what had been a shape once more became a white mist, before evaporating entirely.

For a second, time stood suspended; then Rachel shook off her terror and raced to Duncan's side, dropping down beside him.

His hands were braced on his knees, his head hanging low. He looked white as death, and the realization that she had almost lost him froze her to the marrow of her bones.

"Duncan." She took his face in her hands and smoothed the hair back from his sweating brow. "Oh, God . . . Duncan. Please tell me that you're all right."

His breath rasped in his throat as he struggled to lift his head and turn it in her direction. He stared at her with blank eyes, lifeless eyes, faded hollow spheres that filled her with a fear as powerful as she had experienced moments ago.

"Duncan," she pleaded, shaking him. "Come back to me."

His clouded gaze finally found her. He spoke only one word, but that single word filled her with a dread more chilling and terrible than her earlier horror.

"Gordon."

chapter

9

GORDON. The MacGregor clan's most hated enemy.

The foe Duncan had been fighting right before he had been pulled forward in time.

Rachel shook her head, her confusion and frustration mounting. "I don't understand. How can that be?"

For an eternal moment Duncan remained silent, his body still weak, color barely transfusing his skin.

She gripped his big hands in her own, rubbing them briskly, trying to somehow transmit her strength and body heat to him as her brain scrambled frantically for an answer to what had just transpired.

Something teased the back of her mind, a memory of fire and vows of vengeance. Though she tried desperately to grab hold of it, the images vanished as swiftly as vapor.

Long, tension-filled minutes passed before the dull sheen left Duncan's face and his color began to return to normal. Her relief, however, was brief. As his strength rallied, so did his anger. Blazing fury stamped his features as his gaze swept the room.

He shoved her hands away when she offered her help. He rose unsteadily, weaving on the balls of his feet as if hovering on the edge of a precipice. Then he found his center and righted himself.

His step faltered as he moved to stand in the spot Gordon had so recently occupied. Shattered remnants of Christmas ornaments winked from the floor like iridescent confetti.

"Why?" he demanded, swiveling around to face her, his eyes like ice on fire. "Why is that bastard's hell-doomed soul haunting Glengarren?"

Rachel wanted to wrap her arms around him, hold him tight, tell him everything would be all right. But deep down she knew things would *not* be all right. Something had been set in motion. Something they were powerless to stop.

They had to get away from here. Immediately. Leave Glengarren and not look back. The urgency rattled everything inside her.

"Duncan . . ." she whispered, but he was no longer looking at her.

"Show yourself, ye devil's spawn!" His voice vibrated with escalating anger. "Ye'll not get the better of me again. This I promise ye."

"Duncan, please, listen to me . . ."

"Why is he here?" he shouted toward the rafters, as if demanding an answer from God. "I was denied the pleasure of killing his blackened soul!"

A memory crystallized in that moment, a rush of vivid descriptions . . . gleaned from an old history book.

Rachel closed her eyes and said, in a raw voice, "He died here."

When she opened her eyes, she found Duncan staring at her—his eyes as sharp and dangerous as his sword. "Died in *my* house? How?"

"The fire in the east wing. He set it after you had wounded him. His body was never found. It's believed he perished in the fire."

Duncan's fists clenched at his sides, his jaw tightening into a hard knot of anger. "He always told me that should I ever succeed in killing him, he would haunt me all my days. He has managed tae keep his vow." He slammed a fist into his palm, and Rachel winced at the impact that spoke viciously of his anger and pain. It did not, however, deter the urgency inside her to be away from this place.

"We have to leave here, Duncan. Now."

His flashing blue gaze slashed to hers. "Leave?"

"Yes. I saw the look in Gordon's eyes. He intends to kill you."

His jaw clenched. "And do ye think I fear death, lady?"

"No," she said without hesitation, wishing in her heart he *did* fear death, that he would run away from it, run away with her, stay safe. Stay alive. "I know you don't, and that's what frightens me most. Duncan, please . . ." she begged. Unbidden, the tears began to flow again.

Without a word, he came to her, pulling her into his arms. "Do not fear for me, lass. I promise tae take care. Gordon will not prevail. I have beaten him time and again."

She shook her head, the wildness growing inside her. "No. This isn't the same. Don't you see?"

"I see that his strategy has changed, but that the result will remain the same. He has might, but still no wit. He never did."

Rachel wanted to rail at him, shake him, take him from this place. "He is a different opponent this time, Duncan. This is not an enemy you can face head-on with a sword. He has the advantage. Your strength. Your will. His revenge."

He shook his head, though she caught the flicker of understanding in his eyes, telling her he knew exactly what she was saying, that this time the battle was not simply to take Duncan's life.

But to claim his soul.

"'Tis you I'm worried about," he said, gripping her tighter to his chest, unwilling to face the truth, or simply refusing to believe he couldn't win against Gordon.

"I can take care of myself."

"He means tae harm ye."

"I only care about you."

"He knows I love ye, and he wants tae destroy all I hold dear."

How Rachel had wanted to hear those words, how she wished they could have been spoken at an hour less desperate, her heart less consumed with his safety.

"I love you, too, Duncan, and that's why I beg you to come with me, to leave this place. Surely Gordon cannot follow us."

"Ye ask me tae run away?"

"No. I ask you to save yourself. For me. Please, Duncan."

"'Tis not in my power tae do, lass. This is a battle that

has waited centuries to be put tae rest. There can be no more waiting."

"You don't understand . . ."

"I understand fully," he said softly, his hand trembling as he brushed her cheek, conveying that he had yet to regain his full strength. "I want ye tae depart this place. Go now. Gather your belongings and leave Glengarren and its curse behind."

"I won't leave you."

His grip on her arms tightened and he shook her lightly. "I command ye tae go!"

"No," she said firmly. "Not without you."

His eyes softened a fraction, and his voice became a painful rasp. "I could not bear it should something happen tae ye."

"Then take me away from here. Gordon has lost, don't you see? He's dead. You're alive. Let the past remain where it is, and give us a chance."

A spark of hope warmed in Rachel's chest as he appeared to consider her plea. She knew how much his honor meant to him, how deep this rivalry went between the two clans. But would his love for her prove to be stronger?

Dear God, she hoped so.

At last, he nodded. "I will go with ye as far as town, tae make sure ye're taken care of, but then I must return. I can offer no more."

Rachel bit back the argument that he would not deposit her at some hotel and then return to face Gordon alone. He had agreed to leave with her, and that was all that mattered. Once they were gone from Glengarren and

Gordon's threat, she would find a way to keep him from returning.

She took hold of his hand and tugged him toward the door. "Let's go. Now. Quickly."

He took a step and stumbled, bracing a hand against the back of the couch. To his protest, she wrapped an arm around his waist to help him.

She had expected to stagger beneath his weight, and struggled to keep him upright. He was a big man, and she well knew how solid, remembering the heavy, warm feel of all that muscle and sinew on top of her the night before.

Yet, to her despair, she acknowledged that there was something different about his body, as if Gordon's appearance had robbed Duncan of substance.

The urgency to be gone redoubled inside her, and she prayed they would make good on their escape, that Gordon had been weakened as well, and that he would not have the force to bar their exit.

But as they reached the door, a haunting howl erupted, driving them back. Duncan groaned, and for a terrible moment, she felt him being pulled away.

"Fight him," she cried, locking her arm around his waist, trying to propel him forward as she flung open the door.

She stumbled back, bludgeoned by the cold, biting air that rushed in on her, snow stinging her throat, cutting through her clothes like sharp teeth—no time to retrieve her coat.

Her rental car, covered by a thickening blanket of snow, remained where she had parked it upon her arrival at Glengarren, at the foot of the front steps.

She was forced to beat upon the ice-layered door handle before she managed to jerk open the door, scattering slivers of ice and chunks of snow over their legs.

Duncan dropped heavily into the passenger seat. She slammed the door and then raced around the front of the car, quickly realizing they were going nowhere until she cleared the banked snow off the windshield.

With frantic hands, she swiped at the glass, felt the ice shards cut into her palms. She shut out the pain in her desperation to complete her task.

Once done, she jumped into the car, white-knuckled hands gripping the steering wheel. She stared at the ignition as the jarring realization struck her—she didn't have the keys. They were in her purse. Inside the house.

She had to go back in.

"Where are ye going?" Duncan shouted as she leapt from the car.

"I don't have the keys."

"Rachel!" he bellowed as she dashed away from the car, his protests following her back to the front door, where she momentarily faltered before shoving the heavy portal wide.

Her breath left her in a rush as she spotted her purse on a chair near the library. Ignoring the rising fear that beckoned her to turn on her heels and run, she raced across the foyer, swiping up her purse and clutching it to her as she headed back to the door.

Barely ten feet from her goal, a sudden, familiar pressure gripped her neck, filling her with dread as invisible fingers began to tighten around her flesh, cutting off the scream working its way up her throat.

Her fingers scraped at her neck, trying to pull away hands that were not there, fighting an enemy she could not see . . . one who was far stronger than she, and who she knew would kill her if given the chance.

She struggled against the power holding her in place and forced her feet to move, dropping to the ground to claw her way toward the door, something inside her clamoring that, once outside, she would be free of the menacing hold.

With every ounce of strength she possessed, she fought for her life, unconsciousness threatening as her oxygen-starved lungs sought air, the mounting pressure hauling her back as if she were being sucked into a yawning black chasm that had begun to roil with Gordon's vindictive laughter.

The thought flickered that if Gordon killed her, she would be sealing Duncan's fate. Duncan would avenge her death in whatever way possible. The image galvanized her, pushing her step by tolling step toward the door.

On the threshold, her desperate gaze lifted, seeing Duncan's stricken expression as he stumbled out the car door.

Before he could get to her, the pressure against her throat subsided. She gasped for precious air as she struggled to her feet, praying her legs would not give out or that her mind would not succumb to the overwhelming fear making her body feel combustive.

She fell into the driver's seat, her shaking hands digging in her purse for the keys, only vaguely aware that the contents were spilling to the ground.

At last she found the keys, shoved them into the ignition, and turned. Nothing. She pumped her foot on the accelerator and tried again. The engine grunted and sputtered and then stopped.

Please, dear God, not now. Don't let the cold have drained the battery.

Again the engine whined and labored, before finally roaring to life. Throwing the car in gear, she hit the gas, the tires spinning as she took off down the driveway like the very demons of hell were dogging her heels.

"Rachel . . ." she heard Duncan say, her name barely audible over the wild thumping of her heart, her gaze flying to the rearview mirror, seeing the front door standing open and Glengarren looming over them, its shadow casting a menacing black cloak all the way to the gates marking the entrance to its haunted grounds.

Faster—she punched the gas pedal, racing for those gates, telling herself if she could just get through them, they would be free. That's when she heard the gasping.

Her gaze cut to Duncan to find his chest heaving with the exertion to breathe, his skin as white as the snow clinging to the windshield . . . his very presence growing dimmer, fading with each passing second.

Dear God, what was happening?

Then the answer came to her, swiftly, clearly, and with painful recognition.

They could not leave this property. Somehow, Duncan was bound to it, and should she make it through the gates . . .

She would kill him.

chapter 10

RACHEL SLAMMED ON THE BRAKES.

Tires locking, the car skidded sideways, spewing gravel, sliding over the snow-slick drive, the squeal of grinding brakes ear-piercing as they careened toward the gates—straight toward disaster.

With a muffled cry, she gripped the steering wheel, which lurched from side to side, the gates looming like a gaping abyss before them.

Hurling her partly over the console between the seats, the car suddenly plowed to a stop, the rear mere inches from the property's border and buried in a snowdrift that partially covered the back window, obliterating the sight of the castle in the distance.

Winded, Rachel struggled upright, shook free of the ache in her ribs and turned to Duncan. Panic closed off her throat.

He shimmered, his body mass diffused, breaking up, his eyes half-shut and his chest barely moving. Dear God, he was dying, fading before her very eyes into oblivion.

She turned the steering wheel hard and stomped the gas pedal. The rear tires spun, dug into the snow and mud, spattering the fenders and undercarriage.

The engine roared, the tires whined before they found traction and hurled the car forward up the driveway, toward the house, her gaze shooting repeatedly to Duncan—praying her plan worked.

A cry of relief broke from her lips as his image grew more vibrant and solidified the closer they got to Glengarren.

Coming to a stop, Rachel slammed the gearshift into park, jumped out of the car, and ran—feet sliding on the ice, sending her impacting against the hood before she regained her footing and sloshed through the snow to the passenger door, fighting with the handle that was again covered with ice, slivers jabbing her fingers.

At last she flung open the door and fell to her knees beside Duncan's still form, taking his hand in hers, trembling and numb with cold.

"Duncan," she whispered, her body shaking with the fear of losing him as she pressed his hand to her cheek.

An eternal moment passed before Duncan's eyes slowly opened; he looked at her, smiled faintly, and then swept away a lone tear coursing down her cheek.

Then he said, in a voice that had been stripped of its usual rumbling timbre, "Here I must remain." His words drove home what she had already known.

He could not leave these grounds. Not now.

Not ever.

Until that moment, Rachel had not allowed her despair to take root in the deepest, darkest place inside her. To the very depths of her soul, she had wanted to believe that the days could continue, idyllic and perfect in Duncan's arms, that God had brought this man here for her to love, and that no cruel fate would deny her that happiness. But fate had.

Even if Duncan never returned to his own time, he could not ever fully be a part of her life. He would have to remain locked behind invisible barriers, forever bound to Glengarren, battling Gordon, his life a hell on earth.

"Lady," he said weakly. "Ye must leave this place and forget about me. I am damned."

Leave him? How could she? It would be like losing half of herself. She had waited her entire life for this man, eternity—she would not lose him now.

"I won't leave you."

"There is nothing for ye here but torment."

She shook her head. "No," she murmured, forcing a smile she didn't feel. "Everything I want is here. We'll beat Gordon. Together."

"Nay," he bit out, his strength beginning to return as he swung his legs out the door and grabbed her upper arms. "I'll not have ye in harm's way."

"That's my decision to make, and I've made it. I'm staying."

"Ye are a damn stubborn wench," he said with a growl. Then he pushed away from his seat and stalked around her, the cold wind blowing back his thick mane of black hair and snowflakes flurrying around his shoulders.

The snow, like chips of ice, drove against her flesh as she chased after him, the freezing air cutting through her skin, her gloveless hands numb and her body trembling without a coat to keep her warm.

She caught up to Duncan at the Destiny Stones. A pile of rubble lay scorched and blackened by the lightning that had shattered it.

He stared down at a large fragment of the boulder, partially covered by snow. As Rachel huddled beside him, a fierce blast of wind blew down from Glengarren's rooftop like a mighty breath and scattered the drifts, revealing the words etched on the stone.

Her breath lodged in her throat. This was not some mythical druid boulder, she realized in horror . . . but a grave marker.

Duncan's grave marker.

After more than two hundred and fifty years, weather had barely eroded the words chiseled into the rock.

DUNCAN MACGREGOR
A HERO OF THE SCOTTISH
PEOPLE, WHOSE FIGHT FOR JUSTICE
AND FREEDOM WILL LIVE ON.

"'Tis my grave," he said in a hoarse voice, bringing Rachel's gaze to his tormented face.

What must it be like to look upon one's own grave? To discover with such brutal clarity that no one is immune to death—even heroes.

All these years, people had believed the stones were part of pagan lore. Mysterious. Dangerous. Keeping away from them out of ignorance and superstition.

Had no one ever seen that one man had been laid to

rest in their shadow? Had anyone come to honor the hero who had fought and died for this land, battling for something he believed in?

"When did I die?" he asked, posing the one question Rachel did not want to answer, did not want to even think about.

"It doesn't —"

"When did I die, lady?" he demanded angrily, fierce blue eyes slashing in her direction. "Did Gordon kill me?"

"No," Rachel replied, emotions constricting her throat. "You wounded him badly. In revenge, he torched the east wing of Glengarren, hoping the entire castle would burn down. In the process, the fire became his funeral pyre, which is the reason I believe he is still here."

"Then how did I die, if not saving my home?"

"A group of the king's men surrounded you during a battle that took place down this very hill, at Culloden Moor."

"What day, lady?"

Rachel hesitated, and then said in a barely audible voice, "April 17, 1746."

He raked a hand through his hair and looked away, down the valley toward Culloden. His eyes became distant. His brow furrowed with anguish. "Four months hence in my own time," he uttered despondently. "Four months tae live." He shook his head. "Not enough time. I have so much tae do. My son . . . my clan . . . how will they survive when I am gone?"

"You won't die. Don't you see?" Rachel moved to stand in front of him. "You're here with me now. That time has come and gone. You've escaped your fate."

His gaze dropped to hers. "Have I? And what fate awaits me here?"

"Us." She did not want to think of Gordon or being apart or battles or gravestones. "By some miracle, God has brought you to me, and for that, I am so very grateful."

"Miracle?" His jaw clenched and he stepped away from her, striding to the middle of the stones and whirling around to face her. "Speak not tae me of your God! He has cast me out. Left me here where I cannot get back. All I've ever known has been torn from me. This is no miracle. 'Tis a curse! What future have I? Have *we?* Your God has thrown me into this nightmare tae live eternally, with Gordon plaguing my life—and this ye call a miracle." He turned from her, his fingers curling into fists at his sides.

Rachel wanted to go to him, but knew her comfort would not be welcomed. How could she refute his words, anyway? He was right. Unless history changed, Gordon would remain here to haunt them the rest of their days—until they were all ghosts, doomed to forever drift through Glengarren's dark corridors.

Duncan dropped to his knees in the snow, his hands raised to the sky. "Why have Ye forsaken me?" he roared in anguish. "Why, damn Ye!"

His voice was a pained rasp that went straight through Rachel, piercing her heart, causing tears to slip unchecked down her cheeks.

She went to him, dropping to the ground before him and taking his face in her hands. Though he tried to fight her, she wouldn't let him look away.

"I won't leave you, Duncan." She stared into his tormented eyes, wanting him to see that she spoke the truth. "Whatever happens, we'll face it together. Lean on me, as you have allowed me to lean on you."

She felt him shiver, and knew it was not from the cold. Then, with a strangled oath, he gave himself over to her, drawing her tightly into his arms and laying his head in the crook of her neck.

"I love ye, lady," he whispered, his breath warm against her skin. "I'm sorry for all I've done. Forgive me."

"You have nothing to be sorry for."

The snow began to fall then, dusting them with light flakes, though the sky above their heads was ominous, speaking eloquently of the storm that had only temporarily abated.

They were trapped here, left with only two choices. To return to Glengarren and face Gordon—or freeze to death amid the stones, to allow the cold to slowly numb their bodies until they could feel no more, clutched in each other's arms for all eternity in the place where Duncan had once been laid to rest, so long ago.

To sleep and never wake up . . . *for in that sleep of death, what dreams may come.*

Rachel wanted that. Her parents were gone, and without Duncan, she would have nothing. She was not afraid. No, she was comforted. She had found the answer, and with its revelation came relief.

She eased away from Duncan, pressing a gentle kiss on his lips. Then she sank down to her side in the snow, Duncan's beautiful blue eyes delving into hers, knowing what it was she wanted.

"Lay with me, Duncan."

"Lady . . ." came his hoarse protest.

"Lay with me," she whispered.

Myriad emotions flickered across his face in that moment, a second in time that seemed to go on forever as they stared into each other's eyes, each knowing it might very well be the last time they ever did.

Rachel, already numbing from the cold, reached up and wrapped her arm around Duncan's neck. Slowly, he eased down beside her, his lips, so warm, so full of life, pressed against hers in a kiss that encompassed all their love, a love very few people ever experienced.

A love she was fortunate to have been granted.

He pulled her close. She pressed her cold cheek against his shoulder, unafraid for the first time in a long while. This man of her dreams had burst into her life and pulled her from her despair. Whether he believed it or not, he *was* her miracle. Her salvation.

And as the frigid winds and icy snow bit into her flesh, Rachel hoped that God would grant her one last wish: that if she and Duncan could not be together in this life-time . . . they would be together in the next.

RACHEL DRIFTED IN A DREAMWORLD, a beautiful vision of green meadows and blue skies . . . and Duncan magnificently garbed in his Highland colors, waiting for her at the cliff's edge, one hand reaching out to her.

She smiled and started toward him, wanting to go wher-ever he was going, out there beyond the clouds, beyond pain and sadness. Out where her parents now were.

She didn't feel herself being lifted or the strong arms that carried her. She didn't feel the warm air touch her brow, or creep across her damp body, easing beneath the wet layers of her clothing. She was at peace.

"Wake up, lass," a deep voice said, trying to pull her from her dream, but she didn't want to relinquish her hold on this wonderful place.

She moaned as tender hands gently removed her shirt. She writhed, wanting those hands on her body, stirring her passion, bringing her senses to life.

Pain set in then, tiny needles pricking her skin, jabbing at her in a hundred places. She whimpered and tried to draw back into herself, back into the beautiful dream, the enchantment of this other realm.

The pain dissipated as a sweet warmth pressed against her side, taking away the chill, enfolding her in a safe and protective embrace.

Instinctively, she curled into the hard length beside her, her palms resting against solid flesh, a smile filtering across her lips as her thumbs found the silky disks, heard the slight intake of breath, heat beginning to swell in the pit of her belly and fanning outward, seeping through her bones until none of the chill remained.

"Lie still, sweet," came that same voice, huskier now, familiar . . . endearing.

Rachel's eyes fluttered open, and when at last her world came into focus, she knew all her dreams had been answered as she stared up into Duncan's handsome face.

She did not question this miracle, but embraced it, sliding her naked body up the few inches it would take to reach his mouth. If this was heaven, she never wanted to return to earth.

She sighed ever so sweetly as her lips closed over his, his tongue slipping inside to mate with hers.

She rolled him to his back and moved on top of him, taking control, wanting to touch, taste, love every dangerous, glorious, hard sinew of him.

A breath of delight whispered from her lips as she cuddled the silk-and-steel length of him. He moaned and ground his hips against hers.

Then he shook his head and lightly took hold of her arms. "Nay, lady . . . ye need rest."

"You're what I need."

She moved against him and lowered her mouth to the beautiful, chiseled planes of his chest, finding one smooth pebble and lapping at it with her tongue.

In the next instant, she was on her back, Duncan's darkly alluring body poised above her, his heaviness pressed intimately between her thighs, and she savored the delicious feel of him, reaching down to run a finger across the tip of his silky shaft and then down the length.

His jaw clenched and air hissed between his teeth. "Lady . . . ye must stop. Ye make it difficult for me tae act the gentleman. Desist before ye break my control. 'Tis on the very edge as things stand."

It was only then that understanding dawned on Rachel. They were back in Glengarren . . . in Duncan's room. Reality crashed in on her and her fear swiftly returned.

"What are we doing here?" She tried to push Duncan away, to get up. "We were supposed to die . . . the snow . . . the storm. We could have been free."

He gently shackled her wrists, his weight pinioning

her to the bed. "Not by death, lass. My soul would be damned for all eternity if ye died for love of me."

Rachel struggled against his hold. "But I wanted to! You had no right to deny me." Tears welled in her eyes and coursed silently to the pillow beneath her head. "I want to go with you. Don't leave me here without your love."

"Where I must go, ye cannot follow. But ye'll always have my love." His lips brushed across hers. "Let me prove it to you."

With reverence, he slipped inside her, his gaze locked to hers, holding her captive as she moaned from the pleasure of each long sweep, each thrust that took his possession to the hilt.

Long into the night he loved her, proving his feelings for her time and again. Yet, as the hours ticked past and twilight settled into midnight, the winds swirling around the house in the desperate hours before dawn, Rachel knew that this time, there would be no outdistancing fate.

chapter
11

THEY BEGAN THE NEXT DAY as they had ended the last, living in the moment and trying not to think about what might happen next. Yet the tragedy and despair they had experienced thus far could not be dispelled as easily. Images, both beautiful and horrible, plagued Rachel.

Was it only last night that she had thought to let her worries and fears drift away forever? To be covered by the snow as she nestled close to Duncan on the frozen ground of Glengarren? To embrace that sleep of death in the shadow of his tombstone?

In the light of day, it was almost unfathomable that her anguish had taken her that far, that she had seen no other way out.

Never had she thought to solve whatever heartache might haunt her by taking her own life. It was cowardly. And yet, she knew losing Duncan would be akin to losing herself, that once he was gone, she would never find that integral part of herself again.

In her heart, she believed that, somewhere in time,

they had loved one another, that fate had torn them apart, and they had been searching all this time to find a way back to each other.

Not long ago she would have scoffed at such a tragic, unimaginable notion of lost love, centuries old—until it happened to her.

She was living a dream, a precious fantasy—a fantasy that had transformed into a nightmare somewhere along the way, and she didn't know how to stop them from careening toward disaster. Would she and Duncan slowly erode under the heavy weight of impending doom? Would they lose out on love once more?

Could fate prove to be so cruel again?

Perhaps it was those questions that had led Rachel to such a desperate course of action, believing that, in death, she would have what she could not possess in life.

The uncertainty of that answer had compelled her to find out, thinking to determine the outcome of her own life instead of being propelled by other powers.

Duncan had been the sensible one, of course, not allowing emotions to obscure his focus or make him lose touch with what really mattered most. Life. And the act of living it. He knew that death was not the answer.

But what was? And would they find a solution before Gordon succeeding in killing Duncan?

A chill washed over Rachel, and she hugged herself, gazing out the kitchen window as Christmas music floated softly from the radio on the countertop.

A dense wall of falling snow obliterated the distant church steeples in the village below Glengarren, enclosing them in a cocoon of white.

The sight made her feel as though they dwelt within a snow globe—picturesque, immune to outside influences, encapsulated. And yet, one shake would send the world they knew wildly into a tilt—one careless move by whatever force held them in the palm of its hand would have them crashing to the ground . . . and splintering into a million pieces.

Rachel hugged herself tighter and pushed the thought aside, trying to focus on the moment—and only the moment. It was then that a realization suddenly dawned on her.

Today was Christmas Eve.

She had forgotten all about the holiday, had labeled it as surreal, transpiring outside the small sphere she occupied. It was hard to believe she and Duncan stood on the cusp of a day of celebration while potential destruction loomed above their heads like the sword of Damocles.

Away from Glengarren, Rachel suspected that the hustle and bustle of last-minute shopping was rising to a fever pitch—the shops jammed, families scurrying to wrap presents, and children counting down the hours until Santa's visit. It made Rachel wish she still believed in fairy tales.

She sighed wearily and lifted her gaze to the sky, longing to see a ray of sunshine to alleviate the pall of perpetual gloom that surrounded her and had settled beneath her skin like a sickness.

"What do ye see out there, lady?" came a deep voice from behind her.

A smile touched Rachel's lips as she turned from the

window and faced Duncan. The sight of him never failed to take her breath away.

With the way he looked at that moment—hair mussed, needing a shave, shirt somewhat rumpled, the tail hanging out of jeans that were faded and worn at the knees, and his big body slouched in the kitchen chair, a cup of steaming black coffee in his hand—he might have been a man born of the twenty-first century, just risen from his bed on a lazy Sunday.

He looked so strong, so virile. Invincible. But she had learned the hard way that he was not indestructible—and that the line between life and death was very fragile, as gossamer as fairy dust.

God, how she loved him. The emotion sang in every fiber of her being.

His blue eyes caressed her adoringly. His sensual lips were slightly turned up, sending a warm tingle dancing through her veins, reminding her quite vividly of what those lips had done to her body the night before, how he had wrung every ounce of passion from her with a skill that left her panting his name.

Their sleep had been light, troubled. Waiting for Gordon's next move. Expectancy crackling in the air as they held each other close.

But the night had passed uneventfully, without so much as a bump out of Gordon. And that, perhaps more than anything else, worried Rachel the most.

The house was too quiet, too still. She didn't believe Gordon was gone. No. He was waiting. Watching. Anticipating the moment they let down their guard.

Then he would strike.

She tried to push the thought from her mind and remember her vow to live in the here and now. She would cherish every moment she and Duncan had together, holding those memories close to her heart.

Gripping her coffee cup, Rachel moved across the room to sit opposite Duncan at the table that was littered with the markings of breakfast—scrambled eggs, toast, bacon.

"Good morning," she murmured, leaning over to brush his lips, expecting a brief contact, but he pressed forward and deepened the kiss.

"Good morning, lady," he returned in a husky caress when he eased back. "I missed having ye in my arms when I awoke."

Rachel touched a finger to his lips, her smile changing, wanting to give way to the pain lingering inside her. "I missed being there." But she had needed something to keep herself busy, something to hold back the specters circling her dreams.

His gaze grew concerned. "What is on your mind, love?"

Rachel could not tell him of her worries, her fears. She would not burden him with them. "I was just thinking about my home in Connecticut. Picturing the neighbors bustling about, getting ready for their families to arrive for Christmas, the smell of smoke wafting from the chimneys, children begging to open at least one present."

"Ye give gifts tae each other?"

She nodded. "It's a tradition."

"Like your snowman?"

Rachel's heart was warmed. He had remembered. "Yes . . . like my snowman."

His expression sobered, his eyes delving into hers. "Do ye miss your home much?"

"No," she murmured. "Wherever you are is home."

He averted his gaze and said, "Would that I could take ye tae your real home, lady."

The torment in his voice made her feel as though a mighty hand was squeezing her chest. His remark was a painful reminder that he could never leave Glengarren, that he was trapped forever within its borders—unless they found a way to return him to his own time. But she didn't even know where to begin.

Forces far greater than both of them had brought him here, and something told her that only those forces could take him back.

Duncan rose from his chair and took her hand in his, bringing her to her feet before him. Then, without a word, he pulled her into his arms. She went willingly.

Perhaps he had sensed the turmoil in her, intuited her feelings, as he had done so adeptly from the moment they met. Or perhaps he simply needed to hold her as much as she needed to hold him.

His head dipped and her body tautened in anticipation of his kiss. It was slow and expert, carnal and wet, mouths merging, temperatures rising. He was methodical, and she melted under the sweet pressure and sensuality of his touch.

"Well, now . . . ain't this cozy?"

Rachel started at the sound of a voice coming from the doorway. Her gaze quickly focused around the edge of

Duncan's shoulder. There she found Fergus standing on the threshold, watching them, his murky eyes glinting with far too much interest.

"I knocked, but I reckon ye didn't hear me," he said, his normally ruddy cheeks blanched by cold. Snow clung to his coat and hat, and slush covered his boots, dripping onto the floor in an ever-growing puddle. "Guess I know now why ye looked so uncomfortable when I stopped by the other day. Got yer hands full, I see."

Unnerved by Fergus's sudden appearance, Rachel moved around Duncan, standing squarely between the two men. "What are you doing here, Fergus?"

Without an invitation, Fergus moved into the room, leaving muddy tracks on the floor, his gaze narrowing on Duncan. Hardening. A feeling of unease swept through Rachel, and she wasn't sure why.

While Fergus's demeanor had never inspired a sense of conviviality, there was something about the look in his eyes that made wariness rise inside her.

Nothing about his expression hinted of surprise over finding her in a man's arms—or that the man looked identical to the person depicted in the portrait in the foyer.

In some remote part of her consciousness, Rachel acknowledged that the strains of Christmas music on the radio had become a buzz of distorted electrical interference—short-circuited scratching, like a hundred stations colliding at once. Her disquiet redoubled. Something was not right.

"What are you doing here?" she repeated.

Finally Fergus drew his gaze from Duncan and set it

on her. Rachel gasped at the impact of that solitary look, dark and fixed . . . and churning with some disturbing emotion, making her skin crawl and her body rigid with building fear.

She tried to shake off the slithering sensation working its way along her nerves, telling herself that Fergus had looked at her in such a manner from the start, that his demeanor had always been abrupt, sour.

But he had also worried about her, warning her about the strange goings-on in the castle and telling her to take care. Perhaps he was concerned now?

No, she thought. It was not concern that lit his eyes.

Her gaze shifted, moving down his body: his mouth with its normal grimace, his arm that was virtually useless, his step that had been more of a shuffle—changed somehow.

He edged closer, his lips drawing up in a semblance of a smile. "Guess I was wrong about ye," he said.

"What do you mean?"

"About ye being a nice lass, one in need of safeguarding. Seems ye've found yerself a protector. And by the looks of ye, I suspect he's more than protecting ye." His gaze raked down her body in a crude fashion, and he sniffed the air. "Ye got the smell of rut about ye."

Rachel stared at him in disbelief, his words an unexpected slap. What was happening here? Why was he behaving in this manner?

With a growl, Duncan started toward Fergus. "Retract your words, old man, or I'll retract your teeth."

Rachel threw out her arm to stop him. "Don't hurt him. He doesn't know what he's saying."

"Oh, I know, all right," he said. "I ain't so old that I can't appreciate the lure of a woman's willing body, eager and panting, ready tae be mounted by the biggest stallion." He moved farther into the room, an odd gracefulness belying his crippled leg and damaged arm. "Sinners," he hissed.

She watched in horror as he grabbed a butcher knife from the countertop, his expression twisted into a grotesque caricature as he focused his glinting eyes on Duncan.

"Stop this!" she cried as he started toward them.

"Away, harlot!" He waved the knife at her. "I'll deal with ye next."

Duncan tried to push her to the side, but Rachel held fast to his arms. "No! He's an old man!"

"Stand aside, woman!" Duncan ordered.

Without warning, Fergus lunged. The knife sizzled through the air, missing her arm by mere inches, catching Duncan instead as he shoved her away, sending her spinning to the floor.

She scrambled back against the wall as the men squared off. A scream burst from her lips as Fergus jabbed the knife in her direction, taunting her before whisking it back toward Duncan with dizzying speed.

With a smile that froze her blood, he swung the knife in a wide arc toward Duncan, his intent clear. Duncan jumped back at the last moment, his escape thwarted by a chair that crashed against the table, sending dishes clattering to the floor.

The blade slashed toward his chest and missed. Fergus thrust again, whipping the knife from side to side so the keen blade sang and flashed like a lightning spear.

Duncan dodged each attempt and grabbed the toppled chair, heaving it up above his head, preparing to hurl it at Fergus, whose eyes widened in alarm, as though sanity had suddenly returned to him.

"Duncan, no!" The sound of her cry was scattered, lost amid the piercing cacophony of the radio interference that blasted in her ears.

Duncan tossed the chair aside. The moment he did, Fergus thrust again. Duncan backhanded the old man's arm with a force that sent the knife flying through the air.

Fergus teetered back, his legs suddenly as disjointed as a wooden puppet—his arms swinging bonelessly, and yet the expression on his face was one of smirking, hollow-eyed amusement.

Merciful God, she had seen that lifeless stare before!

In the next instant, Fergus collapsed, sank to the floor in a heap of limbs and snow-sodden clothes, his battered hat tumbling near Rachel's feet where she huddled against the wall, shock shooting threads of numbness through her.

Then came the laughter—maniacal, soulless. Evil. It crashed against the walls with a power that shattered dishes and filled Rachel's head with excruciating pain.

Suddenly Gordon stood in the doorway, flesh and blood, as vibrant in that eternal moment as Duncan, who had planted himself firmly between her and the leering spirit, prepared to wage war to protect her.

"Ye think ye and your whore have power tae deny me my revenge, MacGregor?" Gordon boomed, his voice reverberating through the room. "Ye'll not stop me this time. Your damnable soul is mine! And when I'm done with ye"—he pointed a finger at Rachel—"I'll have *her* soul as well."

With his laughter echoing in their ears, he vanished.

In shock, Rachel stared at the spot where the man had just been standing, expecting him to reappear and finish what he had started.

He had been as human as she and Duncan; his threat very real—a threat he was more than capable of seeing through to its conclusion.

The sound of a pained groan brought Rachel's senses alive, her gaze jerking back to the figure lying prostrate on the floor, looking pale as death. Fergus.

Rachel scrambled over to him. His mouth gaped open and his cloudy eyes stared at the ceiling. "Oh, God," she said in a horrified whisper, lifting his head and cradling it in her lap. "Fergus?"

He stirred and groaned again, momentarily gasping for breath, the air rattling around in his lungs like a pre-death exhalation.

Then, abruptly, the wheezing subsided and he calmed, lying there so still that Rachel believed he had passed away in her arms.

A moment later he moved, gradually turning his glazed, unblinking eyes to hers and reaching up with a shaking, trembling hand to clutch at her arm.

"Wh-what happened, mistress?"

"Don't try to speak—"

"Was it another stroke?"

A sob caught in Rachel's throat as the reality of what had just happened sank into her, crawling through her veins like slow poison.

She looked up to find Duncan looming, his eyes nearly black from the rage that had so recently consumed him . . . yet there was no mistaking the concern and the terror he felt for her safety.

She gave him a barely perceptible nod, letting him know she was fine, before trying to put a smile on her face for Fergus. "What do you remember?"

"Knocking on the front door. No one answered, so I got worried."

Relief flooded her. He didn't know. "How do you feel?"

"Odd," he said, his grizzled brow creasing. "There's naught a pain tae mewl over."

Rachel's gaze flicked to Duncan, knowing the same thoughts were cycling through both their minds; that the situation had grown more dire, that they had to get Fergus out of there.

Duncan's troubled gaze held hers for a long moment before he slipped into the shadowed corner of the room, keeping out of sight as Fergus grew more alert.

"How did I come tae be in the kitchen?" Fergus asked, blinking in confusion as he finally noted his surroundings.

"I don't know," she lied. She could not let him in on what had just transpired, that he had been the human vessel for a madman who wanted her and Duncan dead. Would he even believe her if she tried to explain? "I think I ought to get you to a doctor."

He frowned and shook his head, touching a finger to his temple. "The old noggin feels fine. Won't be the first time I've lost my way since I had the stroke. I suspect it won't be the last."

With her help, he rose to his feet, swaying slightly before finding his balance. "Are you sure you're all right?" she asked, concerned.

"Nothin' that a stiff shot of whiskey won't cure." He patted her hand in a fatherly gesture that seemed foreign to his nature. "Don't ye worry none. These old bones have got life in them yet." He bent to retrieve his hat from the floor and Rachel hurriedly swept it up for him. He nodded his thanks and jammed it on his head. "Sorry tae be troublin' ye. Good day tae ye now."

"Take care of yourself, Fergus," Rachel murmured, watching him leave, the trepidation quivering inside her . . . as well as the certain knowledge that this would be the last time she ever saw him.

As DUSK FELL, so did an impending sense of doom.

Rachel hovered in front of the library fireplace, staring into the flames.

Waiting.

The warmth of the fire did not touch her. The cold had settled in her heart and would not leave.

Since Fergus's departure that morning, she had felt as though she were in a holding pattern, her every sense on alert for the next appearance of Gordon—and he *would* appear, of that she had no doubt.

He had shown them that he could dwell within the living world and outside of it, proven his strength, let them know there was nowhere to hide.

"Here, lady. Drink this."

Rachel turned to find Duncan standing next to her, a glass of warm brandy in his hand. "Thank you," she murmured, taking the glass from him, rolling it between her palms before putting the drink to her lips.

The liquor slid smoothly down her throat, creating a calming effect inside her, taking the edge off her harrowed nerves.

She watched Duncan over the rim, his gaze unwavering, as though silently coaxing her to finish every drop, which she eagerly did.

"Better?" he said, taking the empty glass from her hand and putting it on top of the mantel.

"Much," she replied. "Thank you."

They stood there for a moment, eyes locked, time holding still. Rachel ached for him to make love to her, to help her forget whatever darkness was irrevocably closing around them like an unbreakable web.

She wanted to feel his hardness slide in and out of her, to let her know they were both still alive. The urgency grew with each passing hour.

The only thing that halted her from reaching out and taking what she wanted . . . was Duncan. It seemed as though he was pulling away from her, withdrawing, as if he knew something she didn't. She sensed the change in the very air around them.

She was losing him, and she could do nothing to stop it, nothing but feel the pain escalating inside her and stand helplessly by while it ravaged her.

He took her hand in his. "Come. I want tae show ye something." He drew her away from the fire, across the room to the bay window. "Look outside."

"Duncan . . ."

"Just look, lady. There's something for you."

Taking a deep breath, Rachel glanced out the window and caught sight of what he spoke of. Tears immediately sprang to her eyes. She faced him, words of love and gratitude clogging in her throat.

Consternation etched his brow when he noted her expression. "Why do ye cry, lass? I only thought tae make ye smile." He shook his head. "Damn me. I was wrong. I'll get rid of it."

He tried to walk around her, but she took hold of his arm, stopping him. "Duncan . . ."

"Rachel, sweet lass . . . don't weep so."

"I . . . I can't help myself. You . . . you made me a snowman."

"Aye," he said softly, taking a lock of her hair between his fingers. "I thought it would make ye happy."

"It does," she wept.

"'Twas my gift tae ye . . . for Christmas. Ye said people give presents tae their loved ones. I had nothing else of import tae give ye . . . besides my heart."

"Oh, Duncan . . ." She wrapped her arms around his neck and held him close, as if she never intended to let him go. "Don't you know you have given me everything I could ever want?"

"If it were in my power tae give ye the world, I would do so willingly."

For long minutes, they held each other. Then Rachel murmured, "Thank you for the snowman. It's beautiful."

His response was a gentle brushing of his lips across her forehead. Then he pulled her tight against his chest once more, the colored lights reflecting off the windowpanes and bathing them in soft hues of red and blue and gold.

"I don't have a present for you," she said, looking up into his handsome face.

"I need nothing but you."

"You have me. Always." She leaned up on tiptoe and kissed him.

His eyes had darkened with desire by the time the kiss ended. Rachel responded to that look, and yet she wanted to give him more than just her body.

She realized then that there *was* one thing she could give him, one item she possessed that meant everything to her, encompassed all the love she had ever known in her life.

Her mother's locket.

With a sense of rightness, she reached behind her neck and undid the clasp, letting the cool metal slide into her palm. She stared down at it, thinking about all the comfort it had given her, how the little picture of herself that nestled within the locket had once been so cherished by her mother.

This was the only thing Rachel had left of her parents, her solitary connection to them, and yet, she knew that if they were looking down on her in that moment, they would understand what she had to do.

Taking Duncan's hand in hers, she turned it palm up, letting the locket flow from her hand into his and curling his fingers around it.

She looked up into his beautiful, bewildered eyes and said, "This is my gift to you. It contains all my love, all my hopes and dreams. I want you to have it."

"Nay, lady . . . I cannot take it. It means too much tae ye."

"It means the world to me. This locket was my link to the only things I held dear, the life I knew, my parents. But I see now that I forgot the one thing the locket was truly meant to represent. Love. It was given in love, received in love, and worn in love. Now I give that love to you, Duncan MacGregor, as well as everything I am."

"Are ye sure?" he asked, looking uncertain.

"I've never been more sure of anything in my life."

He wiped a stray tear from her cheek. "Then I accept." He took the gold chain from his palm and fastened it around his neck. The necklace hugged his throat, the medallion reflecting the light as it dangled in the hollow at the base of his neck. "Ye humble me, lady. I pray that I am worthy of all ye have given me today."

He pulled her back into his arms, and as he bent to kiss her, Rachel knew that no man was worthier. Duncan was her soul mate. Her heart's desire.

Her hero.

chapter 12

SOMETHING AWOKE HER.

Rachel's heart thumped against her ribs, and she nestled closer to Duncan, his arms, even in sleep, wrapped protectively around her. She listened hard, staring up into the darkness . . . waiting.

Nothing.

Duncan shifted, and Rachel turned her head on the pillow and found him looking at her. She smiled softly at him, but he did not return the gesture.

She noted then how hot he felt, his body sweating and tense. Was he sick? Or was he, like her, tuning into the sounds around them, alert to any possible danger?

"Duncan?"

He groaned, and she immediately grew concerned. He spoke in a whisper near her ear—garbled words, a fierce sound that caused a dart of fear to jab her, sending threads of icy dread down her spine as the memory of Fergus lying on the kitchen floor came rushing back—visions of Gordon's possession and his threats to destroy Duncan . . . and her.

Struggling to sit up, Rachel kicked back the down comforter and touched Duncan's face. His skin was as hot as the fire in the grate . . . and yet the room felt cold.

She glanced over to the fireplace, saw the flames gyrating brightly among the ashes, but no warmth touched her. Something about that fire unsettled her.

Sliding from the bed, she approached the hearth, her gaze locked on the flames that surged and dwindled, then surged again, as though they were . . . breathing. The ash appeared dark. No red and glowing coals. No crackling logs.

Her hands shaking, Rachel reached, palms out, toward the blazing fire. No heat. Nothing but frigid air assailed her. How could that be?

Edging closer, she stared hard into the lapping flames—then she swiped one hand through the fire . . . and discovered it was no fire at all.

But an illusion.

Fear closed off her throat and buzzed inside her head. Her heart hammering, she turned back toward the bed, her gaze fixed on Duncan's form sprawled over the mattress, shimmering with sweat, the strange red and gold firelight reflecting off his bare chest.

A rumble suddenly shook the floor beneath her feet. Rachel clutched the mantel, holding tight, a cry of alarm drowning among the escalating sound.

Panic rising, she spun toward the window and threw back the heavy drapes, her wild gaze looking out over Glengarren's grounds.

The sky suddenly flashed with a lightning bolt, illuminating rolling black clouds that seethed directly above Glengarren's rooftop.

Again a jagged spear of lightning fractured the night, reflecting off the snow-covered grounds and the gnarled, bare-branched trees.

A roar of wind smashed against the windowpane, driving Rachel back, her breath catching, expecting the glass to shatter from the sudden impact.

Instead, they rattled and pulsated like a living thing, while the howl of the storm careened through the room like a thousand banshees.

She whirled around toward the bed, her cry for Duncan strangled as the room appeared out of focus, disorienting her. She stumbled from side to side, as though trying to gain her balance in a wildly rocking boat.

The furnishings appeared to shift and change, fading in and out, reality juxtaposed against some out-of-kilter nightmare . . . as though the twenty-first century was colliding with the past.

"Duncan!" she cried, at last reaching the bed and grabbing hold of his arms. Duncan's head rolled from side to side and he moaned as though in agony.

She shook him, shouting his name as the thunder boomed and the lightning filled the room, the impact like a cannon blast, throwing her to the floor.

Through a fiery haze that appeared before her, she watched Duncan rise from the bed—his body radiating a dim white glow like an aura.

Slowly, the emanation ebbed and then dissipated entirely. He shook his head, his face a tangle of confusion as he looked frantically around the room.

When he spotted her, he rushed to her side and

dropped to his knees before her, dragging her into his arms and holding her tight.

Rachel clung to him, and together they watched the play of light and fire flash through the room. She cringed as the thunder exploded against the house. This time the impact shattered the windows, pushing the glass inward, scattering jagged pieces around them.

With a howling rush, the wind tore at the drapes, whipping through the room with cyclonic power—hot and cold, the force sucking the air from their lungs.

Duncan groaned, and to her horror he appeared to flicker, his existence as insubstantial as Gordon's—a ghostly blur whose arms around her felt as fragile as the diaphanous bed veil thrashing wildly from the force of the wind.

"No!" she screamed, fighting to hold on to him, but unable to find solid form.

Her gaze collided with his—the reality slamming them both in the same instant. Time had run full circle and had finally caught up with them. And now, whatever power had brought Duncan to her was battling to wrench him back.

Through the growl of thunder came the shouts of men—a melee of angry cries and shrieking horses. Familiar sounds that leached the blood from Rachel's face.

The sounds she had heard the night Duncan had burst into her life.

Duncan jumped to his feet and ran to the window, his hand fisting in the drapes, his body tensing as though preparing for battle.

He turned to her, his image momentarily growing sharper as he looked into her face, the resolve she saw in his eyes like a lance to her heart.

He was leaving her.

"'Tis my men," he said, his voice a painful rip of sound that made grief fill up inside her and tears rise, scalding and bitter, to her eyes.

The plea was there on her lips. *Don't go. Don't leave me. I love you. I need you.*

Yet she had known all along that this moment was inevitable. Every second she had spent in his arms had been stolen, yet no less of a miracle, no less cherished.

She had known the kind of love with this man that few people would ever experience. She had gotten a glimpse of heaven.

He came to her then and knelt beside her, taking her into his arms, holding her tightly, fiercely, his chest heaving with emotion, his lips brushing her face.

"Lady," he whispered in a hoarse voice. "My men need me . . . my clan. My son . . ."

"Duncan . . ." Rachel's heart felt as though it was being torn from her.

"Dear God . . ." He tipped back his head, his face awash in torment. "Why must I choose?"

Tears rolled down Rachel's cheeks as she took his face between her hands. "You have to go." The words longed to lodge in her throat, to never be spoken. But she knew he could not stay, and she would not let him leave with the burden of her breaking heart.

Blue eyes that would haunt her forever delved deeply into hers. "I'll never forget ye, sweet Rachel. Ye'll always be in my heart, no matter where I go or what becomes of me. Someday I'll find ye, and we will be together again. Until then, I leave all my love, my honor . . . and my heart."

She kissed him, deeply, hungrily, wanting to imprint the taste of him on her lips, savoring his touch, absorbing the memory of his body and soul in her every fiber.

"Lady . . ." The word was a haunting whisper . . . then he was gone, torn from her arms as the air erupted with a crash, a boom of thunder shaking the floor and walls.

With a cry of anguish, Rachel pushed to her feet and swung toward the doorway, where a hazy light shimmered. And there, standing on the threshold, was Duncan, once more the Highland warrior, dressed in his kilt and tattered linen shirt, the glimmering sword whose blade was etched with *GRACE ME GOD* clutched in one massive hand.

He looked down the corridor, as if something beckoned him. Then he glanced back at her, despair settling on his face as he held out a hand to her.

"Duncan," she wept and reached for him. One last good-bye. One last kiss.

But he vanished. Where his form had filled the threshold, now only darkness remained.

A sob caught in Rachel's throat and she ran to the doorway, calling his name. She couldn't let him go. She wasn't brave enough to face life without him, to exist in a world devoid of his love.

She fled from the room, racing wildly along the hallway, tears streaming down her face, blurring her vision. She flew down the staircase, through the foyer, threw open the front door, and ran into the raging tempest that drove the winds against her, as if thwarting her attempts to reach him.

Just like the night Duncan had so mysteriously been wrenched from his time into hers, she fought her way toward the Destiny Stones, praying she would find him there, her body numbed to the snow biting at her bare feet or the bitter cold slashing at her with icy, sharp teeth.

Above her the sky collided, and a multitude of lightning bolts careened toward Glengarren, turning the dark into daylight. . . .

And out of the swirling, earthbound clouds came ghostly human shapes—warriors on horseback, frothing animals with flaring nostrils and wild, rolling eyes, the sounds slamming against her ears like cymbals crashing.

And among it all rose the haunting cry of a bagpipe's song—a lamenting aria heartbreakingly mournful.

Massive, snorting horses bore down upon her, their hooves churning and thundering upon the ground. Frozen in fear, Rachel watched them advance, unable to move as they came closer, barreling down upon her.

Duncan! His name was a silent scream.

As though she had summoned him, he appeared, his hair flying, his sword raised above his head. His gaze slashed in her direction, but it was as though he looked right through her.

With a call to battle, he drove his knees into the sides of his black stallion. The horse reared, its forelegs thrashing in the air before its mighty back hooves propelled them forward . . . hurtling them toward Glengarren. And her.

Rachel cried his name and threw her arms in front of

her face, certain she would be trampled to pieces by the razor-sharp hooves of his horse—yet, like a mirage, the animal passed through her.

She watched Duncan ride toward Glengarren's east wing, the house suddenly ablaze with flames that lapped high into the sky, turning the black, churning clouds into the crimson slashes she had seen the night he had appeared.

Stumbling through the high drifts of snow, she followed, the realization of what was transpiring driving her onward, filling her with some macabre fascination—and a terror unlike any she had ever known.

With the dawning horror of knowing what was to come, Rachel's step faltered. She had read about this day in the history book, the time corresponding with an event that had taken place over two centuries ago . . . the predawn hours of Christmas Day.

She was witnessing the moment when Gordon had torched Glengarren out of revenge—when Duncan had waged one last battle against his hated foe—when he had at last sent Gordon to his death.

Damning his vile soul to haunt Glengarren for all eternity.

As the ghostly flames rose into the sky, eating away at the castle's rafters, Duncan jumped from his horse. The beast reared and danced upon its back legs, froth flying from its mouth and its teeth bared in fright.

Wielding his sword, which reflected the fire like a burst of sun, Duncan shouted Gordon's name—the sound a tear of vicious fury as he plunged through the flames and disappeared.

Rachel ran for the house, the spirits of warriors long

dead surrounding her, waging their battle—the MacGregor and Gordon clans clashing with steel blades and fists, their shouts and cries whipped by the roaring winds that pummeled her, driving her back with gale force.

She fought desperately against the storm, finally reaching the burning wing. She hesitated on the perimeter of the blaze, fear of the flames holding her back, but her love for Duncan propelled her forward.

She scrambled over the burning, smoldering ruins—no heat, no flames, the fire could not harm her. It wasn't real, not now, not in her time.

This was all an illusion, history repeating itself, like the soldiers around her—she didn't exist in their reality any more than they existed in hers.

Rachel stopped in her tracks, gasping as she caught sight of the two men, Duncan and Gordon, the fire encircling them, their eyes locked on each other, their bodies tautened, preparing to fight a battle to the finish.

The flames formed a wall before her and streaked over the rafters, eating up the old timber like a famished beast.

Above Glengarren's gaping roof, beyond the high, lapping flames, she watched the black, electrified clouds collide, spitting lightening bolts at the castle, spears of blue and white illumination that centered their fury on the two men battling amid the incinerating inferno.

With a slash of his sword, Duncan drove Gordon back. The man stumbled, his face contorted in fury and pain as the wound Duncan had inflicted in his side bled profusely.

With a roar of outrage, Gordon rallied his strength and deflected Duncan's next assault—metal against metal, crashing as resoundingly as the storm above, sparks flying like charged daggers from the blades.

Gordon braced his legs and wielded his sword in a mighty arc. Duncan met it with a parry that sent the weapon flying toward Rachel, landing near her feet. The ghostly blade spun, reflecting the fire in bright yellow streaks, as if burning with internal heat.

Sweat poured from Gordon's enraged face, his teeth bared as he boomed, "Kill me now, MacGregor, and I'll curse your name all the way tae hell and back! By my blood, I'll have my revenge on ye and all those ye love. They'll suffer my wrath until I can drag their souls down into the inferno with me. This I vow!"

The rafters began to groan then, and with an ear-splitting crack, fiery debris rained down upon them. Gordon stumbled back. Duncan threw himself aside, but not quickly enough to avoid the impact of fire and wood that glanced off his arm, knocking the sword from his hand.

Gordon's eyes gleamed at the advantage afforded him, and with a roar, he threw himself upon Duncan, fists swinging, knuckles cracking across Duncan's jaw, sending him spiraling backward.

Another horrible groan issued from the timbers above them, bringing Rachel's head jerking up. She watched in horror as the beams began to sag, the crack as deafening as the lightning overhead.

Her gaze snapped back to Duncan. She cried his name in warning—knowing even as she did so that he could not hear her, could not see her . . . and worst of all, she could not help him.

With a final curse, Gordon flung himself upon Duncan. They met in a fierce battle for supremacy, bodies impacting, wrestling, stumbling as fire and embers fell to the ground, scattering around them, thick, black smoke beginning to fill the air.

Then the rafters, with a final horrifying growl, shattered in a burst of flames and began to collapse inward . . . toward the men.

As if time ground to a stop, Duncan turned his head, his eyes connecting with hers for an infinitesimal moment, his love reaching out to her across a chasm far greater than either of them could span.

His lips moved, forming a solitary word.

Rachel.

Then, in the blink of an eye, he was gone. Vanished. As was everything else—the sounds of chaos, the horses, the men. Gordon. And the silence was deafening. She stood alone in the cold morning light as her entire world crumbled around her.

With a sob breaking from her lips, Rachel stumbled across the ruins to the spot where she had last seen Duncan, and there she sank to her knees amid the centuries-old scorched rubble, all that remained of the battle . . . all she had left of Duncan.

Covering her face with her hands, she wept with all the pain inside her, her shoulders shaking, the loss filling her up with such wrenching grief she thought she might shatter.

How long she remained there on her knees, the cold whirling around her, pressing her nightclothes against her body with frigid fingers, she could not guess. Time had no consequence in that moment. Seconds. Minutes. Hours. An eternity. What did it matter anymore?

Then, from somewhere, came the sound of bells. They rang across the moor, across Glengarren's ruins, echoing from the village's church steeples, heralding the arrival of Christmas Day.

Blinking hot tears from her eyes, Rachel gazed around her, traveling over the place where only a short time ago flames had raged and men had waged an all-out war to the death. Now their battle cries had long since died, and the ancient rafters glittered with snow.

Overhead, the black, turbulent clouds had changed to white, drifting puffs that parted to allow a single ray of sunlight to spill upon her face. She closed her eyes and tipped her head back to feel its warmth, seeking its comfort.

Then she heard a sound, her eyes snapping open. Squinting against the sun, she threw up her hand to shield the brightness . . . and found a dark figure looming just inside the doorway leading from the main part of the house. Her heart missed a beat.

The figure took a single step forward out of the shadows, revealing a familiar face that made her breath hitch in her throat. It was a man . . . a man whose penetrating blue eyes regarded her with concern.

"Rachel?" he called softly.

"Duncan?" she whispered, rising to her feet, her heart beginning to beat faster as he moved toward her.

He halted two feet from her, and her happiness turned to confusion as reality sharpened. Something was different. He had changed. His black hair was shorter, his skin not so darkened from the sun. He was dressed in a worn, brown bomber jacket, sweater, and faded jeans.

This man was not Duncan. Perhaps, she thought in her grief-stricken mind, he was not even real, but rather an image her mind had created to help console her pain.

She turned away from the stranger, the illusion, and hugged herself. She could look at him no longer. It was simply too much to bear.

"Is everything all right?" he asked, moving in front of her, his arm lightly brushing against hers.

The contact was electric. Jarring. She jumped back, shocked by the force of that single touch as she regarded him from the dark embrace of one of the fallen timbers. This was no phantasm conjured up by her mind. But a real man, one of flesh and blood.

"It's all right, lass. Don't be afraid."

She stared at him, unable to speak. Why was she being tormented? Why had God mocked her by putting Duncan's face on this man?

He stared back at her, his eyes slightly narrowed as his gaze skimmed over her face, obscured now from his full inspection.

"Who . . . who are you?" she managed to say.

He shook his head as though to clear it and replied, "My apologies. I haven't introduced myself. Allow me tae correct that oversight."

He held out his hand to her, and Rachel hesitated in taking it. When she did, she experienced the same jolt that had gone through her when he had brushed so innocently against her. She saw something flicker across his face. Had he felt it, too?

"The name's Duncan MacGregor . . . Lord of Glengarren."

The breath lodged in Rachel's throat, the name rebounding through the room.

"It's nice tae finally get tae meet ye in person, instead of only knowing ye through your letters."

Letters? Rachel's mind scrambled back, recalling the correspondence she had exchanged with the son of her father's friend, remembering one letter in particular that she had received shortly after her father had died.

The words of condolence had resonated so strongly within her . . . giving her the strength to do what she had to do. He had seemed to know exactly what to say to ease her pain.

"Duncan." The word came out a benediction. Until that moment, she hadn't made the connection. He had simply signed his letters "D. MacGregor."

"Aye," he said, an endearing half-grin bringing out the deep dimple in one cheek. "I was named after the man who built Glengarren."

Rachel tried to hold back the pain inside her, but the world seemed to conspire against her, and the tears began to fall.

His smile immediately changed to an expression of concern. "Don't cry, lady," he softly beseeched.

Lady. Duncan had called her that. The memory only made the tears flow that much harder.

Without another word, he pulled her into his arms. She wept softly against his broad shoulder, finding an odd comfort in his embrace, his scent causing a firestorm of raw emotions to spark inside her.

He took her face in his hands and gazed deeply into her eyes, his own searching her features with an expression of wonderment.

"Sweet God," he whispered. "It can't be."

"What?" she said in a choked voice, glancing up at him. "What's the matter?"

"Ye're . . . *her.*"

"Her?"

"The lady in the locket."

Rachel frowned. "I don't understand."

His hand moved from her face to ease down the zipper of his jacket, one finger hooking the edge of his sweater to reveal what was around his neck . . . a gleaming gold chain.

Her locket at its base.

He pressed his thumb to the seam and the pendant flipped open, showing a miniature picture of herself. Her gaze elevated to his and she saw something there, something beneath the bewilderment. A connection.

"How . . . ?"

"I found it years ago, when I was a lad. I had been rummaging around in these old ruins, against my father's wishes, as this section of the castle had been off-limits for as long as we lived here.

"I don't know why I searched beneath this particular pile of fallen debris, but I did. I sifted through the soot . . . and there it was. As soon as I looked upon the beautiful face within the locket, I was lost tae glorious sea-green eyes . . . your eyes."

"I don't understand. Why was it here?"

"I don't know. I always wondered about that myself.

Perhaps it belonged tae my ancestor, the original Duncan MacGregor. He died in the fire that burnt down this wing."

Rachel pulled away from him. "He died?" she said in a pained voice. She had yearned to believe he had survived, that he had seen his men into battle, and that perhaps he had not been killed in the battle of Culloden Moor.

"Aye," he said. "On Christmas Day, 1745. He was engaged in a mighty battle with his most hated enemy—"

"Gordon."

He nodded, giving her a puzzled look. "The story is that the men fought in here, and that MacGregor had the upper hand."

"What happened then?"

"Well, it's strange, but according tae what I've read, MacGregor pushed Gordon out of the way when a section of the rafters caved in, saving the man."

Rachel closed her eyes, the tears seeping between her lashes. "Oh, Duncan," she whispered in a raw, barely audible voice. "You died to save me, didn't you?" He had taken the blow that was meant to kill Gordon so that she would be safe from his enemy. If Gordon did not die, then he could not haunt Glengarren, looking for his revenge.

Duncan put a finger beneath her chin, tilting her face up to his. "Your tears are like daggers tae my heart, lass. Tell me what I can do tae comfort ye?"

Rachel stared up at him, remembering how a Highland warrior had once spoken those same words to her as they stood together beneath the rowan tree, her heart breaking as her parents' ashes floated away on the wind.

As she gazed up into the face that she had thought never to see again, she repeated the words she had said to him then, "Hold me, Duncan. Hold me tight and don't let go."

"Aye, lass. That I will. Always."

And as the man she had loved through an eternity held her tight in his embrace, the sun rose in a fiery ball above Glengarren, bathing them in its warm, golden rays, and Rachel knew then that her wish had been granted. She had gotten her Christmas miracle.

Visit
❖ **Pocket Books** ❖
online at

....

www.SimonSays.com

....

Keep up on the latest new
releases from your favorite
authors, as well as author
appearances, news, chats,
special offers and more.

SIMON & SCHUSTER
A VIACOM COMPANY
www.SimonSays.com

Pocket
Books

2381-01